A BETTER HUMAN

J DONALD

A BETTER HUMAN

Author: J Donald

Line Editor: Regan Schell

Story Critique: Joel Matthew Kremer

Cover Design: J Donald

Book Formatting: J Donald

Paperback ISBN: 979-8-218-85571-0

Hardcover ISBN: 979-8-2954-4886-7

Copyright © 2024 J Donald

DEDICATION

To Arlo

May you always view the world with curiosity

I love you, son

THANK YOU

Julie - for supporting me, my ideas, and my dreams

Mom and Joel - for reading along through the many iterations of Jacob's journey

Christina - for encouraging me to start putting my story to paper

CHAPTER 1

HUMMING FROM THE FLUORESCENT LIGHTS roared over the silence in the room holding Ethan Anderson. Dingy gray-white walls lined this space that was clearly designed for interrogations. The metal table in the center reflected the square grates of the lights in the tiled ceiling. Lifting his head from the cups of his hands resting on the table, Ethan looks at the clock above the door. The second hand moves silently, yet he hears loud echoing bangs with its every twitch. His imaginary slamming of the clock becomes overshadowed by footsteps approaching from the hallway outside the room.

The hollow click of the footsteps pause before the door is forcefully jarred open, revealing a silhouette of a man in the doorway. He watches as Victor enters the room, and for a moment, Ethan remembers seeing his best friend in one of his colored polos, tucked into tan or gray dress pants. His black hair would be naturally curly, and they'd be meeting to talk about their favorite subject — medical science.

Instead, the Victor standing in front of the now-closed door is wearing a dark gray suit, charcoal-black dress shirt underneath and has his hair gelled back. Ethan makes eye contact with Victor, sighs, then looks at the chair across the table that he knows Victor is about to walk to.

Chills tingle through Ethan's spine as the metal legs of the chair are dragged across the tile floor before Victor sits. Gazing with his cold, green eyes, he says calmly, "You look tired."

Chuckling sarcastically, Ethan says, "Do I, Vic?"

"You haven't been home since you tried to take my files?"

"Seems I haven't." Ethan's sitting back, showing he doesn't have patience for this.

Victor leans his elbows onto the table, saying peacefully, "Remember how excited we were after our Better Human breakthrough at the diner?" Ethan slowly blinks and remains silent. "Remember how *nothing* could stop us from achieving our goals and plans together?"

"Don't pretend like you don't know what came between us." Ethan replies with frustration.

Tapping his fingertips together, Victor's shoulders slouch as he sighs and holds a stare with Ethan.

Leaning into the table onto his forearms, Ethan speaks with impatience, saying, "Vic. You had your security stop me from entering the walls, throw me into an SUV, bring me here and hold me in this room for hours now. I doubt that was so we can reminisce about our life before the walls."

"Why were you outside the walls?" Victor asks, suspiciously. He's met with silence from Ethan. He adds, "Where did you go?"

With an aggressive sigh and eye roll, Ethan replies sarcastically, "I was driving around to clear my mind."

"You truly have lost your trust in me."

Realizing Victor is being sincere, Ethan scoffs, saying, "How could I not, Vic? After you…" He pauses when he sees purple veins appear around Victor's eyes, faintly, stemming away as if reaching for his forehead and temples. Cautiously thinking of his next words, Ethan hesitates. He needs to make it out of this room. Angering Victor will only keep him here longer.

"What? After I *what*, Ethan?" Victor asks in a demanding tone.

Ethan exhales through his nose and bites his upper lip while shaking his head, then says, "That outbreak nearly wiped out our species. You'd think that as a Conservation City leader, you'd try to protect people."

Poking his finger into the metal table hard enough to make a drumming sound, Victor yells, "Our people are safer inside the walls than humans have ever been in our history."

"The Outsiders are people, too, Vic."

"The Wasted?" Victor scoffs. He sees Ethan close his eyes with disappointment at him using that term. He continues, "Infected people outside the walls? They're nearly braindead. You're heartbroken over *them*?"

"Nearly braindead." Ethan mocks him. "Who do you think you're talking to?" His voice rises defensively. Victor lessens his lean over the table as Ethan continues. "Did you forget that I studied the infected Outsiders alongside you? Until you terminated the study because of the revelations we were discovering."

"The world saw how the infected behaved. Aggressive. Violent. Acting without rational thought."

Ethan butts in and finishes what he knows Victor is going to say: "And once the infection ran its course, if the host survived, their brains were damaged beyond repair. Only able to perform the most basic of tasks. Unable to speak. I know the propaganda, Vic. But *you* know we were seeing them improve. Function as humans again. Speaking again."

"People can't know that."

"Why, Vic? Because you'll lose your political power ruling the Conservation City?" Ethan scoffs again. "Or because you would lose your ability to test on the Outsiders?" He leans further over the table, showing he's serious, saying, "They're *people*. They deserve safety. We owe it to them to help them. *You* owe it to them."

"We can't risk destroying what we spent twenty years building here inside these walls because you think those Wasted... Infected Outsiders showed *minimal* improvement over being braindead."

"You're supposed to be a leader, Vic."

"You supported me getting this position when the walls went up. You spoke on behalf of me for Volcan Enterprises."

"I supported my friend *before* he changed. Not knowing he'd use that power to test on innocent people. Before I knew that he sabotaged the entire world for a project I *told you wouldn't work*." Ethan yells the last words of his sentence with passion and frustration. After a deep breath, he adds in a calmer tone, "How many failures have you released back outside the walls?"

Victor remains silent. The purple veins around his eyes grow a shade darker.

Hiding his reaction to the change, Ethan changes his direction. "People inside the walls lost all their loved ones from the outbreak. They deserve to know that there's a chance they could be out there alive–"

"And what, Ethan? Have a mass of our people leave the walls on a suicide mission to *maybe* find their loved ones? Yes, I remember our study. And I remember the results. Thirteen percent of infected subjects that were still living showed signs of brain regeneration. *Thirteen* percent. And do you remember how much of the population died during the outbreak?" Victor leans forward as Ethan avoids eye contact. "Sixty percent. Sixty percent of the population died from the outbreak. The violence of the infected killed more victims than it left alive to spread the virus. The chances of any one person's loved one being a healed infected outside the walls is *not* worth the chaos the news would cause."

Ethan sits back in his chair, crossing his arms and glaring at Victor.

Leaning deeper over the table, Victor's expression becomes filled with frustration and arrogance in his vein-covered eyes. "But tell me something, Ethan. Those infected we found with improved brain activity occurred seven, eight years ago. If this meant so much to you, why not just go to CC News and broadcast it to every Conservation City back then? Submit it as anonymous and everyone could be on their way to explore the Outside, searching for their loved ones until they either die out there or are reminded of the trauma they experienced when it first happened." Ethan remains quiet. His heart rate increases as Victor continues speaking aggressively. "You don't need evidence from me to do this. Right?"

Ethan's breathing becomes shallow and rapid.

"So, why try to take files from my office? Why go after me now, Ethan?"

The room is silent.

"Why?" Victor barks, slamming the side of his fist into the metal table. The veins around his eyes grow wider and darker.

Ethan looks at where Victor's fist hit the table and sees a dent. "That's why." He stares longer at the dent, then resumes eye contact with Victor after focusing on the veins around his eyes. "You're testing on yourself. This obsession with your Vitality project has you desperate. You think you can alter

DNA to make humans capable of supernatural abilities, and you're killing innocent people to test it."

"I don't *think* I can alter DNA, Ethan. I already have."

Ethan's mouth opens as he is about to continue arguing, but he instead pauses.

Victor continues. "I have several successful subjects from Vitality. Their neuron counts are elevated and sustainable, allowing subjects to project visions, hear other's thoughts, and another I'm training to cast memories to another–"

"At what cost?" Ethan interrupts, showing disinterest in what Victor was saying.

Victor's eyebrows lower.

"At what cost, Vic?" He repeats the question. When Victor doesn't answer, he says, "How many others had the same fate as that John Doe?"

Victor lowers his chin, casting a shadow over his vein-covered eyes.

"How many *didn't* die, but were released back into the Outside as monstrosities?"

"Why *now*?" Victor responds aggressively. Ethan's head jerks back with surprise. His eyes squint in an attempt to comprehend Victor's question as Victor repeats, "Why now, Ethan?"

"Wh-What do you—"

"You've thrown at me numerous times that you've known about my secret tests I've been doing for Vitality. You tell me I changed fifteen years ago, and I'm not the friend you knew." Victor leans even further toward Ethan across the table that now his legs no longer touch his chair. With adamant eyes, he asks, "Why *now* are you trying to steal my files and stop me?"

Avoiding eye contact, Ethan stares at the table between Victor's elbows.

"This all has to do with Jacob." Victor flashes a vindictive smile at Ethan. "He's about to turn eighteen, graduate, and once he's out from under your roof, he'll finally expose *your* lies."

Nervously gulping, Ethan says, struggling to hold eye contact, "There are no lies, Vic. I've told you numerous times, our Better Human serum didn't work. I've run the tests. Jacob is normal."

Tapping the palms of his hands on the table, Victor speaks confidently. "Here's what I think. *If*, in fact, Jacob *was* normal, you'd have allowed me to take my own sample, even through your reluctance of me testing on your son, just to shut me up and prove it to me."

Ethan's heart palpitates. His eyes don't blink.

"Yeah. That's what I thought." Victor's confidence blends with disappointment.

"Vic. I-I swear to you, he–"

"No, no." Victor stands and holds his palm toward Ethan. "This is *my* turn to point the finger at you." His voice rises with anger. "You know why I need Better Human to work. What it means to me."

"Immortality," Ethan scoffs lightly and mutters.

Pausing briefly, Victor says sternly, "Think of what that would mean for us. For humanity."

"Helping humanity." Ethan huffs. "You care most about yourself."

The dark veins around Victor's eyes fade away as he looks down at Ethan with concern. "Y-You think my intentions are ill? Only selfish?"

"I–" Ethan stutters. His eyebrows lower as his head jerks back at the sight of the veins quickly reappearing around Victor's eyes.

Pointing at Ethan, Victor yells, "How dare you? I want to make our species better. Make humans live to their full potential. After everything our species has been through, we can finally–"

"Our species needs to be protected from *you*." Ethan wishes he would have bitten his tongue.

"That's–" Victor stutters. The veins around his eyes once again fade away. He looks down at Ethan, who is sitting defensively in his chair, awaiting his next words or actions. "You actually mean that, don't you?"

Ethan doesn't move. He watches Victor process his thoughts.

After pacing and rubbing his face, Victor kneels a few feet away from Ethan's chair. The veins are still absent, and his expression is calm. "You're my best friend. We've accomplished miracles together. What happened to us?"

Noticing the change in demeanor, Ethan lowers his defense and says, "Something changed you, Vic. I don't know if it was the political power that got to you, or…" He looks at Victor's chest, then back to his eyes, "All I know is, the secrets, testing on innocent people, m–"

Victor bursts to his feet. Dark purple veins branch away from his eyes again. He scoffs aggressively. "Secrets?" He motions his finger between himself and Ethan. "This here. This… Disdain between us. It's because you keep your secret from me. You keep Jacob from me. When you *know* his DNA is special!" Victor steps quickly toward Ethan, slamming the palm of his hand on the corner of the table as he leans into Ethan's face.

Staring into fully dilated pupils making Victor's eyes look black, Ethan speaks nervously, desperate for Victor to believe him. "Jacob… Jacob is a normal kid, Vic. I'm not keeping anything from y–"

Ethan squints and turns his cheek as he's interrupted by an ear-piercing whistle from Victor. The door opens as Victor steps away from Ethan to greet the young woman walking in with a folder of papers. She glares at Ethan with a stern expression. She reminds him of Amber. Faint freckles are painted across her nose at the top of each of her cheeks. Her hair is braided and resting over her shoulders with strands falling over her green eyes.

"Thank you." Victor smiles and speaks politely to her. She breaks her fierce stare with Ethan to smile back at Victor and leave the room.

Clearing his throat, Victor walks back to his chair, sitting down and sliding the folders to Ethan. Ethan refuses to open the file and says, "I've seen enough of your calculations. You're not going to convince me to support Vitality."

"Open it."

Ethan leans back and rolls his eyes.

Tapping his finger strongly on the folder, Victor leans in and says, "This is a collection of reports from Jacob's coaches, school nurses, doctors. All reporting extraordinary details about him. Top player in every sport. Records shattered. Nurses saying he's never reported sick. Not even a mild cold. The doctor reporting–"

"Jacob being a great athlete isn't proof of Better Human. And we've cured and prevented how many illnesses at Volcan Enterprises? You and I. Remember? 'All the miracles we've done together.' This doesn't prove what you think it does, Vic–"

"The doctor's report is my favorite. Or should I say lack of one," he interrupts, resuming his confident tone. Opening the folder, he flips over pages of handwritten reports from the coach and medical forms from the school. Stopping on the doctor's report, he points and says, "Clean."

"Again, Vic. Jacob's a healthy kid. That doesn't mean he–"

"Last fall. No, two years ago. End of football season. Nobody saw that blitz from the safety coming."

Ethan closes his eyes and sighs.

"Jacob's forearm just–" Victor makes a snapping sound with his lips while twisting closed fists apart. "Poor kid. Wore a cast for several weeks, I believe, right?" Ethan doesn't reply or change his impatient expression. "Seems odd considering this report from the doctor is, well, empty."

They stare at each other in silence. Ethan feels his heart rate pulse on the sides of his neck. He jumps when another ear-piercing whistle escapes between the fingers in Victor's lips.

The door swings open. Expecting to see the young woman again, Ethan instead sees a young man enter the room holding a laptop. He looks older than Jacob and more disheveled than the young woman who entered before. His eyes are bloodshot and dilated. With nearly transparent skin showing blue veins through his arms, Ethan's eyes follow them to IV ports on the back of both of his hands. As he carries the laptop to Victor, Ethan sees he's visibly shaking. The boy meets eyes with Ethan, looking as if he's peering through him, when suddenly he scrunches his face, wincing. Victor grabs the laptop from him and demands he leave the room.

While Victor gently places the laptop on the table, Ethan thinks, *He couldn't have found it.* He thinks about the video he recorded. His plans to stop Victor involved this video that only he knows about. In his old-world home, inside a safe to which only he knows the combination.

Victor opens the laptop. The room is quiet except for tapping and typing on the keyboard. As soon as he stops, he grabs the side of the laptop, turning the screen to face Ethan.

On the screen is a paused video. The image showing Jacob outside their home. An overhead view of their back patio from a camera they don't own.

Ethan gazes at the screen. He looks at Victor, who is already looking back. They stare at each other for a moment, saying nothing. Ethan breaks eye contact and looks back at the screen. Victor moves the mouse pointer over the video and clicks play.

The scene is innocent. Jacob is punching his heavy bag, sending thuds of smacking leather through the speakers. This is normal behavior, as Jacob has been practicing mixed martial arts and boxing after school. Ethan is uncertain what Victor is trying to prove.

Jacob stops and looks toward the bottom of the screen when the sliding door to the patio can be heard opening. Amber steps in the frame carrying a plate with a sandwich. She places it on the picnic table and says, "You need to eat, sweetheart. You've been hitting that thing since you got home."

"Thanks, mom," Jacob replies, taking his gloves off and setting them on the edge of the table. Amber begins to walk back off screen when Jacob says, "Mom, wait."

She turns as he skips over next to her.

"Watch this," he says excitedly. They stand a few feet away from the table as he holds his hand out with his palm facing the gloves.

Ethan's heart races once again.

"What are you doing?" Amber asks, confused by Jacob's small grunts as he focuses with his fingers spread wide.

"Just… Watch." He leans forward. With another grunt, he brings his hand to his chest then quickly snaps it back outward, causing one of the gloves to slide off the table. He turns to his mom, revealing his face on the camera as he's smiling.

Amber shakes her head, saying, "You know I don't like this stuff, Jacob. I'm im—"

Victor slams the laptop shut and pulls it toward himself. Ethan's eyes remain fixed on where the laptop was. "We knew Better Human had the potential to enhance DNA. But telekinesis?" Victor speaks to Ethan who remains staring at the table.

Ethan barely comprehends his words as his mind thinks of how to get out of this.

"How could you keep this from me, Ethan?"

He doesn't respond.

"This is *more* than what we dreamed it could be. Jacob's success could change everything."

"You will *not* use my son like one of your other test subjects." Ethan spits with rage.

"Okay." Victor raises his hands and leans back in his chair. His voice is calm and rational. He lowers his hands slowly, resting them on his thighs. As he watches Ethan hold an angered and worried stare, breathing heavily, he asks, "So, it's true. It *did* work on Jacob?"

Ethan quickly nods.

"You-You've lied to me all these times I've asked about him?"

He nods again.

"Okay." Victor looks toward the door, thinking.

"I won't let you test on him, Vic." Ethan's voice is shaky, yet determined.

"Understood," Victor replies quickly, nodding to Ethan.

Victor stands from his chair and walks to the door where he stops and buttons his suit jacket. Ethan leans back in his chair, feeling his arms tremble.

Turning to Ethan, Victor says, "Let's go. It's time to leave."

Ethan stares at Victor's eyes. They're surrounded by the dark veins yet look sincere.

"Come on." Victor smiles and gestures his head to the door.

As Ethan stands, Victor opens the door. He stops after stepping out to the hall and looks to the side, speaking to someone. He says softly, "It's time."

Ethan walks toward the door when a young man steps inside the room. He's shirtless, but straps cross over his chest in an X. With a smirk, he aims a silver pistol at Ethan. Before Ethan can raise his hands and speak, a flash and bang fill the room.

Ethan's vision goes blurry as he falls backward, slamming onto the floor but feeling nothing. Ethan wants to move his arms but is unable to. He hears voices, but they sound like they're underwater. Realizing he's not breathing, he tries to inhale, but nothing happens, he's stuck, motionless, staring at the bottom of the wall. The light of the room begins to fade and turn gray as a shoe steps in front of his face. The same glossy shoe Victor wears. Ethan tries to speak and yell for Victor, but nothing happens.

The muffled sounds stop.

Everything goes black.

CHAPTER 2

ON THE FRONT DOOR OF house fourteen, road three, section one, quadrant one, hangs a sign that reads, "The Andersons." Within the walls of the new city structures, all housing developments are divided into four quadrants. Inside each quadrant are four sections of housing consisting of eight streets. Each street holds about the same number of two-bedroom houses that look identical. These were designed this way for simplicity, fairness and efficiency, ease of access to stores, schools and businesses, less reliance on vehicular transportation, and most of all, safety from "the Outside."

Inside house fourteen, road three, section one, quadrant one, rings the morning alarm of Jacob Anderson.

"Breakfast will be ready soon, sweetheart!" yells Amber up the stairs. Her strawberry-bronze hair is tied up in a bun.

"I'll be right there, Mom!" Jacob yells back. Thudding rumbles through the ceiling as he is heard jumping out of bed and throwing his usual jeans and hoodie on for school. Once dressed, he slides down the railing of the stairs into the kitchen.

"You and that hair." Amber chuckles as she glances over from the stove at his messy, wavy brown hair falling near his eyes and over his ears.

With a grin and rubbing his hand in his hair, Jacob says, "What? Did I put too much product in it?"

She laughs and shakes her head as she moves bacon from the frying pan to a plate. She says, "Are you prepared for final exams before fall break?"

"Of course, mom," Jacob says with a smirk, sliding to the counter on his socks and taking a piece of bacon.

"Have you thought about shadowing your father while you're off school and considering that internship after you graduate?"

"I dunno, mom," Jacob says singingly, trying to make it obvious he doesn't want to have this conversation.

"Okay, but you'll have to pick a field to work in once school is done," she says, pointing her spatula at Jacob. "You're one of the few kids with good grades in all the fields who gets to choose what they want to do. Not everyone gets to do that."

"I know. I just…" Jacob hesitates. He shuffles his foot around on the floor, then extends his arm and looks at the inside of his elbow.

Noticing, Amber says, "I get it, Jacob." Setting her utensil down, she rubs his shoulder and adds, "You know how I feel about your dad and those tests–"

"He shows me these tests then says it has to be a secret," Jacob interrupts angrily. He is flustered, saying, "Like… Why would I get into that field when I can't even talk about this sh–" He drags out the last word in a shushing sound.

"Jacob," Amber says in a soft, scolding tone with her eyebrows lowering. "I wish that language didn't come so easily to you."

"I didn't say anything, mom," he replies with a smirk.

Unable to fight a returning smile, she shakes her head and says, "Anyway. It's okay. You don't have to choose your field right now. And your dad and I will support whatever decision you make."

Jacob sighs and looks back at the floor. He's worried that if he doesn't choose the same field as his dad that he'll disappoint him.

Leaning to her side to make eye contact with him while he stares at the floor, Amber lifts his chin and smiles, saying, "Until then, just keep being a kid, okay?"

Pressing his lips to fight his incoming smile, he grabs another piece of bacon, bites it and smiles, saying, "Okay, mom."

"Do I get to have any?" Amber chuckles as she returns to finish cooking eggs.

Laughing on his way to the steps, Jacob turns and says, "Where's dad been, anyway? I haven't seen him in three days."

Sizzling from the pan erupts as she flips the eggs. Amber says, "You know how his work is. He and Victor are probably tied up in another project. I'm sure he'll be home today." Her smile fades a bit as she's reminded of Ethan's dedication to his work. She supports what he does, but she will admit her dislike of him being away for days at a time.

He sees his mom's expression of sadness. Pausing, he says, softly, "Mom?"

She looks at him.

"Do I *have* to go to Victor's for dinner this weekend?" he says, trying to make a cute, convincing face.

Sighing while lightly laughing at his forced innocent expression, Amber says, "It's the polite thing to do, Jacob. He's done a lot for us." She plates the eggs. "It's your dad's best friend. Plus, Victor adores you."

Sighing louder, Jacob says, "But, like… His house is weird. Like a creepy-weird."

"Coming from the kid who sneaks out to collect old-world objects," Amber says sternly, pointing at him after placing their plates on the table.

"Yeah, but…" He stutters, "His old-world stuff is… It's *weird*." He drags out the last word with a raspy breath.

Amber unties her apron then hangs it over the back of her chair at the table. Giving a convincing disappointed look, she quickly rolls her eyes, then says, "Okay. Fine. I'll talk to your dad and see what I—"

"Yes! Thank you, mom!" He leaps to her and hugs her.

Grunting from the tight hug, but smiling and closing her eyes, she says, "Just don't make me regret this and you go sneaking over the wall again."

Gasping and backing away from the hug, Jacob says, sarcastically, "What? I would *never*!" He giggles and runs up to his room.

Stepping forward to the stairs, Amber yells, "I'm serious, Jacob! You know how much that scares me! And I just finished breakfast, where are you going?"

His voice muffled through his bedroom door and the hallway, she hears him yell back, "I forgot my backpack! I'll be right back down!"

After enjoying a quick breakfast with his mom, Jacob skips out the front door, along the sidewalk, then onto the street to begin his walk to school. He makes his way to the cross street that leads to the city as Deante, Jacob's best friend, jogs to meet him from street six.

"Yo, nerd!" Deante yells as he approaches, sounding winded. His shoes are untied and flapping as he runs holding his backpack straps.

Jacob stops and waits for him to catch up, laughing at his half-tucked hoodie and his struggle to keep his shoes on while he runs. He makes sure Deante sees him laughing at him before saying, "Damn, man, you gassed? What did you just run, half a block?"

"Man, I ran this *whole* way, bro," he says, catching his breath, while initiating their handshake. "My mom caught me reading that Wolverine comic I found. She did the, 'Don't you *dare* tell me you been outside the walls again!'" He imitates his mom's voice.

"Shit. What'd you say? Did you tell her we—"

Deante interrupts, "*Fuck* no, man. I told her Kyle gave it to me. She'll kill me if she knows we went to the Outside again."

Jacob giggles, "You better hope she doesn't call Kyle's mom. He just got ungrounded from his mom finding all the old cell phones we found."

"Dude, I *know*. I froze, man." He kicks a stone as they walk. "Man, we didn't see Kyle for *weeks* after that. Should I give him a heads up?"

"Either that or roll the dice that your mom doesn't call, I guess. I dunno." Jacob shrugs his shoulders. "My mom's always paranoid that we're going over the walls."

"Shit, man." Deante kicks another stone.

"My dad was pissed when we got caught, but he was also curious about what we saw and found. Kinda wanted to know more about the Wasted and if we saw any." They stop at an intersection and wave to a passing driver in a white lab coat. "I think he only worries 'cause I think he believes there's actually Shriekers out there."

"Really?" Deante asks, shocked. "Your *dad* believes Shriekers are real?"

Jacob chuckles and shrugs his shoulders.

"Ain't no way." Deante shakes his head hard enough that his tossle cap gets loose. "Bad drawings and urban legends is all they are." He waits for a reaction from Jacob. "Right?"

"I guess." His shoulders rise.

"You guess?"

"Yeah, man, I—"

"Does your dad have photos?" Deante uses his arm to stop Jacob in the middle of the street. "Have you seen secret photos?"

With a laugh through his nose, Jacob pushes Deante's arm away and continues walking, saying, "Come on, dude. No. I'd have told you if I did. Plus, my mom hates that he hardly backs her on me sneaking over the walls. She'd flip if she knew he showed me secret pictures. She always just says, 'It's *so* dangerous out there! What if you found those old-ass guns they all had back then.'" He mocks Amber's voice.

"No way your mom said, 'ass,'" Deante says, laughing. "Plus, she should know you aren't going to be aiming those old weapons tryin' to see through that mop-top head of yours." Laughing harder at himself, he jokingly pushes Jacob.

Pushing him back, Jacob says, "Coming from the one wearing that beanie still 'cause you jacked up buzzing your hair."

"Alright. Touché." He pauses, then says, excitedly, "Yo, what if I *do* get Kyle in trouble?" Dramatically holding his face, he adds, "What if I screwed it, dude? He's so close to hacking those devices so we can finally see what kids did in the old-world."

Chuckling at his over-acting, Jacob says, "We'll just do what we did for Renz and get a list of what to find."

"Oh yeah, when Renz believed that Toby and his asshole friends saw a Shrieker."

"Yeah," Jacob laughs. "He didn't come out with us for a while."

Continuing to laugh, Deante says, "Man. He was *really* fuckin' scared even when he did finally join us again." Smacking Jacob's arm, he adds, "Bro. I do gotta find that next issue of Wolverine. Logan got fried to an atom in that last issue, man. An *atom*!"

"Yeah, I've still been trying to find that last *Game of Thrones* book. Someone's gotta have it. They have all the others. Maybe we can run out after school today." Jacob thinks as they keep walking, "Wait, I have basketball practice after school. Shit."

"Man, you're the *best* player by a long shot. You could miss every practice and still start every game."

Hesitating for a second, Jacob says, "You're right. Let's do it!"

They approach the main part of the city where Volcan Enterprises sits behind repurposed commercial buildings. It towers over them as if it's watching over the civilians. As they cross the street to their school, Jacob and Deante nod to others who are walking to work while ignoring eye contact with the few security guards patrolling the streets.

What used to be an elementary school now acts as a school for all grades. The population is small inside the Conservation Cities, so class sizes tend to be around a dozen students. One teacher handles each grade, teaching all classes.

Through the front double doors of the school is a large hallway. To the right is the main office with classroom doors repeating down the hall. To the left is the gymnasium which acts as the cafeteria for breakfast and lunch. Jacob and Deante enter the gym to meet Kyle and Renz at their usual table.

They approach the bench attached to the table where Kyle and Renz are arguing with a group of kids at the other end.

"No, what I'm sayin' is: I don't believe your ass ever left the walls," Renz yells at the student sitting closest to him.

"What's going on?" Jacob asks Kyle as he sits next to him.

"Toby started saying he has pictures of a Shrieker and Renz called him out when he wouldn't show proof," Kyle replies, trying to also listen.

Missing Toby's reply, they hear Renz say, "Really? So how do you get over the walls?"

Toby stutters. He sees Jacob and Kyle snicker at Renz's question. He replies, "It's… There's a…"

Speaking over him, Renz says, "Tell ya what, show me after school. I'll go with you." He turns to Jacob, looks at Deante beside him, and says, "Sup, Jacob. D."

"Morning, bro." Deante bumps fists with Renz.

"You done bullying Toby, man?" Jacob says, chuckling. He watches Toby and his friends whisper and look over at them.

"Man, he's just full of shit," Renz says, arrogantly. "We've been over the walls how many times and ain't ever seen a Shrieker."

"Let him go, man," Kyle mutters, pushing up his glasses.

"What's with you?" Renz asks him, referring to his defeated tone.

"My mom texted me on my walk to school." He holds up his phone, expresses disappointment, then puts it back in his pocket. "Says she needs to talk to me the second I get home."

Deante passes a quick, fearful look to Jacob. He asks Kyle, sounding concerned, "W-What do you think it… It is?"

"I don't know man. I just freakin' stopped being grounded." He leans on the table, holding his face in his hands. He messes up his blonde, spiked hair.

Dismissing Kyle's nerves, Renz asks, "She didn't take those cell phones and tablets we found, did she?"

Muffled through his hands, Kyle replies, "No, I kept them in my closet."

"You hack into anything yet?" Deante asks nervously.

Sighing and revealing his face, Kyle answers, irritated, "I followed the one book I found and got a program running that worked to unlock the tablet. I was gonna show you guys what's on it."

Under his breath, Deante mutters, "Fuck!"

Patting Kyle's back as he now rests his face into his folded arms on the table, Jacob smirks at Deante and says to Kyle, "It'll be alright man. Hopefully it's nothing."

Seeing Jacob's smirk, then looking back and forth between Jacob and Deante, Renz whispers, "What? What's going on?"

Jacob mouths, "I'll tell you later."

Deante lowers his eyebrows angrily, creating wrinkles in his forehead.

"I guess you won't be interested in skipping after lunch with D and I and looting more of that neighborhood we started?" Jacob asks lightly.

"Nope!" Kyle yells through his hoodie sleeve.

"Renz?" Deante asks.

"Uh…" He hesitates, "I probably shouldn't today, to be honest. My dad needed my help with something."

"Fine," Deante says. "Looks like it's just us again." He shrugs to Jacob.

The bell rings through the school to signal classes begin in five minutes. The four of them walk to their lockers then enter Mrs. Ramirez's classroom. They all sit at desks near each other in the back corner of the room. A second bell rings to signal the start of class.

"Alright everyone, please take your seats," Mrs. Ramirez speaks loudly. Her focus is on two students shuffling to their desks. "Mr. Brendel and Mr. Moye. You both still insist on being thirty seconds late every day?"

"Sorry, Mrs. Ramirez," They stutter in unison.

She watches them take their seats. Her curly hair bounces as she turns her head to address the class. Pointing to the dry erase board, she yells, "Okay class. Before I begin, this is a reminder that final exams begin next week. These scores will be considered in your Field Reports. When you all return from fall break, you will turn in your field requests so that your final semesters can be structured accordingly to your field." She looks around the room and asks, "Any questions?"

The classroom is silent with a few heads shaking no.

"If any questions come to you before finals week, please ask me." She gives an assuring look across the room. "Now, as we touched on yesterday, in preparation for your final exams, we'll finish learning about viruses. Specifically, the Vivere Mors virus, or Vi-mor virus for short.

"It transfers quickly between hosts through saliva or blood coming in contact with another person's blood. Infected hosts then become violent, often spreading through biting another person, or attacking viciously and having their blood contact an open wound. Its short incubation time allows it to affect the new host rapidly, which is why it nearly caused the extinction of humans."

She scans the classroom and asks, "Who can tell me why this virus causes the host to become violent?"

Toby's hand whips into the air.

"Yes, Toby," she addresses him.

Toby stands. His tone is arrogant, which is typical when he talks about anything outside the walls. He answers, "The hosts become violent and act on primal instincts due to the virus causing extreme inflammation in the host's brain. Similar to the rabies virus, but with an evolutionary trait to keep the infected alive, it keeps the inflammation extreme enough to keep the host hostile, but not so much as to kill the host, thus killing the virus itself." He sits back down confidently.

"Excellent answer, Toby." Mrs. Ramirez nods to him. "He's correct. Vi-mor is considered to be an evolved form of the rabies virus. It is the first virus considered to act with a parasitic nature.

"With infected Outsiders still living outside the walls, it's important to remind you all how dangerous these infected are." She points to bullet points written under INFECTED on the dry erase board. "Infected are, number one, dangerous. Number two, violent, and will attack if they see you."

As she continues, Kyle turns his head discreetly to look at Jacob and roll his eyes. Jacob acknowledges him and rolls his eyes in return.

"Number four–" Mrs. Ramirez pauses abruptly. "Did I say something you disagree with, Mr. Anderson?"

CHAPTER 3

SPOTLIGHTS MAY AS WELL BE shining on him in a dark theater. Stuttering, Jacob says, "No, ma'am."

Angrily she replies, "You rolled your eyes. I'd like to know what it is you find appalling."

He stares at her nervously.

"Today, Jacob." She's losing patience.

"It's just…" He looks around the room. Everyone is staring at him. "The Waste… The Outsiders *aren't* vicious. They're actually afraid of *us*," he says, matter-of-factly.

"And how is it that you know more than the scientists who continue to study the Outsiders and their—"

Interrupting, Toby yells, "Because he and his friends sneak outside the walls!"

"Toby. You'll raise your hand when you'd like to speak." Turning her head to Jacob, Mrs. Ramirez says, "Is this true, Mr. Anderson?"

Jacob leans on his elbow and squeezes the bridge of his nose. *What am I doing?* He thinks to himself.

As he inhales to give a lie for his answer, he's saved by Mrs. Ramirez breaking the silence, saying, "You know what, nevermind. See me before lunch, Jacob." She returns to the dry erase board. It feels like everyone's stares are burning through him. He closes his eyes and slows his breath to relax himself.

"I'll have all your attention back to the board." The smacking of her hand on the board gets everyone to finally stop looking at Jacob.

Mrs. Ramirez continues to teach about the infected Outsiders and how the inflammation from the virus causes permanent brain damage, keeping the infected host living but acting on primal instinct and rage; only driven to eat, attack, and spread the virus to new hosts. This is why travelling outside the walls is dangerous and forbidden for residents of the Conservation Cities.

Finally, the bell for lunch rings through the school. Jacob just wants to get this meeting with her over with. All the students grab their books and scurry out of the classroom. Jacob takes his time standing and walking to Mrs. Ramirez's desk. He hangs his head, waiting for her to speak first.

"What would your father think of this, Jacob?" she asks politely.

Scoffing, he replies, "I don't know. But can you please not get him involved again."

"I already texted him to call me." She sits forward in her chair and leans to get him to look at her. "It's not a great look for you, being the smartest in the school *and* a troublemaker."

With another scoff, he says, *"Troublemaker*? This was barely me—"

"Kids know – or *think* – you're sneaking outside of the walls? Jacob. Look at me." Taps on the desktop from her finger get him to make eye contact. She then adds, "Whether it's true or not is beyond my control. However, it would be inconsiderate of me to not remind you how *dangerous* and *foolish* that is, if it were true."

He continues to hold eye contact while lowering his head toward the floor, looking through the hair partially covering his eyes.

"The reason I kept you is about your father." She expresses a stern look when she sees him roll his eyes. "He is responsible for saving our species with the vaccine he and Victor Volcan created. Their research of the infected saved us. You second guessing my teachings of the Outsiders is both disrespectful to me and to your father's work."

Jacob looks back at the floor.

"Do you hear me, Jacob?" she follows up.

"I hear you." He shows reluctance in his voice.

"I'll be letting your father know what we spoke of here when he calls me."

"Fine," he mutters. Under his breath he says, "He'll call you if he ever leaves work."

"What was that?"

"Nothing. May I go now?"

"You may." She sits back in her chair. Her head shakes as her disappointed eyes watch him leave the classroom.

Jacob scowls to himself in the lunch line as he replays his conversation with Mrs. Ramirez. He chooses pizza over the second option of grilled chicken and vegetables. Joining the table with his friends who are about to finish eating, he sets his tray down and sits, sighing, ready to tell them about the after-class meeting that made him late for lunch. As he's about to speak, a hand slaps a piece of paper down near his tray. He's looking at a poorly drawn sketch of a person with scribbled out eyes, mangled hair and scars on their skin.

"What do you want, Toby? What is this?" Jacob asks, annoyed. Toby is standing over him.

"I know you don't believe me, but I've seen them," Toby says in a serious tone.

"Whatever, dude," Jacob dismisses him, pushing the paper away.

"I'm serious, Jacob. Why don't you—"

"Because you've never been outside the walls, Toby," he cuts him off. "We've been outside of them enough times to have seen a Shrieker. But they don't exist. They're urban legends."

Toby shows his nerves and looks between Jacob and his friends. Stuttering, he says, "I live in the back of section three. If I crawl out my bedroom window I can climb to the top of my roof." He sits next to Jacob who leans onto his hand. "I kept hearing their screaming and wretched noises. Finally, I took my dad's binoculars up to the roof and, I'm telling you, I saw a Shrieker."

"Even if I believed you, what do you want me to do with this information?" Jacob shows he's bothered.

Toby stands and says, softly, "I was hoping I could meet with your dad and tell him about it."

Jacob stands and gets in Toby's face.

Kyle and Deante burst from their seats and pull Jacob away from Toby. "Just go, man," Deante tells Toby.

"What the fuck was that, bro?" Kyle asks Jacob as they sit back at the table.

"I'm so *fucking* tired of hearing about my dad. I get it. He's *famous* and he 'saved the world' with 'all his tremendous research.'" He waves his arms and imitates Mrs. Ramirez's voice.

Giving him a moment to cool down, Deante, Renz and Kyle stay silent while watching him eat his pizza as if he were racing for the best time.

Finally, Renz says, "Don't you… Don't you think you overreacted just a bit?"

Jacob wipes his mouth and drops the napkin on his tray. He looks several tables over at Toby who is chewing his lunch while staring intently back at him.

Jacob says, chuckling, "Probably. I'll apologize later." He stands from his seat and says to Deante, "We going, D?"

"Oh. That's right. Let's freakin' go!" Deante jumps up, excited. They exit the cafeteria, retrieve their backpacks from their lockers, then sneak out of the front of the school.

A small, wooded area sits between the wall surrounding the city and the last street of houses in section one. In this wooded area is a tall tree with a strong branch that extends over the wall as if it's reaching for the trees in the woods on the other side. Jacob and his friends permanently secured a rope to this branch and use it to repel down the wall and explore the Outside. Deante and Jacob walk to the tree, repel over the wall and began their walk through tall grass.

Breaking the silence when he sees Jacob stewing, Deante says, "So. You wanna tell me what all that was about back there in the cafeteria?"

Releasing a loud sigh, Jacob says, "I dunno, man. I feel like every day in school I have to hear about the shit my dad's done. Kids want to meet him. Teachers remind me how amazing he is.

"But, like, this morning, dude. My dad hasn't been home from work in days. And I see it on my mom's face how much she hates it. I saw her sad this morning and I guess it all just snowballed."

"Damn, bro," Deante says. "He ain't even calling your mom or nothin'?"

"He can't. They don't let employees keep phones on them inside the building."

"Even your dad? A guy that owns half the place?" Deante sounds shocked.

"Nobody. Except Victor. I guess being the city leader grants him the exception." He releases a small laugh as they enter a dense patch of woods.

"Sorry, dude. I can imagine that's—" Deante stops when Jacob hits his arm and points off to the side.

"Look." He's pointing at an Outsider who's peeking at them from around a tree. Their hair is greasy. As they lean and stare at Jacob and Deante with golden irises, their faded shirt hangs off their side with holes worn in several places, and their jeans are nearly white from constant wear. They look to be in their late teens or early twenties.

They stand in place, watching the Outsider watching them. "This guy is one of the *aggressive and violent* Wasted Mrs. Ramirez went on about." Jacob scoffs and steps toward the Outsider, who yelps and runs quickly away from Jacob and Deante.

Chuckling, Deante says, "Why do they tell us they're violent and aggressive?"

"Who knows, man?" Jacob replies, pushing a branch away from his face.

Emerging from the woods, the two of them stand in the backyard of a home covered in green moss. A wooden swing set lies broken on the ground next to a sandbox with weeds replacing the sand.

"We looted this blue one last time, right?" Deante asks, referencing the house in front of them.

"We did. Let's hit this one today," Jacob replies, gesturing to the house to their right. To the left, the yards curve away as the houses sit in a cul de sac.

The house they approach is yellow but tinted green from the same moss, as well as the vines covering most of the brick below the moss-covered siding. They hop over a rusty metal fence and onto a large concrete patio. Cracks run along the cement with tall grass growing through them in patches. A half-evaporated pool holds stagnant black water that looks gelatinous. Deante begins pulling at the handle of sliding glass doors.

"Come. On!" He grunts loudly, pulling at the locked door. "Damn. Why can it never be this easy?"

Picking up a patio stone, Jacob says, "Ever since you found that *one* unlocked house, you hope they're all like that." He laughs then throws the stone through the glass door. Shattering echoes through the silent air. Birds in the nearby tree flutter off into the sky. Jacob and Deante stand frozen, listening inside the house for movement.

"Hear anything?" Jacob whispers to Deante.

Leaning closer to the broken glass, Deante whispers, "Nothing."

Deante steps through the door, knocking a hanging piece of glass to the ground. It shatters but doesn't startle them. He turns, unlatches the lock on the handle and slides open the broken door. "Let me get the door for you, old man."

They both laugh, then Jacob says, "Shut up." He steps inside into the dining room.

Dust fills the musty air, carrying rays of light from holes in the windows covered in vines and dirt. A pot that once held a lively plant, now sits on a grimy dining table holding a dried and withered, brown plant carcass. Deante makes his way to the kitchen on the right. Cabinets are left hanging open. Broken dishes litter the floor along with condiments and empty food boxes. He scans the opened cabinets, then kicks away boxes on his way to the hallway off the kitchen that leads to the front door.

"I'm going to head up these stairs," he announces to Jacob, motioning to the staircase at the end of the hall.

"Okay. I'll look in here. See if there are any of those corny rom-coms Renz enjoys." He chuckles and points to the living room attached to the dining room.

Deante's heavy footsteps through the ceiling are followed by him yelling, "Jackpot!" as he finds a bedroom covered in comic book posters and action figures. Jacob chuckles to himself as he walks up to an end table next to a large sectional couch.

He grabs a framed photo showing a family of three. A woman stands next to a man holding a young boy. They all wear matching t-shirts with a large circle and two smaller circles at the top. Behind them is a crowd of people and a blue castle.

"Things were really different back then, huh?" Jacob says quietly as if the family in the photo were going to answer him. He jumps when a crash on the floor above him sounds.

"Dammit!" Deante yells, sounding muffled through the floor.

"You alright up there?" Jacob yells at the ceiling.

Faint shuffling and clicking of plastic are heard through the floor. Deante is barely audible as he mutters, "These damn bobbleheads. Top-heavy f—."

Jacob laughs to himself while he carefully places the framed photo back into the clean shape it left in the thick dust. A quick look at the stand holding the TV reveals cases of movies. On his way to check the titles, he sees a large family photo on the wall. It's the same family as the one on the end table, but what catches his attention is their faces. Their smiles radiated. Just as he starts to reminisce about his childhood, a disturbing scream bellows from outside. A painful scream.

Startled, Jacob runs quietly to the window. Peering through dry-rotted blinds and leaves outside the window, Jacob sees a man hunched over in agony. He's naked, twitching in the cul de sac, covered in scars and large scabs. One scab on his shoulder is bleeding down his arm. He releases another agonizing cry, jerking his head toward the house, whipping long, dirty, black, greasy hair behind his head, looking at the window Jacob is peeking through.

Before ducking away, Jacob sees his face. One eye has been replaced with dozens of fresh, bloody scratches and a hole streaming blood down his cheek. He is pulling his hand away from his face, as if these wounds were self-inflicted, causing the initial, blood-curdling, scream. His mouth is lipless, with chunks of flesh missing where the lips were, showing he bit them off. All this overtakes the fact that his face is distorted and misshapen.

"Fuck. Fuck. Fuck," Jacob mutters to himself. He scans the room, locking his eyes on the staircase in the foyer. *D!* He thinks to himself as he assumes a crouched position.

Entering the hallway, he ensures that the front door is locked. He quietly walks upstairs, turning down the hallway at the top. Seeing Deante frozen in the window of the bedroom straight ahead, Jacob lightly jogs to him, grabbing his shoulders and turning him around. His face is panicked. "D! We have to go," he speaks sternly but softly.

"Is… Jacob… Is that a… It's a Shr—"

A loud slam hits the front door.

"We need to get downstairs, D. Exit the dining room door through the back where we—"

Another bang strikes the door with a scratchy yelp from the Shrieker.

"Come on." Jacob pulls his arm and Deante follows. They follow the railing lining the staircase and turn to go down the steps. Nearing the bottom, while staring at the front door that is now showing cracks in the center, Jacob freezes as a crashing sound pierces through the foyer and pieces of wood click against the walls.

The Shrieker stumbles inside to its feet and stands in the foyer on top of broken pieces of the front door.

CHAPTER 4

ARMS TWITCHING, THE SHRIEKER SCRATCHES a chunk of flesh from its cheek then jerks its head to look at Jacob with its only eye.

"Go! Go! Go!" Jacob yells, pushing Deante back up the steps as the tip of his sneaker slips off the edge, driving his knee into the hardwood step. Stumbling to their feet at the top, they turn and face a closed bedroom door at the start of the hallway. "In there!" Jacob yells.

From trembling hands, Deante's grip slips when first grabbing the doorknob. He opens the door and runs inside. As Jacob steps into the bedroom, he hears a close screech and feels the Shrieker grab his backpack. Jacob looks at Deante with frightened eyes and closes the door as he's pulled back into the hallway.

Knowing the railing by the steps is directly behind them, Jacob throws himself backward into the Shrieker. It grunts as its back hits the railing. Splitting of wood reverberates off the walls as Jacob's body pushing on the Shrieker causes the railing to give out and send them falling to the staircase.

Jacob lands on the Shrieker. It lets out a weak groan that stops immediately and its limbs go limp, hanging to the step below.

Slowly getting to his knee on the next step up, Jacob taps the Shrieker's bloody cheek. There's no response other than its head moving from the force of Jacob's hand.

Standing and walking to the top of the steps, Jacob says, "D. I think we're—"

He's cut off by a raspy moan followed by rapid breaths as the Shrieker stands, jerking its limbs and screaming until it sees Jacob through the broken railing.

Quickly, Jacob throws his backpack down the hall into the bedroom Deante was in earlier. Bending his knees and raising his fists, he braces for the Shrieker running at him. His nerves send a shiver through his torso. All his training at Dave's Gym never prepared him for a Shrieker attack. He can hear his dad as if he's outside the boxing ring at practice, yelling, "Watch his feet and his shoulders! Predict his next move!" But the Shrieker twitches violently with every move it makes. Now it's closer. It leaves Jacob no choice. He needs to protect Deante. He needs to get them out of here alive.

Jacob swings a punch into the lunging Shrieker's cheek. The bones of his knuckles crack as they connect with its cheek bone. It releases a gurgling scream and holds its hand on its face, shaking its head aggressively. Jacob steps back toward the open bedroom and watches the Shrieker glare at him with its eye and rip skin from where it was hit. It hisses, spraying blood from its bitten off lips.

Jacob scrunches his nose in disgust and watches it step toward him, trying again to predict its next move, Jacob watches its shoulders as it leans forward, preparing to lunge at him.

Its quick, short jerks and twitching arms make it impossible to know how it plans to strike. The Shrieker bursts forward, clasps Jacob's face and slams his head into the wall. Drywall cracks and small pieces tick onto the floor.

His vision blurry, Jacob straightens himself and connects a punch into the chest of the Shrieker, cracking a rib. It yelps and hisses. Spit flies as it haphazardly throws itself at Jacob, tackling him onto his back. Jacob groans as he hits the ground, and it lands on his stomach, just inside the bedroom door.

Screeching, the Shrieker slashes Jacob's face. Its unkempt fingernails rip skin from his cheek. He wrenches from the burning pain. Flailing his arms in a panic, Jacob manages to push the Shrieker back, and with his right arm he swings another jab into its ribs. He hears them crack when he connects.

It screams, spraying blood from its lips again. Clasping its hands over its head, it slams them into the bridge of Jacob's nose. Immediate burning fills his sinuses, and he tastes iron on his tongue. Thrusting his knees isn't moving the Shrieker from his stomach. It slashes through the same wound on his cheek. Writhing and terrified, Jacob slaps away a slash from its other arm. He punches but is slapped away as well. It connects another scrape on his opposite cheek. Jacob keeps swinging, trying to block its wildly attacking arms as the ones he misses scratch his nose, then neck and top of his chest.

A slamming door sounds as Deante bursts from the room he was in. His screaming grows louder and slamming footsteps bang faster when he tackles the Shrieker off of Jacob.

The Shrieker releases a gurgled cry before it thuds onto the floor nearby. Jacob watches as Deante struggles to hold a hand on each of its biceps while it attempts to slash its arms. Deante turns his head as spit flies from the Shrieker's mouth each time it jerks its head to bite at him.

Jacob's breathing is short and rapid. His face is burning as if his wounds are on fire. He tries to yell over to Deante but coughs when air leaves his lungs.

The Shrieker shakes an arm free and swings at Deante, who yells from the scratch on his face. Jacob feels adrenaline rush through him. He rushes to his feet and pulls Deante off the Shrieker, then straddles its chest with his knees. It swings at his face. He catches its wrist while staring coldly into its eye. Jacob aggressively twists its wrist, snapping the bones in its arm. The scream from the Shrieker is gut wrenching as Jacob lets go, dropping the limp, broken arm at its side.

Gritting his teeth, Jacob throws a powerful punch into the eye socket of the Shrieker. Saliva sprays from its teeth as it begins to breathe rapidly, showing that Shriekers can experience fear. Another punch lands on the other side of its face. Then another.

Jacob thinks about pulling back, but can't. He throws punch after punch as bones crack in the Shriekers face. It's no longer responding or making sounds. The head flops from side to side as each punch hits. Blood covers Jacob's arms and is spattered over his face and shirt and trails of blood stream across the floor from each side of its head. He yells as he watches his fists now punching the bloody, caved-in face of what used to be a person. Someone just like him. Someone who lost themselves to an infection. A human being.

Hands grab his shoulders and pull him back, snapping him back into the moment. Deante stares at him with widened eyes, sounding panicked, saying, "Dude. How did you… What the fuck, man?"

Jacob's breathing is heavy. He blinks his eyes tightly and grabs his forehead. "I-I don't know what got into me. I saw it attack you and just… I snapped."

"Snapped?" Deante yells, "You caved its face in." His eyes express shock again as he sees the large gash on Jacob's cheek is smaller and the others have healed and disappeared. "W-What the fuck, bro?" He takes a step backward.

"What?" Jacob is confused. Deante points to his right cheek. Realizing what happened and touching to confirm, Jacob drops his head and says, "Yeah. That."

"*That*?" Deante scoffs. "What is going on with you?"

"Nothing, dude, it's just—"

"*Nothing*? Nothing!"

Standing from the floor, Jacob holds out his arms, saying, "What do you want me to tell you?"

Deante shakes his head with disappointment. Looking at the Shrieker then back to Jacob, he drops his head and says, "Nothing, bro. You don't have to tell me anything." He walks out of the room.

Jacob sighs watching Deante leave. He walks to his backpack as he hears buzzing from his phone inside. The light shining from outside the window has turned a dark, nearly orange, yellow.

As he grabs the strap of his backpack, the buzzing stops. He finds his phone and sees there are four missed call notifications reading: MOM. A text preview is under the missed call notification. Also from his mom, it reads: "*Jacob, I called the school when you didn't come home, and they said you–*" The preview ends.

Crap. Jacob thinks, closing his eyes. He puts the phone in his pocket then opens his eyes and looks out to the hallway. He sees Deante sitting on the top step through the railing. His stare shows he's not well.

Jacob walks slowly to him and sits next to him on the step. Without breaking his stare at the broken front door, Deante says, "That was fucked up, man."

Now looking at the rubble at the bottom of the steps, too, Jacob says, "Yeah."

"We've never seen something like that before." Deante looks at Jacob. Jacob doesn't look back or reply. "You fought it off of us." Jacob's silence continues. He can sense where this is going. "Jacob, how are you…" Deante doesn't finish his question.

"I take boxing lessons, man, self-defense comes naturally to—"

"No way they teach you super strength at Dave's Gym," Deante gestures through the broken railing to the room with the dead Shrieker. "Plus," he points his finger close to Jacob's cheek where the largest wound has slowly started healing, "You haven't explained how you do *that*, either."

Jacob sighs, glances at Deante, then looks back at the broken door. He says, "My dad… I can…" Trying to find the words, he stutters, then continues, "He makes me keep it a secret, D. But, like, I've always had this." He motions to his chest, then his cheek. "I have, like… Abilities. One of them is that I heal quickly."

Deante resumes his gaze down the steps. It's obvious he's thinking. He remembers something and says, "That time you broke your arm in football. You wore a cast for weeks."

"Seriously, dude?"

Deante widens his eyes and jerks his head, waiting for elaboration.

Jacob scoffs, then sighs. "Yeah. It was healed by the next morning."

"This is insane." Deante speaks softly and shakes his head.

"The whole stadium saw the injury, so my dad said I should wear the cast so nobody questioned it."

"Damn." Deante stretches the skin on his cheeks with his hands then looks back at Jacob's cheek. "So, why'd all the other shit heal and that's still there?"

"Just…" He touches the wound. "The bigger the injury, the longer it takes to heal, still."

Laughing, Deante repeats, mocking his voice, "The longer it takes to heal."

"Alright, man," Jacob weakly chuckles.

"So, like…" He hesitates. "What else you do?"

"I don't know that I *do* anything. The healing stuff just happens." Jacob stretches his neck, sighs again, then says, "My dad did this… Thing when he was younger."

"Thing?" Deante asks, puzzled.

"He and Victor made this serum or whatever, and my dad used it on himself. They wanted to find a way to pass better genetics on to their kids. Strength, intelligence, immunity."

"Well, you got the strength down." Deante gestures his head again to the room.

Acknowledging him, Jacob replies, "Yeah." He begins to feel refreshed talking openly about this. Yes, he and his dad spoke during training and testing, but it was always scientific and technical. This feels more natural. Jacob adds, "I can, like, *sense* things."

"Sense things?" Deante asks, excited, "Like ghosts?"

Laughing, Jacob says, "No. It's more like I can anticipate things as they're about to happen."

"So if I threw a rock at you from behind, you'd still catch it?"

Chuckling harder, Jacob says, "No, again. It's more mathematical than that. Like, in basketball, I can watch a player's shoulders and feet and predict what they're going to do next. And when I train for boxing, I can always tell when and how they're going to swing the training pads just by watching their shoulders and hips. And feet, too."

"That's why you're so good at sports and—"

"Yeah. I guess so. Less exciting than eyes in the back of my head, huh?" He jokes.

"More like a great reason why you're the top player in every sport at school. And, I guess, at math."

Jacob chuckles. He continues to feel relief in talking with his best friend about this. He's nervous about what his dad will think knowing someone else knows, but he'll let his future self deal with that.

"I'm still learning, and I'm not perfect." He shrugs his shoulders. "But my dad's been working with me and testing to learn more about what—"

"Testing?" Deante interrupts, sounding concerned.

"It's not as bad as…" Jacob looks at the inside of his arm. His tone sounds disappointed as he says, "He says if he can learn exactly how his serum enhanced my genetics, he could use it as a way to better all of humanity."

"You know," Deante sees that Jacob is sad so he tries to joke, "saying your dad left you outside in radioactive rain or found you in a crashed alien spacecraft would be so much cooler."

"And *that* is why we have to sneak out here to find banned science fiction media," Jacob says. They both laugh. He continues, "But yeah, even I don't fully understand it all. All I know is my dad insisted nobody knows except him, me, and my mom, who absolutely hates it. At least the testing part of it, specifically."

"Hey." Deante gently shakes Jacob's shoulder. "I'm sorry your dad makes you keep this a secret. I can tell that's heavy on you."

"Thanks, man. Yeah. It sucks. I guess I do get it, though. I don't know."

Deante takes a deep breath. He says, "You know what's the worst about all this?"

"What's that?"

"That Toby has been right all along saying Shriekers are real."

"Fuck," Jacob chuckles. "We tell nobody. Agreed?"

"Agreed," Deante laughs, stretches, then stands. "Let's get back."

The walk back to the wall held mixed emotions for Jacob. The Shrieker encounter still gives him anxiety thinking about all the other ways it could have gone. But he feels lighter after speaking openly about his abilities with Deante.

When they arrive at the rope hanging over the wall, Jacob tugs on it then places his foot on the wall, ready to climb up. He looks at Deante and says, "You ever think about how much it would suck if we came back and the rope was gone?"

In an anxious tone, Deante says, "No. But I am now. Thanks for that."

"Just saying that it would suck." Jacob chuckles and climbs up, pulling himself onto the tree branch. He watches Deante climb and helps him to the branch. They both descend the tree and stand at the bottom.

"The only other thing I can tell you is I've moved stuff just thinking about it a few times. I haven't really figured out how to do it *all* the time or on purpose, really." Jacob says with a smile, hoping to get a reaction out of Deante.

With excited eyes, Deante says, "Promise me that as soon as you know how, you show me immediately."

Laughing through his nose, Jacob says, "I promise."

"Oh, and remember, we aren't telling Toby he's right about Shriekers."

"I definitely remember. We probably shouldn't tell Renz, either. He's already scared enough of the Wasted. And *they* leave us alone out here."

"True. Agreed."

They both walk to the street then travel to the second intersection. Stopping at sixth, they say goodbye while doing their handshake and Deante makes his way home. Jacob's pace slows as he walks the rest of the way. For all he knows, he could have more missed calls or texts from his mom. Or both. His phone is in his backpack. He's imagining her sitting at the kitchen table scowling. She'll bring in his dad to join in on the scolding.

"I just agreed to you not having to go to Victor's this weekend, and you repay me by skipping school? To go to the Outside *again*?" He imagines her yelling while he walks only a few houses away from home.

This always becomes even worse when his dad joins in. He wears that disappointed look, making Jacob feel more guilty than he does just knowing he upset his mom.

He stands on the street in front of his house. All the neighboring houses look similar. Once the walls were built around the Conservation Cities, buildings and old neighborhoods were torn down to make newer, smaller, more convenient housing to accommodate a smaller, yet hopefully growing community.

Here we go. He thinks to himself as he rests his hand on the front door. He knows this process well: turn the knob softly, hold it steady and open the door slowly. This will avoid the creaking when the door gets about halfway open – just enough to side-step through.

Jacob turns the knob and slowly pushes open the door. It squeaks. He sighs, immediately hearing Amber's footsteps coming from her bedroom.

She thuds down the steps, turning to face the foyer where he stands kicking off his shoes.

Her voice is loud and aggressive as she yells, "Of all the days for you to skip school. After I *agreed* to let you stay home instead of going to—"

"Mom, I know!" He turns to face her, saying, "I'm sorry, okay, I—"

Her eyes widened in shock. Her jaw drops and her face turns pale. She interrupts, staring at his face, then his shirt, then back to his cheeks. Her eyes glossy, she says, "Jacob. Why the *fuck* are you covered in blood?"

She never swears. This isn't going to be good.

CHAPTER 5

VICTOR VOLCAN IS A FACE and name known around the world. Saving humans from extinction will grant one this type of fame. After claiming the credit for he and Ethan developing their life-saving vaccine, he went on to play a role in designing the Conservation Cities.

Building walls around existing city infrastructures, Conservation Cities were secured within months of the outbreak and vaccine. Residents are required to have the vaccine if they wish to reside inside the walls.

Victor Volcan is the leader of the Conservation City of Pittsburgh; however, given his fame and involvement in designing Conservation Cities and how they share resources, he has a hand in how many of the regional cities operate.

Volcan Enterprises stands tall among the buildings in Pittsburgh. While Pittsburgh had several tall buildings previously, the surrounding ones were torn down to reuse their materials for building the walls and new homes. Standing thirty-three stories tall, it appears to tower over the three-story buildings around it. Large glass windows of offices and laboratories line the outside. The main lobby is a large open room with white ceramic tile floors and floor to ceiling windows for walls, with black metal seating at the base. A guarded security stand is set up at the main entrance, with a large white marble receptionist desk at the back wall next to the elevator.

On floor thirty-three, the elevator chimes, opening the golden doors. In his gray suit, Victor steps into the hallway, his glossy black dress shoes clicking with each step on the floor. He passes a glance at the frosted glass windows of Ethan's office as he approaches the secretary's desk stationed outside the doors of his own at the end of the hall.

"Hello, Ms. Daniels." He greets her with a nod after stopping next to her desk.

Rebecca Daniels is from the Conservation City of Johnstown and graduated last year with high grades and popularity within the city, thanks to her devotion to medical studies. This caught the attention of Victor. Her dream was to intern at Volcan Enterprises, and it just so happened that Victor needed a new secretary after his previous one mysteriously vanished. Connor was one of Victor's favorite secretaries. He was funny, tall, dark-haired, handsome, but known to be curious about the outside. Rumor has it he left the walls and was attacked or killed by an Outsider. Victor sent security searching for him for two days, but he was never found.

"G-Good after… Good evening, sir." Rebecca stands from her chair, clasping her hands nervously in front of her waist. Her blonde pig-tails wave from her quick movement. Victor's demanding presence makes her nervous, but she couldn't be happier to work for such a high-profile celebrity.

Smiling as he does any time he gets this kind of attention, he rests his fingers on the edge of her desk and says, "Call Garret for me. Tell him to meet me in my office immediately."

Garret is Victor's right hand man and the only other known exception to the no-phone rule, given that his company cell phone cannot take photos and is to always be on hand so Victor can summon him.

Dropping into her seat, she picks up the wired phone, says, "Y-Yes, sir," then dials Garret's work phone.

Victor enters his office through the dark oak door parting walls of frosted glass like Ethan's office. He stands inside, looking at more floor to ceiling windows lining the back wall overseeing the city. A matching oak wood desk sits in the center of the room. On top sits a closed laptop, wired desk phone and folders stuffed with papers. The side walls of the office are lined with bookshelves holding medical journals and books. On the right wall, shelves split in the center and a large photo of Victor hangs high above a smaller frame enclosing a piece of notebook paper with a ripped corner, containing the original notes for Better Human.

Sighing and rubbing the back of his neck, Victor walks over to the framed notebook paper.

He stares at Ethan's handwriting reading "gene splicing" with multiple, messy circles of blue pen scribbled around it. Next to it is a poorly drawn pair of jeans. A heaviness takes over Victor as he recalls the moment this happened. He and Ethan laughed. Not because his drawing was funny — it wasn't funny — but because in that moment, they sat in their favorite diner discovering Better Human and finalizing the plans that would become Volcan Enterprises.

Breaking away from his daydream, Victor takes a deep breath then places his thumb on a small metal circle inside the bottom left corner of the frame. A low beep sounds as the entire frame slides to the right, revealing a hidden compartment in the wall. Inside are more folders stuffed with papers and a silver pistol. Victor is reaching for a folder when a knock sounds at his office door. He touches the small metal circle and the frame closes.

"Come in," he barks while turning to the door.

Rebecca opens the door enough to poke her head in. Victor lets out a sigh and says, "I thought you were Garret. Where is he, Ms. Daniels?"

She stutters, "He… He said he would be right up from the… From the morgue, sir."

They stare at each other long enough that it becomes awkward. Victor begins walking to his desk and says, "And? Did *you* need something, Ms. Daniels?"

"Oh… Yes." She chuckles awkwardly. "Um… Penelope from Dover. She asked if you've considered her request for additional security after her last report."

Victor sits and leans back in his desk chair. He rubs his face with his hands, then says, "I told her when she called in her report. Once I see the grades of our graduating class, I'll consider sending her strong security candidates or any of the failures she could mold into some sort of use." He cracks his neck and mutters to himself, "Somehow it's my responsibility to fill her worthless population, offering no graduating kids."

"W-What was that, sir?" Rebecca cautiously asks.

"Nothing, Rebecca. Tell her my offer hasn't changed, and I'll follow up in a month."

"Oh. Okay… Sir." She replies then quickly shuts the door.

Victor spins in his chair and observes the sun falling toward the horizon. The orange sky shines over the buildings inside the wall. The businesses below transition into neighborhoods designed specifically for the Conservation Cities. The back-right portion of the City is under construction. Once completed, Pittsburgh will be fully developed with new housing structures.

A knock at the door sounds.

"This better be you, Garret," he mutters loudly.

"It's me, sir," Garret replies, stepping into the office. He's a well-kept gentleman wearing a gray suit with white dress shirt — like Victor. He's clean shaven with dark brown, gelled-back hair. He walks toward Victor's desk carrying his folded notepad.

Victor spins forward in his chair and motions to one of two chairs at the front of his desk. "Take a seat."

Garret approaches, unbuttons his suit jacket, then sits in the left chair.

"Rebecca says you were at the morgue when she called you here. Getting the samples, I hope." Victor says.

"I was, sir." Garret replies. "But Tommy is reluctant to take the brain sample."

"We got the blood sample?"

"He's given us a sample of Ethan's blood, yes," Garret answers and waits for a response.

"And?" Victor impatiently asks.

"I'll have it examined immediately."

Victor rubs his scruffy beard and says, "Thank you." He stands and walks to the windows. "Jacob is showing telekinetic abilities, Garret."

"I am aware, sir." He watches Victor's gaze strengthen. He asks, "What are you thinking, sir?"

"The N-Strain students. They all show increased brain activity, increased brain cell counts, and they all developed a new strain of neuron cells. Jacob more than likely is carrying these new cells as well."

"I understand that–"

"We need that brain sample," Victor demands.

"Tommy says he won't take a brain sample from Ethan, sir." Garret speaks nervously.

Now facing Garret with his hands clasped behind his back, Victor asks, sternly, "Why?"

Composing his next words thoroughly in his head, Garret says, "During an autopsy, Tommy would only need to cut into the brain if all other testing was inconclusive." Taking a steadying breath while fighting Victor's cold stare, he continues, "Ethan is a high-profile death, sir. CC News will be at our doors and emailing all our staff to get any response about–"

"I'm aware of the media protocol, Garret. Get to your point."

"Okay…" He taps his notepad. "Tommy is afraid of the questions and possible investigation on him as to why he cut open Ethan's brain when…" He taps harder. "When… Cause of death is… Obvious."

Garret drops his head as Victor walks closer to him. Kneeling and forcing eye contact, Victor says, "I'm not asking him to saw Ethan's skull open. I'm asking him to get me a brain sample that he could access through the nose." He stands and returns to gazing out the window. "We need to confirm whether or not Better Human had effects on Ethan."

"And if Better Human worked on Ethan, we won't need–"

Bellowing at the window, Victor replies, "If it worked on Ethan, we won't need Jacob."

"Okay." Garret checks his notes, then asks, "In the meantime, if we need to get the boy to the facility, are you set to—"

"I will get him to agree, Garret." Victor returns to his chair, rubs his face, then leans back. "The kid knows me. He trusts me. His father was the roadblock, and now he's out of the way." His tone is passive.

"I do trust you can do this. But I should alert you to this… We saw him exiting the wall with his friend again. We can have Elliot ready to go next time he goes to the outside."

"That's not necessary at this point in time, Garret."

"Okay, sir." Garret closes his notepad. "I know you're familiar with the media protocol, but we need to discuss the announcement. We're already pushing our luck waiting this long."

"I'll call Amber now." He pulls his phone from his pocket. "After I speak with her, I'll communicate to the faculty in the building, then contact CC News." Setting the phone on his desk, he adds, "The world will know by tomorrow afternoon."

Garret stands, buttons his suit jacket, and says, "Solid plan, sir. I'll make my way back down to the morgue and speak with Tommy."

"Be convincing, Garret."

"Will do, sir," he replies and walks to the door.

Before he can exit, Victor says loudly, "Garret."

He turns to look at Victor.

"Ethan said that I've changed. He didn't trust me to tell me the success he… That *we* had with Jacob." Victor looks at the framed note paper then back to Garret. "Do you think I've changed, Garret?"

Delivering a quick smile, Garret says, "I met you shortly after the walls were built, sir. That was about… Fifteen years ago?"

"Sounds right."

"I'd say you're the same man I've known since we met, sir."

Victor looks at the framed paper again and sighs. He looks back at Garret, who is still standing halfway out the door looking at him. Victor nods and says, "You may go. I'm going to make my first call."

Garret nods and closes the door.

Victor's chest feels heavy as he unfolds his phone and opens Amber's contact. He holds the phone to his ear as it begins to ring.

CHAPTER 6

"MOM… IT'S NOT… I JUST…" Jacob stutters.

"You went to the outside again. I knew it," she yells in a disappointed voice. Pacing, then leaning on the kitchen table, she talks out loud to herself. "I knew he'd do it again. That's what I get for trusting a seventeen-year-old."

"Mom. Just… Listen. I–"

"No." She leans away from the table. Her strawberry-bronze hair is tied up in a bun, as she does before bed. She's pointing at Jacob, saying, "You just wait until your father finds out about this. He will–"

"He's *still* not home?" Jacob interrupts, yelling back. "I'm supposed to be afraid of a guy who's never fucking home–"

"Jacob!" Amber is shocked. She drops her hand and says, "You will *not* use that language toward me."

"Whatever." He kicks his shoes off at the side of the door. They flop aggressively against the laminate tile. "Don't act like you're okay with him being gone every day of the–"

"Your father is saving the world, Jacob. He's *saved* the world. The work he does is import–"

"I see your face *every* day, mom! You think you're hiding it from me, but you're not. You think that's fair for me, to see my mom sad and–"

"This isn't about your father!" Amber clenches her fist. Spit flies from her mouth as her eyes well up with tears. Her breath shaking, she says, "Look at you, Jacob. You're covered in blood. I told you those Outsiders were dangerous, and you didn't listen. You just—"

"It wasn't an Outsider, mom, it was…" He stops himself. Telling her what attacked him will not settle this situation.

"What?" Her voice quivers.

"Nothing." He shuffles his foot on the laminate floor of the foyer.

"What was it? Just tell me. If it wasn't an Outsider, what was it? An animal?"

"It… It was a…" he stutters again. "I'm fine. See? I'm fine. I'm healed. You know I heal faster than anyone–"

"You're not immortal!" Her voice is still shaking. "You think because you are gifted with whatever genetics your father gave you that you can't be dangerously hurt? Or killed?"

Amber's cell phone rings on the kitchen counter. She looks at it across the room and decides to ignore it.

"You're not going to answer? What if it's dad?" He speaks in a frustrated tone.

"If it's your father, then he's on the way home. He can back me up when I tell you that you're grounded."

Flailing his arms, he paces toward the stairs, yelling, "You can't be serious, mom. This is bullshit."

Stepping from the table in between Jacob and the stairs, Amber says, "What did I *just* tell you about cursing at me?"

Jacob and his mom stare at each other. Both are livid. Amber's cell phone rings again.

"Don't move," she demands, pointing her finger between his eyes nearly touching his face. Her voice is angrier than he's ever heard. She walks to the phone and looks to see Victor is calling. She sets the phone down and walks back to Jacob.

"Who was it?" he asks.

"It was Victor. I'll call him back when I'm done with you." Her voice and demeanor are making Jacob nervous. She asks, "What's out there that makes you think it's worth risking your life?"

Jacob forcefully sits on the step. He drops his head and doesn't answer.

She lifts his head with her fingers under his chin. "Answer me. Is it those silly comics? *Those* are worth *this*?" She pulls on his bloody hoodie with her other hand. "Do you realize what we already lost and could potentially lose again?" Her glossy eyes lose anger for a moment as they bounce between his.

He pulls away from her.

"Fine. Three weeks," she speaks.

"What?" He stands. "Are you serious, mom?"

"Four weeks." She points at him. Her cell phone rings again. She looks over at it and Jacob storms up the steps. "You stop right where you are, I'm not done with you," she demands, then walks to her phone. She sees Victor calling again. She answers this time.

"Hello, Victor, can I call you back? I'm in the middle of—"

Jacob listens from the top step.

"Okay. Sure. It can wait a minute."

He hears concern in her voice. He walks slowly to the bottom step to listen.

Amber gasps. He hears her sniffle. "Wh-What hap… How did he…?"

Jacob stands on the bottom step and looks over the banister at his mom. She's slumped against the counter with her hand over her mouth. Her eyes are spewing tears.

"O-Okay." She can barely get coherent words out. "When will you find out what hap—" She's speaking through a lump in her throat. "Yeah. Please. Call me later." She sets the phone on the counter. Her balance failing her, she starts to fall over. Jacob rushes over and catches her. His arms are wrapped around her arms.

"Mom. What's going on?" He helps her stand then walks her to a chair at the table.

Slumped over, her face in her hands, she cries loudly. Jacob kneels and gently grabs her forearms. He says, "Mom. Tell me what Victor said." Suddenly the fight they just had was irrelevant.

Amber sits up, away from her hands. Her eyes are pink and swollen already. She looks at the ceiling, sniffling and waving her hand to dry her tears. "Jacob." She says, weakly, looking back into his eyes, "Your father was killed."

* * *　　* * *

THEIR CONVERSATION LASTS until the morning sun rises. Jacob now lies in bed staring at the ceiling after insisting he shower and try to get some sleep. His mom cries in her room down the hall. Hearing this makes Jacob's heart heavier than it already was.

"Victor said your school will announce this tomorrow," Amber told him. He thinks of this after looking at his phone for the twelfth time with the intention of texting Deante, Kyle, and Renz to tell them the news. At this point, they're already at school eating breakfast without him, minutes away from hearing the news from a speaker in the classroom ceiling.

"Victor said they're investigating the incident, but it involves an accident in his lab with an Outsider," his mom told him after her follow-up call with Victor. This resonates in his mind as he focuses on the spinning ceiling fan above his bed.

"I thought dad wasn't working in the Outsiders department anymore," is what he wanted to say but didn't, because his mom was upset enough.

The spinning fan blades become blurrier as he thinks about his dad spending all his time at work, now obviously lying about what he did there, and when he was actually home, making Jacob keep the most exciting thing about himself secret. *Then you go and get yourself killed?* He thinks to himself, feeling his anger grow and the palm of his hands tingle.

His phone vibrates.

"Dude, where are you?" reads a text from Deante.

Jacob sets his phone beside him, sighs, then looks at his TV next to his bedroom door. It's off, but his focus is on the remote sitting below it on the stand.

Lying on his side in bed, he holds his arm out over the edge with his fingers fully extended and his tingling palm facing the remote. He stares at the remote, thinking about it coming to him.

He strengthens his focus and jerks his arm.

The remote shakes and slides toward him, falling on the floor.

Sighing, Jacob glances again at the message from Deante, sets his phone down again next to him, then rests his eyes.

He opens them and he's outside in the backyard with his dad. Ethan is wearing training pads on his hands, smiling at Jacob. "Alright, bud, let's go again," he says, bouncing back and forth with his knees bent.

Jacob punches with his right hand into his dad's pad. He follows up with a jab from his left into the other pad. Next, he swings again with his right hand, Ethan ducks, stands, and taps Jacob on the cheek with a pad.

"Remember, Jacob, your opponent will see a third punch coming. It's a common combo. Either hesitate on the third hit, countering their movement, or try an uppercut."

"Okay," Jacob replies.

"Go!" Ethan exclaims excitedly.

Jacob swings right to a block from Ethan, swings left to another block. Jacob hesitates with his right swing. He watches Ethan duck, then sees his shoulder twitch. Jacob dodges his dad's pad swing, then punches forward. Ethan sidesteps, then taps Jacob's cheek with his pad.

Ethan chuckles, saying, "That's unfair from me, bud. I told you to hesitate and used that to my advantage. You actually did *very* well with your–"

Jacob throws his gloves off his hands forcefully to the ground and lunges at Ethan connecting a strong punch to his eye.

His dad falls backward onto the hard ground. Jacob steps over him, kneeling and straddling his chest. He swings a punch against his cheek, feeling bones crack. Ethan is smiling radiantly.

Stop! What am I doing! Jacob thinks as he slams another fist into his dad's opposite cheek. His head twists and hits the dirt. He looks back up at Jacob with dried leaves stuck to the blood on his cheek, his eye swollen and bleeding. As he smiles, his teeth show pink with blood.

"I'm proud of you, kiddo," Ethan says, happily.

Jacob cracks both of his dad's cheek bones. He's unable to stop himself.

"Jacob." Ethan looks at him. Both eyes are swollen shut and spewing blood. His cheeks are cracked open, bleeding into his lips as he says, "I love you so much, my son."

Jacob's entire body twitches, jarred awake from the phone vibrating on his nightstand.

What the fuck was that? He thinks to himself.

His phone vibrates again. He looks at the time. He slept for two hours. His phone shows thirteen messages and two missed calls. All from Deante. The messages are from Renz, Deante, Kyle, and other friends from school. All are condolences about his father.

He sets the phone down again without replying. His body is tense from the dream he just had. The more he thinks about it, the more the skin on the back of his neck crawls. He stares back at his door.

"I love you, too, dad."

CHAPTER 7

THE NEXT DAYS ARE A blur. Jacob and Amber spend most hours of the night looking at photographs. An old binder holds photos from when Amber and Ethan first met, the early years of their relationship, and their wedding. A second binder seems to jump many years and has photos of the three of them. Not nearly as many, but photo printing is done less in the Conservation Cities, as the ink and materials are now finite. Jacob asks why the years between the binders were missing.

"We sadly didn't have time to grab them during the outbreak," is Amber's reply. Jacob looks at his father in all these pictures. He thinks to himself, *He's gone. Forever.* But with how often he was at work, sometimes for days at a time, it's hard to feel the difference at this moment.

They also meet with the mortician in a small building in the city. There Jacob learns that the end-of-life process is cremation, and the ashes are returned to the Earth. He also learns that he cannot see his father prior to cremation, due to the nature of his death. The death Victor promises to give more answers about before the celebration-of-life at their home.

Jacob walks from his bedroom down to the kitchen, where Amber is finishing making appetizers for the guests coming to the house. He sits in his chair at the table and stares out the window facing the neighbor's home. Amber sees him wearing his blue suit. The only suit he owns.

"Sweetheart," she says kindly. "You look so nice. You don't have to dress up today, though. I know you don't like wearing dress clothes."

"Oh," he mutters, then looks down at his suit. "I'll… Yeah, I'll change, I guess."

"Are you okay?" his mom asks, addressing his demeanor. "I know that's a silly question with everything going on, but… What I mean is, you can talk to me at any time, sweetie."

"I know, mom. I'll be alright." He sees her calming smile. "Are you… Are *you* okay, mom?"

Giving a warm, bigger smile, even with her eyes, she says, "I'll be okay. Thank you." She turns to continue plating food. She's wearing a green sundress and has her long hair curled. Jacob secretly smiles as he remembers her wearing that only a few weeks ago, when his dad and her went to dinner together. He remembers his dad telling her the color looked beautiful on her, and that he loves it when she wears her hair down over her shoulders. Her shoulders bounce as she lets out a chuckle through her nose.

"What?" Jacob asks as curiosity gets the best of him.

Turning around, she says with another chuckle, "I've been thinking about you and your insistence on sneaking out of the walls to find old-world items."

Jacob drops his head, waiting for another lecture.

Stepping over to him and rubbing the top of his back, Amber says, "I am not condoning or approving your behavior by saying this, but… You're just like your father."

Whipping his head up, he looks surprised, holding eye contact as she sits in the chair next to him.

"Remember you asked me about the photo albums?" she asks. He nods while holding his defensive stare. He's still prepared for the lecture to arrive. "Well. On… *The* day. The day of the outbreak. Victor was sending a car for all of us."

"All of us?"

"Y-Your father and I," she stutters. "As I'm using the minutes we had to pack, then grab photo albums, your father comes down the stairs carrying…" She giggles and wipes away a tear.

"Carrying what?" Jacob's curiosity is piqued.

"This." Amber reaches into the pocket of her dress and hands him a silver watch. He looks at it with confusion then looks at her with a questioning expression. "It's a watch," she says with a chuckle.

"This looks nothing like our watches."

With a smile, but hiding an eye roll, she replies, "I forget how much has changed sometimes." She taps on the face of the watch. "These were another way to tell time. It wasn't *all* just the electronic ones we have now."

Jacob inspects the face of the watch, holding it close to his eye. "How did you even read these?" He holds it, waiting for something to move, then looks at it again. "I don't think it's working."

A tear falls from Amber's eye as she smiles at the watch, then gently takes it from Jacob. A lump fills her throat as a memory resurfaces. She says, "Your father. He… The day he asked me out…" She sniffles, then continues. "He said that later that day, he realized the battery had died while he was in the diner."

Jacob sits quietly as his mom stares intently at Ethan's watch while more tears fall off her chin.

She looks at him with a smile and glossy eyes and says, "He told me that it's proof that time stopped when I said yes to go on a date with him."

Pulling his hand to his mouth, Jacob's eyes squint as he tries to hide his giggling.

Amber stands and lightly smacks Jacob's shoulder, laughing with him. As she hands him the watch, she continues laughing, saying, "Your father was cheesy, yes, but he had a big heart. And he found meaning in a lot of things and kept them close to him. He collected a lot of stuff in the old-world."

She returns to plating food at the counter while Jacob looks over his dad's watch. He recalls memories of his mom and dad laughing together in the kitchen and how they'd make time for dates around his busy job. He tries to imagine his young father asking his mom for a date in that diner.

Time passes with the only sounds being plates lightly clanging and sliding on the counter as Amber works diligently to get ready for the memorial. "Mom," Jacob says to get her attention.

"Yes, sweetheart?" she answers, continuing with her project on the kitchen counter.

"The mortician mentioned how we don't do the 'old ways' anymore for the end-of-life process. Something about not having space for it in the Conservation Cities. What does he mean?"

"Oh." She wasn't expecting that question. "Well. How do I put it simply? Back in the old-world, when someone d... Passed away, often they would be buried."

"Buried?" he interrupts.

"Yes, buried. In the ground. They'd be inside coffins... Wooden boxes, essentially, then buried down into the ground.

Large plots of land were dedicated to this. They were called cemeteries. They were very big, which is why he said we didn't have space inside the walls."

"Oh. Odd," he replies, then stares back out the window. A jarring knock sounds at the door before it opens garnering his and his mom's attention.

"May I come in?" Victor announces himself.

"Of course!" Amber yells happily.

Victor's heavy footsteps travel through the foyer into the kitchen. Jacob looks up at him from the table then stands and shakes his hand.

"You look very handsome, son," Victor states while acknowledging his suit. He catches Jacob glancing at the man standing behind him wearing a nearly identical suit with Victor. "Oh, my apologies. This is Garret. He's my assistant. Or right-hand-man, as they say." He says playfully.

"Hello, sir." Garret nods to Jacob. "And hello, ma'am." He nods to Amber.

Jacob smiles and nods in return. Amber says, "Hello, Garret. Lovely to meet you."

"Very nice to meet you as well. Though, I apologize for the circumstances," he replies. Amber gives a tight smile then returns to finishing her appetizer plates.

"It pains me to open with this, but I feel we should get the difficult conversation out of the way now, if you agree," Victor speaks.

Gulping then stuttering, Amber says, "Uh… Yes. Yes, that's fine. Jacob… Maybe you should wait in your room and let Victor and I talk first." Her eyes gaze at Jacob's saddening face while she slowly looks at Victor for support.

"Fine," Jacob says and drops his head with frustration. Before he can turn to walk to the steps, he feels a firm grip on his shoulder.

"I," Victor draws out his first words, "I would say he's mature enough to hear this." His smile is confident as he looks from Jacob to Amber.

"Oh?" Amber says with reserve.

"I think so. Don't you, son?"

"Uh… Yeah. Yeah." Jacob answers while looking at his mom. The delay in anyone speaking causes his stare to bounce between Victor and his mom's stares. "I, uh… What is this even about?"

"The investigation into your father's death, son," Victor says, squeezing his shoulder harder.

"Oh… Sure. Yeah. I want to hear it," he replies confidently. He wants to hear firsthand what happened to his dad.

"One of the Outsiders in Ethan's lab woke unexpectedly from its anesthesia. It began attacking Ethan's lab partners. Security was on the scene immediately; however, as they took aim to eliminate the hostile Outsider, they missed their first shot, killing Ethan. I'd like to add that it was reported that Ethan quickly pulled the Outsider away from the other lab partners, saving them and demonstrating great bravery." His tone is overtly somber.

Jacob pictures his dad apprehending a wild Outsider and saving people. This warms him, knowing how brave his father was at that moment. Then, he remembers that his dad said he wasn't in the Outsider department at work. Not to mention, Outsiders aren't hostile like everyone makes them out to be.

Noticing Jacob's expression change, Victor says, "Everything alright, son?"

"Yeah… No. I'm confused." He looks up from the floor to Victor. "My dad told us he was out of the Outsider department for years. And I've witnessed Outsiders out…" He hesitates. "Whatever," he mutters under his breath. He doesn't care about getting caught. He wants answers. He says, "I've been to the

Outside. Outsiders see us and they run. They're not hostile like everyone says."

"You're not wrong, son." Victor's grip intensifies further on Jacob's shoulder. Jacob's eyes widen with surprise at the quick response. Victor says, "Your father has been out of the Outsider department for many years, this is correct. However, we've been studying what we hope is a new revelation into understanding the V-Mor virus. This has garnered both his attention and his assistance lately." He glances at Amber, then back down at Jacob. "And to your *personal* observation regarding the behavior of Outsiders: consider yourself lucky that your experience was docile. Outsiders are more aggressive when they're cornered or feel threatened. You should concern yourself more, son. That is a dangerous activity."

"M-hmm," Amber hums from the counter followed by sniffles she's trying to hide.

Victor pauses, then softly clears his throat. His eyes glance at Amber's back facing him from the kitchen counter as he says, "If I may, I'd like to ask you both for approval and interest in something."

"Go ahead, Victor." Amber speaks with a scratchy voice, leaning against the counter. She's wiping her eyes with her sleeve as she turns to face them while forcing a smile.

"Ethan and I had been talking recently about introducing Jacob to our students at our facility."

"Facility?" Jacob and his mom say simultaneously. Amber sounds concerned while Jacob sounds intrigued. "For the medical science trade after school?"

"No," Victor speaks assertively. He's in a hurry to have this conversation before others arrive. "To cut to the chase, we have more students who are like Jacob. Students who *also* have miraculous abilities, who we help to train and understand what they're capable of."

Jacob's head whips to look at Victor. His eyes are wide and his mouth open. As a million questions run through his mind, he only stutters sounds.

Reacting to Jacob's surprise, Victor smiles with the corner of his mouth and says, "You are quite unique, son, and so are the other students. But *your* abilities enhanced your muscular and immune system, plus, unexpectedly, you are demonstrating some telekinetic abilities—"

"He told you *that*, too?" Jacob asks, shocked. His father swore him to secrecy and had given him the impression he followed his own strict rules and told nobody. While it makes sense to him that his dad would tell Victor, he's still surprised to find that he knows about the telekinesis. They only recently began studying this when Jacob accidentally broke a glass in the kitchen with it.

Leaning down, Victor says arrogantly, "Your father and I were best friends, Jacob. He told me everything." He stands, then adds, "Again, while you seem to have telekinetic abilities, I've been working closely with students who show tele*pathic* abilities."

Sighing and expressing disdain, Amber says, "Wh-What's the difference?"

"To put it simply–" Victor begins, but is interrupted by the door opening.

Deante enters loudly. He's wearing his nicest khakis and what he considers to be a formal hoodie — in other words, it's been worn less than ten times and it's not faded or ripped.

He walks past Garret and Victor and shakes Jacob's hand, then pulls him in for a full hug. "Bro, I'm so sorry. How are you holding up?" he asks, looks at Amber, then steps away from Jacob. "Mrs. A. You have my deepest condolences." He kneels and kisses the back of her hand. Victor stands frozen, holding his arm out, as he was about to answer Amber's question. He watches Deante continue as if he's not standing in the same room as him.

With a small chuckle, Amber says, "You're too kind, Deante. Thank you."

"I know these are sad times, but you can still call me D, Mrs. A." He stands and bows.

"Dude, can you *not* be weird?" Jacob chuckles.

Keeping his attention on Amber, who giggles, Deante replies, "I'm just being polite, man."

Jacob shakes his head and laughs. Victor lets out a quick, loud laugh to get attention.

"Sorry. D, this is Victor. And this is his assistant, Garret," Jacob introduces the two of them.

"Hello, sirs." Deante nods to both of them.

"You're not going to kiss *my* hand?" Victor asks.

Everyone laughs as Deante replies, "Not until you've made me award-worthy pancakes."

"Fair deal, kid," Victor chuckles.

Jacob jumps with excitement and says to Victor, "You were telling me about that—"

"Not now, son, we'll finish our conversation before the day is over." He holds eye contact with Amber and quickly shoots his eyes at Deante. She presses her lips together and nods.

Jacob realizes he was about to slip and show them that Deante also knows his secret. He becomes relieved at the fact that Victor shot the conversation down.

"Mysterious!" Deante sings awkwardly to break the silence in the kitchen.

"Uh…" Jacob hums out loud and sees everyone waiting for him to say something. He taps Deante on the shoulder and says, "Let me show you something in my room."

"Deal. It got *real* weird in here *real* quick," he replies.

"Yeah, well, you kinda started that, bro," Jacob lightly nudges him.

They run up the stairs as Amber and Victor watch. "Those kids," Amber says, smiling and shaking her head. "Appetizer?" She holds a plate out toward Victor and Garret.

"Don't mind if I do." Victor smiles and grabs a bacon-wrapped scallop. Garret reaches around him and takes one next.

Jacob shuts the door of his bedroom after Deante enters. "Dude, that was crazy *awkward* down there." Deante speaks as soon as the door shuts.

"Right?" Jacob talks quietly. "Right before you got here…" Holding his hand against the door as if it were trying to push open, he pauses and listens to make sure he hears his mom and Victor talking before he continues saying, "He started telling me and my mom that he and my dad have been talking about taking me to a facility with other people who have abilities like me."

"No shit!" Deante exclaims. He's quickly shushed by Jacob. "Sorry," He speaks quietly. "Are you gonna go?"

"I don't know. I kinda hope so." He walks past Deante, stepping over the clothes he threw on the floor earlier, then heavily sits on the edge of his bed. "Convincing my mom is the hurdle here. I can tell by his approach to the conversation that he knows that, too. My dad probably told him that."

"So, your dad told Victor about you?" Deante asks.

"Yeah. They are best friends, so–"

"I'm your best friend, and you didn't tell me." His face is stern.

"I…" Jacob stutters, then changes his tone to frustration. "I didn't know there were exceptions, man."

"I'm just messing with you, bro. Chill," Deante laughs as he picks up an action figure of Captain America.

Chuckling and relieved he isn't mad, Jacob asks, "Is Kyle still bringing those hacked devices?"

"I think so. He was talking about it in school yesterday."

"Awesome. Sucks I missed–" Jacob is interrupted by a knock on his door. "You're good!" he yells to whoever it is.

The door opens, then Kyle and Renz step into the room. Kyle is carrying a backpack. "What's up, nerds?" Kyle says, sitting on the floor and opening his backpack. "Don't you look dashing." He says to Jacob.

"Says the one wearing suspenders with khakis. You steal that from a Wasted outside the walls?" he laughs, kneeling off the bed next to Deante. They're all waiting to see what Kyle brought to show them.

Kyle pulls out a tablet then pauses as he begins to set it on the floor between all of them. He looks at Jacob with worried eyes and says, "I... I came in here without giving you my condolences, man. I'm so sorry."

"It's fine, dude." Jacob shakes his head.

"Thanks, bro," Kyle replies, resuming setting the tablet onto the floor. He passes another smile at Jacob, then says to everyone, "This is the best one I was able to hack into." He unlocks it and taps on a purple icon shaped like a camera. It loads a screen with a lot of small images.

"You were able to get connected to the servers?" Jacob asks, surprised to see it loaded.

"It took me a long time, but yes." His voice is soft but serious. "All the Conservation Cities communicate through a private intranet. Those *need* internet to operate. Which means that–"

"All the cities have internet?" Renz interrupts with excitement in his eyes and voice.

"Yes." Kyle chuckles at Renz's expression. "I followed that book you found me," he points at Jacob, "and was able to code a hacking software on the laptop we found months ago."

"Nice!" Deante mutters. "A few of those words sound foreign but... Nice."

"Long story short," Kyle continues, "I got into their intranet and used backdoors to get onto the internet it runs off of. We just got lucky that the server that runs this app is apparently housed in another Conservation City somewhere."

"Nice work, dude! This is–" Jacob starts and is cut off by Renz.

"Let's see what you got, man! Enough of the smart shit."

Kyle interacts with the tablet in the center of their square sitting formation. All four of them lean over, waiting to see what his next tap shows them. He scrolls through dozens of images and taps one at random.

Cheering erupts from the tablet's speaker. A girl holds a drink in the air in a room filled with other people dancing. Lights of all colors flash behind her and brighten the screen.

The girl is smiling radiantly and yelling with excitement. She reaches off-camera and pulls in another girl, who joins her wooing. Their faces are filled with bliss as they hold each other's shoulders and sway to the heart-pounding music.

"It's my birthday!" the first girl screams at the other, and they hit their cups together, splashing each drink on their hands, then they tilt their heads back with their cups to their lips, and the video ends.

"What kind of place was that?" Renz asks curiously.

"I don't know. But there are a lot more just like that. Like this one," Kyle says, tapping another video. Heavy knocking hits the door.

"Close it. Close it," Jacob whispers as he slides Kyle's open backpack under his bed. "You're good. Come in," he yells.

The door opens partially. Victor leans in and says, "Jacob. I spoke further with your mother. About what I brought up earlier." Jacob stares nervously. Deante knows, but Kyle and

Renz don't. He's not prepared for the questions he knows they'll ask. "She agreed to allow me to take you and show you around. She said if you like what you see, she'll permit it."

"Seriously? She did?" he asks, surprised.

"The fact that your father wanted this helped sway her," he says lightly.

"What's all this about?" Renz speaks up, having bitten his tongue twice already.

"I'll, uh… I'll tell you about it later," Jacob stutters.

"Is this something you want to do, son?" Victor asks Jacob.

"Absolutely. Yeah. Of course." He stops himself from using another interjection.

"Excellent." Victor opens the door fully. "Let's be on our way." His arms are pointing toward the stairs.

"Wait. Now?" Jacob stutters again.

"We have your mother's support," he replies.

"But the memorial downstairs… It's still–"

"Oh, these things don't last that long as it is." Victor speaks passively. "Besides, you're up here with your friends away from it anyway, aren't you?"

"I… I guess you're right." Jacob looks at his friends. "You guys care if I catch up with you later? You can chill in my room longer; I don't care if—"

"Go ahead, man. We're good," Deante answers with an acknowledging nod.

Jacob stands, excited. He grabs jeans and a hoodie from his closet and folds them over his arm. "I'm going to change real quick before we go. Is that cool?"

"Of course, son," Victor chuckles. "I'll wait for you on the porch."

CHAPTER 8

JACOB CONFIRMS WITH HIS MOM that she did, in fact, agree with Victor to let him see the facility. He made her confirm she was sure three times before he was comfortable believing her. Now he's convinced Victor has magical powers, being able to get her to say yes to this. He steps into his sneakers then onto the front porch.

A large, all-black SUV sits at the curb of his home. It's running but is silent. Jacob tries to peer through the passenger window to see the driver, but the windows are darkly tinted.

The driver's side door opens and shuts, then Garret walks around the front of the vehicle. "Hello sir," he says as he passes Jacob, opening the rear passenger door. "Allow me."

"Uh… Thanks, man," Jacob says as he sits in the back seat. Victor is on the other side smiling at him.

"It saddens me that your father isn't here to see this, Jacob." Victor speaks empathetically. "He was excited for you to reach the age to finally see this place and understand its meaning."

They both break eye contact when Garret shuts his door and begins to drive.

"Yeah, I… I guess it's weird to me to picture him excited about this." Jacob resumes the conversation.

"Why's that, son?"

"Because he was always so stern about me keeping it a secret and telling nobody about *any* of it." Jacob shows some frustration. "Yet you tell me he wouldn't shut up about it with you at work."

"Son," Victor speaks. Resting his arms on his thighs, he taps all of his fingertips together as he continues. "Your frustrations are justified. Just understand that your father had his reasons for everything he did. Protecting you was his top priority."

"Yeah," he replies, turns his head, and looks out the window. Garret slows as they approach a small hut next to the main gate at the wall, where a security guard greets him happily. They interact, then the guard turns and clicks icons on his computer screen until the large gate opens in the city wall and Garret drives through.

"Jacob," Victor demands his attention. "You're about to see the world your father *wanted* you to see when the time came. This is where you'll learn about all that you're capable of."

Jacob forces a smile. As much as Victor insists his dad was excited about this, he can't picture him that way. All he can remember is him saying, "Never show your abilities to anyone, Jacob. Nobody can know about any of this."

Sensing eyes on him, Jacob looks in the rearview mirror, where he sees Garret looking back at him. "How far is this place?" he asks while keeping eye contact with Garret.

"Just a few minutes along the parkway, sir," Garret replies.

"What questions do you have, son?" Victor asks.

"About what?" Jacob asks in return.

"Yourself. Your abilities."

"Oh… I don't know…"

"What were you and your father working on recently?"

"He didn't tell you?" he says with insolence.

Addressing Jacob's attitude, Victor says, "Jacob." He waits for eye contact. Jacob looks at him and he continues, saying, "I'm showing a lot of patience here. I'd appreciate cooperation. I understand your father is gone, but I'm trying to help you and honor his wishes for you."

"I'm sorry." Jacob drops his head in embarrassment.

"It's okay, son." Victor shakes his shoulder lightly. "To answer your question, no, I hadn't spoken with your father about you in a few days."

"Oh." Jacob watches the road ahead through the windshield. "We always worked on boxing and mixed martial arts. He said it was the best source for strength and stamina building."

"Mhmm." Victor acknowledges he's listening.

"And that it's great to know self-defense." He watches Victor nod. "But recently…" Jacob thinks, "I guess he was trying to help me do the thing you mentioned…"

Victor waits for Jacob to finish. After seconds pass, he asks, "What thing, son?"

"The thing where I move sh… Stuff by thinking about it." He motions his arm forward.

"The telekinesis."

"Yeah. That's what you called it."

Leaning to see where they are on their travels, Victor looks out the windshield. He sits back and connects eyes with Jacob, asking, "I'm taking from what you said that you are unable to do it voluntarily."

"I-I can't. No."

"Interesting." Victor looks away through his side window.

"Why's that interesting?" Jacob stares at the back of his head, at his slicked-back jet-black hair. After no response and with little patience, Jacob says, "Victor. Why is that int—"

Whipping his head to Jacob and cutting him off, he says, "The times that you've used telekinesis, were you stressed? Angry? Feeling a significant amount of emotion?"

"Uh…" Jacob thinks. He's feeling stressed right now. "I guess? Maybe. Yeah. I dunno."

"You don't know?"

"I mean, yeah. Sometimes. Maybe most times, but not *every* time."

"The times you weren't angry or anxious and you did it, what were you feeling?"

"I don't know, I–"

"I need you to think, Jacob."

"I am. I am."

"Talk me through a time when you were successful but not angry."

"Um…" Victor's stare is tightening Jacob's chest. The short breaths he's taking are becoming labored. "I, uh… The other night. I was in bed and moved my remote from the TV stand."

"How did you do this?"

"I held my hand out and kept thinking about it moving."

"Did it happen right away?"

"No. It took a–"

"How long?"

"Like… A minute or so? I don't–"

"Did you keep your focus *only* on moving the remote?"

"Y-Yeah."

"And it moved to your hand?"

"Well… No. It moved toward me and fell on the floor."

"Hmm." Victor returns to look out his window.

"What?" Jacob's patience is shorter than before. Not receiving an immediate response, he says, louder, "What?"

"This facility will be good for you, son. We've helped all our students here hone in on their abilities."

"How?"

"By learning what drives their emotions, learning to understand them, then learning how to control them. Once a human learns how to manipulate their own emotions, they can learn how to manipulate another's." Victor's eyes grow thin purple veins around them. He gives a confident smile and holds a stare with Jacob.

"Okay…" Jacob says slightly above a whisper as he feels forced to reply through the silence.

Dropping his smile, Victor rests his head back, saying, "Anger. Fear. Pressure. They have always been a driver for humans to perform or act above mediocrity, proving that we can always achieve better than what we are. The ones who've out-performed everyone else are the ones who learned how to control that driver." His voice grows stern.

"You're saying I have to learn to make myself angry to use my abilities?" Jacob's eyebrows scrunch toward his nose.

"I'm saying that anger is *not* the only way to use your abilities. If you can use them angry, that means you can use them purposefully."

"Oh."

"We'll find which emotions trigger inside you and get you in control of what you're fully capable of, Jacob." Victor presses his finger on Jacob's chest. "Every student here has a unique ability that has proven to be enhanced and more powerful when driven by emotion."

"Uh… Cool." Jacob thinks he understands Victor and trusts his plans. He can see that Victor is passionate about this.

"We're here, sir," Garret announces as he turns into a large parking lot. Abandoned vehicles occupy parking spaces sporadically. Black and green mold trim the lines between the white bricks of what was once a shopping mall. Garret drives toward a very large white garage door. Clean bricks without mold line the sides of the door, showing it was installed within recent years. As he approaches, he presses a button above the windshield, causing the door to open.

Inside is a large room brightened by fluorescent lighting that reflects off the glossy concrete. Three other SUVs identical to the one they're in are parked in the center of the room. Garret drives inside and parks beside them.

"Alright, son. Let's get inside, show you around, and introduce you to the other students," Victor says, his smile radiates with excitement.

CHAPTER 9

THE LARGE PARKING GARAGE ECHOES their steps as the three of them walk to a dark-wood door ahead. Jacob looks around at the pristine white walls lining the place and says, "Was this already here from the old-world?"

"The mall was, yes," Victor says, "But everything you're seeing we renovated to accommodate our needs for the facility." They stop at the door. Next to it is a numeric keypad that Victor types a code into, triggering a clicking sound from the lock releasing. He steps inside the door and holds it open for Garret and Jacob. "Follow me, son."

Sunlight from glass skylights brightens the hallway ahead of Jacob. It is immediately evident where the old storefronts remain and where they were renovated to fit the new needs of the facility. The hallway turns slightly left further ahead, hiding whether the renovations stop or continue further. To Jacob's left is a door reading "Medical One," and to his right is a short hallway with a door at the end, too far to read the name.

Large glass storefront windows remain on the right side of the wall where Victor is leading him. Inside, he can see a massive open room with padding for the floor. Training equipment occupies the far-left corner, while the left wall holds what look to be mock weapons such as bats, swords, and even training gloves. On the other side of the glass is a small sitting area. As Jacob follows Victor past the windows, he sees the short brown hair of someone sitting across from a young woman with brown braids that rest over her shoulder onto her graphic t-shirt. She looks to be close to Jacob's age, maybe a few years older. Her green eyes shift from the conversation she's having with the brown-haired person to look at Jacob. She smiles radiantly, standing from her seat, and waves politely. Jacob's cheeks grow warm as he smiles back and raises his hand for a shy return wave.

Victor grips the extruding handle of the glass door in the center of the large windows. Before opening, he says to Garret, "Go get the others."

"Yes, sir." Garret nods and walks further down the hall beyond where it turns.

"Follow me, son," Victor says happily as he opens the door then steps inside.

Jacob follows and is greeted by the freckled woman who waved just moments ago. She's still smiling but now holds out a hand to shake Jacob's. She says, "H-Hello, Jacob. Nice to meet you." Her voice is positive and friendly.

While he shakes her hand and hopes his smile isn't goofy, Victor says, "Jacob, this is Chloe. I've asked her to assist me with welcoming you here."

"This is Victor's favorite student, Jacob," the brown-haired person says, walking over.

"David. Shut up," Chloe whispers loudly.

"This cheerful young man is David," Victor says with a hint of resentment.

"It's true," David whispers loudly back to Chloe while chuckling. "Hello, Jacob. Very nice to meet you." He firmly shakes Jacob's hand and speaks pleasantly. His friendly brown eyes and smile, while genuine, look tired. He has a short, scruffy beard that matches his short, messy hair. Judging by the barely visible wrinkles at the corner of his eyes, Jacob guesses he's probably close to double his age and in his thirties.

"Hey, David." Jacob smiles politely back. While shaking hands, he looks at Victor and says, "You… You said everyone here has abilities like me, right? So, like… What do—"

"In time, Jacob," Victor interrupts but then adds, playfully, "You'll spoil the surprise."

Surprise? Jacob thinks to himself. His handshake with David has gone on too long.

"Where in the world is Garret and the others?" Victor looks out the large windows into the hall. "I'll be right back, you three." He walks swiftly out of the room and down the hall.

"So…" David sings awkwardly. "How's it feel to have met Victor's prized student and biggest disappointment first?"

"I… I don't understand," Jacob replies, confused, watching Chloe roll her eyes.

"David. Stop." She says sternly.

"Why are you a disappoint—"

"Jacob, don't get him going," Chloe stops him.

"You see, Jacob," David speaks flamboyantly. Jacob watches as he paces around, talking with his arms. "I'm supposed to be the final piece of Victor's *big* project, but it didn't work right." Jacob listens, puzzled. "I mean, it *worked* technically, just not how he wanted."

Chloe steps in front of Jacob and says, softly, "He's not always like this, Jacob. He's having a bad day–"

"Bad day?" David says loudly. "I'm fucking *haunted*, Chlo." He steps close to Jacob and says, "I was supposed to be able to show memories to other people."

"David! He said not to–"

"Who cares, Chlo," David interrupts. Looking back to Jacob, he says, "Anyway. Yeah. I have *my* memories, right?"

"Uh… Yeah. Okay," Jacob replies, unsure if the question was rhetorical or not.

"I can… Poof… Put them in *your* head and let you live through my vivid memory." David makes an explosion sound and gestures with his hand from his forehead to Jacob's.

"Really? That's awesome." Jacob smiles.

"Except that I can't." David speaks disappointedly. "I can't send it to others. But I can relive memories of my own. Very vividly."

"I mean… That… That's still cool, isn't it?" Jacob hesitantly asks.

"Sure, kid. Real cool." David slumps into his chair.

"Jacob, he…" Chloe looks saddened to see David's defeated posture. "He was thirteen when the outbreak happened. Once he got these abilities, he found himself reliving that terrible time over and over again."

"O-Oh. I'm sorry, I didn't–"

"I know, kid. It's fine. I'm sorry for being like this when you first met me." David's voice is still defeated. All three of them turn their heads as the door opens.

Another student walks in. His skin is pale and nearly transparent, showing the veins in his arms. His eyes are bloodshot with purple bags underneath the eyelids. His hair looks blonde but is thin and unkempt. He stares at Jacob as he approaches, then winces and holds his temple when he gets close.

"Dude. I know. I look like shit," he says to Jacob.

"W-What?"

"Jacob, this is Noel," Chloe says.

"He can read minds, kid," David yells from behind him.

"David!" Chloe mutters. Under her breath she says, "This is *not* going how he wanted it to."

"Wow, really?" Jacob asks, excitedly.

"Yeah. It's wondrous," Noel replies, emotionless. He scrunches his face and holds his fist against his forehead, saying, "Jacob. Please. Stop thinking about the questions you want to ask me for a moment."

"S-Sorry, dude," Jacob says. *How do I stop thinking?* He thinks, looking at his feet, trying his best to not think about anything.

Noel leans around Jacob and acknowledges David hunched forward in his seat. "He lived the memory again."

"Yeah," Chloe says, sadly.

Jacob looks back and forth between Chloe and Noel. Chloe looks saddened by this memory David relives, while Noel continues to wear the bothered expression he walked in with. Finally, the silence is broken when Victor slams the door open and walks in with a confident demeanor. Behind him are three more students. They all have perfect muscular tone, which is shown off with their tight tank tops and shorts.

Two of them have straps over their shoulders for holsters on their back. Each holster is carrying two wakizashi swords in the shape of an X. A young woman leads, carrying a metal staff.

"Jacob, I'd like you to meet… What's with him?" Victor starts to speak, then notices David sitting sadly. He asks Chloe another question, "Is he depressed again? From the—"

"Y-Yes. The memory," Chloe speaks softly.

Victor sighs. "Garret. Take David and get him those new meds. See if they help with *this*." He waves it off.

David stands up without being addressed and walks to Garret. Jacob hears him muttering under his breath as he passes. The only words he understands are profanity.

Jacob studies the students standing shoulder to shoulder next to Victor. They carry arrogance in their postures. He quickly notices the young woman on the right looking him over. She is stunningly beautiful in a nearly perfect way. Her vibrant green eyes meet his before she whips her long black hair behind her shoulder, then whispers to the young man beside her. He glances at Jacob and they both chuckle. Jacob brushes off whatever it could be they're laughing about, but he can't shake off the haunting feeling her eyes gave him.

"Jacob," Victor barks, making him jump. "Meet Elliot, Theo, and Jade." He pauses, motioning his hand toward them. Their heads are held upward as if to intentionally look down on Jacob.

He passes a wave and says, "Hello."

"Jacob. These students are successes of the Better Human serum," Victor says excitedly.

"W… Seriously?" Jacob whips his head in shock.

"I'd call it Better Human version two," Victor elaborates. "These students all took the serum and directly received the results, whereas yours were passed to you through reproduction."

"We're also the better version," Elliot speaks loudly and arrogantly.

Jacob looks at him, puzzled.

Elliot smirks. "Yeah. You heard me."

Theo, while chuckling, says, "Come on, Ell, you promised not to antagonize."

"Nah, fuck this kid, man. Look at him, he's–"

"Enough!" Victor's voice is loud and demanding. Jacob jumps, while the three students in front of him snap to attention.

Elliot whispers, "S-Sorry, sir."

"We'll have a private discussion later on about your disobedience." Victor points at Elliot. He steps closer to Jacob and turns him around with his arm on his shoulder. "You met these students already, yeah?"

"Uh… Y-Yeah," Jacob answers, still shaken by Victor's display of anger.

"This is also a special group who have shown amazing abilities from a different serum I developed. I'm still coming up with a name for the serum, so for now it's called the Neuro Strain, or N-Strain for short." Victor walks over to Noel and squeezes his shoulder. Noel is rolling his eyes but not out of annoyance; rather, pain. "This is Noel. He can–"

"He knows, sir." Noel's voice is raspy as he squeezes his temples.

Victor looks to Chloe. "I asked you to—"

"We…" David yells. It's a surprise to all that he snuck back in after getting his meds and is standing in the doorway. "It's our fault, sir. We got to talking and told Jacob our shticks."

"Shticks," Victor scoffs. "And you, Chloe? Did you also tell him and spoil–"

"No, sir! I didn't tell him mine," she quickly answers.

"Good." Victor stands behind Jacob and places his hands on each shoulder. "Before we get to what Chloe can do, we have a surprise for you."

Jacob turns his head to look at Victor behind him. "What sur–"

Victor smiles at him then nods to Chloe. In the back corner of the room is a gray door. Jacob's attention snaps to it as it bangs and opens outward. The room on the other side is dark.

Jacob leans to see who is inside, feeling Victor's hands lightly holding him still. A man walks into the room, turns, and smiles at Jacob.

Jacob's mouth opens as he attempts to speak, but only air gasps out. He's staring at Ethan. He's watching his dad walk toward him.

CHAPTER 10

GOLDEN RAYS OF SUNSHINE SQUEEZE between the blinds at Levelwood Diner. The thumb of an anxious Ethan taps on a notepad while his knee imitates, bouncing under the table of the booth he occupies. He impatiently passes glances between his watch and the glass doors of the entrance, breaking his obsessive proofreading of the scribbled notes on the paper. Engines roar as traffic blitzes by the parking lot that he continues to monitor between checking his notes, the door, and his phone.

Though it's the popular time for brunch, the diner is rather bare, except for a few people sitting at the breakfast bar chatting with the pretty, strawberry-haired waitress who keeps giving Ethan flirty smiles when they make eye contact.

The bell hanging above the front door rings. Ethan looks up to see that, finally, Victor has arrived. Partially standing from his seat, he waves, catches Victor's attention, and motions for him to join his booth.

"I apologize," Victor says, fixing the collar of his three-button golf shirt. It's his favorite red one he wears when he has important plans. "Pittsburgh traffic *is* the worst, and that's a hill I'll die on." He chuckles.

"You're fine," Ethan says quickly.

"You're anxious," Victor calls out. "What's going on?"

"Vic. I think I finally got it." His eyes light up with excitement.

"You got… Better Human? You figured it–"

"Yes!" Ethan couldn't stop smiling if he tried to. Which he's not.

"Well, hello, Vic! Let me guess, you're having your usual black coffee and side of fruit?" the waitress from behind the breakfast bar says, now standing beside their booth.

"Of course, dear. Thank you," Victor replies. He sees Ethan still holding his smile but realizes he's looking at her. Smirking, Victor continues, "Amber, darling. May I be so bold as to speak for my handsome, yet incredibly shy, friend here, and ask if you'd be interested in getting coffee or dinner with him sometime?"

Ethan and Amber blush. She giggles, looks at Ethan, then back at Victor and says, "Tell your handsome, incredibly shy friend that I would *love* to get dinner." Her voice is pleasant and cheerful when she adds, "Tell him I'd love even more to have a date and time to look forward to. Maybe he can provide those details when I return with your coffee?" She winks at Ethan then walks back behind the breakfast bar.

Pretending to be angry while wearing the same, big smile, Ethan leans over the table and says under his breath to Victor, "Why did you… I was going to ask her out… Eventually."

Laughing, Victor replies, "When? I'm not trying to be your best man when I'm sixty."

Ethan laughs through his nose and fidgets with his pen, saying, "I've been… Busy." He watches her interact with a customer at the bar. His cheeks rise higher as he sees how friendly and happy she is. He looks at Victor and says, "Alright. Thank you. You know me too well, man, I'd procrastinate until I–"

"Ethan." Victor is still giggling. "I know. You're welcome." Slapping his hand onto Ethan's yellow notepad, he says, "Now. Pay me back by telling me what you–"

Amber returns to the table. Soft clinks of ceramic chime as she places Victor's coffee cup in front of him. She says politely as she sets the fruit down, "One coffee and cup of fruit." A long awkward pause takes place as she stands, joining Victor in staring at Ethan with anticipation. He smiles with ignorance until finally realizing they are waiting for him when Amber softly clears her throat.

"Oh…" Ethan fidgets with his pen. "Uh… Steranelli's, the Italian restaurant downtown? F-Friday night?" The chime of the bell above the door is the only indication that time hasn't frozen as he waits for her to answer.

"No," she replies sternly with firm lips. Seconds pass with Ethan's heart in his throat. He breathes again when she breaks into a bright smile and says, "I work Friday night. Take me on Saturday."

Victor chuckles while Ethan feels tension leaving his shoulders with a sigh of relief. He smiles back at Amber and says, "Saturday night is perfect."

She reaches over the table and tears the corner off the top page of Ethan's notebook. One of the only areas not covered in scribbles and equations she doesn't understand. "Text me a time and I'll text you back with where to pick me up," she says, writing her number on the torn off paper and sliding it in front of him. She returns to the breakfast bar.

Victor claps his hands slowly and loudly, exclaiming like a sports announcer, "Ladies and gentlemen! The couple you've been hoping to see together is finally going on their first date!"

Embarrassed, but smiling and blushing, Ethan grabs his hands to stop him from clapping and says, softly, "Holy shit. It's a date!"

"It's about damn time!" Victor sips his coffee. "Now. It's also about *damn time* you show me what you have here."

"Okay. Okay." Ethan shakes off his remaining nerves and taps on his notebook. His eyes turn and watch a patron stand up from the breakfast bar then look back at Victor. "Gene splicing isn't the answer we thought it was. We–"

"Is that why you drew a picture of jeans here next to it?" Victor points at a scribbled pair of jeans on the notepad.

"Well, no. That's because I was anxious waiting for you to get here." He chuckles. They share a laugh and agree it's a terrible sketch. "Anyway. We spent too much time on that idea.

"We're correct to be looking at the mitochondria. Altering at *that* level *could* change the entire biology of the host."

"Yes. This is what we've been saying. And I've been saying we should—"

"It's too risky, Vic. You know this. If we alter the DNA this drastically on a living host, we could kill them nearly instantly." Ethan pauses, then adds, "Or, probably worse, altering their DNA could turn them into something unrecognizable. Disfiguring them and likely ruining their mental state."

Victor nods then motions with his hand, encouraging Ethan to continue.

"Okay. So. Look at this." Ethan taps drawings of molecular models and DNA on the notepad. "We needed to be looking at specific cells in the host and alter *those* cells' mitochondrial

DNA, then…" He taps to another drawn model in the corner of the page waiting for Victor to put the pieces together.

Staring at Ethan's drawings and calculations, Victor mutters, "We alter reproductive cells to be passed on n—"

"Yes."

"To naturally alter the DNA through reproduction…" Victor stares at the notes. "Holy shit, Ethan."

"Yeah. The DNA of the partner then combines with the host's enhanced DNA. If successful, the enhanced genetics are formed naturally within the embryo. If unsuccessful, the results are a failed pregnancy."

"Forced evolution," Victor says excitedly.

"I-I… Yeah, I guess so." Ethan smiles.

"This is incredible, Ethan. I could leap over this table and give you the biggest hug right now."

Chuckling, Ethan says, "We're not in the clear yet, Vic. Testing is going to be long-winded, if possible at all. Not to mention getting approval and finding subjects willing to take the serum, which… Will be administered in an unpleasant area, *then* have children, *then* let us monitor and run tests *on* their children. It's a long way to go, and honestly a dice roll that we even get–"

"Ourselves." Victor hits the table with his hand, causing silverware and coffee mugs to chime together. "You said it yourself; the risks are low to the host. Plus, subjects will have to be male as the sperm cell is much easier to alter. We brew up a batch and test it on ourselves, then once one or both of us have children, we test to see if it worked."

"I mean, I guess we *could* do that," Ethan says reluctantly. "But imagine that it does work. Making it public and admitting that we developed and tested this in secret would discredit anything we try to do after."

"We'll let our future selves figure that out." Victor smiles and waves him off. "This doesn't even have to become public. If this works, Ethan, it can be the catalyst to my Vitality project. We could—"

"Vic. Come on." Ethan shakes his head. He hates discouraging Victor from this pipe dream.

"Ethan. You need to support me on this. It's—"

"Do you need a refill, Vic?" Amber approaches in response to him hitting the table.

"I'm sorry, dear, I do not. Your future date here got me excited about something, is all."

"Alright. Well, let me know if you do need anything." She winks at Ethan then says as she walks off, "Just raise your hand this time if you do."

Ethan giggles.

Victor leans in and speaks under his breath. "Think about it, Ethan. You can't tell me that you believe we can enhance genetics to increase muscular strength, immune system strength *and* intelligence, but somehow, we *can't* enhance neurological control in our brains? I've shown you my calculations. They show that it's—"

"Yes, I know. Your calculations do show potential, but it's still too risky, Vic." He hates disappointing Victor. "Even in the safest possible scenarios, you're talking about altering the brain and potentially damaging the host permanently. Even in tests we might think are successful."

"We're talking about neurological enhancement. *Enhancement*, Ethan. Taking the neurons and making them stronger."

"And you think that would somehow grant telepathic abilities?"

"I think it could, yes," Victor says confidently. "Imagine it: subjects learn to use parts of the brain humans haven't used in hundreds of thousands of years. *Complete* control of the brain. Limitless possibilities."

"Vic." Ethan expresses disbelief.

Victor hasn't changed his excitement, saying, "Now imagine this with Better Human. We take the DNA from that host with muscular and cardiovascular enhancements, then combine it with Vitality and enhanced neuron control, we could produce a serum that changes our species forever. We're talking the potential for–"

"Immortality?" Ethan scoffs.

Victor leans back and reaches for a grape. His chest raises the buttons on his shirt as he breathes a swelling sigh.

Another chime at the door breaks the silence at the table.

"Vic. I'm sorry, I know you're serious, I just don't see it," Ethan speaks politely. He sees his best friend is upset. "Even if… And I mean a *big* if here. You're talking *years* of testing."

"Not a problem."

Ethan lowers his eyebrows with frustration. "*With* the data showing what happens to failed attempts. This level of experimentation on the brain could kill subjects or leave them in an unrecognizable state." He sees Victor's expression is blank. "I know that you know this, Vic."

"Maybe so, but with Better Human being successful, that pure DNA will allow us to develop a serum that passes those traits on to any human, the same way we create vaccines! This would certainly make the subjects less prone to failures from Vitality."

"Turning the Better Human subjects into science experiments we continuously take blood and marrow samples from?" Ethan's tone shows disappointment.

Passing a mirrored expression, Victor says, "You're making it sound terrible. We'd make *anyone* comfortable during this process and ensure they're well compensated."

"No." Ethan breaks eye contact with Victor and swirls his pen on the notepad. "We're too far ahead with this. We don't even know that Better Human will work. And if it did… *If* it did… We find a way to better humanity from it *while* ensuring we take minimal samples from the subject. To better our species, not to promote another project that we don't even know could work."

Breathing a defeated sigh, Victor mutters, "You're right." After a long pause, he adds, "If I find an ethical way to test this, would you support me on this?"

Victor is passionate about this. He has been since they met. Ethan pinches the bridge of his nose and decides to take another approach to let him down easy. "I… Okay. Another big if. Say you come up with–"

"We. *We* come up with."

"We come up with an ethical idea, and then a serum for Vitality. We'd never get approval to test on human subjects."

"First off, this would be *years* down the road, so we'd have the success of Better Human supporting us already. Secondly, we could start with patients that are already dealing with mental disabilities or abnormalities." Victor sips his coffee.

"There are hundreds of other medical research projects in that field already that are *much* less risky."

Amber approaches the table and halts their conversation. "Are you two ordering more to eat or drink? Or do you plan to occupy a table that could have higher paying customers for me?" She laughs at her own sarcasm. Ethan joins her laughter.

"We could order an early lunch?" Ethan says, waiting for confirmation from Victor.

"You know what? Sure. Let's get a burger and fries for both of us. To go. Your date and I have a meeting to get to shortly."

"A meeting?" Ethan quickly questions Victor.

"Our realtor found a small place that might be perfect for us." He smiles at Ethan excitedly.

"What! Why didn't you tell me this when you got here?" Ethan is beaming with excitement.

"I wanted to surprise you. Plus, you had some good news of you—"

"I'll go and get your lunches in." Amber interrupts, smiling at both of them.

"Thank you, dear," Victor smiles back. They watch her give their order to the kitchen, then Victor turns to Ethan. "I think this place will be perfect for us to start. We'll have everything we need to start the contract with Bayer."

"Vic… Man, this is incredible. Th-Thank you."

"Just…" Victor hesitates. "You know how important this is to me, Ethan. Promise me you'll consider *trying* to see if Vitality could—"

"Vic. I promise." Ethan watches Amber but doesn't smile as he did before.

"There's a 'but' coming," Victor says, observing Ethan's hesitation.

"But…" He looks somberly at Victor. "I know why you want this. You still have a lot of time. There are other… *Better* ways for you." They stare at each other. "Promise *me* you won't rush this."

"I have time. If Better Human works the way we think it will, that alone could buy me more time."

Ethan sighs.

They stare contently at each other for a moment. Victor looks at Ethan's notepad and smiles. "We start this when we move into this place that we're certain to fall in love with today," he says confidently. "One day this paper will hang next to this… And this." He pulls out two papers. One is their business license, and the other is their first contract to develop a new drug for Bayer.

"You just carry those with you everywhere?" Ethan laughs through his nose.

Chuckling, Victor says, "Not everywhere, but every time we meet with a realtor I do." His expression changes as a thought occurs to him. "One more thing. What about subjects that have more serious mental conditions? Hemorrhages. Brain damage from an injury. Rabies?"

"*Rabies*? You're kidding, right?"

"Of course." Victor chuckles. "Of course."

The rustling of a bag hitting their table interrupts their conversation. "Your burgers to go. Medium-well as you prefer. Fries overdone as *you* prefer." Amber nods to Victor when she mentions the fries. "And your checks. Always a pleasure to see you two! I'm looking forward to seeing *you* soon," she says while smiling uncontrollably at Ethan. She sets the checks on the table then walks to the breakfast bar.

Ethan and Victor pull out their wallets and count cash. Victor sets money on his check and folds up the license and contract. Ethan eyes the corners of his bills, counting to make sure he leaves Amber a bigger tip than Victor.

Watching Ethan count his money, Victor smiles and slides the food to Ethan. Standing, he says, "You ready?"

Setting the money on his check, grabbing his notepad and the food, Ethan stands and says, "I'm ready."

"We're going to change the world, brother." Victor smiles and walks to the door. He waves at Amber on the way.

The bell chimes as Ethan follows Victor. He stops and looks at Amber, who is already smiling at him. She says silently with her lips, wiggling her thumbs, "Text me."

He nods and smiles back, learning that the frequency of him doing this today is making his cheeks hurt. His heart races in a way he hopes to feel forever.

"See you Saturday," he says to her. She raises her shoulders with another smile then returns to a patron sitting at the breakfast bar.

What a perfect day. He thinks to himself.

The bell on the door chimes again as the door closes behind him.

CHAPTER 11

"HEY, BUD!" Ethan says brightly. His voice echoes through the otherwise quiet training room. He walks toward Jacob slowly with his arms held outward for a hug.

"D-Dad?" Jacob stutters, his voice barely above a whisper. He's trying to move his legs, but his feet feel like anvils. "How?" he mutters under his breath.

Victor releases his hands from Jacob's shoulders. Ethan walks halfway to Jacob then stops with his arms still held outward, saying, "Come give your old man a hug!"

"Go ahead, son," Victor says softly, lightly pushing Jacob forward.

Finally able to move his legs, Jacob steps forward, looks back at Victor who nods to him, then continues walking to his dad.

Inches away, he can hear his dad breathing. He's still smiling. Still holding his arms out, waiting for Jacob. A warm tear falls down Jacob's cheek. His lungs are quivering as he fights off crying. Frozen with astonishment, Jacob stares into the unblinking eyes of his father. He reaches slowly and touches his dad's cheek. It's warm.

"I hope you can forgive me, Jacob," Ethan says quietly.

Jacob throws himself into his dad's arms. They both squeeze tightly. Through his crying, Jacob says, "Dad, I'm sorry." His voice is muffled with his face on his dad's shoulder. "I've been so angry that you were gone." He pulls himself away to look into his dad's eyes. With his hands on his dad's shoulders, and more questions filling his head than he can focus on, he asks, "But… Why did…" He sniffles. "Where have you been?" His voice changes from sad to concerned.

"I hate that I missed your game, bud. Mom said you crushed a homerun every at-bat!" He pats Jacob's shoulder. "How's it feel being dad's little champion?"

Jacob shakes his head in confusion. He wipes his tears from his nose with his sleeve, looks back at Victor, who is looking at Chloe, then looks back at his dad. "Wh-Wh… Game?"

"S-Sorry… Jacob… I can explain…" The pitch of Ethan's voice fluctuates aggressively. He continues to smile at Jacob.

"I'm sorry!" Chloe yells, nervously.

Jacob whips around to look at Chloe. Her eyes are glazed with tears as she forces a concerned smile at him. "What the fuck?" he asks, swinging his arms.

She mouths silently, "I'm sorry."

Turning back around, Jacob sees his dad is gone. "What…" he begins to mutter.

"I'm so, so sorry, Jacob!" Chloe exclaims louder. A snicker from Elliot follows.

Jacob looks at Elliot, scowling, when Victor walks over and squeezes his shoulder. "Don't be mad, son, she had limited data," he says quietly to Jacob.

"Limited data?" Jacob pulls away from Victor's grasp on his shoulders and turns to face him. His expression is still angry, his eyes slightly bloodshot from his short crying. "What the fuck does that mean?"

"Language, Jacob," Victor speaks sternly. He leans into Jacob's ear and whispers, "Remember this anger you're feeling. This is the emotion that can drive you to control your abilities."

What? Jacob thinks. He gives a puzzled look to Victor, who waves Chloe over. Jacob looks at her, confused, but she's actively avoiding eye contact by staring at his feet.

"Chloe can project visions into other people's reality. It's how you — it's how we *all* saw your dad here moments ago," Victor explains. He wraps his arm around Chloe, who is still embarrassed and avoiding interaction.

Jacob's fingertips are tingling. He sees Elliot whispering to Theo with an arrogant smirk on his face. They both chuckle and look at Jacob, turning the tingling into a fiery sensation burning through his forearms. He clenches his fists and the weapons on the wall shake, causing Victor to quickly step in front of Jacob, saying, "Relax, son."

Shoulders heaving, Jacob's scowl is fierce as his eyes break away from Victor to see the three other Better Human subjects smirking at him.

"Enough!" Victor turns his head to scold them. They stand at attention and lose their smiles. Speaking loud enough for only Jacob to hear him, Victor says, "I apologize, son. It was insensitive of me to assume you would take this positively."

"I… I did for a… I… I *felt* him. He hugged me," Jacob's angry eyes weaken and drop another tear.

"That's how powerful she is, son." He lightly squeezes his shoulders. It's evident how proud he is of Chloe. He says, "Think about it, Jacob. Her brain is *so* powerful that she can project visions to all of us *and* interact with *your* brain's neurons to imitate sensations. That's the emotional control I've been telling you about. I helped train her. Together we learned that the more heightened her emotions were, the stronger her projections became.

"Once she learned to harness her emotions, she learned how to control her ability."

Jacob can tell Victor wants a response, but he doesn't know what to say.

"She's one of the reasons I'm so close to completing my Vitality project," Victor says softly. Almost as if he didn't mean to speak it aloud.

"Vitality?" Jacob questions.

"I have to see…" Chloe begins speaking, gaining attention from both Jacob and Victor. She wants to explain in her own words what she can do. "I can project anything. But with people, I have to have seen them and heard them speak. Otherwise, it won't be natural. Otherwise, it sounds like when your dad's voice broke."

"So… So, you have a perfect memory, too?" Jacob asks.

"I told you, son, her brain is incredibly powerful." Victor speaks proudly.

Chloe steps over, grabs and squeezes Jacob's hand. His heart beats faster. Her eyes are glossy as she says, "I'm *so* sorry, Jacob. I feel like I violated your privacy."

"I mean…" He stutters. He was just so angry seconds ago, but her eyes look at him with innocence and empathy. Her apology feels genuine. He decides to let it go for now. "It's fine. But if you have to see him to show him… How did you…" He stutters more trying to ask the question he wants to ask. "He mentioned a baseball game–"

"Victor showed me a–" Chloe interrupts then is interrupted by Victor.

"I had your mom send me a video of your father before I came up to your room, Jacob. One that she filmed after a championship game of yours when you were little. I sent it to Chloe before we left your home." He watches Jacob's expression show frustration. "This was my idea, son, and I apologize, again, that it was distasteful."

Jacob's mind is spinning. His emotions are spinning. Of course, the video his mom picks is one where his dad missed his championship game. In his father's defense, this actually didn't happen often, considering his patterns of being at work more than home, but now he's reminded of it. Again. He felt so happy seeing his dad. He felt weightless for a moment. Now he feels frustrated all over again.

"Did you know my dad?" he asks Chloe, curiously.

"Actually, I–"

"For fuck's sake. Are we done coddling this kid?" Elliot yells.

Anger courses through Jacob, creating the sensation in his palms again. It feels like electricity pulsing to his elbows. His fists clench in response before he steps toward Elliot. Elliot, who he just met. Barely. Elliot, who he already dislikes.

A section of wooden staves lean against the wall behind Jade. Victor watches one of them twitch as they did moments earlier. He places his hand against Jacob's chest.

Victor leans close to his ear again and whispers, "Not now, son. This anger, too, I need you to remember it." He pats his hand then stands, changing his focus to Elliot. Dark purple veins appear around his eyes as his demeanor changes. His pupils burn through Elliot as he yells, "That's enough disobedience from you! Go down to Medical Room One and wait for me there." His hand points aggressively to the door.

"Whatever," Elliot mumbles before hanging his head and leaving the training room. Jacob watches Theo and Jade glance at each other, then return to standing at attention.

Victor takes a few steps over to Theo and Jade, saying quietly, but audibly to Jacob, "I expect you two to continue demonstrating the behavior I requested."

"Yes, sir," they say in shocking unison. Both remain at attention, standing perfectly still.

"It's you two who will show Jacob our training regimen and bring him on hunts," Victor says.

Hunts? Jacob thinks.

"Yes, sir." Again, they speak simultaneously.

Immediately switching to a positive and excited demeanor, Victor says to Theo and Jade, "Alright, now show Jacob what he can learn with our training regimen here!"

Theo and Jade smile at each other, then walk to the back of the room where a large rectangle is printed on the padded floor. They stand inside the rectangle on opposite sides. Bowing, Jade twirls her staff, spinning it so fast that whooshing pulses through the room. Theo bows in return, chuckling as he reaches both arms behind him, unholstering his wakizashi swords.

Jade hops forward with a battle cry, swinging her staff at Theo's shins. He laughs, jumping over her attack while swinging his sword overhead. She kneels, bracing her staff over her head, blocking his attack with a loud clang.

Metal scrapes while Theo drags his sword across the staff, then swings ruthlessly with both arms, attacking Jade who twirls her staff, blocking each side back and forth.

"They're good, aren't they, son?" Victor asks Jacob.

"This is awesome," he responds, not breaking his focus on them sparring.

"They're twins. Both took extraordinarily well to my Better Human serum."

Twins. I should've picked up on that, Jacob thinks, realizing they stand the same, present themselves the same, and, naturally, look very much alike.

Victor clasps his hands behind his back. Jacob can see frustration again in his movements. Motioning with a nod to Garret, they walk over to the door. Victor whispers, now inaudible, to Garret. He's pointing repeatedly at the hall in rapid thrusts.

Chloe taps on Jacob's shoulder and whispers, "Are you okay, Jacob? Do you forgive me?"

Already trying to watch both the scene with Victor and the scene with the twins, he slightly turns his head and whispers back, "I'm… Yeah. I forgive you."

She smiles softly. Her posture and lack of interest in the twins show she's used to seeing this training. Even though he's done training with his dad and at a small gym, Jacob can tell they train much more intensely here.

He watches them attack and block each other, sending clang after clang echoing through the training room.

"Jacob." Victor has stopped his conversation with Garret and stands at the door, bellowing loudly. He seems angered all over again. The dark veins around his eyes have gotten darker. The twins immediately stop sparring. Everyone turns their attention to Victor, who says, "Garret will be taking you back home. I promised your mother we wouldn't be long. Say your goodbyes and meet him in the hall." He begins to exit the room.

"Sir!" David yells. Victor stops and looks to him with impatience. "I'd like to continue talking with you about my ideas to work on my abilities."

"*Abilities*? You have *one*, David. And I'm booked. Speak with Garret. I'll see you when I have time." He speaks dismissively, then exits the room. David drops his head in defeat then walks slowly out of the room. Chloe and Jacob watch through the large windows as he disappears down the hall.

"It was nice meeting you, Jacob," Chloe says politely.

Jacob watches Noel exit before turning to Chloe and saying, "Yeah, it was nice meeting you, too. Is uh… Does Victor always get that angry?"

Stuttering, Chloe says, "Typically, only with… Them." She discreetly gestures her head to where Elliot left.

"Later, Second Place." She's interrupted by Theo as he and Jade walk past them.

"Second Pl—" Jacob tries to question the meaning, but they continue walking out the door.

"Well…" Jacob says awkwardly to Chloe. "I guess I gotta go." He points more awkwardly with both of his thumbs behind him to the door.

Chloe chuckles seeing his nerves. "Will you tell Victor you want to come back?" she asks, anxious to hear his answer.

"Of course. Or… Yeah. Yeah, I think so," Jacob quickly answers.

Chloe smiles nervously. "I hope to see you again."

Jacob smiles politely then sets his aim for the doorway. He did not consider the room he's walking out of would create such a mess of his emotions. Sadness. Anger. Loss. Yet, he's still eager and excited to return. Victor says this is what his dad wanted. Maybe training here can be his way to honor that and cope with his loss.

He glances at the staves leaning against the wall and thinks of Elliot. His palms tingle. *Not now*, he thinks. He exits and meets Garret.

Chloe watches him walk beyond the windows then cleans up the few training weapons lying on the floor. She leaves and walks down the hallway to her room.

Each dorm is designed to have a small entryway to an open concept with a kitchenette and open space with a bed and couch. In the back corner is a closet and small bathroom.

She enters her room, kicking off her shoes in the entryway. She looks at the couch against the wall across from her bed. Sitting and smiling at her is Jacob.

"I was hoping to get to talk to you more today," she says to him as she walks to her bed. He follows her with his eyes, saying nothing, just holding his smile. "You have so much innocence." She sits at the foot of the bed across from him on the couch.

Closing her eyes, she takes a deep breath. A tear falls down her left cheek as she opens her eyes, staring into Jacob's. "I really, *really* hope you can help us, Jacob," she says softly, returning a half-smile to his continuingly pleasant, charming smile.

Chloe rubs her face with her hands and sighs. When she removes her hands, she looks at an empty couch with no Jacob. She falls backward onto her bed and stares at the ceiling.

CHAPTER 12

"SO, IF I ASKED HER to, like, make my crush appear and make out with me, she could do that?" Deante asks Jacob in the cafeteria. This question is one of many he's been asking since Jacob told him about the facility on their walk to school.

"If you wanted her to do something weird like that to let you make out with Naomi, yes, she could do that. Since you're too chicken to ask her out," Jacob says, laughing at himself and biting his breakfast pizza. "She'd just need a picture or something to know what Naomi looks like."

"Man, shut up," Deante laughs. "You'll be training with those other students next time? Will they be using the real weapons?"

"Hopefully not at first!" He sees Kyle and Renz walking over to them. "We'll continue this later," he says quickly.

"I'm not going to make it outside the walls today, boys," Kyle says disappointedly as he sits. "I'm still fuckin' grounded."

"We're *literally* going because you said your hacking shit can unlock devices now," Deante says.

"It can!" Kyle defends himself. "I've been stuck in my damn room for weeks now. Learning how to code this software is seriously all I do."

"You're lucky that I'm curious to see more of these online diaries." Deante chuckles while eating.

"This guy sees one video of girls dancing and he's hooked," Jacob jokes, pointing at Deante, receiving a soft punch in the arm in return.

"We'll find you more, man!" Renz says cheerfully to Kyle, shaking him gently while his head hangs in disappointment.

"You're actually going to join us again?" Jacob asks Renz.

"Y-Yeah. Come on, I don't ditch *that* much," he responds defensively. "I also hope I find more of those Avengers movies."

"Oh! I still need that Wolverine comic, too!" Deante yells with his mouth full. "What did you guys tell your parents?"

"Basketball practice and scrimmage," Jacob answers.

Renz says, "That I was hanging at your place. You?"

"Detention," Deante says as he swallows his bite.

Laughing, Jacob says, "You're the only kid who would make up a lie that's going to get you in trouble."

Just as he's about to defend himself, Deante is interrupted by Toby, who sits next to Jacob and says, "Dude. I was on the roof again last night trying to see that Shrieker again. It was super quiet out and as I waited for it to show up, I heard people talking on the other side of the wall!"

Jacob rubs his face in frustration. He says, "Tobe. Seriously, dude. Who would be talking over there? Wasted can't talk."

"I don't know, man, but I'm telling you I heard them. It was a full conversation between at least two people."

"What were they saying?"

"I'm not right at the wall, so I couldn't make out much. Sounded like they were planning something… I *know* I heard them say 'attack' a few times."

"Okay," Jacob scoffs. "Again, man, why are you telling *me* this? What can I even do about it?"

"I just thought your d…" Toby hangs his head. "I'm sorry."

"Yeah," Jacob says impatiently.

"It was probably security, man. Chill," Kyle says. His frustration from still being grounded is showing.

"On the outside of the wall? Since when?" Toby asks. He scoffs dramatically, exchanging stares with each of them at the table. Finally, he says, "Don't you guys think there's more to the outside than they're teaching us here? Don't you think there are secrets they're keeping from us?"

He's met by four sets of eyes, unblinking, when suddenly all four of them break out in laughter. Deante pounds the table with the side of his fist while the others look at each other laughing. Toby drops his head in embarrassment.

"Yeah, dude, no shit," Deante wipes tears from his cheek. "The fuck are we gonna do about it, though? Stop 'em?" His lips buzz as he presses them, unsuccessfully holding off laughter. He pounds the table again, laughing, when the rest of his friends laugh at him.

"Then why do you all sneak out over the wall, huh? Isn't it to find evidence to prove they're lying?" Toby asks Deante, seriously.

Laughing again, then realizing Toby isn't joking, Deante looks stunned. He glances at Jacob and says, "This guy is serious?"

Jacob nods while smiling, trying to hide it from Toby.

Deante clears his throat then answers Toby, saying, "Bro. No. We sneak out to get comic books and movies. And whatever other shit kids had before we lived restricted lives inside twenty-foot walls." He's serious now, too. While taking his last bite he waves off Toby, adding, "Get over this lies and secrets shit, dude, ain't nobody gonna listen to you."

"Dude, whatever," Toby mutters to the table before standing and walking away. Jacob, now laughing through his nose, feels bad that his feelings got hurt, but at the same time, he agrees with Deante.

Class today is filled with test preparations as fall finals are on the horizon. After school, the friends meet at the large concrete circle outside the main doors of the school. Kyle gives them a list of devices to find for him to hack. Tablets, cell phones and laptops. They tell Kyle to enjoy his bedroom and head off toward the tree.

Clouds begin to fill a graying sky on their walk to the tree. Renz climbs first and waits on the branch. Deante looks to Jacob for him to go next and sees him looking sadly at his phone.

"Why the face? Chloe not like you back?" Deante jokes.

Laughing through his nose, Jacob says, "Shut up, bro. No. My mom texted me." He flashes his screen to Deante.

"Hey sweetheart! I know you are playing basketball after school! Just wanted to remind you that your birthday weekend is coming up! Let me know what you want for a special meal and what kind of cake to get (even though I know you'll pick a cookie cake) lol"

His mom always goes above and beyond for his birthday to make it special. He feels heaviness come over him as he thinks about his dad not being here for this one. If he could skip his birthday this year, he would.

Jacob stares at his phone long enough that Deante and Renz make it to the other side of the wall. Renz yells, "Come on, man!"

Jacob types, *"You know me too well, mom, cookie cake is perfect! Maybe just pizza with the scary movie this year?"* He hits send, slides his phone in the front pocket of his backpack, checks the tension of the rope, then joins Renz and Deante.

Time management is meticulously calculated with Jacob and his friends, regarding their travels outside the walls. On days when they skip school or leave early, they travel west to a neighborhood a few miles away. On the days where they go after a full day of school, they travel north, where a large neighborhood is only a one mile walk through woods. Today, they are travelling to Spring Hill, the neighborhood to the north.

Spring Hill is a desolate neighborhood. Single-family, three-bedroom homes line the streets that are now overgrown from tall grass bursting through the worn and weathered pavement. Abandoned cars tell the stories of how the families evacuated, with nearly each street having its own two-car collision rotting at the end of a driveway. Moss and vines hug the siding of every home. Windows are dingy. Roofs are rotted, and any wooden trim or porch is warped and brittle.

Jacob, Renz, and Deante step their knees high out of the woods and through the tall grass between homes, walking to the street.

"Fuck. This breeze is cold!" Deante shivers, holding his shoulders to his ears with his hands in his hoodie pocket.

"Yeah, can we pick a house before the rain gets here?" Renz says with a shaky voice.

Jacob looks down the overgrown street and says, "D, which one did we loot last time?"

"That one." He points to a once yellow, now tinted green house three homes down. He quickly puts his hand back in the pocket.

"You sure? I thought it was–"

"I'm sure, man. Look at the window."

"Ah, yeah, that's right," Jacob confirms, seeing a small X-Men poster taped to the top-left bedroom window. "Let's continue our zig-zag pattern and loot the house diagonally across the street next."

"Deal," Deante says, still shivering.

They jog to the house with vines hugging nearly every brick, exposing just enough to show it used to be red. Deante rustles through the grass and slaps his palms against the front window, then attempts to slide it open, grunting loudly. He mutters through his gritted teeth, "Why... Can't... It just be... Easy..."

"Guys," Renz speaks loudly but cautiously, pushing the front door inward, "I-It was unlocked."

Jogging to join Renz on the porch, Deante says, "I really didn't want to break a window again."

Rain begins to fall gently as Jacob jogs over last from the street. Renz watches him reach the small, covered porch, then squints across the street, asking, "You sure that's not the house you guys hit last time? The front door is open."

Jacob and Deante lean and squint through the misty rain. Jacob says confidently, "No. Definitely was the X-Men house next to it."

"Do you... Do you think someone else is out here looting? That's odd, right? That door's open and this was un–"

Jacob pats Renz's shoulder and says, "Relax, old man. This isn't *that* uncommon."

"No?" Renz's voice is shaky. He's cold and nervous.

"Not at all. A lot of houses were looted during the outbreak. Plus, some people left their homes in a panic and left front doors and garage doors wide open or unlocked." He pats harder. "Take a breath, man. Chill. We're fine."

"O-Okay," Renz says softly.

Pushing the front door open enough to lean his torso in, Jacob stares into the living room and listens for signs of activity inside. The dark rain clouds and vines over the windows offer very little light into the house. Small streaks of gray sunlight beam through the dust particles floating through the room. He grabs his flashlight from the side pocket of his backpack and shines it into the living room. A broken lamp lies in front of a dried-up leather couch with yellow padding protruding through cracked seams. The end table next to it is layered in dust. Leaning further in and shining his light to the right, he finds a littered kitchen. Cabinet doors hang open, some swinging from the bottom hinge. The refrigerator door hangs open, too, showing off dried black residue throughout the inside. Broken dishes, dried puddles from spilled beverages, and a few food items cover the floor.

"Yeah, this place has been ransacked," Jacob speaks while looking up the stairs across the room with his light.

"Sh-Should we move to another house?" Renz asks.

"Nah, most of the looting was done forever ago. All they wanted then was food, medicine, and clothes. The shit we're looking for should still be here." Jacob squints to look down the short hall next to the stairs. He steps inside to investigate further.

Deante steps inside, too, standing in the middle of the living room and shared kitchen. Jacob is at the end of the hallway looking intently at a closet and powder room. Deante walks toward the staircase, makes a suspicious face and asks Jacob quietly, "Do you hear… Humming?"

Shining his light at Deante causing him to block his eyes, Jacob asks, "Humming?"

With cautious steps, he makes his way to Deante when the front door slams shut. Renz stands with his legs wide, using his back to brace the door.

"Renz?" Jacob asks singingly. "You alright?"

"I…" He's struggling to speak due to his rapid breathing. "I was watching you… You two when… When I heard…" He scrunches his face. His lip is quivering.

"Heard what, man?" Deante asks somewhat impatiently.

"Something… Or someone… They ran through the yard right behind me." Renz's voice is panicked.

In a consoling voice, Jacob says, "It's okay, dude, Wasted are more afraid of us than we are of–"

They all simultaneously look to the vine-filled window above the kitchen sink, where rapid footsteps and breathing are heard running past. Jacob walks over and looks through the dust-stained window.

Whimpering, Renz slides his back down the door, sitting and resting his head back against it. He opens his tightly closed eyes. "Guys, I'm not–" His focus changes to the stairs behind Deante. His eyes open wide in horror as he raises his shaking hand, pointing to the steps.

Deante turns to look at the staircase. A young girl is crouched with her hands in front of her feet on the landing of the steps. Dim light barely shines on her faded pink T-shirt and mud-stained, torn jeans. Her head slowly turns as her bloodshot eyes investigate Deante through her matted, greasy hair. Soft, raspy hums escape her nostrils.

"Hey, Jacob," Deante speaks while keeping his eyes on the young girl.

"What's up?" he says through a grunt, still leaning over the sink peering through the window.

"What's the closest we've ever been to an Outsider?" Deante asks, continuing his staring contest with her.

"I don't know, like, the full length of the hall at school?" He stands straight, then asks, curiously, "Why?"

"Check it." Deante points at the girl, glancing quickly to make sure Jacob is looking.

Jacob stands next to Deante and immediately locks eyes with her. He says, "Damn. Yeah, this is a record for us." He watches her breathing. It's fast with short hums still escaping with random breaths. Her eyes switch rapidly between him and Deante. She looks scared. Jacob says, softly, catching her attention, "Hey. Hey. It's okay."

"Are you fucking crazy!" Renz yells. He shuffles on the floor into the dirty living room.

"It's okay, we can let you outside. We're not going to hurt–" Jacob stops abruptly as the girl leaps down from the landing, tackling Deante to the floor.

He lets out an agonized yell as he hits the floor. Whipping her head back, she thrusts her forehead into the bridge of his nose. Her arms flail wildly as she continues to throw her head into his chest and shoulder. He moans as he fights off her arms and headbutts with slaps and jabs with his elbows.

Jacob runs over and grabs her shoulders. He throws her off to the side. She jumps quickly to her feet and stands with her legs bent, looking around the room in panic. Her expression is scared, and her breathing matches her emotion. Renz tiptoes behind her with the broken lamp and swings, breaking the rest of the ceramic base off the back of her head. She drops limply to the floor.

Jacob kneels next to Deante and reaches to move his hand from his bloody nose.

"Let me see, man," Jacob says, moving his hand while he hisses with pain.

"Fuck, man," Deante mutters. "Why'd she gotta do me like this?"

Jacob chuckles and searches his backpack for a rag or spare shirt to hold under his nose. Renz runs around to his other side to help, where he sees Deante's hoodie ripped at the top of his arm.

"Guess we found the source of the humming, huh?" Jacob asks jokingly. Deante lets out a quick chuckle.

"Hold on, D, your arm…" Renz says, pointing at blood near the rip in his hoodie.

"What is it? I fuckin' love this hoodie, man. Shit! Don't tell me it's ripped. Don't tell me!" He lays his head back in disappointment.

Renz looks at Jacob with a concerned look, then switches to Deante. His voice is nervous as he says, "D… She… She bit you."

CHAPTER 13

DEANTE LETS OUT AN EXAGGERATED whimper and panics, saying, "Shit! Oh, shit. Shit. Am I gonna turn?" His eyes are filled with fear and tears.

Jacob chuckles and reaches into his bag for something to bandage Deante's arm.

What are we supposed to do?" Renz squeezes the wound and matches Deante's intensity.

A bandage wrap lies at the bottom of his bag. Jacob grabs it and smiles at Deante while he reaches over him to cover the wound.

Reacting to his calm demeanor, Deante yells, "Seriously, man? How long do I have? Why are you *smiling*?"

Pausing the wrap, Jacob looks at Deante, then Renz, then back at Deante. Both of their expressions are wide-eyed and scared. "Are you… What's with you both?" Jacob asks, sternly. They both reply with quivering lips. "You're going to be fine, bro."

"I… I am?"

"Everyone inside the walls is vaccinated against V-Mor." He tightens the bandage aggressively. "You'll be alright. Worst case, the wound will puss or swell up."

"Damn, man," Deante grunts, reacting to Jacob tightening the bandage. "Ain't gotta be that rough."

"So... Bites would still make us turn without all that..." Renz mumbles while staring into the living room; his eyes are still frightened.

"Do either of you pay attention in biology?" Jacob waits for Renz to answer. He doesn't blink. "Renz?" He turns to see what has his attention.

The young girl is lying face down but rubbing the back of her head. Lightly grunting, she begins to push herself off the floor. Her matted hair covers her face as she sighs and sits on the backs of her feet. She parts her hair, sees the boys staring at her and shuffles frantically backwards, knocking the coffee table aside, then pushes herself into the corner of the room.

Renz, Jacob, and Deante stay still, watching her, waiting in silence to see if she makes another move. She breathes heavily and rapidly, exchanging glances with all their stares.

"Renz," Jacob whispers. "Open the front door."

"Are you crazy! She just attacked D," he whispers back through his teeth, not breaking his stare at her.

"Open the door so she can run out. She's afraid of us. She won't attack again," Jacob whispers back.

"You don't know that!"

"It's worth trying. Just move slow–"

The girl scurries to the window Deante tried opening from outside. Keeping her back against the wall and eyes on the boys, she fumbles with her hands trying to open the window. She yells, her voice scratchy, "M-Ma... Mama!"

All of their eyes widen.

"Mama!" She hits the glass with her palm.

Heavy footsteps pound on the dirt outside the kitchen window. Their heads whip to the wall. Grass wisps loudly from the runner outside speeding past the kitchen wall. Then the front door. Then the footsteps stop when they reach the house near the girl. All their heads follow the noise.

"Rose?" a female voice yells from outside.

"Mama!" The girl jumps up and looks outside. "Ma!" The glass shakes violently as she hits it with her palms again. Her head continues to whip toward the boys in fear.

"Unlock on top. I help push," the female voice yells.

While staring at Jacob and Deante, the girl pats her hands around the top of the window. She looks to find a lock and keeps checking the boys watching her. They remain frozen watching this unfold. She finds the lock and works with her mother to open the window. She rips away vines then reaches her legs out, sliding until she's hanging on by her hands, all while staring at them until she lets go and drops fully out.

Two sets of footsteps stomp quickly away through the grass, onto concrete, then fade into the distance.

"The *fuck* was that?" Deante breaks the silence.

"They… They *do* talk?" Jacob says. They're all still staring where the event took place.

Laying back onto the floor, Deante sighs, rubs his face, then says, "This means Toby was right twice."

Jacob chuckles.

Renz asks, "Twice?"

Deante and Jacob meet eyes.

"What do you mean twice, guys? What was he right about?"

"Nothing. It's stupid," Deante replies dismissively, then hums awkwardly hoping Renz lets it go.

Renz leans over and watches Deante ignore him trying to make eye contact with him. Jacob stares into the living room. Renz says, "Nah, one of you is going to tell me."

Sighing, Deante blurts out, "Jacob and I encountered a Shrieker last time we left the walls."

Renz bursts to his feet. "You're fucking with me."

They reply with emotionless expressions.

"For one, why the f… Why would you come back out here if they are real? For two, why would you bring *me* with you?" His chin shakes from his lip quivering in fear. Renz clenches his fists. There is fury in his grip. His nails leave four tiny marks on his palms.

"It was just one, dude, and Jacob used his special abilities to fight it off," Deante brushes off Renz's reaction.

Jacob sighs and rolls his eyes.

"His what?" Renz is confused.

"Uh…" Deante looks at Jacob. He pulls the strings of his hoodie and tightens the hood, closing it over his face. "Nothing… It's, uh… It's stupid."

Jacob watches Renz become confused. To avoid them going back and forth, he tells Renz everything. His enhanced genetics. His fast healing. The telekinesis, though accidental at the moment. And the facility.

They sit cross-legged between the living room and littered kitchen. Renz asks questions similar to what Deante asked days ago. Jacob explains the situation his dad put him into by making him keep it a secret.

A small pause from the conversation about Jacob allows Renz to ask the other thing on his mind. "Why do you guys keep coming out here when you run into Shriekers and Wasted?"

"Honestly, it's so rare we see Wasted out here. And they're usually watching from afar if we do. As you can see, they're more terrified of us than we are of them," Jacob answers sincerely. "I think she only attacked D because she felt cornered by us."

"I just…" Renz stutters. If I'd have known Wasted were even slightly aggressive, I wouldn't have—"

"Okay, let's be honest for a second," Deante yells through the shirt he's holding against his nose. He interrupts, frustrated, hating that Toby's stories are correct. "Nobody knows for sure that what we saw was a *Shrieker*."

Caught off guard by this defense, Jacob answers, "It looked exactly how the stories portray them. Bloody, chewed-off lips, hissing, twitchy, aggressive and–"

"Ogay I gedit." Deante's voice is quieter and muffled by the shirt as he's holding his head back to slow his bleeding nose.

A ray of sunshine strikes Jacob's eye, alerting him that the sky is turning orange. He says, "Shit. It's going to be dark soon and we haven't found anything for Kyle."

Still muffled through the shirt under his nose, Deante says, "Less eesh chikaroom."

"Dude. Your nose has to be fine by now." Jacob says while laughing at the mumbling he heard.

Holding the rag away and seeing no new blood, Deante says, "Ah. I guess you're right." He breathes freely through his nose. "I said, 'let's each check a room.'"

"Good idea. Just grab a phone or tablet or anything Kyle can try to hack into." Jacob looks at Renz. "Which room you want?"

Renz glances around. He feels a shiver up his spine when he imagines going upstairs, where the girl came from. His other option is the office down the short hallway next to them. Thinking that if there were any more Outsiders hiding in there, they'd have come out when Jacob opened the door, he says, "I'll check that office."

"Cool. We'll check the rooms upstairs." Jacob jumps to his feet. "Let's hurry so we can get back before dark."

Deante and Jacob sprint up the stairs, racing each other and slamming into the railing and walls as they push past each other. Renz gathers his nerves and shuffles cautiously down the short hall past the steps. Leaning his head in slowly, as if he's going to catch an Outsider hiding in a corner, he looks directly to the left inside the door. A tall, plastic plant lies on its side. Dark green paint cracks along the walls, peeling away in areas to reveal pale yellow paint underneath. Floating shelves line the ceiling, holding trophies, pictures, and sports memorabilia. The back wall has two bookshelves on each side with a cherry-wood desk in between. A desk chair lies knocked over in front with a drawer ripped out, broken on the floor and scattered papers trailing to where Renz stands.

A thud slams from the ceiling causing Renz to jump. He pauses, scared, then hears Deante yell followed by Jacob laughing.

He shakes it off and proceeds to the desk. Placing his backpack on top of the dusty desk, he sees, underneath the thick, blanket-like layer of dust, a laptop. Renz wipes off the dust and puts it inside his backpack.

While opening the bottom left drawer, a high-pitched squeak squeals from the rubbing wood. A chill shudders up his spine, only to be relieved by a tablet sitting inside the drawer.

Worth it! he thinks to himself as he grabs it and throws it into his backpack.

"Jackpot!" Jacob yells from upstairs, alarming Renz. He jumps from fear, feeling his heart skip a beat.

I need to get out of here, he thinks, whips the straps of his backpack over his shoulders, and leaves the office to wait by the stairs. Deante and Jacob come thudding down shortly after.

"Find anything?" Jacob asks, excited.

"Yeah. I got a laptop and a tablet. Tablet screen is cracked, but hopefully it still works."

"Check this." Jacob shows off a cell phone he found. "It looks like it'd be heavy but it's actually super light." He investigates the front and back.

"Nice, man," Renz replies, trying to hide that his nerves are shot. "We, uh… We good to head back?"

"I'd say so," Deante answers, ignorant of Renz's nerves.

With a sigh of relief, Renz shifts to the front door and unlocks it. Resting much of his body weight on the handle, he leans outside, scanning and listening for any signs of movement.

Jacob and Deante lean over each of his shoulders and observe the outside with him. After they all confirm the coast is clear, they leave the house and head back to the wall.

Finding three devices for Kyle is exciting. Discovering an Outsider and the fact that they can speak is arguably more exciting. All that considered, the walk back to the wall is quiet. Deante expresses frustrations with these last few outings not providing the comics he wants to find. Renz, while jumping at every light breeze and twig snap, asks a few more questions about the facility Jacob is going to. "Where is it located?" "Where are the other students from?" "Do you like-like Chloe?"

All questions Jacob doesn't know the answer to. Well, except for the last one. But he just met her, so he doesn't know for sure. Regardless, he finds himself excited to go back tomorrow.

Rain begins falling lightly again toward the end of the walk home. Jacob stands at his front door just as the red sun nearly falls below the horizon. He walks in to find his mom sitting in the living room with a blanket on, watching TV.

"How was basketball, sweetheart?" she asks, sounding tired. She stretches as she stands and walks through the kitchen toward him. Seeing his clothes are wet, she adds, "Your scrimmage was outside?"

"Uh… Yeah. The scrimmage was just, uh… Just friends and some kids from the team." He fumbles up a lie. "We played at the park."

"Oh." She hesitates. Joking lightly, she says, "You kids will play your games through anything, won't you?"

Noticing his mom's awkwardness, he uses it to change the subject, so he doesn't have to continue lying, saying, "What's with you? Why do you seem antsy?"

Amber fidgets with her hands, fighting a curious smile. She says, "Okay. I wasn't going to tell you. But… Victor stopped by tonight."

Jacob drops his backpack. He gives a cold, stern look at his mom, expressing immediate unhappiness. "Dad just… You aren't going to tell me you two are–"

"Oh, Jacob," Amber tuts. "Absolutely not. What makes you…"

He shrugs and expresses relief, but they stare in silence.

"Jacob. Ew." She huffs with disgust. "I can't believe you would even–"

"Okay. Okay, mom. I'm sorry I jumped to that. You opened with it and were smiling and I pictured the wors—" He waves off the topic. "So, what did he stop here for?"

"He came to see you, actually."

"Really? Why?"

"He said he just wanted to get your honest take on what you thought of the facility."

His eyes scan the wall then meet back with his mom's. "That's it? What about that has you smiling like–"

"Well, I asked him about it, of course. Since, you know, my *son* keeps me in the dark with these things unless I pry."

Jacob makes sure his mom sees him roll his eyes as he walks past her to the kitchen, placing his backpack on the steps, "Alright, mom, your point's made."

Dragging a chair out from the table, Amber sits and says, "He told me about the other kids — well, young adults — that are there."

"Mhmm." He's shuffled over to the counter to get a glass of water.

"He said there's a young woman there close to your age named Chloe."

Jacob takes a drink then says, singingly, "Mom."

"I just thought… *Maybe…* Victor said you two seemed to get along quickly–"

Briefly choking on water from his eagerness to reply, Jacob says, "She introduced me to most of the others and was telling me about the–"

His mom's cheeks tint red from her smile.

"I just met her, mom. I'm going there to learn about myself. My abilities. What dad wanted me to–"

Amber stands and walks to Jacob. She touches his cheek and says, "Jacob, do you know why I never liked talking about your… Abilities?"

"N-No."

Amber admires her son's eyes. She smiles, saying, "When you were six, your dad showed you which dot in the sky was Mars. And he told you how, years ago, people were planning on flying to Mars. You then spent the next year or so telling me all these stories about how you were going to, 'jump to the moon,' and 'be the first person to fly to Mars.'" She grins.

"I-I remember that. Yeah." Jacob smiles back.

"Nothing was going to get in the way of my little boy being the first man on Mars." She lets go of the grin and it fades away. "Until something did. And do you know what it was?"

Jacob lets his soft grin fade like hers as his answer to the question.

"You started to show your abilities. Cuts and bruises healed on you quickly. Your grades were advanced in elementary school. You got into sports and training with your dad and then stories stopped." Amber's eyes glaze over with tears.

"Mom." He's confused by her sadness. "I just… I grew up. I wanted to learn with dad what it was I could–"

"That's just it, sweetheart. Once you knew you had abilities, your stories to me stopped." She sniffles. "I… We lost so much when the outbreak happened." She pauses and looks up to hold back crying. Her expressions show pain and sadness as she briefly reflects on that time. A tear falls from her eyes. "Having you changed everything for me."

"Mom." Jacob's voice shares both desperation and sadness in his tone. "I… I'm…"

She touches his cheek again and smiles. "All I ever wanted was for you to be a kid for as long as possible." More tears stream from her eyes.

"O-Okay, mom." He doesn't know what to say. His mom is grieving. He wraps her in a hug, and she responds by squeezing his back tightly with her forearms. "I'm going to go shower and lay down, is that okay?" He grunts lightly. Her hug is very tight.

"Of course, sweetheart." She leans harder into the hug as she smiles with her eyes closed.

Loosening his arms, he pulls out of the hug, grabs his backpack and heads for the stairs. After walking a few steps up, he turns and says, "Mom." She acknowledges him. "I love you."

"I love you more," she says softly with watery eyes and her kind, loving smile.

Jacob takes a hot shower, jumps into a clean pair of boxers and basketball shorts, then lays in bed. He turns on his TV to one of the two channels available. Conservation City News. A news broadcast that plays on all available TVs in all Conservation Cities. Tonight's segment is called, "Victories of Victor Volcan."

While it plays a taped interview with Victor, Jacob checks his phone. Texts from Kyle in the group chat reveal his excitement to hack into the devices they found. His TV plays quietly. He likes to fall asleep with the TV on but keeps the volume low, so the noise doesn't keep him awake. Victor is smiling and speaking to the interviewer. Jacob's eyes slowly close.

He opens his eyes the next morning and hops out of bed. As he approaches the stairs from the hall, he hears Amber giggling in the kitchen. By the time he reaches the bottom, he sees Victor eating breakfast with his mom as they chat over her pancakes and bacon. Seeing Jacob at the bottom of the steps, he says, "Oh, hey there, son."

"Why are you here so early?" Jacob asks defensively, not expecting to wake up to this scene in the kitchen.

"My morning started earlier than I anticipated. I rode with Garret to pick you up, and since I knew you'd likely still be sleeping after your adventure outside the walls yesterday, I figured I'd surprise your mother with her favorite flowers." Victor wears the same smile he did with the interviewer on the TV last night.

Jacob looks at the vase of lilies on the counter. *How does he know I was outside the walls?* he thinks. His mom smiles admirably at Victor. *Why isn't she reacting to me leaving the walls?*

Victor stands from his seat and motions to the chair at the head of the table. "Why don't you join us, son? I'll make your plate." He walks around the table and smiles as he passes Jacob, who hasn't left his position standing at the bottom of the steps. As he passes Amber on his way to the counter, he gently touches her shoulder, leans down and kisses her cheek. She smiles radiantly.

"Get the fuck off of her!" Jacob screams, running and tackling Victor into the kitchen table. He tried to fight the reaction but failed.

Victor smiles and chuckles with Jacob perched on his chest, lying between halves of the dining set. Jacob punches his white, shining teeth. Victor continues to laugh, so Jacob repeats a punch with his opposite fist.

"Funny story: I developed the cure for Alzheimer's by accident," Victor says, showing his bloodied teeth with his unending smile.

His jet black, slicked back hair never looked more annoying. Jacob clasps his fists over his head and slams them together into the bridge of Victor's nose. For a second, his giggling stops, then it resumes with blood dripping over his lips.

"Remember this anger," Victor speaks.

Jacob sits atop Victor, he reaches his hands forward, grasping his hands around Victor's ears.

"Remember this anger."

Jacob squeezes his hands, digging his fingertips into the skin of Victor's face. Leaning in, he opens his mouth with an angry scream. As his vocal chords burn, the room begins to shake. Chunks of plaster break off the walls and ceiling, shattering into pieces on the floor. Cracks spread from underneath Victor's back across the ceramic tiles in all directions. Lights flicker and cabinets burst open, throwing shattering dishes and glass shards skimming around them like sand.

His scream is unending as he stares into Victor's bulging face yet smiling teeth. The room vibrates aggressively, and suddenly the walls and ceiling completely cave in on top of them.

Jacob gasps, opening his eyes and looking at the TV playing in his room.

Victor is on the TV. The interviewer shows surprise and asks, "By *accident*?"

"Yes. While working on a different project involving enhancements with the human brain, I found that a calculation I drew for a serum could reverse the damage Alzheimer's does to the brain." Jacob stares at Victor replying to the interviewer.

She says, "Well, Victor, I have to ask what everyone is thinking watching this: what was this other project that could enhance our brains?" Her tone is excited.

"Oh, that's currently undisclosed," Victor speaks playfully. "But it will change the world when it's perfected." He finishes his sentence with the reporter, then turns and smiles at the camera.

CHAPTER 14

RESIDENTS OF THE CITY HAVE a habit of looking at the top floor of Volcan Enterprises when they walk past. With it towering above all the other buildings, its presence and elegance demand their attention. Plus, knowing that Victor Volcan's office occupies the top floor, it's the closest some may get to the public figure.

Little do they know, he stands there now, watching the evening sky drop a rainy mist over perfectly organized housing enclosed in strong, concrete walls, as a loud knock hits his office door.

"Come in, Garret," he demands loudly, turning to watch him enter. "Take a seat." He adds, motioning to the chairs in the front of his desk.

Garret walks over, carrying his notebook. He unbuttons his suit jacket, then sits and leans back in the chair. "I got word that Jacob and his friends went outside the wall after school, sir. Should we–"

"No," Victor says sternly, leaning back in his chair and folding his right leg over the other. Curiously, he says, "After school. They went north, again?"

"Yes, sir."

"How many this time?"

"Three, sir."

Victor's eyes close slowly. Garret notices his tie is loosened and the top button of his shirt is open. At the same time, he sees that Victor's breath is labored. He asks, "Will we get a sample from him in time?"

Keeping his eyes closed, Victor answers, "When I told her about the facility, Amber made a point to tell me how much the kid disliked when his dad took blood samples. I'm going to have to approach this with caution, Garret, especially because we will need more than one." Muttering under his breath, clasping his forehead, he adds, "This would've been much easier if Ethan's samples showed Better Human affected him."

"And you have plans on how to approach this sensitive subject with the boy?"

"I do."

Victor opens his eyes to see Garret looking at him intently. "What, Garret?" he asks impatiently.

"I know that his telekinetic abilities were unexpected, and that you believe they could revolutionize your Vitality project, but our initial need for him was his healing genes. So that we could use that and buy you more time to complete your original Vitality plan–"

"I know, Garret!" Victor erupts from his chair and paces to the window. Other than Ethan, Garret is the only person who could get away with speaking so objectively to Victor.

Victor says to him while looking back at the rainy city, "I've gotten *so* close. So close to what I need Vitality to be. If I can't get David's strain right… This kid's telekinetic abilities can be my answer."

Garret doesn't speak.

"Then… Once I perfect Vitality, enhance the subject's brain and combine that with Jacob's DNA." He clenches his fist with excitement. "*That* would create–"

"Immortality?" Garret finishes Victor's sentence as a question.

Victor turns and asks, "You don't think it can be done? I've shown you the calculations."

"I know, sir, I–"

"Jacob having his healing ability means that the Better Human serum Ethan and I developed worked as intended. This means his cellular integrity will never deteriorate. Which means his organs, muscles, bones, tissues… His body will never age. He'll never grow old, Garret.

"Now, imagine that combined with all three strains of Vitalty. Full control of the mind. We would create the perfect human. Then imagine we give that to the world. Humanity could finally be the *perfect* species."

In a passionate tone, Garret says, "My concern is the time you have to get it done, sir."

Victor returns to his chair and says, "I'll get it done. I've shown you, and *only* you, the formulas. You know that it's possible."

"Getting the third N-Strain sample is the strongest solution. I don't see Vitality working with the boy's telekinetic DNA as a replacement to –"

"Then we'll push to get the perfect subject for that strain. Our time spent with David is done. He's a failed subject."

"Okay… Sir," Garret replies. They exchange silence. Garret's eyes bounce away to other points of the room.

"You have other news for me," Victor says, seeing Garret's hesitation.

After a sigh, Garret says, "Security is reporting small groups of Outsiders surveying near the walls again."

"Wasted are watching the walls. What's the concern? Have they breached them?"

"No, sir," he replies. "The concern is the frequency, and the possibility of their behavior being observed by someone other than security."

"We have our contingency ready in the event that the behavior of the infected goes public. The majority of people inside the walls lived through the outbreak. It'll be easy to maintain the belief that the infected remain vicious and dangerous."

Garret delivers a long blink. With a large inhale, he turns his head and looks out the window at the yellow sky.

"There's more," Victor remarks on Garret's demeanor again.

Referencing his notes, Garret answers, "Chambersburg and Philadelphia have both reported several breaches, as well as attacks from Outsiders."

"Attacks?"

"Small, handcrafted bombs were thrown over the walls in Philadelphia."

"Who all knows about this?" Victor replies quickly. Concern overtakes his voice.

"Obviously, the city leader–"

"Yes, Jason knows. I put that together. Who else?"

"Kristin heard, as she reported with Jason. And…" Garret hesitates.

"Spit it out, Garret."

"Penelope, from–"

"Fucking Penelope." Victor stands again and paces to the window. "Let me guess, she–"

"She demands she receive more security, or she'll go to CC News," Garret says cautiously.

Victor stands with his hands clasped behind his back, looking over the city.

Standing from his seat, Garret rolls his shoulders and buttons his suit jacket with one hand, holding his notebook in the other. He walks to the other side of the chair and asks, "Do we have a response, sir?"

Without turning from his stance, Victor says, confidently, "I'll take care of it."

Garret gives an understanding nod to Victor's back. He exits the office, entering the hall to a warm smile from Rebecca sitting at her desk.

"How is he, Mr. Goodwyn?" she asks nicely.

"He'll be okay, Ms. Daniels," he answers, holding his notebook with both hands in front of him.

"He seemed to look more tired than usual, didn't he?"

"He's a busy man, Ms. Daniels. His position comes with a lot of stress. Nothing to worry yourself with."

"O-Okay." She sounds embarrassed and turns her attention back to her computer screen.

"Why don't you call it a day, Ms. Daniels? It's growing late," Garret says, then walks to the elevator.

Rebecca watches him wait at the doors. A ding resonates through the hall. Garret steps inside the silver elevator, then turns and resumes the stance he held outside Victor's office moments ago. They hold a stare as the doors begin to close. Just before they thud shut, Garret passes her a smile with one corner of his lips.

CHAPTER 15

JACOB WAKES UP FEELING UNRESTED. Knowing his light sleep was from his fear of living out another dream, he sighs and reaches for his phone. It's thirty minutes before his alarm, yet he hears the clang of a pan in the kitchen. Below the time on his phone is a text message from last night. It's from a number he doesn't recognize.

"Hi, Jacob! It's Chloe! Victor gave me your number I hope that's okay… I just wanted to say I'm excited to see you tomorrow!!"

He finds himself smiling. *She's happy to see me,* he thinks. He is already excited to train again. There's a part of him that misses the boxing gym his dad used to take him to, but he hasn't gone because it feels too heavy without him.

He types a message back, saying, *"Of course it's okay! Sorry, I fell asleep before seeing this. I'm excited to see you today, too"*

He contemplates whether to end the sentence with a period or an exclamation mark. After much debate on whether the exclamation mark feels too excited, he chooses to go with it, because using a period feels not excited enough. He hits send.

Garret is picking him up right after school lets out today. Since Victor said he'll be training, he decides to wear basketball shorts with a hoodie rather than jeans. He could change at the facility, but saving the time sounds easier.

Jacob grabs his backpack and heads down to the kitchen, ready to hear his mom's comment about his shorts. He skips to the table and starts eating his bacon from the plate while standing.

Turning to say good morning, Amber says, "Good… Really, Jacob. Shorts? It's October."

Chewing and rolling his eyes, he replies, "Mom. It's fifty degrees. I'll be fine."

Rolling her eyes in return, she chuckles and grabs a small lunch box. While handing it to Jacob, she says, "I know you're going to Victor's facility after school, so I made you a sandwich in case you're hungry later."

"Thanks, mom," he says, smiling. "I'll see you when I get home tonight."

"Aren't you going to eat your–" she begins, then watches Jacob put his egg and remaining bacon on his pancake, then fold it up like a taco. He smiles, shows her his pancake taco, takes a bite, then leaves. Through the blinds, Amber smiles watching him scurry to the road.

Classes are easy this week. All fall final exams. The day should fly by, but Jacob finishes each subject's test early and stares at the clock above the classroom door, counting the seconds to the next subject, to lunch, to the subjects after lunch, then finally to the bell to signal the end of the day. Watching the second hand tick by isn't all wasteful, however. He thinks about his boxing and mixed martial arts training and how it could help him today. He thinks about which training weapon he will pick — if they do happen to use them. And he thinks about Chloe being excited to see him — which adds quick smiles targeted at the clock above the door.

Jacob says quick goodbyes to his friends outside the main front doors, then jogs over the large concrete circle, into the parking lot, over to Garret who awaits outside his black SUV.

"Good afternoon, sir," Garret greets Jacob with a soft bow.

"Hey, Garret!" Jacob replies, giving some effort into hiding his excitement. As he enters the backseat, he sees Victor sitting on the opposite side. Visions of his dream flash through his head.

With a welcoming smile, Victor says, "Are you ready for training today, son?"

Shaking away the replay of his dream, Jacob stutters, "Y-Yeah. Yes! Very excited."

"Good." Victor passes another smile then watches out the windshield as Garret begins to drive. "Now. Jacob." He waits for his attention. "You said that you did boxing and MMA training with your father, correct?"

"Y-Yeah."

"Good." He gives him a serious look. "My intentions are to skip the beginner's regimen. I'd like to throw you in as if you've been training here for several y—"

"Yes," Jacob interrupts.

"Yes?"

"Yes. I'm ready. Throw me in."

Victor nods politely. Jacob waits for him to speak again, but Victor stays quiet and looks out his window. Tapping his heel and bouncing his knee, Jacob's excitement turns to nerves with the awkward silence in the vehicle.

Victor turns his head and looks at Jacob's knee. He stops bouncing when he sees small black veins webbing around Victor's eyes. Victor's lips twitch as if trying to smile, but he turns his head back to the window before they succeed.

Garret pulls Jacob's attention by saying, "Everything okay, sir?"

He watches Garret's eyes focus on the road while they wait for Victor's reply.

"Sir?" Garret says again, now looking at Jacob in the rearview mirror.

"Oh… Me?"

"Yes, sir," Garret confirms.

Jacob leans with each elbow on the front seat's headrests. "You know, you don't *have* to call me sir, man. I'm like half your age." He gives a short laugh to show he's joking.

Garret shows he's unimpressed.

"I'm kidding, man. But, seriously, were you, like, my age when the outbreak happened?"

"I was." He flashes another glance at Jacob then watches the road.

Jacob looks at Victor who is remaining oddly quiet. He continues to talk to Garret, saying, "Was it as awesome back then as it seems? Like… For kids?"

They meet eyes in the mirror briefly. Garret stays quiet, waiting for elaboration.

"It just… It seems like it was a lot… Freer back then for kids," Jacob adds.

"I'm not sure I follow, sir."

"You had movies. And video games. *Arcades*. Electronic diaries you could share on the internet."

"Social media?"

"I guess?"

"How are you so sure we had these freedoms, Mr. Anderson?" They meet eyes in the rearview.

Victor knows Jacob has left the walls. Jacob assumes Garret also knows, but he's not going to admit to it, just in case.

"Rumors," Jacob answers quickly, shrugs, then sits back in his seat. He stares into the mirror watching Garret watch the road.

Offering another look at Jacob, Garret says, "To be honest, Mr. Anderson, you may think that things like social media were luxuries and freedom in that world, but it was more imprisoning than freeing."

Jacob scoffs lightly and says, "We literally live inside giant walls."

They hold a longer gaze in the mirror. Garret breaks the gaze and resumes driving, adding, "Some of the most dangerous prisons don't need walls to keep us inside, Jacob."

Jacob sighs and looks at Victor. Thinking he may have fallen asleep, or that something's wrong, he opens his mouth to ask Garret if he's okay when Garret says, "We're here, sir."

"Good. Your training awaits," Victor speaks loudly, startling Jacob. He smiles with excitement. Jacob sees the dark veins have disappeared from his eyes. "Go on ahead, son. Garret and I will meet you in the training room." Jacob is confused by his silence during the ride that snapped into this. Victor asks, "You do remember where it is, correct?"

"Yeah. Yeah, I remember." Jacob grabs his backpack from between his feet and exits the vehicle. He remembers that he often overlooks the fact that Victor is also the leader of their Conservation City. It's easy to only see him as his dad's friend and business partner. Leading the city has to bring about a lot of stress that not many people would understand.

Finding excitement in his feet the closer he gets to the door to the main hallway, his steps get larger. As he approaches, he realizes he doesn't have a code for the door. He slows to a stop, about to turn around, when the keypad lights up green and the lock release clicks, echoing through the hallway.

Jacob shrugs. *I guess there's a remote release,* he thinks, pushes through the door, then begins his walk to the training room ahead. He's stopped almost immediately when a strong grip grabs his right arm.

Noel stands at the corner of the hallway to the right. The dark bags under his eyes look larger, while the whites of his eyes are tinted pink from all the red veins stemming through, as if they're reaching for his iris. Jacob thinks he's wearing the same shirt as last time he saw him, but he isn't positive. It's very faded and full of holes. The back of his hand has an IV port taped on it. Noel begins to speak but reaches for his temple and hisses.

"Dude. Just… Stop," Noel grunts.

"S… Sorry, man." Jacob is certain that when he thinks about not thinking, it affects Noel the same as when he was thinking. He wants to ask, but he probably heard him think that already. Hoping that maybe he can distract him from what's in his head, Jacob asks, "Is there, like, a range to all that?"

Scrunching his face and pushing through the pain, Noel grunts, "A *range*?"

"Like… Can you be far enough away from people to not read their minds?" Jacob fidgets his hands trying to explain his question.

"Can't say I've had the luxury of testing that." Noel wears a blank expression now. "I can tell you the other end of this mall isn't far enough."

"Damn." Jacob thinks of an idea. "My friends and I read comics we find outside the walls. One has a character who doesn't want his mind read by another guy named Xavier. So, what he does is, he makes a helmet made of material that blocks Xavier from reading his mind. Maybe there's something you can do like that? Maybe to, like, block… Stuff…" Jacob wiggles his fingers next to his head.

Noel's face doesn't change. In fact, he's completely still, only moving his mouth when he says, "Next time Garret refills my Ipenziate to stop–" He hears Jacob think, *what is that?* Noel says, "It's a very powerful sleeping pill."

"Oh."

"Instead of Garret refilling it for me, I'll ask him if we can try a hat instead."

Aware that he struck a nerve, Jacob says, "Man… Look, I'm sorry. I–"

"No. *I'm* sorry, Jacob." Noel finally changes his cold expression to embarrassment. "I'm incredibly tired. You didn't deserve that."

Laughing with relief, Jacob says, "Listen, dude, it's cool. Your response was actually hilarious."

Noel gives a chuckle alongside Jacob's laughter.

Wincing suddenly, Noel scoffs, then mutters, "We're out of time. Dammit."

"W-What?"

"Listen. Jacob. I *need* to talk to you."

"O-Okay? What's up?"

"We don't have the time right now." Noel grabs his wrist again. Squeezing tight and shifting his eyes toward the training room, he says, "Be careful in there. Don't let them–"

The door from the garage blasts open. Victor comes powerwalking through, then stops immediately upon seeing Jacob and Noel in front of him. "Jacob, I see you didn't go to the training room as I instructed."

"I… I stopped him, sir. It's my fault," Noel replies quickly. He jerks his neck and scrunches his nose and eyes.

"Garret. Take Noel for–"

"No," Noel interrupts Victor loudly. "I don't need the fucking medicine." He grasps his temples again. "I need you to stop fucking thinking."

Pointing down the hall, Victor speaks sternly. "Rest in your room, then come join us. And I've told you about your tone with me."

Noel walks down the hall holding his forehead and mumbles, "Yeah."

Victor squeezes both of Jacob's shoulders and says, cheerfully, "Let's get to the room." As they walk by the large windows, Jacob sees Chloe and David in the sitting area. They both look invested in their conversation. Chloe is talking with her hands and making gestures at the side of her head. She stops abruptly when she sees Jacob walking past and waves at him with a large smile.

Victor reaches over Jacob's shoulder to pull the door open, then gives a nudge for him to enter. Elliot stands in the back with his hands on his hips watching the twins train. They're moving slowly and talking as if practicing a new regimen. Jacob watches Theo's shoulders as he readies each of his jabs at Jade. He notices he holds his shoulder higher for his attacking arm. Jade twirls her staff and hits his approaching jab away from her. Even though they're training slowly, her staff spins quickly.

"Everyone!" Victor shouts at the room. Chloe and David stand and scurry over while the others stop what they're doing and stand at attention. Chloe smiles and waves discreetly at Jacob. He smiles back then looks toward the center of the room, waiting for Victor to continue. "We will have to make today's session quick, so we can get to collection before I leave."

Collection? Jacob questions silently. He looks at Chloe for assurance. She raises her eyebrows and forces a tight smile.

"Events have transpired that require my assistance. I do realize that many of you have already been training for hours, and this is not terrible news. My apologies go mostly to Jacob, here." He squeezes and shakes his shoulder while giving an empathetic smile. Turning back to the room, he says, "That being said, Jacob is not new to physical training and is ready to dive in. Theo, you will be his first scrimmage."

"Seriously!" Elliot complains. "I thought that—"

He's interrupted by Victor's stare. No words were spoken, yet Elliot stood back at attention as if he were reprimanded.

"Go on, son." Victor pushes Jacob gently. "No weapons!" He shouts at Theo.

Jacob nervously walks into the painted square on the floor while Theo crosses his arms in front of himself, stretching, and watches him stand in place. He hops, rolling his shoulders and says, "You ready, Second Place?"

Jacob twists at the hips and stretches his neck. With a slight hunch forward, he raises his fists and says, "I'm ready."

Without hesitation, Theo rushes toward Jacob.

Jacob steadies his breathing and scans Theo's posture. He only has a slight angle in his torso from the waist up. His left shoulder is held lower than the right, and he's leading with his left foot. Jacob predicts that he will punch high with his right arm.

Theo's left foot hits hard onto the mat as he releases a groan, thrusting his right fist at Jacob's head. Jacob ducks to his right, dodging the attack easily, then jabs his right fist into Theo's ribs.

Theo lets out a small groan then scoffs, muttering, "Nice."

Jacob holds his defensive posture and watches Theo react. His left leg stands firm as he holds his weight on his right foot behind him. His hands are relaxed, and he begins to push off his right foot, lowering his shoulders.

Knowing he's aiming to tackle him, Jacob side steps, grabs Theo's shoulders and thrusts his knee into his chest. Theo stumbles backward and catches his balance. He smiles at Jacob, stretches his neck, then says, "Okay, Second Place. No more holding back."

Chloe looks at Victor, who is standing with his arms crossed watching Theo and Jacob spar. He wears no expression. "Jacob's doing, uh… He's doing well, right?" Chloe asks him.

Victor remains intent on watching and doesn't reply.

Jacob catches a fist from Theo with his left hand. While gripping Theo's fist, he throws a jab with his right hand which is swatted away by Theo. Jacob gives another soft kick to Theo's chest to push him away and return to his defensive stance.

"I've seen enough. I'm stepping in." Elliot beckons and begins to enter the square. He unsheathes the wooden wakizashi swords from the holster on his back.

"Victor! You can't let him do–" Chloe begins.

He shushes her, holds out his hand and says, "Let it be, Chloe." He keeps his eyes on Elliot, who pushes Theo out of the square. Victor smiles menacingly.

"Remember who the better human is in this room," Elliot speaks arrogantly, then rushes toward Jacob.

Jacob watches both of Elliot's arms reach outward from his sides. He's attacking with both swords. Bracing his feet, Jacob waits for the first shoulder twitch from Elliot. It's his right. Jacob crosses his right arm in front of him and punches Elliot's right wrist, sending the sword to the ground. He twists to block the next sword but is too slow and feels the strike connect into his ribs. Stinging pain rips through his side. Jacob groans then is quickly hit with Elliot's foot to his chest, knocking him backward.

"You think you're the only one who can predict actions?" Elliot stands over Jacob. "You are nothing compared to me." He reaches his sword over his head, preparing to attack Jacob.

Jacob's heart rate is racing. His adrenaline is high. Tingling of electricity rages through his wrists and palms. *Remember this anger, son.* He remembers Victor whispering to him.

"Stop him, please! He's going to hurt him!" Chloe yells next to Victor. Her reply is another hand held outward and a larger grin, as he keeps his focus on what's happening.

"Control your anger. Act with intention." Chloe hears Victor mutter to himself.

Jacob sees Elliot's shoulders shift as he begins to swing his sword downward. Jacob extends his left hand out in a snapping motion. *Come on,* he thinks with a grunt and tenseness in his throat, staring at the sword on the floor. The tingling in his palm is joined by sensory feelings of pressure as if he is touching the weapon when suddenly the sword skips across the floor and into his hand. He holds it over his face, using his right hand against the wooden blade for support as a clunk rings through the room when Elliot's sword connects to his.

Elliot's eyes widen in shock. Chloe gasps and looks to Victor for his reaction. His smile is wider than before.

Jacob sweeps his leg through Elliot's, tripping him and knocking him quickly onto his back. Dropping down with a knee pushed into his chest, Jacob feels anger coursing through him. He pulls his right arm back to throw a punch into Elliot's jaw.

"Enough!" Victor roars. Jacob snaps out of his rage and stands at his feet. Elliot holds out a hand to Jacob for assistance getting up. Jacob stares at his hand, then into his eyes. He's been around him twice and feels bullied by him. *Now he wants me to help him up. I should remind him who just won our—*

"Jacob." Victor speaks delicately, but enough to get Jacob's attention. He sees the anger behind his eyes.

Jacob clasps Elliot's hand and helps him to his feet.

"Good," Victor yells at the room. "I know this was a short training session, but it was successful. Now all of you line up for sample collection."

"Sample collection?" Jacob asks defensively.

He glares at Victor, who glares back at him with his cold, stern eyes.

CHAPTER 16

66 I DID ENOUGH OF THIS with my dad. You can find his archives somewhere," Jacob speaks defiantly to Victor.

The room is silent. All eyes are on Jacob, including Victor's, which are growing dark veins around them as he makes his way toward him. Afraid to make eye contact, Jacob stares at the knot of Victor's tie until it stops only inches away from his nose. He looks up to see the vein enshrouded eyes gazing down on him intently, as if he's processing thousands of thoughts before speaking. Jacob gulps and feels the tingling in his forearms fade as quickly as his anger turns to nervousness.

Leaning in close, Victor says, quietly but forcefully, "Nobody. And I mean *nobody*, Jacob, speaks to me with that tone. Do you understand?" He remains leaned in next to Jacob's face as he awaits his answer; his nostrils are pelting bursts of warm breath next to his ear.

"Y-Yes… I understand," Jacob mutters with a fast head nod.

"Good." Victor stands. "Chloe. Over here." He waves her over to them. She scurries over next to Victor. "Jacob. Your healing ability is unique. *Many* of your abilities are unique. But we have a situation where your healing ability can be studied and used to help people."

Jacob doesn't reply. He holds his left elbow, thinking about all the times his dad had taken his blood samples.

"Chloe." Victor nudges her.

"Jacob," she speaks sadly. "My mom is sick. Very sick. Victor says that he could use your sample to possibly save her. I was hoping that–"

"Is that why you wanted me to come back so bad?" Jacob asks defensively.

"No! No, I swear!" she replies quickly. "I didn't know that you were reluctant to give samples until now. We're all just so used to it, I assumed you were, too…" Her voice trails off.

"Fine. But I'm not agreeing to this becoming a regular thing. I'll do it for her mom," he says to Victor.

"That'll work for now." Victor speaks disappointedly to Jacob and walks over to Garret. He speaks softly and privately to him.

"I'm sorry, Jacob." Chloe grabs the top of his arm.

"It's fine," Jacob replies, looking at his feet. He thought the blood-taking was over for him.

"Listen up!" Victor yells. "Tomorrow we will launch another hunt. Theo and Elliot. You two will go. As will Jacob."

Jacob's head whips toward Victor. *What?* he thinks.

As if hearing his thought, Victor said, "It's important for you to learn and understand what we do besides training, and why. Tomorrow is your last day of fall finals and a half day of school. Garret will be waiting when you get out."

"O-Okay," he replies softly.

"Get the samples, then meet me in my office," Victor commands Garret. "You are first." He points to Jacob then walks to the door and exits.

"Yes, sir," Garret replies. "Over here, Jacob." He points to the chair where Chloe and David are often sitting. As Jacob walks over, Garret opens a small, zipped satchel on the table. It has pockets filled with syringes, vials, and bandages. Jacob sits. "Do you have a preference which arm we use, sir?"

"No… Left is fine." Jacob looks away as Garret quickly begins wiping the inside of his left elbow with an alcohol swab.

"You will feel a pinch and possibly some burning."

"Yeah," Jacob mutters as he's looking at the door. A strong pinch jerks his arm. Stronger than any time his dad took samples. Right after the pinch, a fiery burning sensation travels from his elbow to his armpit. He hisses in response.

"Almost done, sir."

Jacob clenches his fist. He feels tingling in his palms as frustration builds. "All done, sir," Garret says, turning and putting the dark red vial of Jacob's sample in the satchel. Jacob stands and walks over to David and Chloe while Garret begins to take samples from the others.

"You okay, Jacob?" Chloe asks.

"I don't know. I just thought this shit was in the past for me." He pulls his hoodie sleeve down to his knuckles. He sees Chloe looking sad. "The training was fine. And I'm fine. I guess I just didn't expect Victor to pressure me like that."

Chloe shows relief to hear that Jacob was okay with the training. She says, "Whatever Victor has going on is really stressing him. I can tell when he has a lot going–"

"I don't know, Chlo," David interrupts. "Victor wants what he wants and will use his power and stature to force us into getting what he wants."

"What's that mean?" Jacob asks, curiously.

"David, stop it." Chloe rolls her eyes. "Just because you're mad at him doesn't make him a bad guy."

"Sure. Until I become the next Nicholai," David replies.

"Who's Nichol–" Jacob is cut off by Chloe. He really wants to ask his follow up question as he sees how intense David became so quickly.

"David! Victor told us, Nick went back to his Conservation City."

"And you just *love* to believe anything Victor says, don't you?"

She looks at him angry. Her breaths become rapid.

"Why would you believe that, when…" David pauses, then looks at Jacob. Jacob's eyes widen, not expecting direct acknowledgement. "It's no secret here that *everyone* in this room, except for you, are Outsiders."

This is a surprise to Jacob.

David looks back at Chloe. "Why would Nicholai be going back to a Conservation City when nobody else here is from a Conservation City?" She doesn't respond, just continues to stare at David. "Huh?" he reaches for a reply. "He and I had a lot of deep and personal talks. He never once mentioned being from a Conservation City."

"Did you ever *ask* Nick where he was from?" Her voice is stern and matter-of-fact. "Did you?" David doesn't respond. "Right. You had all those chances, but you never asked. You *don't* know. So let it go." Jacob watches them hold frustrated stares with each other, realizing his mouth is open from the shock of seeing Chloe this angry.

Wooden weapons click loudly together, alarming Jacob. Theo and Jade finished their samples and have gone back to training.

"I'm not going to argue with you, Chlo." David sounds defeated. "No, I never asked where he was from. Yes, I just assumed. But we were close, Nick and I. For him to leave and not say goodbye. Not leave a note. It's suspicious."

"David, it could have been–"

"No, Chlo. You know he was the first to take your strain of N. He was supposed to project visions, but could only project to one person." Chloe looks at her feet. "Then you came in and were successful. Suddenly Victor gave Nick the cold shoulder, and then he was gone."

"David…"

"And he's doing that to me now. He wanted more out of my strain of N." David begins to walk away. Turning, he says, "The difference is, I'll decide my fate." He storms off.

"David!" Chloe yells with a shrill voice that fades as she watches him march away on the other side of the windows.

"Second Place is seeing his first performance by the N-Strain drama team," Theo yells over to Jacob. Jade laughs with her shoulders, and Elliot boasts an arrogant huff as Garret takes his sample.

Chloe decides to go after David. Jacob watches as she turns to walk down the hall, then stops in place, dropping her head while her shoulders begin to tremor.

Jacob walks out and approaches Chloe. "Chlo…" He gently touches her arm causing her to immediately turn around. Her freckled cheeks shine from the remains of tears she wiped away with her wrist. She leaps and wraps Jacob in a tight hug. He rubs her upper back as she nestles her crying eyes into his shoulder.

Though the circumstances are unfortunate, Jacob finds a warmth in Chloe's embrace. "I'm sorry you were unhappy about the sample today," she speaks, muffled into his shoulder.

Still rubbing her back, he says, "It's okay. It's not your fault."

She pulls away and looks at him with her eyes, pink from crying, saying, "I'm worried about David."

"He did seem quick to get worked up. Do you think Victor is going to–"

"Not at all, Jacob," she says with confidence.

"O-Oh," Jacob stutters. "Did you know his friend?"

"Not well, no. A lot of my early time here was spent in testing, and in my own room, alone. I really only saw Victor and sometimes Garret most of the time."

Picturing a young, innocent Chloe spending her time alone, being tested on, breaks his heart.

"Will you come to my room and talk with me until you have to go?" she asks kindly.

"Y-Yeah. Sure." There's no way he could say no when she's this upset.

He follows as she walks past the training room where the hallway bends to the left. More storefronts were remodeled to accommodate dormitories. Smooth white drywall stretches along the hallway with doors punched in equal distances apart. A constructed wall is built where the dormitory hall ends, which seems to separate this space from the rest of the mall.

Chloe walks to the second door on the right. Each door has a keypad similar to the one in the garage. She presses four keys, then a click sounds on the door and she opens it and steps inside, holding it with an outstretched arm for Jacob to enter after her.

Jacob stands in the small foyer and investigates the studio setup. Her kitchenette is tidy with fruits in a colored bowl and matching cups and plates neatly stacked on the counter. Her bed is dressed in light pastel purple blankets and pillows. A nightstand holds a small lamp and a framed photo he can't see from where he stands. The wall on the far side of the bed has taped polaroid photos in a collage, and the couch across from the bed holds a laid-out hoodie and small white throw pillow.

"Wow. This is all yours? It's very *you*," he says, impressed.

Chuckling, Chloe says, "Yep. This is my 'humble abode,' as they say. And… Thanks. I think?" She chuckles again, this time nervously, hoping what he said was a compliment.

"Oh. Yes. Sorry, I meant that positively. It's very nice. And cozy. And…" He stutters.

"Thank you." She smiles politely and saves him from his nerves. "Make yourself comfortable." She gestures to the couch. "You want a water or anything?"

"No, thank you," he answers, walking to the other side of the bed to look at the photos on the wall. He sees the TV by the couch on his way. "You get any special movies to watch out here at the facility?"

"No." She stands next to the kitchenette watching him while sipping her glass of water. "Just the big two channels. CC News and that terrible movie channel."

"Hey now, some of those movies are classics from back before… No, you're right. They're pretty awful." He laughs, leaning in to see the photos.

Chloe laughs and walks to the corner of the bed to sit.

Jacob looks at the collage, seeing selfies of Chloe, pictures of her and David, candid photos of the Better Human students training, and a few pictures of different sunsets taken outside the facility. The photo that catches his attention is one of Chloe and a woman with a nasal cannula under her nose.

"Is… Is this your mom?" he asks, pointing at the picture.

She stands from the bed and moves next to Jacob. Grabbing the picture from the wall, she says, "Yeah. This is her." She speaks softly. "This was taken shortly after she got sick."

"Wh-What's… If you don't mind me asking… What's wrong with your mom?" He hesitates, hoping he's not overstepping.

Looking intently at the photo, Chloe says, "Cancer."

Jacob has heard of cancer before. Most of the references are celebratory, because his dad and Victor developed a cure for it shortly after the Conservation Cities were established. Cancer — among many other illnesses that used to be common in the old-world — are said to no longer exist. This is at least true for residents inside the walls. David just mentioned that all the students are from the outside, which could be why cancer, along with the other diseases, still occur. Outsiders don't receive the mandatory vaccines and checkups all the Conservation City residents are required to keep up with.

Chloe hasn't broken her gaze from the photo. Jacob says, kindly, "She looks happy there."

Sniffling, Chloe says, "She's the greatest." Looking away from the photo, now at Jacob, she touches his shoulder and says, "Jacob. I'm very sorry about the other day. Showing your dad without… I was thinking about if it were me and if I could see… I shouldn't have agreed to–"

"It's okay." He looks calmly at her. "I understand the intentions. I do. And to be honest, it was kind of nice getting to see him again."

"Can I tell you something… Something I haven't told anyone?" Chloe asks.

"Of course," he replies immediately. His heart flutters hearing that she trusts him for whatever it is she's about to say.

Stuttering, she says, "I… I want my mom to lose her pain. Even if that means she…" The last words don't make it out.

"Chlo." Jacob's heart sinks. "Victor got my sample. Hopefully he can use it to find the cure he promised you."

She's looking at her feet. A tear falls to the floor. "Y-Yeah."

Jacob sits on the bed next to where Chloe is standing. He sighs then says, "Can I tell *you* something?"

She sits next to him then smiles politely with her teary eyes and wet cheeks.

"I spent *so* much time being mad at my dad. Before and after he was gone." Jacob looks at the floor. "It wasn't fair to him."

"W-Were you close with your dad?"

"Honestly, yes. He probably had no idea I was ever mad at him. He just worked all the time. But when he wasn't working, he made sure to spend as much time with me as he could." He shuffles his foot on the floor. "I was mad because I wanted more time with him. And after he was gone… I was mad again, because I knew I'd never get it."

Chloe rubs the back of his shoulder. Holding the photo in her other hand, she looks at her mom then asks Jacob, "Do you… Do you think I could meet your mom sometime?"

Not expecting that question, but happy she asked, Jacob smiles secretly and says, "Absolutely. She'd love to meet you. She's always asking about things here at the facility."

Heavy knocks hit at the door. "Mr. Anderson." Garret yells from the other side. "It's time I get you home."

"Really? That'd be okay?" Chloe confirms Jacob's answer.

"For sure. We're actually doing a movie and pizza for my birthday on Sunday. I'll make sure with her, but maybe you can come over for that," he says, hoping she likes the idea.

"Okay!" she says excitedly through soft sniffles. Jacob stands and walks to the foyer to step into his shoes. "Will you say hi to me before you head out with Theo and Elliot tomorrow?"

"Of course." He pauses from opening the door to ask, "What… What are these *hunts*?"

"It's where they–"

Knocks hit at the door again. Chloe scurries over to him and wraps him in a hug. "I've never been on one, but I know it's one of the ways they find new students," she says quickly and softly.

"But why call them hunts–"

Pulling away and looking at him, she says, "Thank you, Jacob."

"I… You don't have to thank me for anything." He blushes.

"We… We've needed someone like you."

"For w–"

Knocks slam harder. "Mr. Anderson!" Garret yells.

"I'll see you tomorrow." She smiles at Jacob and nudges him to open the door.

"We can't have your mother worrying, sir," Garret says in a demanding tone.

"I know," Jacob mutters. He follows several steps behind Garret.

As they pass the training room, Noel begins to pass them from the other direction.

Jacob thinks, *He wanted to tell me something.*

Noel stops, briefly, then says, "Yes. I do. Just not with present company." He flashes his eyes to Garret. "Next time, I guess," he adds, then walks on toward the dormitories.

The ride home with Garret is quiet. Jacob spends the ride watching the scenery outside pass by as the moonlight softly lights the sky. Abandoned and overgrown shops sit lonely in cracked parking lots with tall grass and weeds sprouting through. Vehicles sit in their permanent places in patches along the highway. Judging by the position some sit in, they were likely moved to make this trip drivable.

Jacob thinks about tomorrow. What will this hunt be like? If it's how they recruit Outsiders for the facility, why are they called hunts? Tomorrow is also the last day of the fall finals, but that will be easy. Tests don't make Jacob nervous. He realizes he's hungry, so he eats the sandwich from his backpack, then resumes watching the drive back home.

The vehicle stops and reverberates the soft hum of the electric motor as Garret pulls up in front of Jacob's home. Jacob thanks Garret, then exits the vehicle and walks inside. Amber sips her tea as she sits under a blanket on the couch. She smiles happily at Jacob and asks, "How was the first day of training, sweetheart?"

"It was good," he says, kicking off his shoes. He sets his backpack on the steps as he passes through the kitchen. A bowl of popcorn is on the coffee table. Jacob eats a piece before sitting on the couch next to his mom. She's watching the evening CC News segment.

"'It was good,'" she mocks his voice jokingly. "That's all you're going to tell me?"

Shifting to face his mom, he eats another piece of popcorn, chuckles, then says, "You always hated hearing about my boxing and stuff. I'm sparing you those details. Doing you a favor." He smiles.

"Sparing me the details? How thoughtful." She chuckles, sipping her tea. "You are right, though. You didn't get hurt or anything, did you?"

"No, mom." He sits back, watching the TV. "The one kid is an asshole, th—"

"Jacob! Language."

"Sorry, mom. But he is." He leans for the popcorn again, this time sitting back with a handful.

"How are the other kids? How's Chloe?" She says her name singingly.

Laughing gently through his nose, he says, "Other kids are pretty cool, actually. And Chloe is really cool. Really nice."

"Don't make me fight the details out of you, Jacob. I may not *train* like you and your dad did, but I'm not scared of you!" she teases and gently punches his shoulder.

Jacob laughs. "I dunno, mom." He blushes. "She's very nice to me and wants to make sure I am happy with things at the facility."

"That's nice!" she says happily.

"Yeah." He decides not to tell his mom about the samples. "Her, uh… Her mom is really sick, I guess."

"Oh. That's sad. Will she be okay?"

"I… She doesn't seem sure." He stares at the popcorn in his hand.

Amber gives an empathetic smile. They both watch the TV.

"Mom." Jacob opens for a question. "Would you care if I invited her to come here to join us for pizza and a scary movie on my birthday?"

Amber's face lights up.

"It's not, like, a date, mom, it's–" He smiles at her reaction as she interrupts him.

"Jacob, that is very much okay!"

"Good, cause I kinda already sort of invited her," he chuckles nervously.

"You like this girl, don't you, sweetheart?"

"Mom!"

She smiles seeing how red his cheeks are. This is what she wants for her boy. "Maybe we can do something more than pizza. Maybe–"

"Pizza is fine, mom." He can't stop smiling. "It's easy, and we all can enjoy just–"

A red banner flashes across the TV screen, reading ALERT. Jacob and Amber's phones blare sirens. They both look at their phones and see they're broadcasting the same footage as what's on the TV.

CC News anchor, Jennifer Kremer, sits at a desk above a new red banner reading: BREAKING NEWS. Her expression is distraught, her voice is serious yet professional as she says,

"We interrupt the broadcast with breaking news. Earlier today, we learned that Conservation City leaders Kristin Brown of Chambersburg, Jason Taylor of Philadelphia, and Penelope Connor of Dover were found murdered.

"At this time, investigations are underway, and we will alert all of you to any updates on this tragic matter."

Amber, covering her mouth in shock, mumbles, "This is terrible."

Jennifer continues: "Our on-scene reporter, Brock Frantz, interviewed Victor Volcan moments ago in Pittsburgh. Here is what he had to say."

The TV transitions to Victor standing outside Volcan Enterprises with Brock. Brock speaks into his CC News branded microphone, asking, "Victor. It's known that you have a close relationship with many Conservation City leaders, *especially* these three who have been tragically killed. Did any of them express any matters or concerns of threats to you?"

Victor speaks matter-of-factly, saying, "They did not."

"Have you had any contact with security teams in these cities as they have started their investigations?"

"The incident is fresh, but I have, Brock," Victor speaks in an assuring demeanor. "Most importantly, I will continue to be working closely with all three teams to ensure we find answers and justice for these tragic events."

Brock expresses compassion as he asks, "The city residents are going to be restless and feeling uneasy. Can you provide any insight at all as to what may have transpired or words of confidence for the people of these cities?"

"Of course," Victor speaks confidently. "While our Conservation Cities are the safest form of civilization ever built, they are not without fault. Breaches do occur, even with the best security teams guarding the walls.

"Most of us were around during the outbreak. We're aware of the nature of the infected. The Outsiders. Were they to breach these walls and reach the–"

Brock interrupts. "Are you saying Outsiders killed these leaders?"

"I don't have that answer, I'm just giving information as to all the possible factors. Were it Outsiders, or defiance from a resident, or residents, you can all be sure that we will get to the bottom of it and act accordingly."

Jacob and his mom stay glued to the TV.

"What about replacing the leaders? Will you have a hand in choosing the next candidates?" Brock asks.

"In time, Brock, yes, they will be replaced. And yes, I will ensure that, while all three will be difficult to replace, we will find excellent leaders to fill these positions."

Brock nods to Victor.

Victor pulls the microphone toward him, smiles politely at the camera and says, "Until the cases are closed and new candidates are confirmed, for the time being, I will step in myself and lead these cities."

CHAPTER 17

THE EXPRESSION ON HIS MOM'S face last night is the first thing on Jacob's mind as he wakes the next morning. She looked worried and scared. Almost immediately after the broadcast interview with Victor, she said goodnight and went up to bed.

He doesn't hear cooking in the kitchen. Hoping this means there's still time to sleep, he checks his phone. In three minutes, his alarm will sound. The disappointment of not getting more sleep is shrouded by the mystery of his mom not being awake and cooking.

Jacob sighs, stretches, and gets out of bed. He walks to his dresser and grabs a pair of socks and jeans. While putting on his socks, he observes the top of his dresser, which is littered in comics he's found from the outside. A stack of movies is in the corner. They're not from the outside. They're horror movies gifted from his parents. Since he was ten years old, every year on his birthday, his parents gave him a horror movie from the old-world. Each movie was one of their favorites. They'd celebrate his birthday by having one of Jacob's favorite meals, sharing a cake, then making popcorn and watching the newest horror movie as a family. This is a tradition Jacob's always looked forward to. As he stares at the collection from the years prior, he feels heaviness around this year's tradition. In two days, it'll be his birthday. In two days, it'll be the first tradition without his dad.

After putting on his jeans, he searches through his pile of worn hoodies on the floor. Deciding that they're all due for a wash now — even his favorite green one — he returns to the bottom dresser drawer and grabs a gray zip-up hoodie.

Before turning to go down the steps to the kitchen, he looks in his mom's bedroom. The door's open and her bed is empty. *Odd,* he thinks. She's awake but not cooking. He thuds quickly down the steps and finds her sitting at the table with a bowl of cereal, a milk carton, and an empty bowl next to her. She's staring out the window.

Turning to look at Jacob, she forces a smile and says, "Hey, sweetheart. Is cereal okay this morning?"

"Yeah. Y-Of course." He shifts to his seat, setting his backpack next to his chair as he sits. "Are you okay, mom?"

"I'm fine. I just didn't sleep well is all," she says, unconvincingly.

"Is it the news we saw before bed?"

She lowers her eyebrows questioningly.

"You… You just seemed really upset after it," he stutters.

Amber sighs and rubs above her eyes. "There's a lot I miss about the old-world. But the best part about the way we recovered after the Conservation Cities were built was less disease, and no more violence." She pushes the box of cereal to Jacob. "There was so much evil in that world that I thought we left behind."

Jacob replies with a tight smile and makes his bowl of cereal.

"Last night… Seeing that those leaders were murdered… It just reminded me of before. I'm sorry, sweetheart."

Chewing his bite of cereal, he gives a surprised expression to his mom. He didn't expect an apology. "Iss ogay mum," he mumbles with a full mouth and bringing his hand to his chin to catch the milk spilling from his lips.

She chuckles with a relieving smile. He always makes her smile. It's the same as how Ethan always did.

Swallowing quickly, he asks, "Do you think it's what Victor said? A Wasted th–"

"Jacob. I hate that you use that term," her voice quickly becomes stern along with her disappointed head shake. "They were once people. They became sick. They don't deserve a derogatory name."

"S-Sorry," he replies. "I just don't see how an Outsider would breach the wall in each city and only attack the leaders and no other citizens."

"Well, maybe it happened late at night or early in the morning. You know how busy Victor is. I'm sure all the leaders are putting in late and early hours. Traveling alone on the streets. It's possible."

"I guess."

"Plus, that infection makes these people dangerous and unpredictable. Nobody knows how or why they do what they do. That's why we needed these walls."

"Yeah," Jacob says, stirring his cereal. He chooses not to debate the Outsiders' behavior with his mom. For several reasons.

Amber gasps. "Oh no."

"What?" He immediately turns around and looks where her eyes went. The front door.

"You're going to the facility again after school, and I didn't make you food for later when you're hungry." She bursts from her seat. "Let me throw something together for–"

"Mom." He stands and gently holds the tops of her arms. "It's fine. I'll be fine." He smiles politely at her.

"It'll be quick. You won't be late for sch–"

"Mom. I'll just get a second lunch and pack it to take with me. Give yourself a break."

Reluctantly, she asks, "Are you sure?"

"I've never been more sure."

"I'm sorry, I just–"

"Mom, it's okay." With a reassuring look, he continues, "I promise. I do have to go, though." He steps over and grabs his bowl, shoveling his last few bites of cereal, then throws his backpack over his shoulder and walks to the foyer to put on his shoes. "I'll see you tonight."

"Have fun and be safe, sweetheart." She's sitting back in her chair at the table, smiling at her son.

"I will." he says, then walks out the door and makes his way to school.

Deante runs to meet Jacob in his usual fashion: untied shoes, backpack bouncing while nearly falling off his shoulder, and out of breath since he left late and ran the entire way. Jacob smiles and chuckles as he waits for him to catch up at the intersection.

"Watching you barely make it here every day will never get old," Jacob says, laughing.

"Man…" He's short of breath. "I'm too gassed to think of a comeback." He adjusts his backpack straps, and they begin to walk to school. "How was training yesterday?"

"It was good. Victor let me dive right into it. Then I got to see what the dorms there are like for the students."

"Oh?" Deante is surprised by this. "They give you, like, a tour or something?"

"No. Chloe invited me back to hers."

"Oh!" His surprise turned to excitement and curiosity.

"Not like that, dude." Jacob smiles and shakes his head. "She was upset and wanted—"

"Your sexy shoulder to cry on?"

"Someone to talk to," Jacob corrects him. "Her mom is sick."

"That sucks."

"Yeah."

"Thought you would've–" Deante holds his hand to his face and makes obnoxious kissing noises.

"Dude." Jacob laughs. He pushes Deante as they walk. Interlocking his fingers inside his hoodie pocket, his voice lowers as he says, "Victor pressured me into taking a blood sample."

Deante's expression changes to serious. "Dude. For real? He, like, *made* you give a sample?"

"Yeah. I, very unsuccessfully, attempted to fight it. But I guess he thinks he can research the special genetics that allow me to heal and fabricate some sort of cure for Chloe's mom. So, at least it's for something beneficial."

Deante makes an explosion sound and gestures with his hand next to his head. "Still bullshit you were pressured, bro." Jacob laughs lightly through his nose before they walk a block in silence until Deante says, "Speaking of your dad. You doing alright with all the talk of those city leaders and everything?"

"What do you mean?"

"Well, they mentioned the possibility of an Outsider killing them. With how that all happened with your dad and an Outsider, I wasn't sure if…" He struggles to find words to finish his thought.

"Oh," Jacob answers. "I really didn't connect those dots." He shrugs.

"I guess that's good, then."

"Yeah. My mom was really worked up about it, though."

"Mine was, too."

"Yeah? Something about the old-world being violent, too?"

Deante flashes a blank look. "I didn't ask," he answers, disappointed with himself.

Jacob chuckles.

They finish their walk to school and arrive at their breakfast table to join Kyle and Renz. Catching them up on their conversation, Renz says, "Guys. Kyle has more shit to show us after school."

"What do you got?" Deante asks, excited, sitting heavily onto the seat.

"The phone you found." Kyle points at Jacob. "This kid has photos and videos of himself and his friends doing all kinds of stuff."

Deante and Jacob look impatiently at Kyle. When he doesn't elaborate, Deante says, "Like what?"

"Going to these places to watch movies on *massive* screens. Riding bikes everywhere. One of the videos, they're in a crowd of people and filming other people playing music real loud and lights flashing everywhere," Kyle says.

"Concerts," Jacob says, confidently.

"Concerts?" Renz asks.

"My dad's told me about them," he replies.

"Oh."

"We've been best friends for forever and I still forget that your parents *actually* talk to you about the old-world." Deante chimes in.

"Mostly just my dad," Jacob corrects. "My mom not so much."

"Still," Deante replies, "It's more than we get."

Kyle clears his throat and continues, "This kid did a lot and recorded, like, all of it. But I've got one better."

The others wait for him to tell them. He sits with an excited smile switching eye contact between each of them.

"Dude, will you just spit it out already?" Deante yells impatiently.

Chuckling, Kyle says, "Remember how I said that I got connected to the internet by breaking through Volcan Enterprises intranet?"

They all nod.

"Well, curiosity got the best of me, and I wanted to see how much I could access through their intranet and–"

"What did you find?" Renz asks, tapping anxiously on the table.

"Well… Technically nothing." They all drop their shoulders with sighs. "*But* I got to their database, I just need a log in and password."

"Can't you hack that with your software… Thingy…" Deante wiggles his hand.

"I *could*. It just feels too risky. They *have* to have security measures that would catch someone trying to hack in."

"They do," Jacob says. They all look at him questioningly. "My dad, guys. Remember. He worked there." They all nod their heads in understanding. He laughs and shakes his head at them. He adds, "Man, if we can get into that, we might be able to access their security cameras."

With a confused stare, Deante says, "And?"

"And see if we can find the video of what happened to my dad."

"Why would you want to see that?" Deante follows up. "That's kinda fucked up."

"Not to see... Just..." Jacob stutters. "To see the security guard that killed him."

"And do what with that knowledge?" Deante is asking sternly.

Jacob looks frustrated and embarrassed. "Forget it."

"Anyway," Kyle changes the subject. "I want to show you all this after school."

Deante and Renz are excited. Jacob, disappointed, says, "I'll miss it. I gotta go to that... Thing with Victor again."

Renz and Deante look at each other, and Kyle notices. He says, "Wait. Am I the only one that doesn't know what this is?"

Stuttering, Jacob says, "I just haven't had the chance to tell you, man. We talked most about it when we went to get you those devices. You were–"

"Grounded. Yeah. Figures," Kyle says, flustered. "Tell me now."

Jacob shakes his head.

"Why not?" Kyle asks, confused.

Jacob nudges his head to the other side of the table. "Because of the eavesdropper over there." He refers to Toby, who is ignoring his friends, sitting twisted in his seat watching Jacob and his friends talk. Deante gives Toby the middle finger.

The last day of tests before fall break is easy for Jacob. The subject is biology, which he has taken an extra interest in. Before the day lets out, the school plays a message from Victor over the loudspeakers. This is common any time something news-worthy happens in the Conservation Cities. Usually, this is assurances that breaches have been handled, or new trades were set up with other cities. This time is serious. He repeats a lot of what he said in the interview, assuring that their city is safe, and that answers will be given as soon as they're discovered.

Jacob leaves the school hoping to spend a few minutes with his friends. As he approaches them in the concrete circle, he sees Garret already waiting in the parking lot. He says goodbye to his friends and makes Kyle promise to show him the hacked devices during fall break in exchange for his explanation of his project with Victor. Kyle agrees, as long as he is ungrounded, like his mom promised he would be.

"Good afternoon, Mr. Anderson," Garret greets Jacob as he approaches the vehicle.

"What's up, Garret?" Jacob replies as he gets in the back seat. He looks across, expecting to see Victor, but the seat is empty.

"No Victor today?" He asks as Garret sits in the driver's seat, puts on his seatbelt, and begins driving away.

"Not today, sir," he replies to Jacob, looking through the rearview mirror. "He had other matters to attend to."

Assuming it deals with the news last night, Jacob doesn't ask any more questions. He watches out the window. The scenery is familiar to him now. The rusty yellow bridge they cross leads to a long dark tunnel. Shortly out of the tunnel is the sign overgrown with moss and vines that reads "Parkway Plaza."

Jacob rests his head back and closes his eyes. His nerves about this hunt begin to grow strong in his chest. He thinks of a question to ask Garret. Opening his eyes to start the conversation, he finds himself in a brightly lit lobby. He's walking briskly forward as people in white lab coats scurry past him. A young brunette woman sits behind a large marble welcome desk. She greets Jacob with a polite smile as he passes. A large Volcan Enterprises sign hangs behind her on the wall.

Unable to control his actions, he continues past the woman at the desk and stops at an elevator, presses the call button, and waits. Jacob tries to look around but can't move his head. He's stuck staring down the hallway next to the elevator, where more people in lab coats walk in and out of doors.

A chime sounds, and the doors drag open. Without control of his own, Jacob enters, turns, presses the number thirty-three, then on a keypad next to the floor buttons enters the code seven, three, five, three. The button thirty-three lights up yellow with another chime. His eyes look up at the digital sign above the door that reads: L. The doors begin to close as a hand reaches in and stops them. As they bounce back open, Ethan rushes in and stands next to Jacob. He smiles, leans in front of Jacob, checks the floor, then watches the doors close.

"Dad?" Jacob tries to say, but nothing comes out. He's looking directly at the profile of his father.

Ethan sips his cup of coffee, turns to Jacob and says, "Well, Garret, I see we both have been summoned again."

Garret? Jacob thinks to himself.

Now he's replying, but in Garret's voice. "Yes, it seems we are, sir."

"Wonderful," Ethan replies, sarcastically. He watches the numbers change with each ding as they ride upward.

The doors open after the last chime on floor thirty-three. Ethan exits first, then Jacob follows. He sees the sign in front of the first office reads "Ethan Anderson." They continue walking to the end of the hall. As they approach the desk outside of the far office, Jacob greets the young woman at the desk, involuntarily saying, "Good morning, Ms. Daniels."

In a chipper tone, she smiles and says, "Good morning, Garret! And hello, Mr. Anderson!"

"Hi there, Rebecca, how are you?" Ethan replies. Jacob can tell by his dad's expression that he doesn't want to be here. "Is he ready for us?" he asks.

"I-I'm great, thank you!" she replies, nervously, attempting to put her hands in her pockets but awkwardly rubbing her hips when she's reminded her pants don't have pockets. "Uh… Yes, I believe he's expecting you; you can go in!"

They enter Victor's office, where he sees Victor standing in front of large windows, staring out at the city. He turns to both of them, motions to his desk and says, "Have a seat."

Immediately, Jacob begins to walk over but stops when Ethan says, "Skip the formalities, Vic. Why'd you ask me to come up here?"

Jacob watches Victor walk over to Ethan. With a stern look on his face, he speaks calmly and asks, "How's Jacob?"

"He's fine," Ethan replies quickly, saying nothing more.

Why do they look like they hate each other? Jacob thinks to himself.

Victor scoffs and steps over to his desk. He rests his hand on a folder, keeps a calm tone, and says, "I want you to look over something with me. I think I'm finally close to breaking through with–"

"I told you I want no part of this project, Vic," Ethan cuts him off.

"You haven't seen what I want to show you, Ethan. I think you'll find my tests to be–"

"I've seen enough of the things you *didn't* want to show me."

Victor steps back toward Ethan. His chin lowers to keep eye contact as he looks down on him. He stands a head's height over Ethan. The tension still feels thick, but Victor remains using a calm voice when he asks, "What might you be referring to?"

"Your tests are unethical."

Victor raises his chin and hums with a grumble.

"Your *unsuccessful* subjects?" He states it as a question. Pointing to Jacob, he adds, "Does Garret here know where you send them? What they become?"

Victor looks across the room and meets eyes briefly with Jacob. He turns angrily back to Ethan. Shoving his finger at Ethan's chest, Victor's eyes sprout the purple veins as he opens his mouth, starting to yell, when suddenly Jacob is watching through the windshield as Garret parks in the brightly lit garage of the facility.

Noticing Jacob's startled expression, Garret asks, "Are you okay, sir?"

With quick breaths, Jacob thinks, *What the fuck was that?* He answers, "Yeah. Yeah… I think so."

He senses Garret looking at him in the mirror. Nervous, Jacob rubs his forearm and feels a bump inside his elbow where Garret took a sample yesterday. He immediately lifts his hoodie sleeve and sees it. A small lump. Pressing on it doesn't move it. It doesn't hurt to touch it. But something is there. An object. Underneath his healed skin.

CHAPTER 18

WITH A FIRM GRIP ON his backpack strap, Jacob lifts it from the seat next to him and exits the vehicle. He races to the door, forgetting there's a code to get in, requiring him to wait for Garret. He shuffles his feet and rubs the lump in his arm through his hoodie sleeve.

Avoiding eye contact with Garret, he listens to the beeps of his key presses. The latch clicks and Garret opens the door for Jacob, who bursts through.

"Do you know where to go, sir?" Garret asks, loudly, as Jacob has walked across the hall.

Stopping, then replying quickly, Jacob says, "Yes. Yeah. Uh… It's right over…" He points behind him to the training room.

"It's in this room down this hallway." Garret points down the hall directly to his right at a lonely dark gray door.

"Oh," Jacob stutters. "I'm going to go say hi to Chloe then I'll head there."

"I'll go and let the others know you'll–"

"Yeah. Thanks, Garret," Jacob yells as he turns and rushes to Chloe's room.

Arriving at her door, he knocks rapidly. Chloe opens the door slightly, sees Jacob, then opens it fully. "Jacob! Why the aggressive knock–" she sees him fidgeting his hand through his messy hair and reads the look on his face. "Jacob, what's wrong?"

"Can I come in?" he asks, breathing quickly.

"Of course." She steps aside. He rushes inside. Drinking a soda and walking to the opposite end of the dorm is David, turning and moving to the photos on the wall. He nods at Jacob.

"Hi, David." Jacob returns a nod, then waits while Chloe closes the door.

"How's it going, Jake?" David replies.

"Just Jacob, man," he corrects him.

"Sorry… Didn't mean to–" He stops, then says to Chloe, "Chlo, when did you update these photos? I love them!" He points to the wall.

"I added a few the other day after going through my shoebox of pic–"

"Look at this," Jacob says to Chloe, lifting his hoodie sleeve.

She looks at his arm, puzzled, noticing only that he shows no small scab from where the needle took his sample or any normal bruising around the area. She shrugs. "I don't—"

"Look." He shakes his arm then presses his finger to his elbow.

She leans close to where he's pointing. "That?" She pokes the bump.

"Yes. That. Garret put something in me when he took my sample. I knew something was off when it burned. I also think he gave me something else when he took the sample from me."

"Something else?" She chuckles softly then touches his cheek. "Jacob, that's just a port they put in when they take the first sample. It's a little silicone tip that—"

"A port?" he asks, still shaking off his anxiety.

"Yeah, we all have them, man." David answers, making his way over to them. "It's a silicone piece they put on your first needle just to make it easier for them to *get in there* when they go for their next samples." He chuckles and imitates a needle stabbing his arm with his fingers.

"Yeah, see?" Chloe shows him her arm. David does the same gesture.

Jacob looks at the same bump in both of their elbows. He shoves his sleeve back down, sighs and says, "Well, I still don't like this. I didn't agree to multiple samples."

"Maybe Garret didn't know that?" Chloe shrugs.

Pacing to the kitchenette counter, Jacob says, "Then… What was that vision?"

"Vision?" David asks.

"I…" Jacob leans and thinks of how to explain what happened. "It was on the ride here just, like, daydreaming. I blinked and all of a sudden, I was reliving a memory. But it wasn't mine. It was Garret's, but, like… I was watching it through his eyes. I think I read his mind."

Eyes widened, David says, "That's… That's an N ability. I thought your dad used–"

"Better Human. Yeah. He did." Jacob shares David's surprise.

"Victor did say your abilities are more unknown because the enhanced genetics were passed on naturally. Maybe Better Human also gave you forms of our N abilities, too?" Chloe chimes in. Jacob stares at her, deep in thought.

"Have you done this before? Read someone's mind?" David asks, curiously.

"No. Never." Jacob stands up from leaning. "Then what's even more confusing is the memory itself."

"How so?" Chloe asks. David nods to show he wants to know as well.

"It was at Volcan Enterprises. Garret was with my dad in an elevator. Both were going to Victor's office. When we get there, I'm watching my dad and Victor interact and…" Jacob pauses.

"And?" David shows impatience.

"They just… There was so much tension between them." Jacob speaks in a concerned and confused tone. "Like they hated each other."

Chloe asks, "Weren't they best friends?"

"Y-Yeah. They were."

David adds, "Maybe…" He's pacing, waving his arm as he speaks through his thought. "Since it's Garret's memory, you're just seeing *his* perception of it. Altered to his interpretation of the event?"

Chloe and Jacob look at each other and shrug. What David says makes sense. Jacob says, "I guess… Maybe that could be possible."

"Why don't you try to see if you can read one of our minds?" Chloe says with anticipation.

"I have no idea how I did it, though," he replies.

"First time I learned to control mine was when Victor wanted me to push a memory to him. I'd lived *many* memories by accident before that, but couldn't do it voluntarily," David explains. "It was like meditation. I thought of a memory, closed my eyes and took a deep breath. Found myself reliving when my dad took me to Kennywood. Ever since then, it works every time."

"You should try that!" Chloe says, excited.

"I… Sure. Why not?" Jacob says reluctantly. This sounds like a lot to him.

They all walk into Chloe's living area. Jacob sits on the edge of her couch while David and Chloe stand in front of him.

"Okay. Now sit back, relax, take a deep breath, then focus on one of us to see if you can read our mind," Chloe speaks with so much excitement she bounces twice on her toes.

David taps his chest and says, "Try me, first."

Jacob pushes back into the couch. He closes his eyes, inhales deeply, then exhales strongly, puffing out his cheeks with the force of his breath. Clearing his thoughts, he's ready. He opens his eyes and goes cross-eyed, as David's nose is nearly touching his.

"Anything?" David's anticipation radiates through his wide, excited eyes.

"Dude. No. And why are you so close?" Jacob leans his head back.

"I thought it might help you *connect* to my mind," David replies. He steps back then kneels on the floor in front of the couch. "Try again. I'll stay still right here."

"Okay," Jacob says. He closes his eyes, inhales, then exhales.

"I'll even tell you a memory," David says. "It's my first day here. I'm seeing my living quarters. Walls are white, my room is similar to–"

"Not helping, David," Jacob interrupts. His eyes are still closed.

"Sorry." David chuckles.

Jacob opens his eyes.

"Anything?" Chloe asks.

"Nothing." Jacob shrugs. "Maybe it was a fluke."

"Did you focus as hard as you could?" David asks.

"Uh… Yeah. I think so."

"How hard did you focus?" Chloe asks next.

"I… I don't know how to answer that," Jacob replies, confused. "Let's just forget about it and–"

"One more time." David slaps his hands on Jacob's knees. "Full focus. All serious. I'll go through it alongside you."

"Fine. One more time," Jacob agrees.

"Alright. Eyes closed." David moves his hands to his own knees. Jacob closes his eyes with David. "Inhale." They both inhale slowly. "Exhale. And focus on the silence. Focus on finding a memory." They both sit in meditation as Chloe watches, waiting for something to happen.

David hears the silence of their room slowly grow into a familiar, unsettling noise. He opens his eyes and finds himself in his old-world home. Sirens are blaring outside. The curtains are illuminated by pulsing red and white lights. The TV speakers combat for dominance with the sirens, playing a broadcast alarm on the local news channel while a banner flashes, reading: "Virus spreading across the nation affecting local counties — Allegheny, Washington, Westmoreland, Beaver…" The news anchor is frightened. She is speaking but can't be heard over the commotion outside. New sirens have arrived and join the chorus of the existing sirens, now casting blue lights on the curtains with the red and white.

As he's about to walk to the window and see what's happening, David's mom bursts in from the kitchen with a phone to her ear. She speaks into it loudly, in a panic, "Matthew, you *need* to call me back. Something is happening here. I think that plague is in our neighborhood. Please tell me you're on the way home–" She looks at her phone, touches the screen, then quickly brings the phone to her ear. "Emily! Have you made it home?"

"Mom?" Thirteen-year-old David pulls on her hand. She pulls away, pacing to the window and cautiously peeking through the curtains as if she's expecting to find someone looking in.

"Have you heard back from mom?" David's mom asks into the phone. "Yes, I think it's here–"

"Mom?" David grabs her hand for her attention. His eyes are watering from fear. Outside, more yelling has started.

"Hold on, honey," she replies to him in a tone she thinks is calming. Talking into the phone, she says, "If it's all over Monroeville, it's definitely here." Her voice quivers. "No, he hasn't. And he's usually home by now from–"

A vehicle crash is heard outside, followed by violent screaming. David looks at his mom for comfort. She's holding the phone away from her ear and staring out the window.

"I gotta… Call me back if you hear from mom, Em." She puts her phone into her pocket. David is staring at the TV, where the broadcast shows an aerial view of a mall with hundreds of people running in the street. They pile onto a vehicle, slamming their arms at the windows. He watches as they drag a person out of the car until his mom steps in front of him and says, "Davey. I need you to go upstairs and hide in your closet."

"Why? Where's dad? What's happening out–"

"Davey. It'll be okay. I just need to ask the officers outside if they've seen your father's car trying to get to our street." He watches her bottom lip quiver. "Just hide in your room, and don't come out until you hear me call for you. Okay?"

A woman screams outside from far away. Officers yell, "Get back inside! Now!"

David looks at the window. He's stiff and unable to move.

"Davey? Do you hear me? Don't come out until you hear me say it's okay."

He nods yes but stares at the window, listening to the horrifying sounds. His mom stands and walks to the door. She waits, watching him, gesturing for him to go upstairs. David feels frozen in place but forces himself to move. Once he starts walking, he transitions to a full sprint with his hands hitting the higher steps, galloping up to his room. He rips the comforter from his bed, dives into his closet and hides under the blanket, listening for his mom.

More screams find their way through the walls into his ears. David remains huddled, refusing to move. *Don't come out until you hear me say it's okay.* He replays his mom saying this in his head to drown out the officers yelling orders and crashing and banging and more screaming.

Another cry from outside catches his attention. This one sounds like his mom. Her scream is followed by the officers yelling, this time more aggressively, along with loud shots of gunfire that cause David's shoulders to jump with each piercing crack. Several finishing shots are accompanied by more yells that quickly fall silent. He pulls the comforter away from his head and listens intently for sounds to resume. A slam into the door startles him. Then the door opens and quickly slams shut. He hears panting with soft groans. It's his mom.

David escapes his closet and runs to the top of the steps. He transitions his head slowly between each railing, looking at his mom, who is sitting against the front door. She is sitting with her back against the door. Her breathing is labored and her arm drips blood that is spewing from dark red holes in her shoulder.

It looks like someone bit her.

"Davey, go back to your room," she says weakly, grasping her shoulder and hissing from the pain.

"Mom, what happened?" he asks. His voice is shaky. His arms quiver as he grips the posts of the railing.

"I just… I needed to see if your dad…" She's struggling to keep her head up to look at him.

"Mom?" He shifts down the railing toward the top of the steps.

"Honey… Go back to your…" Her head and weakly pointing hand falls limp.

David slowly and quietly shifts his hands along the railing until he sits at the top of the staircase, looking down at his sleeping mom. He waits and stares, watching her breathe, watching the blood pool below her arm, and watching the news on the TV show footage of hordes of people tearing through towns and cities, attacking each other viciously. Minutes pass as he's hypnotized by the sounds outside. The blood reaches her resting hand on the floor.

Her arm twitches.

She's finally awake.

"M-Mom?" David speaks barely over a whisper. He sees her entire body twitch. Her head jerks toward the news anchor speaking on the TV. "M-Mo–"

She whips her head toward David. His mom's eyes are no longer recognizable. Her pupils are dilated and fully black. Her mouth hangs open while she moves her bottom jaw slowly back and forth while weak wheezes escape from her throat as she sits there staring through him.

David wants to go back to his closet where he felt safe under his comforter. He bends his knee and places his foot on the step behind him slowly.

His mom effortlessly leaps to her feet. She releases a sound that sends chills down his spine; a screech and growl combined. She lunges to the steps and sprints toward David, barely keeping balance, hitting off the wall, reaching the top where she tackles him onto his back.

David screams, flailing his arms that are quickly pinned down by her hands. She hisses and leans all her weight onto his arms while staring with her black eyes, sending saliva dripping onto his neck.

"Mom, you're scaring me!" he whimpers.

She throws her head toward his neck. David lifts his knee into her chest, stopping her. She lets go of one of his arms, hitting his knee away. He quickly pushes on her shoulder with his free hand, trying his hardest to get her off of him. She shrieks, slaps his arm from her shoulder, and thrusts her head into his side, digging her teeth into his ribs.

He feels her teeth slip off his bone and rip through his skin and muscle. Fear and adrenaline give him the strength to pull his other hand free and pull the hair on the back of his mom's head. "Mom! That hurts! Stop it!"

The bite digs harder. She begins to grind her teeth further and deeper into his side.

His slaps turn to fists as he slams them repeatedly into her skull to stop the pain.

She pulls her head into the air. Not because his punches got through, but because she needed to breathe. A burning pain soars through his side as oxygen hits his wound. He sees blood soaking his mom's chin. His blood.

She sighs, jerks her head back, and begins to send her teeth back into him. He pulls both of his knees back and pushes both his feet into her stomach, extending his legs with all his strength. His mom flies backward down the stairs. Her head slams against the wall, then off the steps near the bottom. He sits up, clutching his side, and sees his mom lying motionless at the bottom of the steps.

David crawls his way to her.

"Mom?" he cries. Tears of fear and pain drop from his eyes.

Her legs and torso lie across the bottom steps with her shoulders and head on the floor. Her eyes are open, staring lifelessly across the room. She hasn't moved.

"M-Mom?" He kneels next to her head on the floor. Pressing her cheek doesn't get a reaction. Hesitantly, he slowly leans his ear near her nose, ignoring the droning sirens, listening for her breathing.

He hears nothing. He feels no air.

David sits cross-legged next to his mom. The sound of the sirens grows muddy as his vision blurs. He's desperate for water as his body temperature begins to spike. The pain in his side has gone numb. He wipes his forehead and sweat covers his hand.

His head feels heavy. His eyes want to close. The sirens and new broadcast sound muffled now. He reaches back to balance himself but collapses to the floor, falling unconscious. His legs twitch hard enough to wake him. Sirens still pulse, the TV mutters and lights the room glowing white and yellow. He tries to move his limbs but barely gets a finger to twitch. His consciousness fades to black.

David twitches again, waking himself. This time he's in Chloe's room. Jacob is leaning over him.

"Bro. Are you okay?" Jacob asks, concern fills his eyes.

"No. Not at all," David mutters. A tear falls from the side of his eye.

David sits up from the floor, rubbing his watery eyes and sighing. Jacob has returned to sitting on the edge of the couch, next to Chloe. They both look at him with concern in their eyes.

David asks Jacob, weakly, "Did you… Did you see that, too?"

Jacob shakes his head.

CHAPTER 19

DAVID STANDS AND ADJUSTS HIS shirt, angrily tugging at it as if he finds it responsible for what just happened. "All that for nothing. Great," he mumbles to himself. "I'm gonna go. I'll, uh… Yeah." He walks quickly to the entry and slides his feet into his shoes.

"David…" Chloe stands, then doesn't move. They look at each other quietly. She gives him a sad expression, lost for words. David opens the door and leaves.

"That was…" Jacob stutters.

"Yeah." Chloe stares at the door. "He lived the memory again."

"What is… Has he ever told you what the memory is?"

"No. I think the only person he ever told was Nick."

"I feel like it's my fault. I came in overreacting to–"

"It's not." Chloe sits next to him. "It's happened to him before. And you weren't overreacting. We still don't know how you read Garret's–"

Knocks pound at the door. "Mr. Anderson. I've been instructed to take you to meet your peers," Garret yells from the hall.

"Mind," Chloe finishes her sentence.

"Peers," Jacob scoffs. He stands and zips his hoodie. "Thanks, Chlo."

"For what?" she asks sincerely.

"For trying to help me figure this all out." He twirls his hand by his head. He walks to the door and puts on his shoes. "I've never been able to… It's just nice to talk openly about all this." His hand rests on the doorknob. "Hey, my mom said it's cool if you still wanna join us for pizza and a movie Sunday."

"Yes!" she beams. "I'd love to."

"Cool," he smiles back. He opens the door as Garret begins knocking again. They look at each other awkwardly, as his hand is held in the knocking position. "I'm here, Garret."

"Great, sir. Let's get going." Garret drops his hand and walks toward the training room. Jacob passes a smile and waves to Chloe.

"See you Sunday!" she says in a chipper tone, smiling and waving back.

Knowing Jacob is approaching, Noel exits the training room before he passes. "Hey," Jacob says quickly, stopping to chat.

Noel holds his hand out, defensively scrunching his face, saying, "Just… Don't start thinking a bunch of shit."

"Okay. Okay. I won't. Listen…" Jacob glances at Garret, who is several feet away waiting impatiently. He asks quietly, "When you read minds, do you, like, *see*, people's thoughts or memories?"

"No," Noel answers. He sees disappointment in Jacob's eyes, so he elaborates, "I hear thoughts. Like loud whispers."

"Oh," Jacob replies. "I just… I–"

"Not now, Jacob," Noel says, glancing at Garret with his eyes.

"No?" Jacob asks.

"Not with an audience."

"Oh." Jacob sees Garret standing with his arms crossed in his peripheral vision. He shows an impatience that is unusual compared to his commonly calm demeanor. "I have an idea," Jacob whispers loudly. He thinks, *I think I read Garret's mind.*

"I know," Noel answers.

It worked! Jacob expresses excitement. *But how did you know?*

"I heard all of you thinking when you were in Chloe's room."

Wow, you do have range with that. Do you know how I did that?
"Yes."

You do? Can you tell me?

"Not with the audience, Jacob."

Jacob taps his foot anxiously. *Fine. Hey. Didn't you have something to tell me?*

"Yes. But again, not with the audience." He winces and holds his forehead.

"Mr. Anderson," Garret speaks loudly. Jacob assumes that's Garret's version of yelling.

Jacob goes to say bye to Noel, but he sees him walking toward the dorms holding his head. He walks to Garret, who turns and continues down the hallway by the garage door.

As they approach the door, Jacob rolls his eyes when he hears Elliot's voice from the other side. Garret opens and holds the door for Jacob. As he walks into the smaller garage, he sees a workbench on the left wall with tools and small weapons sitting next to maps with hand-written markings on them.

"'Bout fuckin' time," Elliot says to Jacob, looking him over.

Jacob thinks of a response but decides to keep it to himself.

"Victor said he instructed you two to show and explain everything to Jacob," Garret speaks to Elliot and Theo.

Theo starts to reply but is cutoff as Elliot walks to the workbench, barking, "Yeah. Sure."

"I'll be ready to take you home after the hunt, sir." Garret nods to Jacob and exits back to the hallway.

"Here," Elliot yells to Jacob, tossing him a hunting knife and folded map.

Jacob catches them, then shows the knife and says, "Really? This? When you two have those?" He references the wakizashi swords on their backs. They're both dressed in more clothing than they were during training. Both are wearing long sleeves under tight-fitted shirts and black cargo pants with boots.

"Don't worry, Second Place, we'll protect you," Elliot says with an exaggerated sad face. He laughs then heads toward the main door next to the garage door. "Let's go."

Theo shrugs to Jacob and steps ahead behind Elliot. He's noticeably being more polite toward Jacob than past interactions.

The early evening sky is dimmed by gray-white clouds blocking the orange sun. A light, misty rain fills the air. Jacob looks at the map he was given to follow their planned path. A square is scribbled in pen over a portion of the mall with a dotted line protruding from that square through a dim green section, ending where streets resemble a neighborhood. Small circles and Xs are scribbled over tiny squares that indicate houses they've looted.

"Is this where we're headed–" Jacob asks, ending his last word sharply as he realizes they've walked faster while he was reading the map. He jogs to catch up, confirming they're following the dotted line as they enter a wooded area down a small hill at the edge of the parking lot.

Aside from a few looks from Theo, they continue to walk as if Jacob wasn't there. Halfway through the wooded area, Elliot chimes in with, "You getting scared back there, Second Place?"

Jacob scoffs silently and follows his place on the map. When they exit the woods up ahead, they'll be in the backyard of a house in the neighborhood. All the houses close to this wooded area have an X marked on them with a few circles.

"What do the circles represent?" Jacob asks, wondering if they're even listening.

"You can't figure it out for yourself?" Elliot says arrogantly. "The X means we didn't find anything but checked the house. The circle means we found shit. Simple enough to put together."

This angers Jacob, though he does agree that he could've figured that out on his own. Theo looks back at Jacob and offers a tight smile. Jacob stares through the strands of hair over his eyes, then looks back at the map.

Leaving the woods and entering a backyard, Jacob looks up from his map to see the house ahead is half charred wood and siding. Ashy streaks reach into the unburnt half as if it was stopped by the massive growth of foliage hugging the home. He continues walking while observing the burnt insides through the broken windows when he trips, looking down to find bones of an animal with a chain leash disappearing in the grass. He crumbles the map in his hand and jogs to meet Theo and Elliot. They're standing at a three-way intersection with the perpendicular street running straight ahead.

"Alright, Second Place. The end of this street is where we left off last time. You'll see on your map the last X right here." He smacks Jacob's crinkled map with his finger. "We'll start at the unmarked house right after it."

"What are we looking for? Neither of you told me," Jacob asks with an irritated tone. Elliot begins walking away.

"Living infected fuckers," Elliot yells back.

Theo stands with Jacob. He hesitates his first steps, showing that he's waiting for Jacob to walk alongside him.

Walking with Theo, Jacob asks, "We're looking for… Outsiders?"

"Yeah. But they can't be altered," Theo answers.

"Altered?" Jacob asks.

"Fucked up eyes," Elliot yells. He's far ahead but can still hear the conversation.

"If their eyes are an unusual color, Victor doesn't want them," Theo elaborates.

"Oh." Jacob watches Elliot turn and walk to the front door of their destination. "Why?"

"He never said," Theo replies.

Elliot kicks open the front door. Dust clouds up and rushes out of the home. He waves it away from his face and says, "Tell ya what, SP. Since we got a late start because you were pissing around with Chloe, how about *we* check this house for hiding fuckers," he motions to himself and Theo, "and you check the house across the street?"

Theo gives another nervous smile to Jacob, then looks away. "Whatever, man. Fine," Jacob says. He pockets his map and walks across the street. He hears Elliot yelling followed by glass shattering.

Jacob arrives at the front of the house and notices the window next to the small porch is mostly open. Confirming the door is locked, he walks to the open window, pushes it open further, and climbs in. He lands in a small living area. It opens to a large foyer where the front door is located, with a fancy wooden staircase that leads up to an open hallway with two doors on each side.

The walls of the living area are lined with multiple large framed family photos with two adults and two children occupying all of them. All look older in each picture as they progress on the wall. All are wearing dressy clothes and sitting in the same pose for each photo. The furniture is well-kept, and, other than being dusty, looks like it wasn't used often.

Jacob exits the room into the foyer. Beside the stairs, the foyer leads to a kitchen. He walks in to find it left as most kitchens are: ravaged with all the non-perishables taken.

While stepping over broken ceramic dishes, Jacob sees a large room with the biggest couch facing the biggest TV he's ever seen hanging on the wall. His eyes widen with excitement. *Movies!*

He takes a large step over more broken mugs and plates and sees an unopened box of protein bars among the broken boxes of pasta and cereal. He kneels gently on the floor and opens the box. Inside are all the bars with wrappers intact, not having been tampered with. The expiration dates are years old, but he shrugs. He's had expired protein bars before; they're just dry and chalky. He shoves them into his hoodie pockets.

Standing and proceeding to the living room, he hears shuffling above him upstairs. Freezing in place, he watches the ceiling, listening to light footsteps scurry and stop after the sound of a door shutting.

Stepping carefully back through the kitchen, he walks softly to the steps and tiptoes to the top. Halfway up, a step creaks under his weight. He pauses, hears nothing move, and continues.

The door to the left would be where the footsteps came from. He turns the doorknob slowly and pushes it open, peeking inside the room. It's a large bedroom with a king-sized bed in the center. One nightstand is on each side, both with open drawers. The closer stand has its contents spilled on the floor beneath. In the back of the room are two doors parted by a nook with a bench and window in the back. One door is left open showing a bathroom. The other is closed.

Jacob thinks the closed door is a closet and could be where the footsteps ran to. He moves quietly past the unmade bed, scanning the bathroom as he approaches the closet. An empty shower enclosed by glass doors and a lonely toilet confirm nobody is hiding inside.

He opens the closet door. Clothes hang lining the walls ahead. Underneath, tucked in the back of the closet, are two young Outsiders. A boy and a girl. They're both wearing sweatshirts and sweatpants that are frayed to confirm they're from the old-world.

Jacob kneels slowly in the doorway. They both look to be younger than ten years old. "Hi," he says softly. "Can… Can you understand me?"

The little girl nods. Her eyes are golden yellow. The young boy cowers in fear from Jacob, staring with wide, pale purple eyes.

"I'm not going to hurt you. Okay?" The girl nods again. The boy remains still. "Are you hungry?" Jacob asks, taking a protein bar from his pocket and holding it out for them to take. The girl quickly grabs it from his hand.

"Thank… Thanks," she mutters.

"Do you come to this house often?"

They both shake their head.

"No. Okay," Jacob rubs his mouth. He watches the little girl rip the plastic from the protein bar, break it in half, and give half to the little boy. They eat as if it's the first food they've had today. "Is your house… Do you live near here?"

The girl nods.

"Okay, good, do you—"

"Everyone helps find food," the girl speaks well. "We wanted to, t-too."

Jacob smiles nicely. "That's very admirable of you both. Do you want more?" He holds out another bar. She grabs it just as quickly as last time. Laughing through his nose, he says, "I'm sorry if I startled you."

She nods. "Heard… Heard noises." She points at him.

Chuckling, Jacob says, "Yeah. That was me. I'm sorry." The boy catches his attention, trembling in the corner. "How about I help you get out of here and get back home?"

They both nod in unison.

"Yo, Second Place!" Elliot yells from outside. Jacob sighs and rolls his eyes. "It's not getting brighter out here!"

The little boy tries to run but is stopped by Jacob's hand gently pushing against his chest at the closet door. He holds his finger to his lips and shushes quietly. "It's okay, stay here."

"Come on, man!" Elliot screams. An explosion of wooden pieces rattles through the house as he kicks in the front door. The boy squirms and pushes past Jacob, then sprints out of the room.

"Wait here," Jacob says quickly to the little girl and chases the boy.

"Well, what do we have here?" He hears Elliot speaking playfully from the foyer. Jacob exits the room and looks down the stairs to see Elliot holding his hands on the little boy's shoulders. "Great find here, Second Place!" he says, smiling up at Jacob.

Theo stands in the open doorway watching through the sides of his eyes as if he doesn't want to see what's happening.

"The young ones are good finds. Young blood. Plenty of time to let the serum work and train," Elliot says, patting the boy's head. Jacob sees the boy shaking. "You know what I mean, SP?" Elliot passes another arrogant smile at Jacob.

Kneeling in front of the boy, Elliot tuts and shakes his head, saying, "One *little* problem." He stands back up and looks at Jacob. "The eyes are fucked."

Jacob watches Elliot reach behind his back. "No!" Jacob screams.

In a swift motion, Elliot unsheathes a sword and swings it over his head, bringing the blade down over the boy. Jacob turns his cheek, closing his eyes as he hears an abrupt whimper followed by silence, then a thud of limbs hitting against the hard floor.

CHAPTER 20

ELLIOT PUSHES THE BOY TO the side with his foot. Laughing, he says, "Whelp. Guess we mark this house as an X and move–" His eyes look behind Jacob.

Jacob turns to see the little girl peeking out of the room, down at the little boy. She's covering her mouth with her hand while sobbing.

Elliot steps over the boy and begins to walk up the steps when Jacob says, "No."

"No? Who do you think you are to tell me, 'No?'"

Elliot continues walking up toward Jacob.

His palms tingle through his fingertips. *Remember this anger.* Jacob feels a sensation rush from his chest and through his right arm as he thrusts his hand toward Elliot. Without touching him, Jacob feels pressure in his palm as he sends Elliot flying backward down the stairs and into the wall next to the front door.

Jacob descends the stairs. With a menacing grin, Elliot pushes himself to his feet, keeping his back against the cracked wall and his eyes locked with Jacob's.

"That's the stuff right there, Second Place. I knew you had it in you." He pushes off the wall.

Jacob watches Elliot's left shoulder twitch. He remembers his fake-out at training. Hoping his prediction is correct, he raises his left arm to block a strike from Elliot's right hand after he fakes with his left. He's correct. A painful thud sounds as his forearm stings. Quickly, Jacob counters with as strong of a punch as he can throw. His fist lands a powerful hit to Elliot's left cheekbone.

Jacob feels the bone shatter under Elliot's skin. He falls back into the already cracked wall, sending crumbling drywall to the floor around him, holding his hands to his eyes.

Elliot writhes in pain with his palms against his face and elbows twisting from side to side. Jacob stands with clenched, white-knuckled fists. Theo remains still, watching from the front door. Elliot's groan turns into a maniacal chuckle as he slides his hands away from his face, smearing blood from his fingertips across his forward. His lower eyelid has detached and hangs slumped over his skin from the broken cheek bone, exposing the bottom half of his left eye.

Pushing himself away from the wall, Elliot slides the short distance between him and Jacob. He moves as if there are wheels on the bottoms of his boots. Jacob's eyes watch both of his legs for signs of his next move, but neither are twitching or moving. Elliot swings his right arm to throw a hook at Jacob's ribs. Jacob steps to his right, avoiding the hit, but steps into Elliot's intentional attack —his hand clutching Jacob's throat.

His grip is intense. Jacob's breathing immediately becomes raspy. He puts his hand around Elliot's throat in return but is too distraught to grab a strong hold before his arm is slapped away.

"I gave you a fuckin' warning, Second Place. I fuckin' told you who the better human is.

"You think *this* means anything?" Elliot points to his sunken eyelid. "This is nothing. Do you have any idea how many others like you I've killed?" He speaks with an immense amount of pride. Jacob's breathing is becoming audible and wheezing as Elliot's fingers gripped around his neck sends pain deep into his throat to his tonsils. Saliva foams from his lips as his attempts to breathe become labored. Elliot forces Jacob backward toward the kitchen while he continues speaking, "Maybe I tell Victor one of the Rejects got you. I tried to save you, but I just didn't make it in time." He sarcastically tuts. His evil smile intensifies.

Rejects? Jacob thinks while choking.

"Theo. Get over here and hold," Elliot demands. He's pushed Jacob up against the countertop. The hold on Jacob's throat has made him weak from the shallow breaths providing little oxygen. He wants to throw jabs to free himself but can't even gather the strength to raise his arm. He turns his eyes to Theo, who hasn't moved from the front door or replied to Elliot. Instead, he's remained still, watching in shock.

"Theo!" Elliot turns his head slightly.

Theo hangs his head and walks past them, squeezes between the counter and Jacob, then wraps Jacob's arms behind his back, locking him in place. "I'm sorry," Theo says very quietly, under his breath.

Elliot keeps his evil smile and sends a punch into Jacob's ribs. This connects as Jacob is taking a strong inhale after his throat is no longer being clutched. His lungs fill with sharp pain as the air is forced out. Another punch connects to Jacob's cheek, whipping his head to the side. He's too weak to pick his falling head back up after his chin rests on his chest.

He hears Elliot unsheathe his other sword with a scoff. Jacob stares at his feet, helplessly.

"Elliot. We can't–" Theo stutters. Another disappointed scoff is made by Elliot.

Jacob's head lifts as Elliot pulls it up by a fistful of his hair. Their eyes are inches apart. "You're *very* lucky I'm not allowed to kill you." His eyes show a hatred Jacob's never seen before. Small pupils staring deeply at Jacob along with his twitching cheeks reveal that he is truly resisting the urge to kill him. Elliot's sunken eyelid drips a single drop of blood to his upper cheek. "Yet," Elliot adds. He lets go of Jacob's hair, dropping his head. "Let's go, Theo. Leave him."

Theo begins to let go of Jacob's arms and realizes Jacob has no strength in his legs. He slowly lowers Jacob to the floor.

"Now, Theo." Elliot demands from the foyer as he picks up his sword by the steps then exits the house.

Theo rests Jacob against the countertop so that he's sitting upright. Weakly, Jacob moves his eyes to look at him. Struggling to catch his breath, Jacob barely is able to ask, "Is… Is it…" He shifts his posture and groans in pain, "Killing Outsiders…"

Theo knows he's trying to ask if this always happens. He's kneeling in front of Jacob. They keep eye contact and Theo nods somberly.

"Wh-Why do you–" Jacob barely whispers with raspy breath.

Theo says, "He… He'll kill her if I don't–"

"Theo!" Elliot screams from outside.

"W-Who?" Jacob wants to say but is trying too hard to breathe.

Theo stands and walks quickly out the front door. Jacob watches them get to the street and walk back toward the facility. His head slumps to the side as he loses consciousness.

Thunder roars and startles Jacob awake. He finds himself lying on his side where Theo left him. A stale orange glow shines through the soft rain outside the front door. Jacob sighs, realizing he's been unconscious for a few hours.

Pushing himself to a sitting position, he notices his throat feels better but still has a light bruising pain where Elliot hit his ribs. His punch was powerful.

Jacob thinks of the little boy and sees the top of his head sticking out from below the bottom step in the foyer. He can't leave him lying there. Not when the little girl knows he's there. He needs to see if she's still here.

He stands and brushes the dust from his clothes. Walking slowly into the foyer, he stops at the little boy, looks at him and gives a slow blink, speaking softly, saying, "I'll be right back."

Upstairs, he pushes the bedroom door open slowly. The closet is wide open and empty. The nook between the closet and bathroom has a now-open window. Jacob walks to the window and leans out, looking down. The back of his head is hit with cold rain. Below are small bushes with the bush directly below the window flattened.

Jacob sighs and goes back downstairs to the boy. He remembers seeing a small garage on the side of the house. He walks back to the kitchen, stepping on the broken dishes and discarded food items. No need to be quiet now, he figures. He opens the door before the large living room, revealing the inside of the garage.

With the flashlight on his phone, he shines around and finds what he was looking for. A shovel.

After grabbing the shovel, he walks back through the kitchen, outside the front door, and surveys the side of the house. Between the homes is a row of tall trees. Between two of the trees is where Jacob decides to dig.

Soft flashes of lightning, followed by low rumbles of thunder, light up Jacob's progress as he digs the hole he now stands over. He stabs the shovel into the ground next to him, sighs, then walks back into the foyer.

"I'm sorry," he whispers, kneeling his wet knee next to the boy, gently flipping him over. He notices the boy's faded shirt has a black and red Spider-Man logo with "Miles Morales" in cartoon graffiti underneath. "He's one of my favorites, too," he says, softly.

Carefully placing his right arm under the boy's knees and his left behind his head, Jacob lifts him from the floor. Retracing his steps back to the hole, he carries the boy, saying, "My mom told me this is how they did this in the old-world. Or… At least I think it was something like this." He stands at the edge of the hole. He kneels next to it and gently places the boy inside. The soft dirt squeezes between his fingers as the weight of the body presses against them. Realizing the boy is lying directly on the dirt, Jacob says, "She said they used to use boxes." He looks around in the dark rain. "I'm sorry, I don't have one."

Watching the rain land and wash away the dried blood on the boy's face, Jacob stands and takes off his zip-up hoodie. After folding it to the length of the boy, he kneels back down. While softly laying it over him, he says, "You didn't deserve this," he sighs. He wonders if the little girl was his sister.

The rain soaks his T-shirt and jeans while he finishes shoveling the dirt back into the ground, burying the boy. Jacob stands next to the mound wiping away his wet hair from his eyebrows. The sky has turned dark. The storm has passed, but the rain persists. It's time to make his way back.

His map has become soggy and unreadable. Shaking his head to himself, he says, "Figures." He can follow the street back to the intersection, then straight through the woods should bring him back to the parking lot of the facility.

As he turns and begins walking down the street, he thinks about everything that transpired. He starts with how quickly Elliot overpowered him. How did he adapt so quickly? He thinks about Elliot saying, "How many others like you I've killed." Who does he mean? Other Better Human subjects? Or just other subjects? Nicholai?

Headlights from behind Jacob shine at his feet, and his shadow parts the white-blue light as it grows quickly, getting closer to him. Jacob stops and turns, squinting at the bright headlights. He holds his arm to shield his eyes as they turn off, only shining soft, yellow lights. He immediately recognizes the vehicle. It's Garret's.

The vehicle slows down to a stop. Jacob walks past the driver's door to the back. As Garret opens his door, Jacob stops it with his hand, saying, "I'm fine, Garret." He enters the back seat. As soon as he sits, he rests his head back and stares out the windshield.

"I brought you a towel, sir," Garret speaks and offers a towel to Jacob.

He grabs it and dries his messy hair, saying, "Thanks." Next, drying his face, he says, "I guess Theo and Elliot told you where I was."

"Theo did, sir. Elliot marched directly to the medical room."

Jacob audibly sighs. He folds the towel and places it behind his head, then looks out the side window while Garret navigates the neighborhood. Many of the houses have front doors hanging open or knocked completely onto the floor. He can picture Elliot's annoyingly satisfied grin as he kicked in each one of them.

Garret hears Jacob's sigh and sees him through the mirror. "Theo mentioned the three of you were attacked?" He phrases as a question.

"Yeah," Jacob mutters. "That's one way to put it."

"Is that not true, sir?"

Through the corner of his eyes, Jacob looks at Garret in the rearview mirror. Garret's tone seems genuine and concerning, but Jacob replies, "Sure. Yeah."

The drive becomes silent while Jacob watches the abandoned homes pass. The darkness of the night with the rain brings a new sense of eeriness to the stories these homes tell. Yards with rusted vehicles sitting with the doors open, as if the person was forced to evacuate. Maybe to save someone or themselves. Porches with furniture hanging through a window, as if an attempt to escape or enter was halted suddenly. Even the tall grass feels as though it's hiding something inside of it. Something that wants to be found, but Jacob doesn't want to find.

As Garret drives onto the parkway, he says in a more chipper tone, "So, are you excited for your two weeks of fall break, sir?"

Surprised at Garret's invitation to small talk, Jacob stutters, "Uh… Yeah. Yeah, I am."

"You know, back when I was in school, we didn't get the seasonal breaks that you get. We had three months off for the summer."

"My dad had mentioned that before." Not in the mood to chat, but realizing Garret is actually trying, even calling back to Jacob's prior inquiry to his childhood, Jacob replies, "Do you think you'd have preferred your way or this new way?"

"Hard to say, sir."

Jacob chuckles quietly. That reply is more on-brand for Garret. But it was nice that he made the attempt. Deciding to take advantage of the moment, Jacob asks, "Hey Garret, what is a Reject?"

"Sorry, sir?" Garret replies, requesting clarification.

"Elliot mentioned it. He referred to something called a Reject."

"Oh," Garret stumbles. "They're the same as what I believe you kids in the Conservation Cities call Shriekers."

"Hmm," Jacob mumbles. He watches them pass the same cars on the parkway, thinking about Theo's demeanor during the fight. He seemed nervous, like he disapproved of Elliot's actions. Theo confirmed that it's common for Elliot to kill Outsiders. But does Victor know he does this?

He'll ask Victor himself, but Jacob decides to start with Garret. Turning his head to look at Garret in the rearview, he finds himself sitting in front of Victor's desk. He's in Garret's mind again. Victor's eyes are surrounded by dark veins; more than he's ever seen on his face.

He learns they're mid-conversation when he speaks as Garret, saying, "The subject you hoped would replace David? From the last hunt?"

"Yes." Victor sounds frustrated.

"And you're certain it failed?"

"They became ravenous, began twitching, biting themselves, scratching open wounds." Victor waves his hand without empathy. "The serum basically destroyed all the neurons in the brain, like with the other rejections."

Rejections? Are those Rejects? Are Shriekers Victor's failed subjects? Jacob thinks, unable to speak. He and Victor stare at each other.

Victor answers their questioning stare, saying, "It's been part of the process. It either works, giving the subject miraculous abilities, or it fails, and they turn into th... You know this, Garret. It's why we use Outsiders and not city people."

Another pause in conversation is broken when Garret says, "You gave them the same strain that you gave to David?"

"Yes. Well..." Victor stands from his seat. Defensively, he says, "Altered, of course. David is the second subject that only re-lives their own memories. They *need* to be able to *project* the memory to another person. The strain is clearly targeting the cerebrum as intended, I just need it to *f*–" He hisses through gritted teeth, clenching a tight fist, stopping himself from cursing as he walks to the side wall of his office to a framed piece of notebook paper. Jacob can't make out the writing on the paper from where Garret is sitting. He watches Victor press his thumb against the corner of the frame, triggering the frame to slide to the right. Jacob tries to lean in his seat to get a better view but is reminded he has no control. He sees a stack of folders and a pistol inside.

"Chloe and Noel are perfect subjects for their strain," Victor says as he grabs the folder on top of the stack. He walks to the desk. "Once I finally find a third subject and perfect *this* strain, I can combine the three and have a perfected Vitality serum. One that works without fail." He sets the folder near them, opening it and revealing the top page.

The top of the page reads NEURO STRAIN – VITALITY PROJECT. Stage 1 and Stage 2 are highlighted and checked off with Chloe's and Noel's names next to them. Stage 3 has two names: Michelle Maro, crossed out, and David Rowel. Drawings of DNA and pictures of brain scans and molecular models are taped and drawn underneath, with calculations that Jacob does not understand. He tries to take it all in before Garret moves his eyes to Victor. Victor's expression looks weak. Seeing the veins this close reveals red skin between the dark stems branching around his eyes.

"We need them to find a good subject when they go on their next hunt," Victor says adamantly.

Garret asks, "How much time do we have, sir?"

Victor gives a concerning look. Jacob can't stop focusing on his eyes. Victor's expression is sad, but his eyes look lifeless. Victor opens his mouth to respond.

"We're here, sir," Garret exclaims. Jacob jumps, startled, realizing he's back in the vehicle, parked outside of his home. "Are you okay?" Garret asks.

How am I doing this? Jacob thinks, showing frustration.

"Sir?" Garret reiterates.

"Yeah," he replies. Curiosity getting the best of him, Jacob asks, "Did I fall asleep?"

"Seemed like you did." Garret chuckles. "Didn't stop you from mumbling, sir."

Jacob looks at the headlights shining on the street.

"Nothing understandable, of course." Garret delivers another soft chuckle to reassure his point.

Forcing a laugh through his nose, Jacob says, "Thanks, Garret. And thanks again for the towel."

"You're welcome. See you soon, Mr. Anderson."

Jacob exits the vehicle and stands at the edge of the porch while Garret drives away. So much happened today. So many questions remain stirring through his mind. Are Shriekers actually failed subjects? Does Victor know what Elliot does on hunts? Does Victor know Elliot wants to kill Jacob?

He decides Victor will know. And he'll get his answers.

CHAPTER 21

WITH HIS HAND ON THE doorknob, Jacob sighs. He's about to open the door, get scolded, and will have to give an explanation for his absence yesterday. It's for good reason that he missed, but it's not fair that he ignored the messages and calls on his phone.

"Are you ready to explain yourself?" Deante says to Jacob as soon as he opens the front door.

Jacob glances back at his mom in the kitchen, nervously, then says to Deante in a loud whisper, "Quiet, man, she still thinks I hung out with you—"

"Hello, D," Amber yells politely from the kitchen.

Smiling and waving past Jacob, Deante says, "Hello, Mrs. A. My mom said you two had another lovely Saturday bargain shopping."

"We always do, D. Even though bargain shopping is much different these days, it's still fun to do," she replies with a chuckle.

"Oh, I'm sure, I'm sure," he yells at her, giving an angry look at Jacob, who is still blocking the partially open door. "I'd say my Saturday was normal, but your son decided to–"

"I'll be back in a few, mom, we're going to go to the–" Jacob stutters, slips on shoes, and shuts the door quickly behind him. Not expecting to be outside and having been lounging all morning, he's still wearing his basketball shorts from bed and a zip-up hoodie with no shirt underneath. He glares at Deante with frustration.

"*You're* frustrated? Bro… *You're* frustrated?" Deante releases an exaggerated scoff.

"I texted you this morning saying I'd explain later, bro." Jacob shoves his hands into the hoodie pockets and extends his arms as a cold breeze passes across his exposed skin.

"After an *entire* day of ignoring me. You reply *this morning*. We *always* hang on Saturdays when our moms shop. It's *been* our thing, dude."

"I know, man, it's just that I was–"

"It's not just that, Jacob. You're doin' this training and facility shit — which, like, I'm not mad at you for, I want you to figure your shit out — but that already has you missing shit you never used to."

"I'm sorry, D, I–"

"But then *our* Saturday, bro. *Our* Saturday. I thought that wouldn't get cut, bro. I did." He pats his arms in disappointment at his sides.

"D…" Jacob stutters. He's still holding his arms stiff from the chill in the air. "Listen, dude, Friday was absolutely crazy."

"I'm listening." Deante exaggerates his angry expression.

Looking around as if he expected to find onlookers listening to his conversation, Jacob checks in all directions, then speaks at a low volume. "First, I'm sent out on a hunt. Which is apparently where they find Outsiders to use as subjects.

Second, I *actually* find these young kids, I think siblings, in one of the homes. Third, that asshole, Elliot, I told you about–" Deante nods. "He just… He comes into the house and kills one of them." Jacob speaks passionately.

"What?" Deante loses his angry look and is quickly invested.

"Yeah." Jacob pauses for a moment. "Then he tries to kill me, dude."

"What?" Deante yells.

"Yeah." Jacob nods strongly. "But that's not the craziest part—"

"How… Okay. Go on."

"Before Theo stopped him, he mentioned his plan would be to tell Victor that a Reject attacked and killed me." Jacob pauses, knowing Deante will ask a follow-up question.

"What's a Reject?"

"They're what we've been calling Shriekers."

Deante tenses with excitement.

"There's more," Jacob says.

Deante's eyes widen.

"I think Shriekers… Or Rejects… Whatever they are… I think they call them Rejects for a reason. I think Victor makes them."

"Okay. Okay. Okay. Hold on." Deante gestures his palms downward. "*Makes* them?"

"I think they're his failed subjects. When whatever he's giving them is rejected by the subject's DNA. Like, if a serum doesn't work, it turns them into… Shriekers. Rejects."

"W-What makes you think this?" Deante shows disbelief.

Jacob sighs and rolls his eyes.

"What?" Deante asks.

Jacob realizes he hasn't explained the situation with Garret's memories to Deante yet. He also doesn't want to have to explain it right now. Talking with his hands still in his hoodie pockets, Jacob bounces anxiously and says, "Promise you'll let me explain later."

Side-eyed, Deante says, "Promise."

"I've been reading Garret's mind, D."

Deante exhales and paces to the edge of the yard. "No you didn't," he yells, then walks back to Jacob. "No, you didn't make me promise to learn shit later and then drop that on me."

Jacob glances nervously at the front door, then continues gesturing with his hands in his hoodie, saying, "I saw a memory of Garret's where he was talking to Victor about this. *All* of this."

Deante is shaking his head while pinching the bridge of his nose.

"D, *this* is why I missed yesterday," he says sincerely.

Tossing his arms to his side, Deante says, "What? You gonna say now that you teleported back in time and tried preventing the outbreak or some shit?"

"Bro." Jacob rolls his eyes. "No. But I *have* to know if this is true."

"And?"

"*And* I spent all that time yesterday looting through every corner of my dad's office. Every file. Every notebook. Every drawer."

"And?" Deante sings louder.

"Fuckin' nothing, bro," Jacob says disappointedly. "I thought, worst case scenario, I'd find his login credentials scribbled somewhere so we can get into the Volcan Enterprises database through Kyle's program. But I didn't even find that."

Deante shrugs and sighs. Jacob copies the gestures. They stare while glancing away occasionally.

Finally, Deante shrugs again and says, "You missed seeing some cool shit Friday after school." His tone is intended to make Jacob jealous.

Chuckling, Jacob says, "Yeah? What did Kyle show you guys?"

"Dude, these kids had *everything* back then. And they *did* everything. Music. Art. Fuckin' adventures. Dancing. It's cra–"

"Jacob," Amber yells from the door. Deante and Jacob turn and look at her. "Cookie cake is done. You better shower up and get ready soon."

"Bro." Deante sounds embarrassed. "It's your fucking birthday."

Jacob chuckles.

"I'm the worst friend ever. I'm sorry. Happy birthday, bro."

Laughing, Jacob says, "You're fine, dude. Let's say we're even."

Deante laughs with him. Sarcastically rolling his eyes, he says, "Alright. Fine. We're even." He extends his hand for their handshake. "Enjoy your date tonight." He winks.

Stuttering, Jacob decides to just smile and say, "Thanks, man."

Walking away down the street, Deante yells back as Jacob is opening the front door, "You better tell me how today goes. And about that other shit. Don't forget!"

Jacob shakes his head, laughing, then walks inside.

Before jumping in the shower, Jacob is scrolling through yesterday's text conversation with Chloe to see what time she's coming over when he receives a text saying she's on her way. He feels his heart beat faster. He races through his shower, throws on a recently washed pair of jeans, swipes a few extra passes of deodorant, then finds a plain green t-shirt to wear. He skips downstairs, where his mom has his cake on the table next to a small, wrapped gift and a card. She smiles and shakes her head, thinking how this is the hardest she's seen him get ready in eighteen years.

"Do I—" Jacob begins to speak when he hears the squeaking brakes of Garret's vehicle outside. "Do I look okay, mom?" He asks quickly, bouncing anxiously on his toes.

"I thought this wasn't a date?" she jokes.

"Mom." He slaps his hands at his sides and gives a stern look.

"You look like you always do, sweetheart."

He increases the sternness of his stare.

"Which is *always* handsome," she adds, raising her eyebrows and giving a sarcastic stern look back.

Jacob's nerves spike when knocks sound at the door. He exhales, then walks to the foyer and answers the door. Chloe is smiling brightly with Garret standing a few steps behind her. Jacob notices a slight smile in the corners of his lips.

Chloe is wearing one of her graphic T-shirts depicting another band he hasn't heard of, faded ripped jeans, and sneakers. Her braided ponytail falls over her shoulder as she raises her hand to wave, then reaches for a hug.

While in the hug, Jacob meets eyes with Garret who says, "Hello, Mr. Anderson."

Standing back from the short hug, Jacob replies, "Hey, Garret."

"I'll be back to pick you up later this evening, Ms. Parker," Garret says to Chloe. "You both enjoy your time." He bows then walks to his vehicle.

"Bye, Garret!" Chloe waves.

"Uh… Come on in," Jacob says nervously, standing aside and motioning toward the kitchen.

Chloe steps into the foyer and looks around her, then into the kitchen and says, "Wow, your home is lovely."

"Th-Thanks."

Amber walks to the edge of the kitchen near the foyer and smiles, waving to Chloe. "Uh… Mom, this is Chloe. Chloe, this is my mom, Amber," Jacob says. His mom chuckles, finding his nervousness adorable.

"Hello, Mrs. Anderson." Chloe steps in front of Jacob and reaches to shake her hand. As Amber reaches for her hand, Chloe adds, "You are *so* pretty."

With a big smile, Amber says, "Hello, Chloe, it's very nice to meet you, and you're too sweet for saying that. And you may call me Amber." She gestures to the kitchen and says, "Come in, make yourself comfortable. Can I get you something to drink?"

As they walk in the kitchen, Chloe says, "Yes, please. Your home is beautiful, Amber."

"Thank you very much. Would you like water? Soda?" Amber asks.

"Water is perfect, thank you," she says, staring into the living room.

Amber hands Chloe a glass of water and says, "We were going to get pizza for dinner today, is that okay?"

"Of course."

"Any special toppings?"

"I'm good with anything!" Chloe says confidently.

Antsy, Jacob says, "Mom, I'm going to show her my room real quick."

With a serious expression, Amber points at him and says, "You'll keep your door open."

"Seriously?" Jacob says, embarrassed. He leads Chloe to the stairs, stops and says, "Oh. Mom. I need to borrow your phone for a sec." He reaches out his hand. "But… You can't ask why."

"Why?" Amber asks suspiciously, grabbing her phone from the counter.

Jacob tightens his expression and raises his eyebrows while shaking the hand he's stretching outward. Amber walks over and sets her phone in his hand. Her expression is still suspicious. "Thank you," he says, then heads up to his room.

As they enter Jacob's room, Chloe's eyes widen as she sees the superhero posters on his wall, action figures and stacks of comics on his dresser, and guitar leaning against the wall. His messy bed and clothes on the floor catch her attention next, making her giggle.

"So-Sorry about that." He shuffles over to the hoodie on the floor and kicks it under the bed.

"Jacob, this is *so* cool." She walks over and picks up a comic book. "Did you get all this stuff from the outside?"

"Most of it, yeah," he says. "Some of it my dad gave me."

"Really?" She sounds shocked.

"Perks of running the business, I guess." Jacob shrugs.

Chloe sees him scrolling through his mom's phone. She sets the comic down and covers the screen with her hand. With a concerned look, she says, "Jacob. Your mom is *so* sweet. Are you sure about this? The last thing I want to do is make a bad impression."

"Yeah. She'll love it," he says confidently.

Chloe leans over the phone to show with her eyes that she doesn't believe him. "You hated it. Remember?"

"I didn't *hate* it. I just didn't expect it. How about this? How about I ask her with you there. Will that make you feel more comfortable with this?"

"Yes. Definitely."

"Perfect," he says, excited, handing her the phone. She watches a video of Ethan and Amber dancing to a slow song in a room full of people watching and smiling. Seeing the love between them puts a smile on her face.

Jacob sits on the edge of the bed watching Chloe. She pulls the phone from her ear, taps the screen then hands it to Jacob.

"Chlo…" Jacob speaks hesitantly. "I read Garret's mind again."

"You did?" she asks, surprised, sitting cross-legged on the floor. "Did you do it on purpose this time?"

"No," he says, disappointed. "But I was thinking about something Elliot said on the hunt, and then the memory I saw from Garret was about that same thing. So… Maybe I influenced it?"

"What was the thing?" Chloe asks.

"Rejects."

"Rejects?"

"Chlo, the conversation between Garret and Victor seemed like Victor might be doing some shady stuff," Jacob says with concern in his eyes.

"No," she says quickly. "I don't think–"

"Chlo. It's not like he'd be open about it to us if he is."

Shaking her head, Chloe says, "No, he wants to help people. He wouldn't do anything that would–"

"Pizza will be here in fifteen minutes." Amber yells from downstairs.

"Let's continue this later. There's more I want to tell you, but we should probably head back–"

"Yeah," Chloe chuckles, interrupting Jacob. They both make their way back to the kitchen.

Amber has put snacks on the table: chips and pretzels in bowls with dips and glasses of iced tea by their seats. She invites them to play a card game while they wait. It arrives during the game, so they eat and continue playing. Chloe and Amber quickly warm up to each other.

"Once your internship is over, will you be a researcher at Volcan Enterprises?" Amber asks Chloe.

"I really hope so," she says, excited. She looks at Jacob, saying, "We never talked about… You never told me what trade you'll do after school."

"Yeah…" Jacob mutters. "I haven't really decided yet."

"That's okay!" Chloe says, assuring him after seeing him embarrassed.

"I think it's time for the yearly tradition," Knowing the after school subject is a touchy one, Amber tries to cheer up Jacob and chance the subject while sliding a small gift to him. The yearly horror movie.

Opening the card first, Jacob sees his dad's handwriting inside. It reads:

JACOB,

HAPPY 18ᵀᴴ BIRTHDAY, BUD! THIS YEAR, WE FINALLY DO IT, WE FINALLY GET TO MY ALL-TIME FAVORITE!

CAN'T WAIT TO WATCH THIS WITH YOU!

LOVE, MOM AND DAD

Every year before this, Jacob would look up after reading the card and see his father beaming with a smile and radiating excitement from across the table. Jacob bites his tongue to fight the urge to cry but releases a single tear when he tightly closes his eyes. He sniffles, wipes the tear away with his wrist and says, "I'm sorry."

"It's okay, Jacob," Chloe says. Her eyes are tear-filled.

Amber kneels next to him in his seat. She says, "Your dad loved this tradition." Jacob smiles through another tear falling and nods. "You were his entire world, Jacob. His pride and joy." She places her hand on his cheek and wipes a tear with her thumb. "I see so much of him inside you." A tear falls from her eye. "All he ever wanted was for you to be curious of the world," Looking at Chloe, she adds, "Which is why *I* was the only one upset about this kid sneaking out of the walls."

Jacob chuckles and says, "Thanks, mom."

Amber puts both hands on his cheeks and says, "My *eighteen*-year-old." She leans up and kisses his head, kneels back down and says, with teary eyes, "Promise me something." Jacob offers a smile. "No matter how old you get… Don't ever stop being my boy that's going to fly to Mars."

Jacob stands and hugs his mom. Chloe sniffles from her seat. "Okay," Jacob says, sniffling, wiping his eyes, "now, I… Well, *we* have a surprise for you."

"Oh?" Amber looks at Chloe who's smiling, then back to Jacob.

"But… Just to be sure. I have to ask." He says in a serious tone, "If you could dance with dad again, would you want to?"

"W-Wha- I don't understand."

"Like… Would you want to see dad and dance with him one more time if you could?"

"I… I don't… No," she stutters. She gives another confused look to Chloe, then back to Jacob. Jacob is looking at her with a shocked expression. She repeats, "No, I wouldn't."

"Oh." Jacob looks to Chloe who is looking at him with a surprised expression. "I've seen you watching your wedding video on your phone… I thought if you could–"

"Jacob." Amber grabs his shoulders gently. "I loved your father. Deeply. And I miss him dearly."

"But… You wouldn't want to dance with him again?" He looks into his mom's soft gaze. Glancing back at Chloe, he looks back to his mom and says, "Chloe can–"

"Sweetheart." Amber squeezes his shoulders. "You know how much I miss your father, right?"

Jacob nods.

"And you miss him just as much."

Jacob nods, this time with tear-filled eyes.

"That knot you feel. In here." She touches the center of his chest. Jacob nods again. "That's reminding you of all the love you have for your father," she says. "The hardest part of loving someone is knowing that one day, no matter what we do, we're going to lose them. But that's also what makes loving someone so beautiful."

Jacob stares at her. Her eyes water as she reaches again to touch his cheek.

"We never forget the loved ones we lose." The corners of her smile catch teardrops falling over her cheeks.

Jacob sniffles. "I-I'm sorry I–"

"Don't be," Amber says. "It was a sweet thought. Even though I have no idea what you were planning to do if I said yes." She chuckles. Chloe and Jacob chuckle with her.

Chloe catches Jacob's attention and quietly mouths, "Told you!"

"It's… We can explain another time." Jacob replies to his mom while sending a sarcastic smirk back to Chloe. Exhaling a loud sigh, Jacob says, "So… *The Conjuring*?"

Chloe and Amber laugh as Amber grabs the popcorn bucket and points to the living room, saying, "Blankets and pillows are ready for us."

They sit on the couch with Chloe in the middle. Jacob says, "This was dad's favorite?"

"Oh, Jacob, when I told him I hadn't seen it before, I got a lecture on how creative the director was when filming this movie, and he had me watch it at least twice a week for months," Amber says, giggling.

Jacob presses play and they commentate, laugh, and jump at the scares. Late into the movie, Jacob nudges Chloe to show her that Amber has fallen asleep.

Chloe looks up at Jacob. She smiles, lunges forward and kisses his cheek. He smiles back at her as she looks back at the TV, then rests her head on his shoulder.

Jacob gently moves his arm from the back of the couch and wraps it around Chloe's shoulder. In a few moments, Garret will be here to pick her up and this will be over. For now, though, he takes it all in.

What a wonderful day, he thinks to himself.

CHAPTER 22

THE FIRST OFFICIAL DAY OF fall break sees Jacob waking with a smile. This has always been Jacob's favorite time of year. His birthday, fall break for school, permanent hoodie weather, and scary movies playing on the normally lame movie channel are the top reasons why it's his favorite. Those, along with a good evening with Chloe, are the reasons for the smile.

He's admittedly nervous to ask Victor about the Rejects, but he's known Victor his whole life, and he's certain the conversation will be fine. Everything will be explainable and the mystery surrounding it all can be put to rest.

He jumps out of bed and grabs the hoodie he kicked under it yesterday to throw on with his shorts. He finds his mom cooking breakfast in the kitchen – a pleasant sight after last night.

"I know you're leaving for training this afternoon, so I figured you'd enjoy a bigger breakfast this morning," she says as he sits at the table.

"Awesome, thanks," he replies.

"Well, I do have to ask, after all. How would I have been able to dance with your father?"

"So… Chloe's ability…"

Amber nods and smiles.

"Chloe can project visions," Jacob says. "I asked her if she'd be okay with showing dad and having him dance with you."

Amber smiles at Jacob, then continues cooking.

"It's why I asked for your phone," he continues. "She needs to have seen and heard someone in order to project them accurately. Especially with voices and stuff. So I showed her the video I've seen you watching a lot."

"Wow." Amber shakes her head in awe. "That stuff has always been fascinating to me. But I've never even begun to understand the world your father worked in."

Jacob presses his lips and gives her a tight smile. She sets a plate of eggs, pancakes and bacon in front of him.

"Dang, mom," he says at the sight of all the food.

"I told you. *Big* breakfast." She chuckles.

He laughs and takes a bite of the pancakes. While chewing, he asks, "Hey, mom. Did dad ever mention him and Victor not getting along?"

Lowering her eyebrows, Amber says, "No. Not at all. Why?"

"No reason," he says and continues eating. Amber looks at him with confusion, but Jacob doesn't see it. She brushes it off.

After a few more bites, Jacob asks, "Did dad ever mention a project called Vit–"

A knock sounds at the door.

"Who would that be?" Amber asks, surprised.

Jacob stands and says, "Maybe it's D?" He approaches and opens the door slightly, peeking outside, and finds Garret standing on the porch.

"Garret?" he says questioningly.

"Hello, sir."

"You're early. Like, very early."

Garret clears his throat. While fidgeting with the top button of his suit jacket, he awkwardly jokes, saying, "I... Got ahead of the traffic, sir."

Jacob laughs through his nose. "My mom and I just started having breakfast. Mind waiting a bit?"

"Uh... Sure, sir," Garret replies. "I'll wait in the vehicle."

"Cool, thanks." Jacob shuts the door and returns to the kitchen table.

"Was that Garret I heard?" Amber asks.

"Yeah. He's super early," Jacob answers with his mouth full.

"Did you invite him in?"

"No?" Jacob replies, shrugging. "Should I?"

"It is the friendly thing to do, Jacob," she answers sternly. "I'll go invite him in."

"No. Mom. It's fine." He shovels his last two bites in his mouth. "I'll go early and then hopefully be home early." He runs upstairs, kicks off his shorts, throws on jeans, runs back downstairs, then shuffles to the foyer to slide his feet in his sneakers.

"Weren't you going to ask me something a bit ago?"

"Huh?" Jacob thinks with his hand on the door. *Vitality.* He shakes his head and says, "It can wait until later."

"Are you sure?" Amber asks from the kitchen.

"Positive."

"Just don't leave me hanging. Promise?"

"Promise." He smiles and leaves the house, jogging to the vehicle.

Jacob enters the backseat. No Victor again. He hoped to have the conversation on the way there. But it's fine, he'll ask him at the facility. Buckling his seatbelt, Jacob shifts his shoulders and contemplates seeing what Garret might know.

"So… Pretty early today, huh?" he awkwardly starts a conversation.

"My apologies, sir."

"It's cool. It's cool." Jacob watches out his window. He needs to casually get Garret to talk about Rejects. Moving his eyes to the rearview, he looks at Garret in the rearview and says, "Hey, Garret. So, like, what *are* Rej—"

He's watching the elevators open to the top floor of Volcan Enterprises.

Oh, come on! he thinks to himself.

He walks toward Rebecca's desk outside of Victor's office. Looking left as he walks, he sees inside the glass windows of Ethan's office. It's dark and boxes are stacked around the desk in the center. The plate holding his dad's name outside the office door is removed.

"Hi, Garret!" Rebecca exclaims as he approaches.

"Hello, Ms. Williams." He nods.

She places her hand sideways on her mouth and whispers with concern in her eyes, "He doesn't look well today." She points with her other thumb to Victor's door.

Garret doesn't reply. She gives a quick smile then resumes her work on her computer.

The view of the city outside the large windows is the first view upon entering the office. Victor is leaned back in his desk chair resting his arm over his eyes. Standing in the doorway, Garret clears his throat, then says, "Good morning, sir."

Victor sits up, revealing the worn expression on his face. His five o'clock shadow is thick, he's breathing heavily, and his eyes look tired but don't show the dark veins. He says, "Good morning, Garret."

Garret moves to the chairs at the front of the desk, pauses before sitting, asking, "How was the trip to Chambersburg?"

"Long. Uneventful. But they were more cooperative than Dover," Victor answers quickly.

Jacob is staring into Victor's strong gaze. Nobody speaks.

Finally, Victor asks, "Chloe say she enjoyed last night?"

"She seemed pleasant and excited on the ride back from the Andersons', sir."

Wait. This memory is from this morning? Jacob thinks.

"Good," Victor mutters weakly. He rises from his seat and walks slowly to the framed notebook paper, opens the safe behind the frame, then stands, breathing heavily for several seconds. He pulls a folder from the middle of the stack, then walks back to the desk. Sighing heavily, exasperated, Victor looks at Garret; the dark veins have appeared around his eyes. He says, "I'm out of time, Garret."

Garret doesn't reply, he just holds a stare looking over Victor who opens the folder. Inside, the top page reads BETTER HUMAN – TRIAL with a photo of Jacob paperclipped to the top.

What the fuck? Jacob thinks watching Victor flip pages and stopping at NEURO STRAIN with a picture of David clipped to the top. The edge of another picture is sticking out from behind it but not enough to see the image.

"They didn't find any candidates for another test subject on the last hunt," Victor speaks. His voice is weak. "And even if they did, I'm questioning the time that would be available."

"A subject to transfer memories, sir?"

Victor nods. "Promise me you see this through if–"

Garret nods.

"All the subjects for this strain were failures." He speaks with disappointment, pushing the folder away from him. Pages fall out onto the desk but Jacob can't see what they say as

Garret holds his focus on Victor. "All the others needed a *few* tweaks to get successful subjects. But I can't crack this one." He points his finger at Garret. "It's time, Garret. The boy's sample we took at the beginning of the week worked on Elliot. His busted eye healed in hours."

"Jacob's blood sample?"

"Yes." Victor replies with a devious smile.

Jacob feels his heart skip a beat.

"What are you thinking, sir?" Garret asks.

"I need a stronger sample from the boy," Victor demands.

Jacob feels like his heart is beating in his throat.

"He was unhappy about the original sample, sir. I don't foresee him agreeing to–"

"We can't give him a choice."

Another minute of staring transpires. Victor stands from his lean over the desk. He says, "I'll need more than blood samples. I'll need marrow and brain tissue."

Stuttering, Garret requests elaboration. "Brain tissue?"

Pacing, Victor says, "Without the time to fully research what drives his healing factor, I need to be sure I have all possible samples to work with."

"You said Elliot healed from the blood sample. Wouldn't that mean–"

"Elliot has a version of Better Human genetics. It's more than likely a significant factor as to why it worked with only a blood sample."

Garret sighs. "How many subjects have survived a brain tissue sample being taken from them?"

Victor stops with his back turned to Garret. He speaks softly, saying, "Why are you going here, Garret?"

Jacob hears Garret's sigh inside his sinuses. "To be sure you've thought this through sir."

Victor remains still staring out the large windows. The quiet becomes so thick that Jacob hears wind pulsing against the glass before Victor mutters, "Three."

"Out of how many, sir?"

"Thirty-eight."

Silence overtakes the office again. Victor walks slowly back to his chair. The dark veins have spread to the sides of his face and forehead. His weak expression holds a stare with Garret as he says, "I need you to make this happen."

"And if this kills the boy?"

"It would be an unfortunate casualty," Victor replies. His eyes roll back and close as he lays his head back, looking as if he passed out.

Jacob feels his own breathing become rapid while Garret stands from his seat. He leaves the office, nods to Rebecca while buttoning his suit jacket, then walks to the elevator. He steps inside and presses the L button. As the doors close, the metal mirrors a nearly perfect reflection. Garret stares into his own eyes, which feels like he's staring directly at Jacob.

"Wake up, Jacob," Garret says, holding the stare.

"Wake up, Jac—"

Jacob gasps. He's in the vehicle. It's parked in the facility's garage. He sees Garret staring at him in the rearview mirror.

"It's… It's been you," Jacob says. His heart rate is elevated. His breathing is rapid. "You've been projecting these memories onto me."

Garret nods.

"You're the successful third strain?"

Garret nods again.

"D-Does… Victor know this?"

Garret shakes his head.

"Why are you showing me this?" This is one of hundreds of questions spinning through his head.

"He cannot get your samples, Jacob."

Jacob looks around the garage and grips his backpack with a white-knuckled grip. "Why? How... Why can't... What do I do? Why'd you bring me here if he's–"

"He will use anything and anyone to get to you. And he knows you are close to Chloe. You need to get Chloe and get out of the facility."

"H-How? I–"

Garret holds the keys in the air for Jacob to see, then sets them in the cup holder. "Five, eight, nine, one," He says, then exits the vehicle.

What? Jacob thinks. He escapes from the rear seat, leaving the door open, and walks quickly to the door. He turns to see if Garret is coming to enter the code, then realizes what those numbers were.

He enters them on the keypad, which releases the lock on the door. Jacob pulls the door open and bursts through, ready to dodge past the training room and get to Chloe's room, when fast footsteps approach from behind him and a hand grabs his wrist.

Stopping him and turning him around is Noel. He's more disheveled than ever. His skin is pale, the whites of his eyes are completely red, and purple bags lie underneath both of his eyes. He pulls Jacob's hand over and places a piece of paper in his palm. He says, "Take this."

Jacob looks at the note. It reads:

1793 Cameron Dr – NORTH of the city
1004

589 Long Street – WEST of the city

"What are these?"

"Jacob." Noel's expression becomes serious. He winces as he is hearing all of Jacob's thoughts screaming inside his head, then fights it off with a scrunched face, saying, "I saw your father the day he died."

"What?" Jacob replies, shocked.

"Victor was with him. They were fighting about… You."

Jacob's jaw opens to speak, but he says nothing.

Noel continues, holding his forehead, "Your dad knew what Victor was up to. I heard him thinking while he was being interrogated by Victor. He recorded something and hid it in a safe at the house he and your mom lived in before the near-extinction.

"He wanted to stop Victor by getting his files and the recording to CC News."

Jacob feels a lump in his throat. He stutters, then asks, "This is the–"

"The address to his house in the old-world." Noel winces again.

"The numbers underneath?"

"The combination to his safe."

Jacob looks at the note, then asks, "What's the second address?"

Grasping his forehead with both hands, Noel grunts, "You're about to find out."

Running footsteps and panting approaches from the dorm hall. Chloe runs to Jacob and Noel, sobbing. She says, frantically, "Jacob… David is gone!"

"Gone?"

"Look!" She shoves a heavily wrinkled piece of folded paper into his chest.

Jacob unfolds it and reads:

Chloe,

I had to leave quickly. Noel told me everything. That they're done working with me. I can't let Victor decide my fate.

I will forever appreciate our friendship.

Don't come looking for me.

-David

Chloe grabs Jacob's arm and says, "I don't care. We *need* to find him. He's not well."

Jacob gazes at Chloe. Her eyes are pink and swollen from crying. He's not changing her mind, and Garret said he needed to get her out of here. This may be the perfect opportunity.

"I'm going to grab my backpack, and we can go. Meet me down at that small garage." She motions her head down the hall, then runs back toward her room.

Noel looks intently at Jacob and says, "You'll need to find him soon. You don't have much time."

CHAPTER 23

"MUCH TIME UNTIL WHAT?" Jacob asks suspiciously.

Noel's glossy eyes bounce between Jacob's. He takes a breath and says, "David has a bottle of my sleeping pills." He watches Jacob's eyebrows lower. "He intends on taking all of them."

"Will that..."

Noel nods. "He intends to never wake up."

Frustrated, Jacob says, "Why would... Why would he do that?"

Noel steps closer to Jacob. He says sternly, "Stop fighting the thoughts in your head, Jacob. I can hear them. You're putting the pieces together, you just don't want them to fit."

Jacob bites the inside of his cheek as he waits for Noel to continue.

"With the shit we go through here, we're forced to find our own peace."

Jacob closes his eyes and pinches the bridge of his nose. "Okay. Okay," he mutters. Holding up the note Noel gave him, he points and says, "This is where he's going for sure?"

"Yes."

Jacob sighs and walks toward the small garage.

"Jacob," Noel says. Jacob turns to see his eyes are filled with tears. "When Victor gets here and sees it's only me, he's going to question me."

Jacob waits as Noel stutters.

Pointing to the IV port in his hand, Noel says, "If I don't give him answers, they switch the medicine that helps me sleep with a chemical that burns and feels like my brain is on fire. I… He uses it to get information out of me."

"Noel, I," Jacob watches him squeeze the corners of his eyes to stop the tears. "I'll… We'll find a way to stop him."

"It's not that, Jacob. I'm telling you how long you have until I tell him where you are going."

Eyes widened, Jacob replies, "What? Why… You can't… Can't you lie and–"

Noel shakes his head with more tears falling from his chin to his shirt.

"I… I understand." Jacob hugs Noel, patting the top of his back. "I'll find David. I'll find my dad's safe. We'll stop him before he does anything else."

"Your father was terrified. He didn't know how to stop Victor and protect you at the same time."

"We're going to finish what my dad started."

"He'll send the others after you," Noel warns Jacob.

"I'll figure it out," Jacob replies. He stops talking when he hears footsteps echo as Chloe sprints back from her room. Her ponytail bounces off her shoulder. She stops and stands next to them catching her breath.

"Let's go," she says impatiently, then scurries to the small garage.

"I'll see you as soon as this is all over, Noel." Jacob nods and jogs to join Chloe.

Chloe enters the garage then immediately runs to the exit door. Jacob stops at the workbench and sorts through the maps that are available.

"West of the city," Jacob mumbles as he sifts through them. "We're west of the city here." He confirms with a map showing a circle where the Conservation City lies and a square signifying the facility.

"Come on, Jacob," Chloe yells from the door she's holding open.

"Hold on." Jacob searches for Long Street in the directory. He finds it, finds the coordinates, then locates the street. It's not far from where he was on the hunt.

"What are you doing?" Chloe asks with little patience.

"Noel told me where David was going. It's right here, not that far aw–"

"How does he know?" Chloe interrupts.

Jacob raises his eyebrows and answers with his eyes.

"Oh." Chloe forces a chuckle. "That makes sense."

"Right outside the door, we'll cut through this patch of woods. Jump to this street and walk here, cut through these houses and that brings us to Long Street."

Shrugging at how quickly he displayed his plan, she says, "Okay, I'll follow your lead."

Chloe stays close to Jacob as he references the map while they walk through the woods. They emerge at the three-way intersection and begin walking down the street ahead.

Jacob folds the map and sighs. They'll be following this street for a few blocks.

"You want to tell me what's going through your mind?" Chloe asks, referring to his slouching shuffle.

"It wasn't me reading minds, Chlo," he says. She looks at him, puzzled. "It was Garret showing me his memories."

"H-How do you know this for sure?"

"He told me."

"But Victor has been saying he needs to find a subject that can do that. Why would he need that if Garret can–"

"He said Victor doesn't know."

Chloe's face scrunches in frustration. "How wouldn't Victor know this?"

Jacob shrugs and opens his mouth to reply when a shriek pierces through the air. Both of them freeze. Jacob scans the area around them and sees a Shrieker up ahead on the road. Its arms are held outward, twitching violently with its head circling in quick, jerking motions.

"Over here," Jacob whispers, pointing to the house on their left. They walk quickly off the street. Jacob watches the Shrieker. Its head jerks toward them, then its entire body freezes. *Please don't see us...* Jacob stands stiff while Chloe hides against the house. His fear is confirmed as it lunges into a sprint toward them, releasing a high-pitched growl.

"We have to run," Jacob says quickly, motioning for Chloe to leave her hiding spot. "Through those trees and the next yard!" he yells ahead at her.

Glancing behind him, he sees the Shrieker turn off the street and run through the yard toward them.

All he can think about it protecting Chloe. He needs to stay ahead of the Shrieker, but also stay between it and Chloe. He watches ahead as Chloe enters the next backyard. Jacob can hear its raspy breathing catching up behind him.

Chloe turns at the front of the house. Jacob feels his lungs burn as he pushes his sprint faster, only a few paces away from turning the corner behind her. As he turns, she pulls him down between small bushes and shushes him. Adrenaline is coursing through his veins so much that he feels them stretching his skin. She points to the road.

Jacob looks to the street and sees himself standing and looking calmly off in the distance. Heavy footsteps and breathing from the Shrieker burst past them, hissing and sprinting toward Jacob's copy.

His copy runs — faster than Jacob is physically able — away from them down the street. They watch as the Shrieker relentlessly chases Jacob's copy until they're far out of sight.

Laughing while out of breath, Jacob says, "That was an incredible idea."

"Thank you," Chloe says pleasantly. "Was that a… Reject?"

Jacob nods, brushing small leaves out of his hair.

"They're horrifying."

"Yeah," he replies, standing from the overgrown shrubbery. "All the times my friends and I have been outside the walls, we never saw them. Now, I've seen two in just a few weeks."

Jacob brushes off his hoodie while walking toward the street. A house, three down on the left, has the bed of a pickup truck sticking out from the front wall. Two other cars are crashed behind it, occupying the edge of the yard and the road. He turns and looks above the stop sign near them and sees the street sign reads, LONG ST. "This is where we want to be," he says, checking the house numbers, confirming the direction they need to go. "This way." He points the direction his copy lured the Shrieker away.

Seven houses down, they walk past a dusty police car filled with dents all over the sides and hood. It's parked sideways on the street with a line of cars on the other side. Jacob tries to look inside as they pass but the windows are brown and covered in years of dust and dirt. They arrive at the address Noel noted. A yellow-sided home with white shutters and white front door, all tinted green from moss and vines growing along the trim.

"This should be it," Jacob says, looking at Chloe, who is fixed on the front door.

"What do you think he's doing here?" she asks nervously.

"I, uh… Chlo, there's a chance we may not like what we find. Are you sure you want to–"

"Yes," she interrupts, and walks to the door.

The front door is unlocked. They both step inside into a living room that looks as though someone violently ran through, destroying and flipping furniture and knocking the TV face-down on the floor. Dark stains are on the floor under their feet and near the steps to their right. Ahead is an opening to a kitchen. Labored breathing can be heard from the other side of the wall.

"David!" Chloe yells, and runs toward the breathing.

Jacob tries to catch her, but she gets away quickly. He hears her gasp, then yell, "David, what did you do?"

Jacob turns through the opening and sees David hunched in a chair at a dining table with a fallen chandelier on top. He is actively trying to keep himself awake and focused on Chloe. His arm rests on the table next to an empty pill bottle.

"Chloe," he says weakly.

She approaches, kneeling next to his chair. Beginning to sob, she gently grabs his arm.

Moving as if it weighs a hundred pounds, David lifts his head and looks at Jacob. He forces a weak smile on his pale face and says, "Hey, Jake."

"Hey… David," he replies softly.

"We can help you, David. It's not too late to get them out of your system. Let's just go back. It's not far. We can–"

"Chlo." He slowly grabs her hand and tries to sit up. "I… This is what I want."

"But… Why, David?" Her voice quivers.

"I'm haunted by my own memories. It's no way to live."

"You've been training to control… What if…" she stutters. David squeezes her hand, slowly shaking his head.

"Thank you, Chlo… For always being… For everything." David speaks slowly.

He looks up at Jacob. The corners inside his eyes have small red veins creeping in. His pupils are dilated. Through their stare, Jacob sees a tiredness in David's eyes, but not a kind of tired he's seen before. Not one that desperately needs sleep, but one that needs peace. The weakness behind his heavy eyelids beg for a long-fought battle inside to end. As David's eyes grow glossy, Jacob feels a tightness in his chest. He nods to David while giving a tight smile.

Jacob touches Chloe's shoulder and says, "Come on, Chlo. We should leave him be."

She looks at David while tears rush down her face. He touches her cheek and says, "Thank you for being my greatest friend. I promise, I'll be living my favorite memory when I go."

Chloe lunges forward, squeezing David in a hug. Jacob watches him smile as he weakly wraps his arms around her.

She holds the hug until David's arms drop, then stands next to Jacob. David is showing that keeping his eyes open is a struggle. He forces another smile and says, "Goodbye. Thank you for being… Friends…"

He watches Jacob put his arm around Chloe as they quietly walk away and leave the house.

David looks at the wall across the room as he allows his eyes to close. The curled strips of peeling paint heal and become a vibrant green. The broken chandelier now hangs beautifully above his head. On the table in front of him is a mostly eaten bowl of chocolate chip ice cream. Behind him, he hears the evening news playing in the other room. He sees his nine-year-old hand grab the spoon and take the last bite.

"Alright, my little sweet treat monster, it's time for bed!" his mother's voice sings as he's tickled from behind.

Young David giggles and turns in the chair to see his mom smiling brightly at him. She's just as he remembers. Long brown hair. Comforting blue eyes. She's wearing her purple long sleeve pajama shirt and matching pants.

"Okay, mommy!" he says, hopping out of his chair. He races through the living room past the glowing TV, bursts up the stairs while smacking his hand between the posts of the railing, then sprints into his bedroom. Dark blue walls are lit by the glowing lamp on the nightstand next to his bed. He dives in, pulls the covers up to his chin and looks at the glow in the dark stars he haphazardly put on the wall above his bed as he waits for his mom to come into the room.

She walks in and sits on the bed next to his legs.

"Mommy?" he addresses her.

"Yes, my darling?" she asks, resting her hand on his leg over the covers. Her precious little boy loves to ask questions to delay going to sleep — it's a part of the routing she'll cherish as long as she can.

"Where do we go when we close our eyes forever?" David asks.

With a comforting smile, she leans forward and says, "That's an amazing question with an amazing answer."

"It is?"

"Yes, it is." She pinches his cheek. "You know why?"

"Why?"

Whispering as if she is sharing a secret with him, she says, "Because when we close our eyes forever, we get to go to the most beautiful place we can think of. And all our favorite people go there with us."

"So, like, our most favorit-est place ever?" David asks.

"Yep," she says confidently. "Anywhere you can dream of, dear." She smiles and rubs his head.

"And anyone I want will be there when I go?"

"Anyone you want will be there," she sings, petting his hair, holding her comforting smile.

"So, grandma, grandpa, our dog Boomer… All of them will be there?" She nods. He continues, "And my best friend, Jimmy. And *you'll* be there, too, mommy?"

"They'll all be there!" She rubs his cheek. "And of course I'll be there. You know I'll *always* go everywhere with you." She leans in and kisses his forehead. As she stands from the bed, she says, "But you don't have to worry about this for a long time, Davey. Okay?"

"Okay, mommy," he says, smiling, watching her walk to the door. She closes it most of the way, then looks back at him.

"Goodnight, my little Davey."

"Goodnight, mommy."

She turns off the bedroom light.

David looks at the ceiling, seeing the glow from the stars in his peripheral vision. He takes in hearing his mom tell him goodnight one more time.

One last time.

He slowly closes his eyes, falling asleep. Forever.

CHAPTER 24

HEAVINESS WEARS ON JACOB AND Chloe like a weighted vest. Chloe's is heavier than his, as she has fallen behind, shuffling on the street. He sees her walking with her head hanging and tucks the map into his hoodie pocket, waiting to walk next to her.

Jacob takes in the houses on the street as they continue on slowly. The stillness of their surroundings feels quieter than usual. Untouched mailboxes hold envelopes with time-stamped dates of when the world almost ended. Each home's interior paints a portrait of another family's last day inside. He listens to Chloe's sobs become softer while focusing on a gray-blue home on their left. The front door contains seven small holes with pieces from them on the porch. A blackened, bloody handprint streaks from the middle of the door to the bottom, where a tattered pile of clothes sits with dried bones protruding from the arm and leg holes. Jacob wonders if the person inside made it out.

They pass a few more homes and weave through a cluster of totaled vehicles at an intersection. On the other side of the wreck, Chloe stops and waits for Jacob to look at her. Her braided ponytail is messy, hanging over her shoulder. She shrugs to Jacob and says, "Where are we going? This isn't the way we came."

"We need to get north of the city. To this address," he replies, holding up the piece of paper from Noel.

Chloe squints at the address, then says, "North of the city? That will take us hours on foot." Her voice carries impatience Jacob hadn't heard in her before. "We need to get back to the facility and tell Victor what happened here."

Sighing, Jacob says, "We can't go back there." He turns and continues walking in the street.

"Why, Jacob?" Chloe yells as she walks to keep up with him.

Jacob keeps walking and doesn't reply.

"Jacob." Her tone is angry. "Why aren't we going back?"

He continues walking as if he doesn't hear her.

Chloe runs to him and grabs his shoulder. They stand in the middle of the street surrounded by tall standing weeds protruding through large cracks in the worn pavement. The silence in the air softly echoes their conversation. She says, "Talk to me. Why can't we go back?" She detects his reluctance to make eye contact with her. Leaning to catch his attention, she adds, "What's at this address that's so important?"

Frustrated at the realization that there's no way for him to avoid this, Jacob looks at her and says, seriously, "Proof of everything Victor has been up to. That's what is at this address."

Chloe steps back and expresses disdain, saying, "Proof of what? What is it that you think he's up to, Jacob?"

"What happens when a subject doesn't take well to his serums, Chlo?" he asks angrily.

"I… I don't–" she stutters, looking around.

"They become one of those things that chased us."

"You don't know that–"

"And what is this *Vitality* project he's trying to piece together?" He stares at her, waiting for an answer.

Chloe sniffles and is now the one avoiding eye contact. He sees her fidgeting with her hands, uncomfortably. Changing his tone, he says calmly, "He wants to take more samples from me, Chlo." She looks at him now, showing she's listening. "He wants my brain tissue, and he doesn't care if it kills me."

Shaking her head in disbelief, she says, "No. Jacob. No. He wouldn't let something kill you. You're his best friend's–"

"Chlo, even David didn't trust Victor. Your closest friend. I heard him twice telling you he–"

"David was disappointed in himself. And he coped with that by taking it out on Victor."

Jacob scoffs. "Why do you insist on defending Victor?"

"Because after all the tests and experiments I went through, being poked and stabbed and told these tests could take the *miracles of my genetics* and bring cures and enhancements to the world… Maybe, just *maybe*, I'd like to hope that it's still worth something, Jacob." She stares at him.

Deciding he doesn't want to argue with her, Jacob shakes his head, turns and continues walking. Chloe sighs, then yells, "Where are you going? We *need* to go back to the facility."

Turning to face her again, Jacob says, calmly, as to not stir another fight, "I'm not going back, Chlo."

"What has you so convinced that what you think is true, Jacob?" she asks, her voice defeated.

"I told you. Garret showed me his memories. He showed me Victor speaking it. He told me I'm the–"

"Jacob," Chloe interrupts. She rubs her hands on her face then through her hair, causing more strands to come loose from her braid, laughing sarcastically, saying, "And you think that's genuine?"

Expressing confusion, Jacob says, "Why wouldn't it be? They are *his* memories?"

"They can be fabricated, Jacob. Changed to show you *whatever* he wants you to see."

Shrugging his arms in exasperation, he sighs and says, "Why would he–" He freezes when he sees Chloe's expression change.

She raises her hand and snaps her finger. Amber appears next to her. But instead of seeing his mom as he's used to, she's bloody, her lips are bitten off. She's hunched over, swaying her upper body from side to side as if looking for someone. Her eyes are dilated and bloodshot. A patch of her hair is missing as if ripped from her skull. She shrieks, freezing her movements when she makes eye contact with Jacob. Chloe lowers her hand and Amber sprints toward Jacob.

Raising his hands to his face, bracing for impact from his mom in Shrieker form, Jacob groans, watching with one eye over his arm as she hisses, jumping toward him, then disappears right before attacking him. "See?" Chloe tilts her head. "If I can show you anything I want, why couldn't he?"

"Whatever, Chlo," Jacob speaks angrily. He turns to walk away and finds his dad standing behind him.

Arms held outward, Ethan smiles and says, "Hey, bud! Come and give your old man a hug!"

Jacob walks forward and pushes his dad to the side, out of his way. Appearing directly in front of him is Chloe. She tilts her head to the side, raises her eyebrows and says, "I can show you whatever I want. Just how Garret could."

Allowing his shoulder to aggressively bump into hers, he walks past, yelling, "Stop!"

Elliot appears in the yard to the right, charging at Jacob with his fists clenched, ready to strike. He jumps unnaturally high into the air. Knowing that Chloe will make Elliot vanish, Jacob ignores the projection.

As Elliot quickly approaches Jacob, he doesn't disappear but instead connects a powerful punch with Jacob's cheek.

Waves ripple through his cheek where Elliot's knuckles drive into his skin, sending a thick stream of bloody saliva from his lips and down his chin. Elliot is now gone. Jacob wipes his chin with his sleeve, turns to Chloe and yells, "Are you serious, Chlo? What the f– " He stops himself and turns angrily away from her to keep walking.

Standing in front of him is his dad again. He's holding his arms out, smiling, but this time he's bloody, wounded, and twitching like a Shrieker. His voice wavers in pitch as he says, "Victor was my best friend, Jacob. Why would he want to hurt you?"

Jacob shoves his dad to the ground. He turns to Chloe and screams, "Enough! Okay? Enough." He sees her angry expression glaring at him. Scoffing and rubbing his face angrily, Jacob marches back toward Chloe, asking, "Fine. I'll entertain your idea. What motivation would Garret even have to fabricate memories about Victor and show me?"

"Who do you think would take over?" she asks.

"What?"

"If Victor was framed and removed from leading the city. Who do you think would take over?"

"You think Garret would–"

"Of course he would. These cities always go with the direct assistant. Someone that already has an 'in' and knows how things operate."

Jacob rubs his eyes in frustration, then runs the back of his hand across his bottom lip. Only a small amount of blood remains. He rolls his eyes then looks at her and says, "No. Just… No." He turns and walks away.

"You're not even going to think about the possibility that he could–"

"No, Chlo." Jacob turns back again. "I only had to think about it for a second before I realized it's crazy."

Scoffing, Chloe says, "Right. And your theory isn't."

"There's something there, Chlo. I can feel it in my gut. And I think, deep down, you know there's a chance it's true." He looks at her intently.

"And what if you're wrong?"

Shrugging his arms, Jacob says, "I'd rather do this and find out I'm wrong, than do nothing and find out I was right."

Wind rustles through the tall grass in the yards next to them as they stare at each other in silence. Jacob thinks about Garret telling him to keep her away from Victor. He thinks that right now, at this moment, he's close to failing that request.

In what feels like a last chance effort, Jacob calms himself and says, "How about this: come with me to this address. If there's something there, we look into what it is and consider pursuing it. If there's nothing there," he sighs, "I'll drop it."

"Fine."

"Fine?"

"Yeah. Fine." She waves her arms. "I'll go with you. Just… Where are we even going? Show me on the map."

Jacob unfolds the map and shows her the path they walked since leaving David's old-world home. "Here's the facility." Jacob points at the rectangle drawn over the mall. He finds a tightness in his chest from his frustration with Chloe as he speaks. With short words, while sliding his finger to the right of the map, he says, "Here's the city." Moving his finger up, he adds, "Here's the address north of the city." Rustling the map, he pokes his finger back at where he started explaining, saying, "And we're here."

Expressing the same shortness of patience with her voice, Chloe says, "So, we're just going to casually walk from here and swim across this river?" She mirrors his poke on the map.

Her sarcasm strikes a nerve as he replies, "Do you have any better i–" He stops. *The keys.* Garret left him keys.

Chloe widens her eyes and twitches her head at Jacob, waiting for him to finish.

"Follow me," he says, folding up the map as he starts walking toward the facility.

"Jacob," Chloe yells. He turns around and sees her holding her arms out with confusion. "Are you going to tell me where we're going?"

"To the facility." His words are still short.

"You literally just fought me on going there."

"Just…" Jacob rolls his eyes and motions his arms forward. "I have a plan. Okay?" He turns and continues walking.

Chloe mutters, "Whatever," and walks behind him.

They follow the path back in silence. Arriving back at the facility, they enter the small garage, passing the workbench holding maps and tools. Jacob grabs a folded knife and puts it in his back pocket.

Quietly, to avoid anyone hearing him, Jacob opens the door to the hallway. Dim lights shine across the center of the ceiling tiles, reflecting off the ceramic floor. They crouch and tiptoe ahead to the turn and look around the corner, confirming the facility is unoccupied. The only noise they hear is their own breathing. Standing up, they walk to the left, entering the large garage.

Jacob remembers the parking spot from earlier and locates the vehicle with the keys inside. Not wanting to speak to Chloe, he points forward and walks toward the vehicle.

As he's opening the driver side door, Chloe asks, "Have you driven before?"

Annoyed that her tone shows she's also still frustrated, Jacob says, "No."

"Let me, then." She waves him away and steps in front of him, entering the driver's seat.

Rolling his eyes, he walks around the front of the vehicle. Lights turn on with an echoing clang as they illuminate the other half of the garage, triggered by his motion. He enters the passenger seat, closing the door and asking while buckling his seatbelt, "So, *you've* driven before?"

"Yeah." Her reply is short. She presses the garage door opener on the visor.

Jacob watches her push to start the vehicle.

"You keep forgetting that how *you* grew up inside the walls is much different than how it is out here," she says defensively, putting the vehicle in drive and accelerating out of the garage.

CHAPTER 25

JACOB LEANS THE SIDE OF his forehead against the passenger window, peering inside the abandoned cars along the parkway as he listens to the phone ringing on his left ear.

"Where you been at, bro?" Deante answers.

"Hey, D," Jacob replies with his head turning, following a vehicle he saw a corpse inside.

"What's all that wooshy noise?"

"We're driving. Chloe and I."

"Oh," Deante says singingly. Switching his voice to serious, he says, "You're with your girl, why you sound defeated?"

"It's a long story." Jacob leans forward in his seat. "Listen. We're going to have to do the Power Play. Can you get Kyle and Renz on board and meet Chloe and I at that house we last looted north of the city?" He catches Chloe quickly glancing at him in his peripheral vision.

"Damn. The Power Play. Yeah, I can get them on board." Deante stutters the last words, preparing to ask, "You want to tell me why you sound like your mom took away your comics again?"

"Yeah, I'll explain it all there," Jacob replies. Wanting to give Deante something, he adds, "It has to do with my dad. He hid shit about Victor in his old-world home. We need to get it, and we'll probably need Kyle to hack into it."

"What kind of shit? Bad shit?"

"Would someone hide good shit?"

"Holy shit."

"Yeah." There's a pause in the conversation while Jacob resumes observing the lines of rotted and overgrown vehicles they're driving through. "So… Make sure Kyle brings his hacking stuff."

"Got it. I'll get them together now, and we'll head out right away."

"Cool. Thanks, man."

"Sure thing. Hang in there." Deante gives a short chuckle and says, "Tell your girl I'm excited to meet her."

Jacob rolls his eyes and involuntarily sends a short laugh from his nose. "Later." He ends the call.

While putting his phone in his pocket, Chloe says, "So… Power Play?"

His head quickly turns to look at her. He wasn't expecting an attempt at conversation yet. He replies, "Yeah. It's where we each tell our parents we're staying overnight at the other's house."

She forces a smile from the corner of her mouth.

Elaborating, he says, "We'd do that so we could sneak outside the walls and not have to worry about–"

"Yeah. I put it together, Jacob," she cuts him off.

Feeling a knot in his chest from her interruption and short tone, Jacob drops his head.

With a light chuckle, she says, "I didn't realize you all were such rebels."

Jacob looks at her through the corner of his eyes and smiles. It feels good that she is joking with him. He opens his mom's contact on his phone and stares at the screen, contemplating what to say, realizing it's another lie to tell her, then decides not to do it now for Chloe to hear. Instead, he puts the phone back into his pocket, sighs, and looks ahead as they approach the downhill portion of the parkway where they can see the entire walled-in Conservation City.

Volcan Enterprises stands looming toward the western gate, as if to remind them that it oversees the whole city. The northern and eastern walls hold the redesigned neighborhoods with the same copy-and-paste houses sitting the same distances apart.

They both admire the view as they approach the city, passing the western gate. Up ahead, the road is untravellable due to abandoned cars blocking the highway. These were never cleared, as trade routes didn't need to travel in this direction.

"Pull over up here. We'll have to walk from there." Jacob points above the dashboard.

Chloe pulls the vehicle over on the shoulder of the road and turns the engine off. They both exit the vehicle and observe their surroundings. Beyond the congestion of the vehicles crowding the streets sit old brick buildings with broken windows and doors. Street signs on the sidewalks are bent over, nearly touching the concrete. Further away is a tan-brick police station, where faded and ripped clothes lie scattered across the front with gray bones sticking out of the pile.

"How far is it?" Chloe asks as she turns her attention away from the devastated buildings. They stand next to a concrete guide rail at the edge of the highway. She leans over, looking at the short drop to tall grass.

"Well, from our rope–" He sees her whip her head toward him with a questioning expression. "It's… The rope we use to get over the walls from inside. From there it's not a far walk at all. But I think our walk along *this* wall will be longer."

Jacob hops over the guide rail into the tall grass. He turns and offers his hand to help Chloe. She ignores the gesture and hops over confidently. They begin walking along the wall through the grass. Layers of trees up ahead are losing their leaves, and the remaining leaves are turning different shades of brown and orange. As the two of them enter the wooded area, Chloe wraps her arms around Jacob's arm.

Jacob hides a smile of relief, happy that this might mean that both their frustrations are subsiding.

Used to the stillness and quiet of their surroundings, Jacob looks around as they walk along the wall, hoping they're approaching familiar territory for him. Assuming this walk would take about the same time as his walk to school, he is realizing it's much longer. Looking at the combination of block and poured concrete, combined with the length of this walk, he appreciates what it must have taken to build this quickly during the outbreak. He feels Chloe's squeeze on his arm tighten with each twig snap and tree rustle when a strong wind blows through the woods.

They finally step out from the patch of woods, and off to the right, in the distance, Jacob sees the rope from their tree hanging over the wall. "There it is," he says with relief. "Not too far from here now."

The warm yellow glow of the sky begins to deepen in color as they walk through the tall, overgrown grass. Through another small patch of trees, it brings them to the neighborhood. They cut through the backyard of a house with a rotted swing set barely standing on the legs of decayed wood.

The glass storm door is shattered next to a concrete patio with large patches of weeds and grass growing between the cracks.

Chloe sighs when they arrive in the street. She gazes ahead at the line of houses in front of her. Shutters dangle on vines wrapped over windows. Sun-stained and rusted cars occupy driveways overgrown with tall weeds. "It's so… Sad," she mutters quietly.

"Yeah." Jacob looks around with her. This is not his first time here, but it feels the heaviest. As if each family's fate is scripted by the condition of the home. "We're heading to that house up there on the left." He points ahead and begins walking.

As they approach the house, Chloe asks, "Do you think your friends are here already?"

Jacob steps quietly onto the porch and says, softly, "I feel like we'd have heard them if they were."

He turns the doorknob slowly, confirming it's still unlocked. Opening the door quietly, he steps a foot inside, peering into the living room. The dark-orange glow of the sun casts a shadow in front of him.

Inside the shadow stands a tall figure. It's standing still; not moving.

CHAPTER 26

THE DIMMING, SETTING SUN AND mostly vine-covered windows allow for little light to shine in the living room on the figure. It continues to stand with its back facing Jacob. If this was a Shrieker, it'd be twitching. Jacob crouches and walks quietly and slowly toward them, holding the knife from the workbench tightly in his hand, just in case. With light footsteps he gets closer, still unable to make out the figure standing in the shadows, when suddenly Deante yells from the steps, "Bro! You made it!"

Jacob is startled. He looks at Deante, then back in front of him to see Kyle turned around, smiling, holding a tablet in his hands.

"What's up, Jacob?" Kyle says, noticing Jacob's heavy breathing. "What's got you worked up?"

"I thought... It's nothing," Jacob lies. He puts the knife back in his pocket secretly, hoping nobody noticed him holding it. "Your tall lanky ass is creepy standing in the shadows, though," he says to Kyle with a forced chuckle.

"You must be Chloe," Deante says, shuffling past Jacob to introduce himself. "I'm Deante, but you can call me D." He kisses the back of her hand.

Chloe looks at Jacob and they share a soft smile. Jacob rolls his eyes and shakes his head playfully.

"Hi, D," she says with a smile.

"Where's Renz?" Jacob asks.

"Oh, he's checking to make sure all the doors and windows are closed and locked. He was pretty paranoid about it," Deante answers.

"Got it!" Kyle exclaims, shaking the tablet in his hands. He sees the three of them staring at him. "The city's Wi-Fi… I got in," he mutters as he unplugs another device from the tablet.

"So… What's the plan, then?" Deante asks Jacob.

"Okay," he says, pulling the map from his pocket. Snaps of rustling paper travel from the floor as he kneels and slides his hand from corner to corner. The door down the short hall past the steps opens and Renz exits. "Hey, man," Jacob greets him.

"H-Hey," Renz says, scurrying quickly to the group. "H-Hi. You must be–"

"Chloe. Hi, Renz." She smiles and shakes his hand.

"We're here." Jacob lands his finger on their location. "The address for my dad's old-world home is here." He traces roads a short way. "If we follow the streets through this neighborhood, and reach *this* main road, here… Follow it to *here*… That'll take us to the neighborhood with his house." He looks up to see all of them following his route. "Shouldn't be more than maybe an hour to ninety minute walk? We crash here for the night then leave when the sun rises?" He speaks both sentences as a question and waits for a response.

They nod their heads and Kyle says, "I like it. Sounds great."

"I saw a closet upstairs with a bunch of sheets and blankets in it last time we were here," Deante says. "Might be dusty and shit, but we can just shake 'em off or whatever."

Chloe shrugs and says, "Works for me."

"Girl. You get first dibs to pick a bed if you want," Deante insists. "They're probably pretty gross and dusty but, like, you do you."

"I… I'm fine wherever, D," She replies.

Renz says nervously, "Why don't we all just bring stuff down here and crash in the living room? Probably safer from–"

"From what?" Deante chuckles. "This might be the first house without a caved-in door or broken window. We're fine dude."

Seeing Renz is legitimately nervous, Jacob says, "Renz is right. There's enough space here we can still be out of each other's business or whatever." He scans for agreement, sees relief in Renz, then says, "Better if we're all together for the night."

"This person's tablet had movies downloaded on it," Kyle says, holding up the device, adding, "We can play one while we lay here."

"Alright. Cool." Deante gestures to show it's not a big deal to him.

"I also brought snacks," Kyle says, stepping next to the couch, grabbing his backpack and opening the top to reveal protein bars, bottles of water and bags of potato chips.

They all exclaim with excitement. Deante says, "Good thinking, bro." He looks into the living room at the broken lamp from their encounter days ago and says, "Let's clean up and find our places before the sun completely sets."

They all agree. Jacob says, "I'll catch up last, I'm gonna go call my mom and do my part of the Power Play." He motions his phone to them.

"Make it quick, dude, you owe us the story about whatever is going on. Remember?" Deante says.

"I remember. I'll fill you all in after this."

The front upstairs bedroom has a dormer window that leads to the roof on which Jacob sits, fidgeting his dad's watch between his thumb and fingers while staring at the reddening sky. A half-moon peers through transparent coulds, looking over Jacob. He thinks about the phone call he just had with his mom where he lied and told her he was staying overnight at the facility, promising he'd be home tomorrow evening.

Scuffling on shingles catches his attention. He looks over to see Chloe's sneakers hanging out the window, getting their footing, then her knees exiting after. She stands, catching her balance on the sloped roof, and offers a polite smile. "Is it okay to–"

Jacob nods.

With her arms held outward for balance, Chloe carefully walks over to Jacob and sits close to him. She sits with her knees at an angle, mirroring him. Wrapping her arms around her knees, she looks at Jacob's hand shifting the watch between two fingers.

He sees her look at the watch and says, "It was my dad's. My mom gave it to me after…"

After giving him a comforting smile, she leans in close to the watch, squinting. She sits back upward and says, "It died at eleven fifty…" She sings the last syllable, leans back in then quickly back and adds, "Three."

"You can read this?"

"Of cour–" Chloe chuckles, stopping when she sees the puzzled look on his face. "You can't?"

Jacob smiles and blushes with embarrassment, shaking his head.

With a hearty laugh, Chloe says, "You city kids."

He sends a short laugh through his nose before looking back at the watch in his hand. After a minute of quiet, they both look up at the purple to black gradient now blanketing the sky. Stars begin to appear like little holes being poked through a canvas. Jacob turns to Chloe and says, "Chlo, I'm sor–"

"I'm sorry, too, Jacob," she interrupts. "I just… I don't know what to make of all this. Then David…"

"I know," Jacob speaks softly. Forcing another laugh through his nose, he leans toward Chloe, bumping her shoulder and says, "I must've had you really pissed off, huh?"

She tilts her head and creases her eyebrows.

"Victor said our abilities strengthen when our emotions are heightened. And your projection of Elliot *really* hit hard." His chest bounces as he laughs while pointing at his cheek.

Joining him, but with an embarrassed laugh, Chloe stutters, "I am *so* sorry about that."

"It's fine, I promise," he says, softly.

She gently, and briefly, rubs his shoulder.

They both resume looking at the sky, watching stars begin to flicker where the gradient of red and orange turns black. A peaceful quiet defines the solitude of the neighborhood around them. Sighing, Jacob holds up the watch and breaks the silence, saying, "My mom told me the story behind this watch. My dad never fixed it because he said it stopped when she agreed to go on a date with him. Told her it was proof she made his time stop… Or something like that."

"That's so cute," Chloe says with a smile.

Another short chuckle leaves Jacob's lips. "Yeah. They… They had this *whole* other life before the walls. Before me. And I feel like I barely know anything about it." He glances at Chloe and sees she's listening intently. "There are, like, a million questions in my head that I wish I would've asked him before he…" Jacob stares back at the watch.

A light breeze whispers through the swaying trees around them. Chloe remains silent, observing Jacob, waiting to see if he is going to continue.

He sighs, clasps the watch in his fist, and lays back onto the roof with both his hands behind his head. He watches Chloe lay back, then looks at the stars in the sky and says, "One of my favorite stories he did tell me was that there used to be this plan in the old-world to send people to Mars. If they did it, it was going to be a one-way trip. The people wouldn't be able to come back."

"That's terrifying!" Chloe exclaims. "Why would anyone do that?"

Laughing, Jacob says, "Research, I guess? He said they had whole departments in the old-world that focused entirely on studying space. The plan was to find out if we could terraform Mars and make it habitable for humans. They did away with that in the Conservation Cities. It wasn't considered *necessary*."

"Wow," Chloe says softly.

"Yeah." Jacob holds his eyes still and lets the faint shimmering of the stars freeze in his vision. "There was a time when we'd spend almost every Saturday night looking at the stars, and he'd tell me everything he knew about 'the world outside of our world,' as he called it."

"That sounds really nice." Her voice is quiet.

Releasing a sigh, Jacob continues, "I can still picture him laying next to me in the yard. I'd tell him I was going to do it. I was going to fly to Mars *and* come back to tell him about it. He'd smile and say, 'Don't ever think that you can't. How can we ever give ourselves limits when everything out there has none?'" He pauses, looks at Chloe, who is looking back with the most peaceful and calming expression. He rolls his head back to look at the sky and says, "Anyway. That's what my mom was referring to when she said–"

"'Don't ever stop being my boy who's going to fly to Mars,'" Chloe delivers Amber's quote. He looks at her, surprised. She says, "I… The way she said it. The way she looked at you. I could tell it meant something."

"Yeah," he says quietly, once again resuming his stare at the sky.

"Jacob?" Chloe mutters. He turns his head to her. She leans over and kisses him.

His heart races. The warmth of her lips on his feels magical. He closes his eyes and lets this moment last as long as he can.

She leans away, smiling, and her hand rests on his cheek. They smile radiantly at each other and lie back down on the roof to admire the sky once more. This time, their shoulders are touching and their fingers are intertwined.

*** ***

CHLOE AND JACOB took in the peace of the night for a few more minutes, then made their way back to the group in the living room. Jacob filled them in on all the details up to them meeting at this house. They watched a bad movie on Kyle's hacked tablet, laughed together, and fell asleep.

Jacob wakes from a small ray of sunshine beaming through the cracks in the vines on the far window in the living room. He stretches, leans up on his arm and sees Kyle sitting on the dusty couch, tapping away on his tablet.

"Good morning," he chuckles to Jacob.

"Hey, man," Jacob groans with another stretch.

Renz startles himself awake hearing them talk. His eyes are wide as he whips his head around the room in a panic. Jacob and Kyle laugh loud enough to wake Chloe and Deante.

Kyle passes out protein bars to everyone as they sit up, stretch repeatedly, and all grunt and groan to wake up. They eat and gather themselves, agreeing they're ready to get an early start.

Dew covers the long grass in the yard and fallen leaves on the road. They walk north, all moving slowly, yawning and listening to Deante hum the song from the credits of last night's movie.

Renz kicks at stones and weeds standing through cracks in the road, while the sound of the soft wind singing through trees and bushes is interrupted by Jacob unfolding his map as they approach an intersection.

"This is the main road we're looking for," he says, looking up from his map to see his friends looking around in awe. Across the road are storefronts with wrecked cars occupying the edge of the road and parking lot. Construction vehicles sit abandoned in a beveled pit of patchy grass and weeds. Cars litter the road, parked haphazardly as if the drivers were crashing to get through the traffic.

"Ugh," Renz exclaims and turns his head, but not before pointing at a vehicle not far from them. The windshield is broken with darkened, gelled blood on the edges. Inside is a rotted corpse buckled in the driver's seat.

"Do you guys see that?" Deante asks, anxiously.

"Yeah. It's pretty gross," Jacob replies.

"No… *That.*" Deante points to the right up the road. Past the line of cars is the top of a giant wall made of rusted scrap metal and wood panels. "Is that a wall to another Conservation City?"

"Conservation Cities have concrete walls. Not whatever that is," Kyle answers.

"Wh-What do you guys think it–" Renz begins to ask but is interrupted by an ear-piercing screech from behind them.

Jacob quickly turns around and surveys the surroundings. So many cars occupy the road, it's impossible to know if something is crouched between them.

"All of you run that way," he says to them, pointing down the road toward the wall. "A couple hundred feet ahead, take the first left. Find the first place you can get inside and I'll meet you all there."

"Jacob. Are you sure?" Chloe asks, nervously.

"I'll be fine. I'll get rid of it," he answers, keeping a hard focus for any movement. He hears nothing. Which means his friends haven't moved either. He turns and yells, "Go!" He watches them walk fast toward the metal wall.

Jacob begins walking toward the shriek. "Show yourself," he yells. Another screech sounds. It's closer but isn't visible. Jacob climbs on the roof of a sedan. *Where the fuck are you?* he thinks. It shouldn't be this difficult to spot a Shrieker with how twitchy they move.

Jacob stomps on the roof of the vehicle and yells, "Show yourself–" He sees it. Between two cars, only six vehicles away, twitches a head and arms. It sees him now, too.

The Shrieker jerks its torso to run toward Jacob, smacking its arm into a window, shattering it. It yells out in pain but runs between the vehicles toward him. Jacob jumps down from the roof of the sedan and jogs backward to an open spot on the road. He steadies his stance, fists raised. Watching the Shrieker's movements as it approaches.

Its arms twitch violently. Its face is missing skin and muscle on its cheek. Scratches rip through its tattered shirt, revealing slashes in its skin. He watches its footsteps, hip movements, shoulders and arms but can't predict what it's going to do from the sporadic twitching. It's too close now. It lunges at him, slashing both arms at his face. Jacob blocks one but feels the burn of its nails across his cheek near his eye.

"Fuck!" Jacob groans. The Shrieker loses its balance. Jacob grabs it shoulders and throws it off to the side, into the passenger door of a pickup truck. Metal thuds and dents as the Shrieker drops to the ground, groaning and releasing an eerie cry.

It begins to push of the truck. Jacob lifts his knee and drives the treads of his shoe into its chest, kicking it back into the dented door before it falls to its side.

Growling, it now leaps to its feet, crouches forward, and hisses violently at Jacob.

"Oh, shit..."

His breathing instantly becomes heavy as his feet stomp into the pavement in a full sprint through the rusted wreckage of vehicles. He wants to turn and see how close the Shrieker is, but gets his answer as he hears it breathing behind him.

Ahead, the vehicles are cleared off the road, pushed far into the field on the left. He sees the open pavement in front of the large metal wall. Even closer to the wall, over the crest of the road, are his friends, kneeling on the ground with their backs facing him and arms held in the air.

A bang rings through the air followed immediately by a sharp whizzing past his ear, then a gurgle from the Shrieker and thud on the pavement. Jacob turns to see the Shrieker lying face down. He stops running and watches a pool of blood begin to form under its head.

"Put your hands up and drop to your knees!" a voice yells through a megaphone.

Jacob sees the torso of two figures in green hoods standing over the wall — one holding a megaphone, the other holding a rifle with a smoking barrel, pointed directly at him.

"Put your hands above your head and drop to your knees, or we *will* shoot," the voice says again.

Jacob glances once more behind him at the dead Shrieker while slowly raising his hands. He looks at his friends, who are tens of feet in front of him. Chloe and Renz are shaking nervously.

"On your knees! Now!" The voice has lost patience.

Jacob drops to his knees. The pavement stabs through his jeans into his skin. Loud gears clang repeatedly as a latticed metal gate in the wall begins to rise.

Through the squares in the gate, Jacob sees three more hooded figures standing, waiting for the gate to fully open.

CHAPTER 27

A METALLIC BOOM SOUNDS TO signal the gate is stopped. Before the hooded figures move, the one in the center yells, "Nobody move!"

All three wear dark-green hooded jackets, brown cargo pants, and bandanas over the bottoms of their faces. They walk through the gate and move toward Jacob's friends, who remain kneeling on the ground with their hands in the air. Instinctually, he wants to stand and protect his friends, but with the hooded guard over the wall still aiming a rifle at him, it's safer for him to remain still.

The figure in the center walks with their hands latched behind them. The other two walk on either side carrying rifles. As they walk in front of Jacob's friends, the figure in the center yells, "Are all of you together?"

Nobody moves or speaks.

"It would be wise to answer me." Their tone changes to impatient. "Are all of you together?"

Chloe and Deante nod silently.

"And that one is with you?" The center figure kneels in front of Deante and gestures to Jacob.

Deante nods.

"Which of you is in charge?"

Renz and Deante point back to Jacob. Jacob closes his eyes to hide that he's rolling them. He sighs as he opens his eyes to see the figure in the center stand, look over at him, and begin walking his way.

"One of you, stay and watch them," they demand, and one of the armed hooded figures remains standing in front of the friends while the other two walk to Jacob.

Their combat boots thud on the pavement as they approach him. The unarmed figure kneels in front of Jacob. They pull back their hood and reveal long, bright-red hair. Jacob stares into their golden-yellow eyes as they pull the bandana under their chin. Freckles spread across their nose and under their eyes. Jacob gulps, waiting for them to speak.

"What's your name?" they ask him.

"Jacob," he replies quickly.

"My name is Trissa." She stares at Jacob as if awaiting a response.

"Hi, Trissa," he offers as a reply.

"I'm responsible for keeping the walls safe at this compound." She points her arm behind her at the walls. Jacob notices the two figures above the wall are still there. The one on the left is still aiming its rifle at him.

"Is your compound some kind of smaller Conservation City?" Jacob asks, scrunching his face as he adjusts his knees on the uncomfortable pavement.

Trissa scoffs and says, "Conservation City. No. Far from that. This compound was built for *our* safety *from* Conservation Cities. There are many others around here. This one is the most elaborate. And the only one nearby with walls," she says proudly.

There's a pause in the conversation as she surveys Jacob. While she looks over him, he hears Renz sobbing up ahead.

"Put your arms down, kid," Trissa demands Jacob. He sighs with relief, dropping his arms so quickly he scratches his knuckles on the street. She turns her head, yelling behind her, saying, "Tell the rest they can put their arms down. Any sudden movements and they get the same fate as this Ghoul."

Ghoul? Jacob thinks, then realizes she is referring to the Shrieker behind him.

"Why are you here at our walls?" Trissa asks sternly. Her eyes bounce between his, waiting for his reply.

"We just… We stumbled upon your walls on our way to a neighborhood just north of here."

"What is your business in the neighborhood north of here?"

"It's a long, convoluted story," he replies.

"Not sure if you picked up on your surroundings, but you're not going anywhere anytime soon, kid," she says, arrogantly. "Indulge me."

Jacob closes his eyes and exhales with frustration. He opens his eyes and says, "My dad hid… *Supposedly* hid evidence against Victor Volcan in a house north of here, and I need to find it."

Trissa hums and looks over him again. She asks, "Which home is this evidence hidden in?"

Jacob looks at her coldly and says, "I'm not telling you that." He inhales sharply from his nerves.

Trissa leans in close to his face. Her eyes shift between his rapidly still. She smiles, leans back, slaps her hands on her thighs and says, "Fair enough."

Whistling and waving her hand in the air, Tissa motions for the figure on her right to lean in. They hunch forward, revealing the same golden-yellow eyes by staring at Jacob. She speaks into their ear, saying, "Take the group to the cafeteria. Feed them well. Offer them fresh clothes if they wish." Holding her stare at Jacob, she adds, "I'll be in with this one after a few more questions."

"Yes, ma'am," they respond assertively. Standing quickly, they return to Jacob's friends, yelling, "On your feet. Follow me."

Jacob continues the stare between him and Trissa while watching in his peripheral vision as his friends stand and follow the hooded figures through the gates. He hears his jaw crack in his temples as he grinds his teeth together. Glancing above the walls, he sees the megaphone figure has left. The one with the rifle remains at attention, but is no longer aiming at him. His friends disappear behind Trissa, and their footsteps fade away as they walk into the walls. Wind gusts around Trissa and Jacob, twirling leaves between them and over their bent knees.

Finally, Trissa asks, "What kind of evidence do you hope to find on Victor Volcan?"

"I think he's done terrible things. And I think my dad knew and hid evidence of it out here."

"And who is your dad?"

"Ethan. Ethan Anderson."

Her eyes widen slightly as her stare strengthens. Squinting her eyes, curiously, she asks, "Ethan Anderson? Does he not work alongside Victor Volcan?"

"He did."

"*Did?*"

"He was killed. By an…" He stops speaking and drops his head.

Trissa looks at the top of Jacob's head. His messy hair hangs over his forehead. When he lifts his head to resume the conversation, she says, "I'm sorry." She then asks, "What are your plans if you were to find this evidence against Victor?"

He speaks while shrugging his arms. "Find a way to use it to take him down. Remove him from his authority and power. Get him away from being able to do his terrible things."

She scoffs and looks away, thinking. Jacob leans in slightly at the side of her face and neck. The edge of a large scar creeps into her neck from under her shirt and jacket. She snaps her head back at Jacob, stands and says, "Let's get you back to your friends. I'd like to speak to the leader of this compound and then speak with all of you. Come with me."

Jacob grunts as he stands to his feet. He adjusts his hoodie and looks back once more at the Shrieker that is now lying in a large pool of its own blood. He turns back to Trissa, who has walked toward the gate and is nudging her head for him to follow.

Inside the gate, Jacob is taken aback by the view. The street they arrive on travels through to the far wall, where another gate is guarded. In the twenty-foot space between the street and the left wall are gardening plots of different vegetables being tended by many residents of the compound. Jacob surveys his right, where old homes have been demolished to make plots for many small one-person huts. In the back corner stands a four-story building with many windows, resembling a modified apartment building.

He follows Trissa along the road, receiving cold stares from residents walking across the street. Those tending to the garden stop and stand to watch Jacob as he passes. He notices some of their eyes are golden like Trissa's and the guard's. Kids play in a small field between the homes and a row of larger buildings they seem to be heading toward.

They turn onto a gravel path, making their way between a line of fabricated shops built with the same repurposed materials as the huts. The first building on the right has WASHROOMS scratched in the dark wood. Across the path on the left reads ARMORY next to an open door. Jacob looks inside to see many residents wearing cargo pants, combat boots, and tan long-sleeved shirts. The walls are lined with rifles and shelves of ammunition. In the center of the building sits a large table, where nine to ten people are standing around overlooking whatever is laid on top of it. Jacob walks on the tips of his toes but is unable to see.

The next building reads OFFICES, across from MEDICAL. Trissa stops at the last building on the left reading CAFETERIA. "Your friends are safe in here," Trissa says as she opens the door for Jacob.

The inside reminds him of a half-sized cafeteria at school. The far wall has serving lines, and residents behind it are preparing meals and food. Picnic-style tables line the eating area in three rows. Sitting in the center row are Jacob's friends. Chloe looks past Renz and Deante, stands, and waves to him.

"Jacob!" Chloe shouts.

Trissa nods to Jacob and says, "Join your friends. I'll be back shortly to talk further."

Jacob makes his way to the table and sits next to Renz across from Chloe and Kyle. The four of them have plates of scrambled eggs, toast, and sausage links. Jacob is immediately interrogated by Kyle.

"What's happening? What did she say to you?" he asks. All of them look at him waiting for his response. Deante is the only one without wide eyes as he takes another bite.

Jacob rubs his face and leans his elbows onto the table. Speaking through his hands, he says, "She wanted to know what I'm looking to find at my dad's old place, and what I plan to do with it if I find it."

"Shit, man," Deante mutters with his mouth full. "Dude, though, this breakfast is excellent. Way better than those protein bars we had at–"

"Are we going to get out of here?" Renz asks nervously.

"Yeah, man, for sure. We'll–"

"This is for you," a high-pitched voice speaks to Jacob. He turns to see a teenage girl setting a plate of food in front of him. Her eyes are brown. Her hair braided but messy. Her appearance makes him think about the girl he found on the hunt.

"Th-Thank you," Jacob stutters and smiles politely at her.

"What's next?" Chloe asks him.

"She said she was going to talk with the leader, then come talk to us. After that, we'll ask to leave," he answers. Not having much of an appetite, he stabs a few scrambled eggs and takes a bite. The door opens behind him.

They turn their attention to the door and see Trissa walk in with a taller man with short gray hair and a full gray beard. Jacob recognizes him from among the people he saw in the armory. He's wearing the same tan shirt, cargo pants, and combat boots the others were wearing.

Trissa approaches them and greets them, saying, "Jacob. Jacob's friends." She nods to each of them. "This is Isaac. He's the leader of this compound." She points to Isaac.

He nods and says, "Welcome to The Wasteland."

"The *Wasteland*?" Deante asks as he just took another bite of his food.

Chuckling, Trissa says, "It's an inside joke, mostly. We're aware of the nickname you wall-dwellers have given us *Outsiders*."

They all stare awkwardly at Trissa.

Chloe stutters and says, "I'm not a fan of that nickname and have never said it."

"You're not from the walls, correct? You're one of us?" Trissa asks confidently.

"H-How did you know?" Chloe asks, shocked.

"You have a tell," Trissa answers but immediately moves on. "Anyway. After my discussion with Jacob, it seems we all have a common goal." She's met with intriguing eyes from the group. They watch her as she grabs a wooden stool from the corner of the room and brings it to the end of their table to sit. Isaac stands over her shoulder with his hands cupped in front of his waist. Trissa says, "We are planning to take down Victor Volcan."

The cafeteria goes silent. Chefs cooking food is heard from the back of the room alongside Chloe's stuttered breathing in reaction to Trissa's statement. Jacob tries to reach under the table for her hand but can't reach far enough.

After clearing his throat, Kyle asks, "Why… If I may ask… Why do you all want to go after Victor?"

Isaac lightly scoffs. Trissa rolls her shoulders then answers. "What he's done to our people here from The Wasteland. Along with other infected outside of our–"

"*Infected*?" Renz involuntarily yells. "But you seem… Normal."

"Yes… Sorry, I didn't catch your name," Trissa replies.

"R-Renz. Lorenzo," he answers, looking at the table.

"Yes, Lorenzo, we're infected," she repeats.

"Still? Like right now? Currently?" Renz replies quickly.

Trissa scrunches her eyebrows and asks them, "Everyone outside the walls are permanently infected. You all don't know this?" She watches them shake their heads while Chloe nods. Shaking her head, Trissa then continues, "Yes. Everyone outside your walls is infected. Infected and forgotten by the leaders of The Walls." Her voice grows angry with each sentence. Jacob and his friends continue to look on with undivided attention. "As the infection took over the world, people died. People killed each other. People ravaged for survival. The ones who got protected and taken into the safety of The Walls — they were the privileged. The wealthy. The powerful.

"The rest of us were left out here to fight and hope for safety. If you weren't among the chosen to live in a Conservation City, the chances of becoming infected were nearly one hundred percent. Attacks from infected were inevitable for the first several years. If you didn't die from the attack, then you became another infected host.

"Early stages of the infection made us primal. Unable to control our actions, reacting on instinct, and viciously attacking anyone we would see." Trissa becomes choked up and sniffles. She clears her throat and looks intently at each of them, saying, "But you know the worst part about that stage?"

They remain silent, waiting for her to answer.

She says, weakly, "You eventually come out of it. And you remember everything you did in your state of uncontrollable rage. You remember the faces of those you hurt… Or killed. You remember your responsibility for spreading the infection to those who you attacked."

The group watches her fight back tears. A pin drop could be heard in the cafeteria.

Isaac rubs Trissa's back as she gathers herself and says, "Stage two, after the infection had run its course, our consciousness returned, but we could barely function. We spent years roaming, able to think but unable to speak. Able to do just the basics of movements.

"Then stage three, those of us remaining found each other and learned how to be human again. We gathered in groups and built our own communities. We learned to live in our own peace — outside The Walls."

Trissa slams her fist on the table. Jacob and his friends jump. She speaks loudly and angrily, "*Then* after those *years* of rebuilding, our people who scavenge for supplies and hunt for food for the compounds get killed… Or captured and disappeared — by soldiers sent by *him*." She looks away.

Jacob gulps.

"These soldiers that hunt *us* aren't wall-dwellers. They're different. Altered. They carry swords and travel together. Sometimes three of them. But always the same two."

Elliot and Theo, Jacob thinks to himself. Chloe sniffles, catching Trissa's attention.

Trissa pauses, then says, "We know that Victor Volcan is responsible for this."

Deante and Renz look at Jacob from across the table. What Trissa is saying matches what Jacob told them all last night. Jacob drops his head slightly and sighs. He hears Chloe sniffle again.

Finally, Isaac speaks. He says, "We've trained a group of soldiers we call Watchers."

He's now met with their intent stares.

"They're soldiers who can get close to The Walls and observe, listen, and gather information and bring it back to me without being caught."

"Awesome," Kyle mutters.

Trissa says, "Our Watcher teams have recently delivered proof we've needed to confirm the ties to Victor." She looks at Isaac.

Isaac nods then says, "One team followed Victor to his facility in Robinson Mall. There, they watched soldiers leave that matched the descriptions brought back to us by survivors of groups attacked.

"A second team communicated with a compound outside of Chambersburg. While Victor was there at the Conservation

City, that compound reported two younger civilians were captured."

Chloe gasps. The rest of the group listen with widened eyes.

Trissa speaks, saying, "Now, with this information, combined with Jacob saying you're on your travels to find evidence against Victor as well…" She watches them nod. "We can help take him down."

"How?" the group asks in unison.

Trissa looks at Isaac. Isaac turns to the group and says, "We can all work together. I have been training an army for several years, along with our neighboring compounds. In just over a week's time, we will be launching an attack on The Walls and taking down those responsible for killing and capturing our people."

CHAPTER 28

ISAAC IS MET WITH LOOKS of concern, confusion, and worry. Even the staff in the kitchen seem to have stopped working and join the silence. Finally, Kyle speaks up. "When you say, 'attack,' do you mean… *Attack*?" He draws out the last word waiting for an answer.

Isaac says, "We've compiled a large amount of firepower. Firearms, ammunition, grenades, Molotovs. Other compounds have been training soldiers who will be joining us.

"The attack will start with grenades and Molotov cocktails thrown over the walls. We have limited amounts of C4 to use to blast open a breach in the wall closest to Volcan Enterprises headquarters. Once inside, we'll–"

Trissa interrupts, her eyes show that she doesn't want him to divulge all the details. She says, "We have waves of soldiers trained appropriately to complete the mission laid out for them."

Jacob glares back and forth between both of them. With a concerned tone, he says, "Our city is filled with innocent people. People who could be harmed when your mission is to get Victor."

"There will be casualties, Jacob. There often are with wars," Trissa says calmly, with a serious tone.

"*Wars?*" Jacob and Deante say simultaneously.

Jacob stutters, but speaks passionately, saying, "Guns are banned from Conservation Cities. Only a small number of security guards at Volcan Enterprises are armed. Nobody will be able to defend themselves."

Trissa and Isaac remain expressionless, looking at Jacob.

"It would be a massacre," Jacob says loudly, begging for a response.

"I told you outside," Trissa speaks sternly. "We're not the only compound in this area. There are many. Each hiding throughout several neighborhoods. *All* have been subject to their people being abducted or murdered. Then, if the abducted come back, they're turned into those Ghouls. Imagine your loved ones taken from you and coming back like *that*." Her golden eyes look through Jacob when she says, "Our people outside the walls have suffered enough. I'm sorry to inform you that there will be casualties, but for too long we've been defenseless. It's our time to fight back. It's our time to stop Victor for good."

Chloe wishes she was next to Jacob so she could squeeze his hand under the table. Breathing rapidly and thinking frantically, Jacob takes a gamble and says, "What if there's another way we can work together? A less violent way. With these files my dad hid, we can negotiate something. Right?"

Scoffing, Trissa says, "Sorry, kid, but the time for negotiation is ov–"

Jacob interrupts. "Listen. I… The evidence my dad kept on Victor is thorough. I find that, then get it to CC News, they broadcast it to all Conservation Cities… All you would have to do is help us deliver it to their headquarters in Cleveland. Victor will be done for. No more of his soldiers, or projects, or Shriekers."

Isaac and Trissa look confused.

"Ghouls, sorry."

"How do you know they'd broadcast this?" Trissa asks, skeptically.

"They'd have to," he replies.

Isaac and Trissa continue to look skeptical.

"They'd *have* to," he speaks adamantly. They remain quiet, looking at him. He adds, "CC News is one of the few things that isn't running out of our city. So Victor doesn't have his hands in it. There's no forced loyalty there." Jacob holds his eye contact confidently with Trissa. "Give it a chance. Let me find what is at my dad's house. If it's enough, we'll solve both of our problems *peacefully*." He watches them look at each other. He sighs and says, "If… If I find nothing or it's not enough… Just let us get our parents out of the city before you attack."

Trissa holds a stare with Jacob. He notices small scars on her forehead and between the freckles on her nose. She leans close to Isaac's ear and whispers for some time. Renz leans over the table, trying to hear, but is unsuccessful.

Isaac nods and Trissa leans away. He says to the group, "We'll give this a chance."

The group looks at each other and softly cheers. Isaac holds up his hand and adds, "*But*… With the exception that we revisit this after we see the evidence you find. If we feel it is insufficient to take down Victor publicly and politically, we *will* continue our plan of attack."

"Fine," Jacob says quickly and confidently. "Deal." He stands, showing he's ready to go.

Isaac steps toward him while holding his palm outward. He says, "I'll be sending one of my newer recruits with you on your venture."

"What? Why?" Deante asks before Jacob can, still speaking with his mouth full.

Kyle says in a frustrated tone to Deante, "How are you still eating?"

"I'm still hungry," he replies defensively. "And I paused during Triss's whole thing."

"Consider this insurance for us," Isaac answers. "We'll also have you leave a member of your group here in The Wasteland as well."

"I…" Jacob stutters.

"We're just covering our bases, Jacob," Trissa says politely. "While you seem like a trustworthy group, we still need to protect ourselves."

Jacob looks at his friends. They all switch between looking at each other, trying to figure out what each other is thinking. Kyle speaks up, saying, "I'll stay."

"You can't," Jacob responds immediately. "I'll need your help accessing the drive my dad stored."

Kyle nods and expresses frustration that he forgot.

"I'll stay," Renz and Deante say together. They look at each other, surprised. Deante holds a fork in his mouth as he takes a bite of eggs.

"D. You stay and plan a housing contingency with Trissa in case our families need to come here," Jacob speaks, thinking on his feet and surprising himself. Trissa meets eyes with him and nods in agreement.

"Got it, bro," Deante replies. Renz drops his head.

"Hopefully they can afford the hit on their food supply with you staying here," Kyle leans in and lightly punches Deante's shoulder.

"Hey!" Deante speaks with another bite entering his mouth.

Isaac claps his hands together. "Sounds like we've got a game plan. I'll grab our recruit and bring him in for introductions. I'll also bring our map of the area and help plan your quickest route to the destination. Then you can be on your way." He nods and leaves the cafeteria.

Trissa preps to stand while saying, "Is there anything else you need before you go?"

They all shake their heads. Jacob stutters and says, "C-Can I ask a question?"

"Of course," Trissa says kindly.

"I've seen other Out…" He hesitates.

"It's fine, Jacob. That one isn't offensive." She smiles.

"Your eyes. Some Outsiders have eyes like yours. But some don't. Is that–"

Smiling again, Trissa points to her eyes and says, "Side effect from the infection." She sees Jacob and the others waiting intently for her to elaborate. "Stage one of the infection should've killed anyone that had it. Thankfully, our bodies persisted, but not without compromise.

"Even though we fought off the effects of the infection, it remains active in our blood."

Renz chokes and coughs.

"Getting to stage two and finally stage three," she gestures to herself, "our DNA changed naturally to become immune to the virus. Since we couldn't fight it, we learned to live with it.

"That change in the DNA, for some of us, affected other areas as well." She points to her eyes again. "But I kind of like it." She laughs lightly.

"I-I like it, too," Chloe says softly. Trissa smiles at her.

Jacob gives her a tight smile. He says, "I've ran into younger Outsiders and they don't seem to have the same language skills you all have."

Nodding with an impressed smirk, Trissa says, "Our youngsters are born into a challenge."

"How so?" Renz asks curiously.

"They're born infected, but the infection hasn't run its course. We've been trying to learn through observing children as often as we can. It seems as though something has to trigger the infection to activate, causing their bodies to react, then, unfortunately, go through the stages of infection." She's met with widened eyes. She says, "Yeah. What we've documented is severe injuries have seemed to trigger it for some, while most tend to go through it during puberty. We monitor our preteens all very closely." She pauses, then adds, "Then some, but very few, have triggered the infections randomly.

"But this is why you likely saw a younger Outsider speaking slower or broken English. They were likely in late stage two of their infection."

"Wow," Chloe says, shocked.

The cafeteria door swings open, then Isaac, followed by a young gentleman, walks in. The young man is wearing the same outfit as Isaac and the others Jacob saw in the armory. He also wears a bandana under his chin. His hair is buzzed short, and his brown stubbly beard surrounds a gentle smile as they approach the table.

"Everyone, this is one of our newer recruits, Kilian," Isaac introduces him. Kilian waves and greets everyone with a short bow. Isaac continues, saying, "Kilian here has completed our regiment for security and army training. He'll be a welcome companion for your journey. I'm sure of it." He pats Kilian on the back. In his other hand is a large rolled up map. He unrolls it over the table and gestures for Kilian and Trissa to help hold the ends down.

Sketches and notes are drawn over streets and areas of the map. Red Gs are noted by neighborhoods, which Jacob thinks represent areas where they've seen Ghouls. A square is drawn where their compound is, with circles in neighborhoods all around it. *Those must be the other compounds,* Jacob thinks to himself as he continues to look over the map.

"This is where you'll find Cameron Drive." Isaac points to a street northeast of the square signifying The Wasteland. "This way here is the most direct path." He slides his finger over a light green area between them and the neighborhood of Cameron Drive. "This area is acres of old farmland. Mostly overgrown grass with a decomposed barn and stables. A small patch of trees at the other end brings you to Richard Drive. Cut through the houses and you'll be standing on Cameron."

Jacob nods, learning the map and the path they'll take.

"You can take this. We have several copies." Isaac rolls the map and hands it to Jacob. Looking at the group, he says, "You all need anything else before heading out?"

Renz stutters, asking nervously, "Weapons?"

Chuckling, Isaac says, "I can't give you weapons, but Kilian here will be armed and ready to protect you if you happen to need it." He hits Kilian's back again.

"Yes. I will, sir," Kilian speaks, standing at attention. Jacob watches him push out his chest. He's eager to prove himself to Isaac.

"Alright, then." Isaac smacks his hands on his hips and says, "Gather up what you need and head to the gate. I'll have them open it for you when you approach."

They all nod and smile at Isaac. Each of them take turns introducing themselves to Kilian with a handshake. He maintains his pleasant energy and smiles with confidence at each of them.

Outside the door they stand as residents walk by. Some are walking children to the small field to play. Others are carrying clothes into the washroom. Jacob notices several of them giving them side-eyed glances as they pass.

"Guess I'll reserve spots for our families in case we need 'em?" Deante shrugs and says to his friends.

"It looks like it's barely a three-mile walk. We shouldn't be long, man," Jacob says, trying to assure him.

"Just, like… Don't do anything super cool or find anything awesome without me, okay?" Deante says.

Jacob laughs and smirks, saying, "Okay."

Smiling, Deante says, "Other than the compelling evidence about Victor. Everything else, keep boring."

"Got it." Jacob chuckles again, then he and Deante do their handshake. The others say bye to Deante, and they walk back to the road to make their way to the gate.

"Approach the gate!" yells the hooded figure on the catwalk made of planks and wooden studs that runs along most of the wall.

They walk within a few feet of the gate and stop. The hooded figure pulls a lever on the catwalk, triggering the large gears to turn and ring with loud metal clanking.

Jacob inhales and rolls his shoulders as he watches the gridded metal gate raise in front of him.

CHAPTER 29

KILIAN'S PISTOL SENDS A CRACK through the open field they stand in. The bullet pings with a loud chime and spark.

"Damn! I didn't think you could hit it twice in a row!" Kyle exclaims, referring to a second indent on a metal shovel head fifty feet away, leaning against a rotted barn. Kilian stands with a proud expression.

"This barn was where we had our target practices before we took hay back to the compound to make target dummies and boxes," Kilian says as he holsters his pistol. The barn is dry-rotted and dilapidated, surrounded by moldy bales of rolled hay and rusty, overgrown equipment. The roof is sunken in, ready to collapse from the next storm that passes through. Holes occupy random places where slabs of wood siding are hanging on by a single rusty nail.

"Alright, one more target," Renz speaks up.

Jacob shifts anxiously, saying, "Come on, guys, I want to get to the house and make it back before dark."

"Fine. This place smells like shit anyway."

Chuckling, Kilian says, "It's the hay. You get used to it. Bothered me when we were carrying loads back to the compound, but after a while you–"

"Ain't no way you get used to that, man." Renz shakes his head.

The tall grass is nearly to their hips as they walk with high knees through acres of farmland. It's still damp near the ground from the morning dew hours ago. As the group walks to progress on their journey, a crash sounds from inside the barn now behind them. All of them turn and watch around the barn for movement.

Kilian holds his pistol with both hands in front of him. Jacob sees he's breathing heavily. A slam crashes against the wood as if something inside threw itself against the wall of the barn.

"Something must have crawled in there," Jacob says to Kilian. He's pointing at broken pieces of wood at the base of the back wall of the barn. It's small, but large enough for a person to crawl into.

Kilian nods, fixing his eyes and aiming at the hole.

Another loud crash sounds from inside, this time accompanied by an odd-sounding screech.

"What is that?" Renz asks nervously.

They all watch intently, waiting for something to exit the hole in the wall. The high-pitched screech sounds again, followed by rotted wood bursting outward from the side of the barn. Tumbling through the wall then shuffling to its feet is a panicked and distraught deer. It runs quickly through the tall grass away from the group, toward the street.

With a sigh of relief, Kilian lowers his pistol and holsters it on his hip.

"Shit, man," Renz says, exasperated.

Kyle chuckles and pats him on the back, saying, "Lighten up, man."

Renz grunts and walks with the group. He says defensively, "Even Kilian looked nervous." He points ahead to Kilian, who's walking next to Jacob and Chloe.

"I'm…" Kilian says, "I'm just prepared." His voice sounds hesitant.

"We're fine, guys, it was a false alarm," Jacob says, finding himself struggling with unrolling the large map Isaac gave him while he walks. Stopping to control the map, he sees where the corn field ahead is marked. He looks up, confirming that up ahead, at the other end of the field, are the tops of the trees they need to walk through. "We'll go straight toward those trees."

Caved-in stables sit in the back of the field covered in green mold. Chloe sees them and says, "I wonder what happened to the horses."

Kilian stutters and says, "Just… Don't look inside." He gives a nervous glance at Chloe.

Through the fields and woods, a small breeze whispers to them as it flows through the rotted corn stalks and the lonely trees extending their leafless branches. The groups' footsteps echo the snaps of sticks and dried leaves covering the forest floor as Jacob leads them into the neighborhood. Chloe holds his hand, intertwining her fingers with his. She speaks softly to him, asking, "What do you think Trissa meant when she said I have a tell?"

"Hmm?" Jacob looks at her, showing he wasn't fully listening.

"Trissa said I have a tell. Remember? What do you think she means by that?"

"Oh." He looks ahead. They're finally twenty feet away from leaving the woods. "I don't know, Chlo. Your eyes are a brighter green… Like how her eyes are golden… Maybe that's…" He stops when Chloe pulls her hand away from his and touches next to her eye.

"You think?" she asks.

"I dunno." He shrugs. "Just a guess."

They emerge from the woods into the backyard of the pale blue-sided house. A collapsed wooden deck lies over the patio that is also overgrown with moss and some other brown, furry growth. They're standing next to a black metal fence that surrounds the yard and contains a pool with rings of stains along the walls from the moldy, dark-green water evaporating into the gelled substance it currently consists of at the bottom.

"Jacob." He hears Kyle whisper loudly from behind him. He looks back and sees Kyle pointing to the yard next door.

Next to a pile of rotted wood that used to be a shed is an Outsider leaning around the back, looking at Jacob and his friends. He hears the click of Kilian's pistol.

"Stop," Jacob says loudly but under his breath. He pushes the pistol down. Kilian's arms resist but still lower with the gun as he gives a shocked look at Jacob. "It's an Outsider, not a Shrieker." He gestures his head toward the road and says to the group, "Let's keep going."

Looking at the map, Jacob feels his shoes hit pavement. He stops and confirms what Isaac told him. They can cut through the houses across the street and arrive at Cameron. Making sure everyone is together, he turns and walks through the first yard.

As he passes the house, he notices the large front window is shattered. Curtains sway from the soft breeze, revealing the wall of the room inside. Jacob sees splatters of blood across the wall overtop family pictures that are still hung. He looks at Chloe who's looking ahead. He's happy she didn't see inside the house, but quickly thinks he'd rather her have seen that than what they find in the backyards.

Between the yards is a large pit. Blackened grass and dirt are permanently singed in a circle. In the center of the circle are piles of bones and ash.

"What the f–" Renz begins to mutter aloud, but is shushed by Jacob. Jacob is slowly turning his ear listening for any suspicious sounds.

"We should just keep moving," he whispers loudly and begins to softly step through the high grass in the yards.

They pass the houses and emerge on Cameron. *One. Seven. Nine. Three,* Jacob thinks as he checks house numbers. In front of him is 1785. "Only a few this way." He points and starts walking.

Jacob stops in front of his destination. He's looking at a two-story house with green siding and light brown bricks around the base. A covered front porch is overgrown with vines, except for where it's been cleared out and maintained. Near the street where they stand is a light post wrapped in the same vines hugging the porch and the sides of the house.

"Are you okay?" Chloe asks after seeing Jacob's deep stare at the house.

"Y-Yeah. Just thinking… They had a whole different life in there," he replies.

Kyle moves next to Jacob and squeezes his shoulder. "You ready to do this?"

Jacob nods his head, looks at Kyle, then at Chloe, and walks to the front porch.

The boards under his feet bow with each step and creak loudly. He observes patio furniture that has sat through years of weather strewn across the porch. Some pieces sit upside down with the cushions next to them, ripped and tattered. Grass and more weeds have grown through the cracks between boards and intertwine through the frail and broken furniture.

Jacob imagines his mom enjoying her morning tea, sitting on this porch, taking in the scenery that was once much more beautiful than the rundown homes behind forests of grass that defines the view now.

She probably knew the neighbors well. She likely walked these streets and waved to them on their porches. She lived a whole life out here that Jacob knows nothing about.

He shakes off this daydream and walks to the front door where he sees an open, empty cooler sitting next to the white railing. He rests his hand on the doorknob, wiggles it to test if it's locked. It's not.

Inhaling and closing his eyes, he thinks, *Here goes nothing.* He turns the handle, opens the door and steps inside his parent's home.

CHAPTER 30

JACOB WALKS INTO A LARGE foyer. The still air carries the familiar dust particles showing off streams of sunlight beaming through gaps in the vines covering the windows. Ahead is a staircase that leads upstairs to an open hallway lined with wooden railings. He sees three doors from where he stands. A small hallway leads ahead to an open kitchen. To the immediate left is a dining room that connects to the other side of the kitchen. On the right is a small family room with a small couch and a lamp standing behind it in the corner. Novels and small figurines line bookshelves on the wall next to the sofa. On the outside wall hangs a large photo.

"This is more… Tidy… Than what we're used to seeing. Isn't it?" Renz speaks quietly. He sees Jacob taking everything in, but he wanted to speak his thoughts.

"Yeah," Jacob mutters, barely audibly.

Kyle and Renz wander down the hall toward the kitchen. Kilian stands at attention at the door while Jacob and Chloe walk into the dining room. She follows him as he begins to pace around a square, solid-wood dining table in the center of the room. Large abstract artwork hangs on the walls, and in the corner of the room stands a floor to ceiling curio cabinet containing fancy dishware.

As Jacob walks toward the table, he envisions his mom and dad enjoying breakfast together. This is where they shared meals before their new home. He paces around the table, running his finger along the edge leaving a trail in the dust. His eyes focus on the areas of the table with dust cleared off in front of two chairs.

He walks through an open doorway into the far end of the kitchen. In front of him and to his left are doors that he ignores and steps into the large kitchen. Usually, every kitchen out here is ransacked and looted, leaving broken dishes and unwanted food items scattered across the floor. This isn't the case in his parent's house. The countertops are organized. The floor is clean. All the cabinet doors are intact. Even the kitchen island holds four unopened water bottles neatly standing in the far corner.

My mom must've loved this kitchen, Jacob thinks, seeing that it's double the size of their kitchen now. Ahead, past the opening to the hallway from the foyer, is a large living room with a large sectional sofa and big screen TV hanging on the wall. To the right of the TV stands a shelf holding gaming consoles and dozens of movies. Jacob chuckles to himself seeing Renz and Kyle already finding and looting through all the movies and games.

Renz turns when he hears Jacob in the kitchen and says, "Dude, your mom and dad had *so* many movies."

Laughing softly, Jacob replies, "Yeah, my dad was quite the movie nerd. I think he sucked my mom into it as well."

He leaves Kyle and Renz in the living room to continue checking the collection and walks into the small room off the foyer. A large photo hanging on the wall catches Jacob's attention as he enters. He stands in front of a photo of his mom and dad from their wedding. His dad is in a suit, leaning back, smiling and holding his mom in the air with his arms around her waist. Her smile beams with happiness. She's wearing a long white dress and holding a bouquet of flowers in one hand, mirroring his immense happiness.

"You can see how much they loved each other," Chloe speaks, reminding Jacob she's behind him.

He gives a tight smile while looking over the picture. Chloe taps on his shoulder and says, "Look at this."

On the wall by the opening to the foyer hangs another large photo. In the picture is Jacob's mom and dad, with his mom holding a small child. Jacob's eyebrows lower as he leans in, inspecting the child in the photo. He rubs away a layer of dust to see it clearer.

"Jacob, I thought you were born inside the walls," Chloe questions.

His nose is nearly touching the picture as he looks at a child resembling him, saying, "I… I was." His voice sounds unsure of his answer.

"Do you think…" Chloe begins to speak, then says, under her breath, "Nevermind."

"What? You can say it."

"I… I was thinking… Could your dad… A-And mom… Have lied about your—"

"About my age? W-Why… For what reason?"

Chloe shrugs and looks at her feet.

"It wouldn't… Doesn't make sense." He looks back at the picture. Renz and Kyle laugh loudly in the next room. Jacob breaks his stare at the photo and walks to the bookshelf to find other photos of himself in the room.

Novels and figurines line the top shelves. On the bottom shelf sits a lone photo album in the center. The spine reads, "College." The open space to the right of the album looks like it would fit two or three more. Those are the ones his mom took when they had to evacuate the house. The figurine in front of Jacob depicts a wood carving of a woman holding a newborn. The base reads, "A Mother's First True Love."

Jacob turns around and looks directly at the family portrait again. He stops himself from thinking more about it and says to Chloe, "Let's look upstairs for his office."

"O-Okay."

As they walk past Kilian, who's still guarding the door, Jacob nods to him. At the top of the stairs, he pushes open the door on the left and looks inside. It's a large master bedroom. "Not the office," he says to Chloe.

The next door opens to a bathroom. Jacob looks inside long enough to see that it doesn't have a broken medicine cabinet with contents littered across the floor, as other homes usually do.

Approaching the end of the hall, there are two doors across from one another. The door on the right is partially opened. Seeing a small bed through the opening, Jacob chooses to look inside.

Light purple walls line the room with white floating shelves holding children's books and small stuffed animals. An area rug with baby tigers and lions lies in the center of the floor. A small bed with white posts above the mattress sits against the wall with a rocking chair next to it. Hanging above the bed on the wall are large letters: ALI. On the floor by the chair lie the letters C and E.

Alice?

Chloe is standing on the tips of her toes looking over Jacob's shoulder into the room. She wants to ask Jacob about what they're seeing, but decides not to when she hears his breath stutter.

On top of a small dresser sits a framed photo. Jacob bursts into the room and grabs the picture. He's looking at a younger Ethan smiling with his cheek against a small, smiling child who resembles a young Jacob, except with two short ponytails tied on her head.

Angrily, Jacob looks at Chloe, flashing the picture, saying, "How could they…" He shakes his head and scoffs. Under his breath, he says, "Of course they could. They kept *me* a secret from an entire city."

"Jacob. What are you saying, I can't hear–"

"I have, or… I had a sister." He now sounds sad. "They never told me."

"Maybe there's more to this. Maybe there's a reason they never told–"

"What reason would that be, Chlo?" He keeps the picture gripped in his palm as his arms swing outward. She watches his lip begin to tremble as he continues. "Could it be the same reason I was never told about the facility? Or you and the others? Or given a reason why I had to keep my abilities a secret? Or…"

Jacob pauses and finds himself lost in the picture.

Slowly stepping toward him, Chloe softly says, "Jacob. I know it's hard to understand now, but I'm sure they were trying their best when they decided not to–"

Pulling away from her hand reaching for his arm, Jacob speaks angrily with watery eyes. "Everybody is lying to me, Chlo. Victor. My dad.

"I thought the one person that never would lie to me was my mom. And now…" His eyes release drops of tears as they move from Chloe back to the picture. She waits while he processes a thousand more thoughts in his mind. Finally he looks back at her and asks, "What if you and my friends are the only people I can trust?"

Chloe's heart drops. His eyes hold a heavy sadness that her words won't mend in this moment. As she is about to step forward to wrap him in a hug, she's interrupted by a roaring voice.

"Jacob!" Kyle yells from downstairs. "We found the office!"

Chloe watches Jacob look at the picture in his hand and says, "Jacob. I'm sorry."

"Whatever." With a flick of his wrist, he throws the picture at the wall. Light chimes of glass hitting the floor reverberate through the otherwise silent room.

"Everyone I trusted has been lying to me, Chlo."

She closes her eyes then looks back to Jacob. As she begins to speak, he pushes past her to exit the room and says, "Let's go find what we came here for."

Chloe bends over to pick up the picture, shaking off remaining pieces of glass inside the frame.

They head downstairs and see Kilian has left standing guard the front door. Back through the kitchen, Jacob sees everyone standing in a room through one of the doors he passed earlier.

The office is painted dark green with oak wood trim around the base of the floor and decorative chair rail. The far wall is lined with dark oak bookshelves full of medical journals, medical books, and trinkets his dad must have collected. Off-center of the room, in front of the shelves, sits his dark wood desk with a small lamp in the corner, a picture frame standing underneath, and a closed laptop on top. Pictures of Pittsburgh hang on the walls next to framed and signed jerseys from sports teams.

"Do you guys see a safe or something nearby?" Jacob asks as he takes in the sight.

Renz points toward the floor by the bookshelves.

Walking around the desk, Jacob sees a small black safe on the bottom of the far-left shelf. As he kneels, he observes a shelf full of bobble-head sports figures, a signed football, and several sports cards encased in hard plastic. He pauses as he sees a Venetian Volto mask lying next to its stand. While running his finger along the sharp edge under the nose, he observes that the bottom half of the mask is completely missing. He kneels down and sits on the backs of his feet, checks Noel's note and enters the code on the small keypad on the door of the safe. A barely audible beep sounds with a click. Jacob turns the handle, and the safe opens.

Inside are two small journals and a flash drive on top of them. Under the flash drive sits a small note that reads:

WORK:

EANDERSON - YtRk52p@7

Elevator: 1245

HOME:

EANDERSON - AmberAlice2068

Passwords? Jacob thinks. "His elevator code is the same as our garage door code," he says with a light laugh.

Met with a confused look from his friends, he flashes the journal and stands, then turns to tell Kyle to get his computer ready. He sees Kyle has his backpack open on the floor and his laptop powering up.

Kyle smiles and says, "One step ahead of you, bro."

Jacob stands next to Kyle as he inserts the flash drive on his laptop then clicks to open a folder with a file inside.

"It's not password protected," Kyle mutters. "Guess that makes sense if he was planning to turn this in." He clicks and opens a window with a paused video showing Ethan sitting at the desk Kyle and Jacob are leaning over with a play symbol over his face.

"You want the honors?" Kyle says to Jacob as he pulls the chair out for him.

"Y-Yeah. Sure," Jacob says nervously. He sits in the chair in front of the laptop. Chloe, Renz and Kilian walk around the desk behind him ready to watch. He takes a slow inhale, then exhales.

Jacob presses play.

CHAPTER 31

STARTLED AWAKE, ETHAN QUICKLY SITS up in bed. The clock reads 07:39, twenty-four minutes after his alarm normally sounds. He gets out of bed, puts on khakis and a dark-blue button-up shirt, then walks down to the kitchen where Amber is making breakfast.

"Did I sleep through my alarm?" he asks as he sits at the table.

"I thought you could sleep in for once, hon," Amber replies, plating eggs next to pieces of toast.

"Babe, I need to be punctual, my team relies on–"

"You just spent two straight days at work. They can manage if you're a little late today." She sets the plate in front of Ethan. He looks at her as he leans and ties his brown dress shoes. After glancing up the stairs, she whispers loudly, adding, "You missed his scrimmage. You know how excited he gets when basketball starts."

Ethan rests one elbow on his knee and holds his head in that hand. He lets out a defeated sigh as he scratches his fingers through his hair.

"Take some time off, honey. Victor can handle whatever it is you're–"

"Victor isn't involved with this project," he interrupts, dismissing her suggestion.

"What's going on with you two? The tension at our last dinner with him didn't go unnoticed."

"We're… Figuring it out... Business disagreements." Ethan grunts as he leans and ties his other shoe.

"I hope so. He's done a lot for us."

"Yeah," Ethan replies under his breath. Amber doesn't hear him over Jacob's loud footsteps barreling down the steps.

"Oh, hey, dad," Jacob says, surprised to see him. "You off today or something?"

"Nah, bud. Late start this morning," he mutters, taking a few bites of his breakfast, ignoring a stern glare from Amber.

Jacob air boxes and asks, excited, "You wanna take me to Dave's gym after work today? He said I'm ready to start sparring against Malik."

Ethan wipes his lips with his napkin, aware of, but still dodging, Amber's stare. He stands and says, "Knockout Master Malik? You must really be impressing–"

"I do *not* like the sound of this," Amber intentionally interrupts.

"Mom. It's fine. I'm not *full on fighting* him. It's just another level of training." The attitude in Jacob's voice could not be stronger.

Catching Amber's looks toward their son and his tone, Ethan quickly says, "Tonight. I'll take you to Dave's." He holds his hands up, palms out, waiting for Jacob.

Jacob bounces on his toes and softly throws a right hook at Ethan's right palm.

"Right!" Ethan yells.

His other hand punches Ethan's left hand.

"Left!"

Ethan throws a soft swing that Jacob ducks, then pretends to hit Ethan with a slow-motion uppercut.

"Counter!" Ethan sings dramatically. He shakes his hand in Jacob's hair and says, "Ice cream after?"

"Shit, yeah!"

"Jacob!" Amber yells.

"Sorry, mom."

Ethan walks quickly to the door, then before closing it when he exits, he says, "I'll see you both later."

"Bye, dad!"

"One minute, sweetheart," Amber says softly to Jacob, before scurrying out the front door.

"Ethan," she yells, watching him close the car door. As she jogs barefoot to the driveway, she yells, again, "Wait." They hold eye contact as the hum of the window lowering buzzes. She says, "I don't know what's going on with you, but you don't hide it as well as you think. I notice. Your son notices."

"Babe, I'm sor–"

"I know you are. And I know your work weighs on you. But I'm used to seeing that on you." She pauses and admires her husband's face. "This is different, Ethan."

He sighs and stares at the eyes and freckles he fell in love with.

"Whatever it is. Please figure it out. Please…"

"I will. I… I am trying," he stutters. She touches his cheek then walks back to the house. "Amber." She turns to look at him. "I love you." He smiles.

She smiles back and says, "I love you."

Amber's words replay in his head on the drive to work. This is the spark he needed. Victor's pressure about Jacob has gotten stronger over the past months. Ethan's managed to dodge any attempts at blackmail, but his luck could be running out. He needs something of his own. He just needs proof.

"Beautiful morning, Mr. Anderson," the guard greets him as he enters the building. "Later than usual."

"Good morning, Zayne." He flashes his badge.

"You know I don't need to see that." Zayne laughs and waves off Ethan's gesture. "But you do owe me somethin' now."

Ethan lowers his eyebrows and tilts his head.

"Come on, man. It's almost October. What movie are you givin' the boy this year?"

Ethan smiles. "*The Conjuring.*"

Zayne claps his hands ecstatically. "Finally!"

"Finally is right." Ethan places his phone, wallet and keys on the security table then steps through the metal detector. "The classic."

"*The* classic, Mr. Anderson." Zayne replies commandingly as he grabs Ethan's phone and places it in one of the many small lockers next to his guard stand.

"You get the costumes for the kids yet?" Ethan asks, putting his keys and wallet back in his pockets.

"Wife's getting them this weekend."

"You know the drill, show me pictures," Ethan yells as he walks away.

"Will do!" he hears Zayne yell back at him.

Ethan takes the elevator to floor twenty-three, where his research lab is located. The doors open to a short hallway with thick-glass security doors to a brightly lit medical lab. He taps his badge on the card reader and enters.

Two women in white lab coats and goggles sit at a large table covered with papers, beakers, and medical machines. They are talking softly over a tablet as Ethan walks past them, saying, "Good morning, Whitney. Good morning, Emma."

"Good morning, sir," Whitney replies. She's Ethan's newest lab partner, having just finished the internship with Volcan Enterprises, and her enthusiasm shows in her voice. "We're seeing positive results with your Multiple Sclerosis cure."

"Good," he replies, arriving at his desk. "How many test subjects are we monitoring now? And for how long?"

"S-Seven. Seven, sir."

He unlocks his desk drawer, notices a pause, then says, "And for how long, Whitney?"

"One… One is at two weeks. The others are six days." Her voice sounds defeated.

Ethan sighs. He grabs his journal. He and Victor each bought one together in college, when they began to discuss ideas for their future in medicine.

He sets it on the table, opens it, flips past early drawings and notes, past his scribbles and documentations of Better Human, then stops and thinks.

Victor's journal.

If he finds Victor's notes on his Vitality project, he can use those as a means to stop him from asking about Jacob.

"I have to go. Keep documenting, and I will follow up with you both later." He puts his journal in his pocket and rushes to the door. Turning to Emma and Whitney he says, "Don't be disappointed in the small number of subjects. Population is small and conditions are rare. Keep up the good work." He doesn't wait for a reply and leaves the lab, running to the elevator.

The elevator doors are barely open on floor thirty-three when Ethan pushes his way out. Rebecca stands at her desk and begins to stutter as Ethan approaches with his aggressive walk, cutting her off, saying, "Is Victor in his office?"

"N-No, sir."

"Good. Let me in," he demands.

"B-But he doesn't–"

"Rebecca." He forces a stern look.

Ethan enters Victor's office and walks directly to the framed notebook paper on the wall. He presses his thumb onto the metal circle in the corner of the frame, triggering it to slide to the right, revealing the safe. A stack of folders sits on the bottom shelf under a silver pistol. Ethan moves the gun to the top shelf and pulls the stack of folders out, looking inside the safe for the journal.

It's not inside the safe.

He walks past the large windows overlooking the city, sets the stack of folders on the desk, and sits in Victor's chair. Wood squeaks as he forcefully pulls open drawers, finally opening the top left drawer which contains the journal.

The first pages contain Victor's passwords — almost hundreds scribbled out as they've been updated — and Victor's own notes for their Better Human project. The next pages list their ideas for new, non-addictive pain medicines for their first Bayer contract. He turns past Victor's notes reading BETTER HUMAN [FOR LIVING SUBJECTS]. He rolls his eyes as he skips through pages of drawings, plans, and details about testing. They're nothing but copies of their original Better Human serum, except for this being injected into the bone marrow of a subject, hoping for immediate results to satisfy Victor's impatience.

He stops turning the pages when he reads VITALITY – NEURO ENHANCEMENT.

This is it, Ethan thinks as he runs his finger over Victor's drawings of neurons and calculations next to genetic data.

Victor's early designs from soon after college to a few years after he became leader of the Conservation City.

All the pages are molecular drawings, formulas, and notes. No logs of studies. Ethan is positive they exist. But where?

There. He stares at Victor's laptop.

Ethan opens the laptop and looks at the login screen for Volcan Enterprises' database. While he has access to all the data in the network, he's certain that what he's trying to find will be in a private folder that only Victor has access to.

Referring to the password list in the journal, Ethan logs into the database as Victor. He sees the files and servers he's used to seeing listed on the left of the screen. Security, vaccines, shipping logs, contracts, employee data — all the usual, with the exception of the folder at the bottom titled Vitality.

Opening this folder reveals four sub-folders inside: Strain One – Thought, Strain Two – Memory, Strain Three – Perception, and Vial One.

Inside Vial One's folder are video logs dated to the year Ethan is suspecting. Starting with the earliest date, he clicks the file to play it.

-APRIL 4, 2063-

A young Victor sits at a desk in a lab unfamiliar to Ethan. The walls are concrete and the brief view of the metal tables in the background are old furniture from their first days of Volcan Enterprises, confirming that this secret lab was in the basement of their building where they were storing old spare furniture and equipment.

Victor looks into the camera. His appearance is that of someone Ethan hasn't seen in many years. Victor is wearing his white lab coat over a green polo and not one of the many dark gray suit variations he wears now. His hair is medium length and loosely spiked in the front instead of the now long and slicked back look. He's clean-shaven, and most of all, carries a look of innocence in his eyes that Ethan has forgotten his best friend once had.

Victor begins speaking to the camera, fighting a smile. "I've completed a strain of Vitality that is ready for testing on a live subject. This… This could be revolutionary for our species. My calculations show that, if successful, neuron counts should double, as well as neuron size. Once enlarged, their strength will show increases upwards of eighty-seven percent. This *should*, in theory, grant the subject telepathic abilities.

"How? I predict that larger, stronger neurons can interact with and traverse through electrons outside the body, allowing for telepathic, and even telekinetic, abilities."

He rustles papers that are on his desk off-screen. "The infected outside the walls are reported to have grown docile and passive, no longer attacking on sight, yet showing a decline in mental state. If true, I hope to capture one and use them as a test subject." His arm moves forward, pressing on the keyboard, ending the video.

Ethan vigorously rubs his face, then clicks the next date.

-APRIL 27, 2063-

Victor is in the same lab with a similar appearance, but with a maroon polo under his lab coat. He wears disappointment in his eyes as he says, "It's been over three weeks, and I've been unsuccessful in my attempts to find and capture an Outsider to use for testing Vitality.

"I've attempted to talk with Ethan and show him my calculations, but he continues to lack support for this project." Tilting his head and staring away from the camera, he thinks, then says, "I can… I need to be able to prove to him that he can trust me. Trust my data and research again.

"All I need is to show him that this *is* possible. All I need is a subject from outside the walls. Just one. I know it'll work."

Victor ends the recording. Ethan plays the next.

-MAY 11, 2063-

"Security reported finding a Jane and John Doe collapsed and unconscious outside and close to the walls," Victor speaks enthusiastically to the camera. "I immediately ordered them to be delivered here to my lab." Victor points to the side, but only himself and the background are visible on the camera. "They were malnourished and unresponsive upon arriving. Six years have passed since the outbreak, yet they both were somehow uninfected. I entertained the thought that they could be from another Conservation City; however, their blood samples also confirm that they did not receive a vaccine.

"The female I believe to have been in her mid-forties, and the male in his early twenties. I assume they were mother and son. Unfortunately, Jane Doe did not survive after receiving intravenous fluids.

"John Doe has shown an increase in vitals with the fluids, but is unresponsive. He will be my first test subject." Victor looks eager as he clicks to stop the recording.

-MAY 19, 2063-

Victor stands, leaning into the camera, speaking as if he's in a hurry. "One week has passed since administering Vial One of Vitality to John Doe. Brain monitoring shows strong activity, but the subject remains unresponsive verbally. His eyes have opened, and he reacts to light and movement.

"I will continue to monitor."

-MAY 21, 2063-

"John Doe is speaking." His eyes are wide with excitement. "Very few words of incoherent and basic English, but this is clearly a sign that his brain is healing.

"Will continue to monitor." Victor walks away and speaks off-camera to someone. It's mostly inaudible and faint. He steps back into the video, clicking the recording off.

Ethan taps the desk anxiously. "Come on. Give me something, Vic," he says, clicking the next video.

-MAY 24, 2063-

As this video starts to play, Victor immediately appears nervous, saying, "John Doe is eating solid food. His motor functions are normal. His speech is still incoherent." Closing his eyes, he sighs audibly. Looking back at the camera, he speaks shakingly, "A lab assistant from the main floor wandered into my lab down here, looking for a spare centrifuge. She saw John Doe strapped to the medical table. I approached her to explain what she was seeing when her expression and posture changed. She looked at me with unusual eyes and spoke to me as John Doe.

"I know this because he used her to tell me information she would not have known. His mother's name. Her name was Freda. She told me what I gave him to eat over the last three days." Victor pauses, then says, "I asked what his name was but she... He couldn't remember his name or their last name. He said his brain felt like it was on fire.

"Then, suddenly, like a switch flipped, her eyes became normal and scared. She ran back to the elevator. I… I followed her and explained everything I could to her."

Victor looks to the side then back to the camera and says, "She understands now that this is revolutionary and knows not to speak of it."

The video ends. Ethan mutters out loud, "What the fuck, Vic."

He plays the next video.

-JUNE 1, 2063-

"John Doe is speaking better, but with broken English. He's responsive to questions, so I've asked him if he is able to control telepathic abilities, such as how he communicated through Janice."

Janice? Ethan's stomach drops.

Victor's hair is disheveled and messy, his green polo has all three buttons undone, and he looks nervous and shaky as he continues in the video. "He is telling me that he felt a tingling in his temples as he looked at her. When he focused on the sensation, he felt the ability to speak through her and even control her movements.

"He…" Victor shudders. "He said that in doing this, he has tethered himself to her." He looks off-camera for a moment, then looks back, speaking softer, "He told me where she lives, and that he watched her every day since he…" He motions from his forehead to the camera with his fingers.

"Even though the address he spoke was correct, I couldn't believe all of it, so I asked him to prove it. Within minutes, Janice arrived at the lab again. He then had her repeat a conversation that he and I had earlier in the day."

Gulping, Victor says, "After she left, he… He reached his hand toward me and showed me one of *his* memories. I saw it as if I lived it. He was with his mom searching for food outside the walls. I…

"I'm becoming more terrified. I'm afraid to ask for Ethan's help, but I need it. I… I may not know how to control this."

Ethan immediately plays the next video.

-JUNE 3, 2063-

Victor's eyes are bloodshot as if he hasn't slept. His hair and apparel are the same as in the last video, with the addition of a stubbly beard growing over his neck and face. His voice is frail and shaky as he says, "John Doe won't tell me his name after showing incredible improvement in speaking and motor functions. I still have him strapped to the medical bed, though he is beginning to ask to be removed. I have been fearful that he will control me as he did Janice, but it seems he is still tethered to her and unable to tether to more than one person."

Victor rubs his face aggressively. He looks ashamed as he speaks to the camera, saying, "When I asked him if he is able to break the tether, he shook his head. He said that he believes the only way to disconnect… To destroy the tether with her is to destroy her brain… Or for her to… For her to…"

He stares at the ceiling. "I can't let him–"

The office doors burst open and Victor walks in. His black hair is slicked back. He's wearing another dark-gray suit with a black dress shirt underneath. "What are you doing?" he asks Ethan.

Without hesitation, Ethan stands from the desk chair and points at the laptop, saying, "Mind control, Vic? Your Vitality project was *fucking* mind control?"

Victor stares at Ethan without blinking.

"Do you realize how dangerous that is? How reckless?" Ethan's voice rises as he speaks. "How f–" He shakes his head in disappointment. After a moment of holding a stare with Victor, he asks, "What happened to Janice?"

Victor raises his chin and remains quiet.

"She needed to *die* to be untethered from John Doe?" Ethan walks to the side of the desk. "Did he kill Janice?" When Victor doesn't reply, he adds, "She was reported missing, Vic. You went on CC News begging for help from the other cities to find her outside the walls. All that time, did you know she was killed by this John Doe?"

Victor clasps his hands behind his back, remaining in place, not responding.

"What happened to this John Doe?" Ethan asks, impatiently, as his other questions go unanswered.

No reply from Victor.

"Answer me!" Ethan yells, sending spit flying from his lips. His eyes roar with rage.

"I did what was necessary," Victor replies calmly.

Ethan's fingers stab into his palms as he clenches his fists and breathes heavily. His eyes could burn a hole through Victor.

"I found Janice, and she looked unwell. I told her to hide until I dealt with John Doe." He sees Ethan express distrust in his words. "I made a mistake creating that serum, Ethan." He steps forward, lowering his hands to show he's sincere. "I... I had to stop him. Though, I do fear John Doe killed Janice before I got to..."

"You killed the John Doe?"

Victor drops his head and closes his eyes, sighing through his nose.

For a moment, Ethan feels empathy, but then he thinks of the other folders in Victor's private files and says, "But instead of learning from this, you decided to split it into three serums? To test on *more* subjects?"

"I *did* stop, Ethan. For a while. But then an idea came to me, to single out parts of the cerebrum. Isolate and target specific neuron functions with a less potent serum. This would grant me more control with the successful subjects. Then, once successful, their DNA samples can be combined and used to create the perfect serum." Victor steps toward Ethan, speaking excitedly, "Ethan, I've already perfected two of them. Once the third strain is successful, I'll *finally* have it. If you could see what they're capable of, you'd understand that I–"

Ethan holds his hand up to stop Victor. He closes his eyes and inhales, then looks at him, saying, "Stop." His eyes are glossy. "Do I not already hold enough of your secrets, Vic?"

Victor sees Ethan's lip tremor. He knows it's from both anger and sadness.

"Look at you," Ethan says, scanning Victor from head to toe. "You…" He points back to the laptop while keeping his eyes dancing between Victor's. "What changed you, Vic?"

"I…" Victor stutters as dark veins stem around his eyes.

Ethan's eyebrows lower as he shakes his head and says, "What have you done to yourself?"

Victor blinks his eyes weakly. "I'm running out of time, E–"

"That's on you." Ethan points his finger at Victor. His lip quivers. Victor's shoulders sink. They stare for minutes without speaking.

"If… If Better Human worked on Jacob like we intended for it to… All I'd need is a small sample and it could buy me time." Victor speaks calmly. "Once I perfect the third strain for Vitality, we could combine it with Jacob's DNA and make our species–"

"Immortal?" Ethan interrupts as he picks up the folders from the desk. "I've told you many times now, Vic. Jacob is *normal*. Better Human didn't work."

Victor sighs disappointedly. He looks at Ethan with sadness in his eyes surrounded by purple veins. He says, "Do you have any idea how much it hurts knowing your best friend doesn't care that you're dying?"

Ethan squeezes his eyes shut and tightens his lips, ready to speak. Instead, he says nothing and walks to the door. He gets halfway and turns to Victor. "My best friend died a long time ago."

Victor's head drops. Before turning to the exit, Ethan hears the doors open behind him. He turns to find Garret standing between him and the doors. Ethan rolls his eyes at Garret's gray suit and gelled hair. With a sigh of defeat, Ethan mutters, "Of course. It's you."

Garret and Victor meet eyes. He receives a nod from Victor, then says, "I'll take those from you, Mr. Anderson."

Ethan shoves the folders into Garret's chest. He looks back at Victor and says, sternly, "Leave me and my family alone."

Before Ethan closes the door, Victor yells for him. Looking at each other, Victor says, "Your family is the only family I have."

A tear falls as Ethan blinks, then he leaves the office. He walks quickly to the elevator. As it descends, he touches his pocket, confirming Victor's journal is there. His breathing is rapid. He closes his eyes and calms himself before reaching the bottom floor.

Driving directly to his old-world home outside the walls, Ethan parks on the street, grabs protein bars from his glove compartment, and walks to the porch.

Entering the house, he walks to the kitchen, confirming there are still six bottles of water on the island as he counts them. He then enters his office, sits in his desk chair, inserts a battery pack and flash drive into his laptop, and powers it on.

He enters his password to log in, then clicks the program he needs to record. A window pops up showing the camera's view of him and the wall and shelves behind him.

Ethan takes a large inhale, pauses, then clicks record.

CHAPTER 32

"MY NAME IS ETHAN ANDERSON." Jacob watches his dad nervously look around the room and adjust his posture. Ethan clears his throat and breathes slowly, leaving a long pause quiet enough that Jacob can hear his friends breathing behind him.

"My name is Ethan Anderson," he repeats, speaking those words quickly before adding, "I am of sound mind and body as I am recording this."

Jacob gulps.

"Victor Volcan has been developing experimental serums and testing them on Outsiders." Jacob's friends gasp as Ethan speaks. "He's been testing a serum he calls Vitality, which he believes can grant the subject enhanced brain functionality, enough to give them telepathic abilities."

Ethan closes his eyes and gives an expression of deep sadness that Jacob has never seen on his father.

"Victor and I started Volcan Enterprises with the goal to help people. To… Better humanity." He takes a large inhale and rubs the scruff on his bottom jaw. "This was our plan since we met in college. So much so that we developed an experimental serum together that we called Better Human." Jacob feels a lump in his throat as his dad continues. "It was a serum that would enhance DNA through the reproductive cells, passing on better immunity, strength, and intelligence to future offspring.

"We knew it was a pipe dream that would be rejected by any pharmaceutical company. And with little risk in the serum we created, we decided to test it on ourselves in secret."

"What the fuck?" Kilian mutters as Ethan takes another reflective pause.

"The plan was to monitor its effect once one of us or both of us had kids, while we built Volcan Enterprises from the ground up. But then the outbreak happened.

"The outbreak Victor created."

"What?" Jacob and his friends yell simultaneously at the monitor, as if Ethan can hear them.

"He..." Ethan rubs his face. "Victor had calculations for Vitality early on. He knew that the risks with experimenting on the brain were high, and that he'd never get FDA approval to administer to the public. Even through a trial study. So, he decided to *create* a need for his Vitality serum. He thought that if a village of people were to contract a rabies-like virus which affects the brain, he'd have an opportunity to pitch his 'brain enhancing' project to our contacts at Bayer. Thus, granting approval through emergent need.

"So... He developed the Vi-Mor virus and tainted a batch of flu vaccines that were scheduled to be delivered to a small town in Pennsylvania. At the same time, a strong strain of influenza began to spread, causing cases of flu vaccines to be rerouted and shipping Victor's tainted batch all over the world."

"Dude, holy shit," Kyle whispers to Jacob, who remains focused on his dad's video.

"I did not know he was responsible until a few years after we were inside the walls." Ethan holds his face in his hands and pauses long enough that Jacob thought the video froze. "Victor is dying," Ethan removes his hands and speaks in a softer, yet serious tone. "He was diagnosed with a heart disease that is incurable, but able to be slowed via medicine. His time is running short.

"He was desperate then, and he's desperate now. He believes that if he can perfect Vitality and combine those results with our first project, Better Human, that he can create a serum to make humans immortal.

"This may sound delusional, but his plan is possible. It's also dangerous. He claims to want this for humanity and to better our species, but the truth is: he wants it for himself."

The room is silent waiting for him to continue.

"If he's not stopped, he will continue to test on innocent Outsiders until he completes his project. From what I've seen in his files, I believe he has two of the three strains completed. The successful subjects are alive and demonstrating telepathic abilities. But these successful subjects don't come without a cost.

"Each strain has documented failures. Outsiders he has captured, tested on, and the serum causing a negative take to the subject. The failures from his experiments don't die, but become nearly braindead, acting violent, often hurting themselves, and he releases them back outside the walls, documenting them as rejections."

Shriekers. Jacob thinks, as Renz whispers the same to himself.

"He's close to perfecting Vitality. Which makes him more adamant with his questions about my son, Jacob. He hopes to learn if Better Human worked on him so he can use Jacob for Vitality. I've told him it hasn't.

"But the truth is… It has."

Jacob feels Kilian's gaze staring into his neck.

"The evidence for all of this resides in Victor's office, in a safe behind the framed notebook paper on his wall. He has video logs in private folders on his computer that confirm his testing on Outsiders. The password to access his files are inside this," he shows Victor's journal on the camera. "I tried to get these files and was stopped by Victor. I will continue to try and retrieve these files and turn them in with this video; however, I fear he may go to extreme measures to stop me."

Ethan stares off-camera for a moment, then looks back, saying, "I don't know what will happen if he does. Nobody knows about this video… Or my plan." Ethan scoffs, shaking his head. He mutters softly, "What the fuck am I–"

His hand reaches to stop the recording. He pauses, then says, "If… If *that* happens and I… If someone finds this, Victor can *never* know about Jacob."

Ethan stops the recording.

"D-Did… Did Victor k-k–" Renz mutters.

"Kill my dad?" Jacob interrupts, keeping his eyes on the paused image of his father. He bursts from his seat and closes Kyle's laptop. Pulling his dad's laptop from underneath, he slides it to the edge of the desk and looks at Kyle, saying, "You need to power this up. We need to access his files at Volcan Enterprises and find the security footage from the cameras."

"Jacob… I… I don't think I–"

"Try," he demands.

"I don't have a power supply, man, the thing's probably a brick," Kyle defends himself and opens Ethan's laptop. He presses repeatedly, holds the power button, then points to the black screen and says, "See? Nothing."

"Fuck." Jacob fidgets his hands and rubs his face.

"You… This is what you wanted to find, isn't it? Evidence against Victor?" Renz asks. "This is it right here, man, you–"

"My dad thought he was going to kill him. And my dad *is* dead." Jacob holds his arm toward the laptop. "Victor told my mom and I that security footage showed my dad being shot by accident at work. I *need* to know if it's true. I need to see it for myself."

Nobody speaks. They all see the determination and fear in his eyes.

"Let's get back to The Wasteland and show this to Trissa." He stacks the laptops and hands them to Kyle. "They have some kind of power running the shit in the cafeteria, right?" Nobody answers. "*Right*?" He asks Kilian directly.

"Y-Uh… Y-Yeah," he stutters.

"Good. Let's go," Jacob commands and walks around the desk. Moving quickly through the kitchen, he waits at the front door for them to catch up. Kyle stops next to him, adjusting his backpack on his shoulders. Kilian and Renz stop behind Kyle.

Chloe squeezes past them and stands next to Jacob, gives him a concerning look and says, "Jacob. Tell me where your head is. Are you okay?"

His eye contact is brief as he nods his head. He looks at the ground, then back to his friends and nods.

Jacob steps outside onto the porch and sees Theo standing in the front yard with a sword in his hand.

CHAPTER 33

"WAIT HERE," JACOB SAYS TO his friends as he begins to close the door to keep them inside. They all stare past him at Theo who remains still, looking at Jacob.

"Who is that?" Renz asks, nervously.

"He's…" Jacob looks back at Theo, then back to Renz. "I'll take care of it," he adds as he closes the door and turns to walk toward Theo.

Chloe, Renz, and Kyle run into the dining room and watch through the large window.

"Why are you here?" Jacob speaks loudly, stopping several feet away from him in the tall overgrown grass.

"I have to take you back, Jacob," Theo replies. His voice is shaky. Jacob notices his breathing is rapid and short. This wouldn't be from his travels here. This is because he's anxious. "You have to come back to the facility."

"I'm not going back there, Theo."

"You…" Theo sniffles. His eyes are glossed over. He says with his bottom lip shaking, "Jacob, he'll… He's going to kill her if I don't bring you back."

"Jade?" Chloe mutters.

"Who's Jade?" Kyle whispers.

"His twin sister."

They speak quickly, resuming their attention outside.

"I'm sorry," Jacob speaks compassionately. "But you know why I can't go back."

Using his left hand to wipe tears off his cheek, Theo then joins it with his right hand on the hilt of his sword.

"Don't do this, Theo," Jacob says, cautiously.

"I don't have a choice–"

A bang fires from behind Jacob as he watches Theo's right shoulder whip backward. A stream of blood ejects from the back of his shoulder. He drops his sword and holds his hand over where a bullet ripped through, wincing, screaming, "Fuck!"

"Jacob, step back toward me, I have your cover," Kilian yells from the porch. He's standing with his pistol aimed at Theo.

In an exasperated tone, Jacob says, "Not necessary, Kilian. I told you I had this handled."

"He drew his weapon, Jacob. He was preparing to attack."

Releasing a grunt, Jacob ruffles his hair with frustration. He loses sight of Theo, then sees he's knelt down in the tall grass on one knee, holding his hand over the wound. "How bad is it?" Jacob asks.

"I'll be fine," Theo responds, without making eye contact with Jacob.

Stepping toward him, Jacob says, "There's a place not far–"

A metallic thunk sounds from close by, turning Jacob's focus up the road. More crushing metal sings from that direction as he sees a Shrieker standing on the roof of a rusted car. It's standing with bent knees. Its tattered clothes sway wildly as it's shifting its body in circles with its arms extended and head jerking, pointing its ear toward their direction, trying to locate something. That something being the gunshot.

Holding his hand out toward Theo, Jacob quietly shushes him. Turning slowly in the tall grass toward the house, he reactively crouches as another gunshot rips from the porch. Jacob sees Kilian's smoking pistol aimed at the Shrieker.

Immediately looking for the Shrieker's reaction, he sees it falling off the hood of the car.

"Okay. Nice sho–" Jacob is interrupted by a deathly scream. The Shrieker leaps back onto the vehicle. Squeaks from rusty shocks are heard as the car rocks aggressively back and forth. The Shrieker opens its mouth wide, releasing a roar while scratching its fingertips into its elongated cheeks, leaving dark red lines behind.

It leaps high into the air and far off the vehicle toward them, landing into a neighboring yard, disappearing momentarily into the grass. Kilian's pistol clicks as he arms his next shot, waiting for the Shrieker to appear from within the tall swaying blades.

Rustling and crunching grows louder as it runs on all fours toward them, finally revealing itself in the yard next door. Kilian immediately fires, missing the Shrieker.

"Come on, man," Jacob yells nervously.

Another shot rings but misses.

"I'm not used to shooting moving targets, man, I–"

He fires again, hitting the Shrieker's chest, sending it back into the tall grass just as it enters their yard.

Jacob quickly demands, "Get inside–"

A gross hiss gurgles from the slowly standing Shrieker. Saliva bubbles from its brown, exposed teeth, combining with the blood dripping down its cheeks, sending pink streams over its chin. Kilian shoots, sending a bullet through its forearm. It looks at the hole in its arm, then whips its head toward Kilian, lunging itself into a full sprint in his direction.

Kilian fires, missing the Shrieker, allowing it to quickly grapple him and throw its head into his shoulder, pinning his pistol between their bodies with the nose against its chest. Jacob and Theo begin to run to his defense as another shot fires, exploding a red mist and chunks of flesh from the back of the Shrieker. Kilian screams in agony as he falls backward with the limp body of the Shrieker falling on top of him. Jacob hears grunting from Theo and looks over to see him lying in the grass, holding his neck, which is protruding blood from under his fingers.

Forced to make a decision between the two of them, Jacob rushes to help Kilian, pulling the dead Shrieker off of him. Jacob immediately sees a ripped chunk of skin and muscle hanging from the bottom of his neck next to a dark-red hole with scratches from the Shrieker's teeth extending from both sides. Blood pours from the exposed tissue as Kilian's shaking hand slowly reaches toward the gaping wound.

Jacob grabs his wrist and helps him put pressure on the bleeding. With his two hands and Kilian's hand, they are failing at slowing the blood from adding to the large pool growing in the dirt underneath him. Kilian turns his head to look at Jacob. His face is pale and his eyes are weak. He speaks with a raspy voice, saying, "I... I don't want to die, Jacob." Tears fall from the corners of his eyes.

"I..." Jacob breaks eye contact and pushes harder on his injury. His teeth are gritting inside his mouth. He looks at Kilian and says, "I know." His voice stutters.

"My legs are cold. I can't feel your hands anymore."

Jacob leans all of his body weight into his hands. Through his tightly gritted teeth, he mutters, "No. No."

In a weak whisper, Kilian says, "I'm dying, aren't I?"

Thrusting his weight into his hands, Jacob watches Kilian's head fall to the side. He rests backward, sitting on the backs of his feet, letting his bloody hands fall at his sides. Jacob releases a scream of anger. As his voice trails from the air leaving his lungs, a cough from behind him reminds him that Theo is lying in the grass.

Crawling through the tall green blades, Jacob kneels at Theo's side. His hand is oozing blood between his fingers pressed against his neck.

Now helping him hold pressure, Jacob asks, "How did this happen?"

"The bullet from… From the back of the Shrieker. Hit…" He points at his neck with his other hand. Theo begins to sit up, causing Jacob to resist and hold him down. Theo grunts, "He… He gave us your sample."

Jacob lets him sit up, giving a confused look.

"Victor gave us samples from your DNA. It gave us all your healing ability," Theo says as he stares at the porch, still holding a hand on his neck. "It healed Elliot's eye. It will heal this."

He said my sample was for Chloe's mom, Jacob thinks. "He gave it to *all* of you?"

"Me, Jade, and Elliot, yeah."

Releasing a sigh, Jacob stands, holding his hand out to assist Theo to his feet. As he finds his balance, Jacob says to him, "You still need to get the bleeding to stop before you get too weak. There's a compound nearby. It's in that direction. Keep going south, look for rusty metal walls, and go to the gate. When they stop you, tell them I sent you."

"Th-Thanks. Is that where you're staying?"

"Yeah." Jacob looks over at Kilian's body lying next to the dead Shrieker. "I'll be there after I figure out what to do with him. When I do get back, we'll figure out a way to save Jade."

Theo nods, picks up his sword, sheathing it in his back holster, then walks in the direction Jacob pointed.

Renz, Kyle, and Chloe cautiously walk outside and over to Jacob, who is standing over Kilian's body. Chloe wraps her arms around Jacob's arm and rests her head into his shoulder.

Renz leans over Kilian and pulls a chain from his neck. "My dad told me about these. He had them from when he served in the old-world." He hands Kilian's dog tags to Jacob.

"We need to do something with him before we head back," Jacob says to them.

They search Ethan and Amber's home for shovels, finding two in the garage. After checking the fenced-in backyard, they dig a hole next to wildly overgrown shrubbery lining the inside of the fence. Together they carry Kilian back, burying him gently into the grave. For several minutes, they stand next to the grave in silence.

On the walk back, their footsteps repeat a rhythm of breaking twigs and leaves. A cold wind repeatedly cuts through, sending a chill over their skin and carrying a whisper of leaves rustling. They're brought to a stop when Jacob holds his arm out in front of them.

"You've got to be kidding me," Renz says, angered and nervous. He's looking at a young kid standing ahead of them in the woods. She's staring at them with bloodshot eyes.

"It's fine. It's just an Outsider," Jacob speaks, stepping slowly in her direction. Her appearance is what they're used to seeing in wild Outsiders: faded shirt from the old-world that's been worn repeatedly along with dirty jeans that show they've been climbing and crawling through these woods for years. "She should run from us," he says, quietly.

The girl jerks to attention, locking her elbows and knees. Her bloodshot eyes start widened and full of fear, then switch quickly to anger. She roars and sprints toward the group. Her arms flail as she runs at full speed, kicking up dirt and leaves under her feet. Jacob steps up to console her when she pushes him aggressively away, knocking him onto his back. She pushes Chloe to the ground, then runs directly into Renz, sending them both into the dirt.

Renz screams in panic as his arms push rapidly against her. He pushes her away and scrambles to get to his feet when she gets on all fours and jumps on top of him.

Kyle throws his backpack to the ground and grabs the girl's shoulders, pulling with all his strength, unable to get her to budge. Her arms are next to Renz's head and her head is writhing on his shoulder. He screams in agony.

Chloe runs over with a thick branch and swings, connecting with the girl's head. She falls to the side, unconscious. Renz sobs, moving his hand below his ripped shirt and bloody shoulder.

Jacob rushes over and helps him to his feet. Renz is crying uncontrollably. Jacob taps his uninjured shoulder and says, "You'll be okay, bro. It's not bleeding too much. We'll get back and get you fixed up."

"Jacob." Renz barely can speak through his sobbing. "I don't have the vaccine."

CHAPTER 34

KYLE AND JACOB ARE PANTING breathlessly through the tall grass of the farmland as they carry Renz with his arms around their shoulders.

"We're almost there!" Chloe yells to them from several steps in front of them. They can see the rusty metal walls as they pass by the rotted and moldy barn.

"Hang in there, Renz," Jacob pants.

"I'm… I'm sor…" Renz can't finish. His head bobs weakly as they run. Jacob feels the arm around his neck twitch. With every other step they take, Renz's head hits against Jacob's cheek, revealing his skin is hot from a spiked fever.

"We need to hurry," he speaks to Kyle, knowing they're both running on adrenaline at this point.

As they approach the gate, Jacob screams weakly, out of breath, "We need Isaac or Trissa." The guard pulls their hood back and looks over them with concern. "Now!" Jacob yells demandingly. The guard speaks into a radio.

While they wait, Jacob taps his foot impatiently, unable to calm his nerves. Feeling heat resonating off Renz's entire body now, he inhales, ready to yell for help when he sees Isaac running to the gate.

"Open it," Isaac yells up to the guard on the catwalk. He and Jacob stare at each other through the rising, unprofessionally welded squares. Clanging rings through the walls as it opens. Seeing a faint bruise on Jacob's face, blood on Jacob's arm, worry in Jacob's eyes, and Renz barely conscious in between him and Kyle, Isaac asks, cautiously, "What happened?"

"He got bit by an… By an Outsider."

"You're all from the walls, right?" Isaac looks at Chloe, saying, "Except for you?"

Chloe drops her head.

"We are, but he's not vaccinated like the rest of us." Jacob answers. "I felt him twitch, I think he–"

Isaac quickly ducks under the half-open gate and takes Renz from Jacob and Kyle. He speaks into his radio, "I need two from medical at the west gate, *now*." Adjusting Renz's arm over his shoulders, Isaac asks, "How long ago was he bit?"

"T-Twenty… Thirty minutes?" Jacob answers. Boots thud as two residents dressed in their soldier apparel run to Isaac.

"Take him to the isolation room in medical. Get him restrained in a bed and connected to IVs. We have maybe thirty minutes before he fully turns," Isaac orders the soldiers. They nod, each taking a side of Renz, and they walk down the street.

Jacob rubs his face aggressively and sighs. When he moves his hands, he sees Isaac looking around them, confused. He looks at Jacob with a questioning stare. Releasing another sigh, Jacob pulls the dog tags from his pocket and hands them to Isaac.

Staring at the tags in the palm of his hand, Isaac slowly blinks, then asks, "What happened?"

"We were attacked by Shriekers… Ghouls. He… He fought to protect us and…"

Isaac looks to the sky, then back into the compound, muttering, "Maybe he *was* too innocent for this." He snaps his head back to Jacob, Chloe and Kyle. "Your friend. How is he from the walls and not vaccinated?"

"He said his dad was a city judge. During the outbreak, their vehicle was ambushed on the way to the walls. His dad was stabbed, so they rushed him and his mom into the medical unit inside the walls, bypassing the security checkpoint where the vaccines were being mandated." Jacob inhales. "By the time they got acclimated, they figured they were safe inside the walls and didn't act on it. Renz was born without them passing the immunity to him, and they were too embarrassed to admit it, so they kept it a secret," Jacob finishes, seeing an impressed look from Kyle as he repeated almost word-for-word what Renz told them as they carried him through the woods.

Isaac shakes his head and rolls his eyes. "Did you find what you went out for?"

They all nod.

"Good. Let's get inside, get you cleaned up, fed, and meet with Trissa. Take your time showering and changing. I need to deliver this news to the others." Isaac holds up Killian's dog tags.

Jacob is the last one to get to the cafeteria, as he stood in the shower under the hot water replaying Kilian's dying words, Renz getting attacked and infected, and his dad's words from the video. The video he hears ending now, as he sits at the table in a brown long-sleeve shirt and cargo pants, picking at food on a plate in front of him, while Trissa, Isaac, and Deante finish watching.

"Dude…" Deante mutters and looks at Jacob.

Jacob tightens his lips and raises his eyebrows. He watches Trissa and Isaac whisper with one another.

"This is a lot," Trissa speaks, motioning to the laptop. "You'll still need the files your father mentioned to go along with this if you expect anybody to believe it."

"I know." Jacob nods. He continues to stab diced potatoes with his fork.

"Even with all of this, it's still a gamble to go after a powerful political figure like Victor. There's no way of knowing if this CC News will air it no matter how much evidence you give to support it."

"We won't give them a choice," Jacob answers quickly. He looks up from his plate and sees everyone at the table looking at him, waiting for him to elaborate. He says, "CC News broadcasts their alerts to all TVs and cell phones. If they refuse to air this on Victor, then we will."

"*We* will?" Isaac questions.

"Yes."

"How?" Trissa, Isaac, and Deante ask simultaneously.

"Kyle will hack into their system."

"I will?" Kyle asks, looking over the laptop.

"Yes," Jacob insists. "You've already hacked into the Volcan Enterprises database. While I get the files my dad talked about, you can work to hack into CC News' database." He's looking at the continued surprise on their faces. "You can use the passwords from the diary my dad showed and find Victor's private data. We send that, there's no way they can deny taking him down."

Trissa raises an eyebrow and nods. Her and Isaac whisper again, then she says, "How much time do you need to get the files from Victor's office?"

"A day." Jacob answers, now pushing around corn on his plate.

"A day?" Isaac questions Jacob's confidence.

"I'll make it happen. I'm going to Victor's office tomorrow morning." Jacob stops moving his fork and lowers his eyebrows as he looks at Isaac. Jacob's forearms and palms pulsate with electric tingling the more he thinks about the idea of Victor being responsible for his father's death.

"O-Okay. We'll hold off our attack of the city while you do it. We'll continue to be a source of help for whatever you need."

"Thank you," Jacob says. Kyle opens Ethan's laptop and begins clicking and typing.

"Understand that if this doesn't work, our plans to attack will resume."

Jacob swirls his fork, combining the potatoes and corn on his plate. He watches them intertwine and roll off his fork, then says, "Just… Let us bring our families here before you do."

Isaac nods in agreement.

"Is there anything any of you need at the moment?" Trissa asks. She watches them look at each other.

"Is Theo here?" Jacob asks.

"I'm sorry… Who?"

Jacob returns her confused expression.

"W-Will Renz be… Will he–" Kyle stutters, pausing the loud typing he was doing on the laptop.

"He has a very long road ahead of him," Isaac answers compassionately. "I don't want any of your expectations to be misguided. It will be a long time before he's the person you remember."

A fork clangs against a plate, bringing everyone's attention to Jacob, who is leaning on the table with his head in his hands. He's rubbing his face aggressively, struggling to keep his thoughts composed.

Chloe rubs Jacob's back gently and presses her lips together for a forced smile she gives to Trissa.

Jacob sighs and looks off into the cafeteria.

Trissa gives a concerned smile to Jacob, who doesn't see it, then says, "Stay as long as you need. You can keep using the power supply," She says to Kyle, "We'll be in the next building if you need us."

"I got in," Kyle announces.

Jacob breaks his stare and looks at Kyle. Trissa stands and moves behind Kyle, looking over his shoulder.

"Your dad's login worked. I'm in the Volcan Enterprises database." Kyle shows excitement at his discovery.

"Can you access security footage?" Jacob shows a little enthusiasm at this revelation.

"P-Probably. I just need to figure out how to navigate this syst–"

"Sir, we need you at the gate, immediately," Isaac's radio sounds.

"What's going on?" Isaac responds. A click of white noise sounds when he releases the button.

"We've got two people here matching the description of the attackers our scouts reported."

Isaac bursts from his seat as does Jacob. "You all stay here, I'll handle it," Isaac demands, then quickly leaves.

A moment of silence holds in the cafeteria as everyone trades glances and gestures of concern. Trissa looks over Kyle and meets eyes with Jacob. Seconds pass as they stare, then Jacob turns and exits the cafeteria. He hears Trissa yell his name but continues to run, passing the buildings down the dirt path, then turning onto the street. He sees Isaac standing at the gate, waiting for it to open, the orange glow of the sky casting a black silhouette of the two outside the gate.

As he gets closer, he hears Elliot's voice saying, "...Looking for Second Place. Give me him and I'll leave you all alone."

Isaac yells over the turning gears, "I don't know who it is you're speaking of, but I can assure you, we do *not* negotiate deals by offering up our people. Turn away now and–"

"There he is," Elliot says singingly with an evil smile.

Isaac turns and sees Jacob arrive at the gate. "I told you I will handle this," he says, angrily.

"They're here for me. Let me–"

Isaac pushes against Jacob's chest and exits the gate. He walks toward Elliot. Jacob sees Theo standing next to Elliot. They stare briefly, then Theo looks to the ground, embarrassed.

Standing in front of Elliot, Isaac motions his arm to the guard on the catwalk and says, "As you can see, we are well guarded. I'll say it one more time. You should leave."

"*One more time,*" Elliot mocks Isaac. "That's cute." He scoffs, then in a swift motion, reaches a hand behind Isaac's right shoulder while pushing his other hand against the front of his left shoulder, spinning Isaac around and grappling his neck. He raises his right leg, pulls a hunting knife out of his boot, and holds it against his throat.

Trissa sprints next to Jacob and gasps as she watches Elliot holding Isaac. Isaac looks directly at Trissa and speaks softly saying, "It's okay. It's okay."

"Let him go!" Trissa yells from the gate.

Elliot smiles devilishly at Jacob and says, "Give me Second Place, and this old man is all yours."

Jacob steps forward and feels Trissa's arm hit his chest, telling him to wait. He looks and sees her eyes scolding Elliot.

Isaac mutters nervously, "Trissa… Don't–"

"Guard, fire!" Trissa yells, pointing at Elliot. A bang roars through the sky, echoing off in the distance. The bullet pierces through Elliot's left eye and out the side of his face in a cloud of red mist. His hold remains on Isaac as his head whips to the side.

Elliot laughs quietly as he turns his head back to Trissa. He's grinning as blood pours down his face from the hole where his eye was.

With a scoff, Elliot says lightly, "I *just* got that fuckin' eye fixed, too." He laughs and releases the arm grappling Isaac against him. Then he quickly jerks his other elbow outward, slicing his blade across Isaac's neck.

Isaac's eyes widen in fear. He pulls his hands to his neck but is stopped when Elliot wraps his arms behind his torso, holding Isaac upright and, with his other hand, pulling Isaac's head back, making Trissa, Jacob, and the guard watch.

Gurgling and coughing emerge from Isaac's mouth as he moves his jaw. His body begins to squirm slowly, and his face slowly relaxes. Elliot throws him forward, and Isaac lands hard against the concrete.

Jacob watches as Isaac lies still over his own blood pooling under his neck. His hands feel like they're on fire as the tingling in his palms extends to his elbows. He sprints forward toward Elliot.

Laughing, Elliot hunches forward, throwing his knife far off to the side, ready for this fight with Jacob. "Bring it, Second Place."

Jacob sends a powerful punch into Elliot's forehead. His head jerks back, then he lowers his eyebrows and returns a punch to Jacob's cheek.

His head whips to the side, then back, then Jacob swings a left hook to the side of Elliot's good eye. Elliot absorbs the hit, returning a left hook of his own toward Jacob's face.

"Close the gate!" Trissa yells. Her demand is followed by gears clanging.

With the tingling in his arms still burning, Jacob yells, whipping his right hand in the air, blocking Elliot's swing.

Elliot groans from the force of the hit. Jacob raises his knee and kicks Elliot's chest, sending him stumbling backward.

Reaching his left hand outward, Jacob spreads his fingers with his palm toward Elliot. He feels pressure pulsing through his fingers as he thinks, *stop*. Elliot expresses shock as he comes to an immediate halt with his arms held outward. He's leaning backward on one foot, off-balance, but unable to move.

Jacob closes his fist, feeling resistance as if he's squeezing a tennis ball, then pulls his left arm back in, launching Elliot toward him. Elliot groans. He's moving chest-first through the air toward Jacob, who swings a powerful punch into the hole in his face, sending Elliot backward onto the ground.

Jacob screams as he falls forward, swinging his right fist at Elliot who rolls to the side, forcing Jacob's fist into the concrete. He releases another scream as the bones in his hand snap from his knuckles hitting the pavement, leaving cracks and small pieces of gravel around his fist.

"Jacob!" Chloe yells. Jacob, kneeled on the ground holding his injured hand, glances over and sees her standing at the gate with her fingers gripping between the square holes. Deante and Kyle stand in shock next to her.

Jumping to his feet, Elliot yells at Theo, saying, "Feel like helping at all?" Theo steps backward, nervously. Scoffing, he says, "Fine. I don't need your fuckin' help anyway." As Jacob begins to stand, Elliot bursts forward, punching his right cheek. Jacob hears a cracking from his orbital bone and tastes iron in his mouth. He spits blood onto the street then pushes off his feet, uppercutting Elliot's chin with his good hand. As his head whips back, thick, red liquid ropes stream through the air from his missing eye. Elliot stumbles backward, then catches his balance.

Blood rushes down Jacob's cheek from an open gash. Elliot stands a few feet away with blood covering the left side of his face. His white teeth show through the red as he grimaces at Jacob.

Noticing that Jacob's right hand is hanging limp and bloody, Elliot laughs and says, "You could've made this easy, Second Place."

Jacob spits blood from his mouth.

"All you had to do was listen to Victor like the rest of us." Elliot wipes blood from his face with his forearm. New blood immediately streams and fills it back in. "You'll never know what you're truly capable of, like me. The *better* human." He hears Chloe whimper from the gate and looks at her, then back to Jacob and chuckles, saying, "Even your girlfriend knows to listen to Victor. She knows that none of us would be anything without him."

Elliot laughs as he watches Jacob clench his left fist while his right arm remains limp and injured. Jacob says, "You're wrong."

Elliot scoffs.

"*You* have no fucking idea what I'm capable of," Jacob says, reaching forward. Feeling confirmation in his palm as he thinks about pulling Elliot, he sees Elliot's eye widen with shock. Jacob pulls his arm in, sending Elliot toward him. He swings his left arm, punching Elliot's good eye.

"You killed that boy." Jacob screams.

Elliot reaches his arm back with a roar leaving his lips. As he swings the punch, Jacob raises his left hand and clasps his fingers into a fist, thinking about grabbing Elliot's arm. In an instant, Elliot freezes. He gasps and looks frighteningly at Jacob. Swinging his right elbow, Jacob attacks Elliot's bloody half of his face. Blood sprays through the air as his head whips to the side.

"You killed Isaac." Jacob screams loader.

Jacob watches Elliot struggle to keep standing as he wipes the blood off his face, shaking the blood from his hands, then stumbling a step toward Jacob. As Elliot scoffs, then opens his mouth to reply, Jacob thrusts his left hand forward, feeling the tingling rush from his shoulder to his palm, launching Elliot through the air backward and landing on his back, sliding along the pavement.

A raspy breath escapes his lips as Elliot quickly shuffles to his knees while Jacob walks toward him.

Breathing rapidly, tasting blood, feeling blood run past his chin and down his neck, Jacob stands and watches Elliot breathe slowly on his knees with his arms slouched at his sides and his head hanging forward.

"Get up," Jacob demands.

Elliot smiles slowly. Thick maroon blood flows down his chin as his lips spread into a teeth-showing smile. He begins to laugh. His torso shakes with each chuckle. His good eye twitches as it's surrounded by purple swelling. The whites of it are red. The hole in his face is still seeping blood down onto his bare chest and the straps of his sword holster. His laugh is quiet but becomes more menacing as his eye peers into Jacob.

Chloe's voice screams Jacob's name as a warm sensation burns through his chest. His breathing becomes labored and difficult with the urge to cough, but his ribs feel like nails stabbing his lungs. He gags as blood fills his mouth from his throat. His vision fades in and out of blurriness while Elliot gets to his feet.

Jacob's head drops and he sees a sword piercing through his chest. *Theo?* he thinks as he tries to speak but can't, as his breathing is shallow now. His body jerks backward and burning rips through him when the sword is pulled from his body.

Jacob falls to his knees and sees Elliot's boots directly in front of him. He hears muffled cries from Chloe and yelling from Kyle and Deante. Bangs from their fists hitting the gate sound like low frequency bells far away. His head whips back when Elliot kneels and grabs a handful of Jacob's hair.

"You better not fuckin' die before I get you back to Victor," Elliot mutters. Jacob struggles to keep his eyes open while staring at the hole in Elliot's face.

Elliot throws Jacob's arm over his shoulder and heaves him up, carrying him like a bag of sand. He begins to walk away, stopping when he sees Theo staring at the gate. "Fuckin' come on," he barks.

Chloe watches Theo hang his head and walk beside Elliot. Jacob's arms hang next to his head, hair swaying and bouncing with each step Elliot takes. She cries and hangs from her hands, still interlocked in the holes of the gate, watching Jacob's limp body be carried off into the distance.

CHAPTER 35

A LOW, STEADY BUZZ HUMS endlessly in Jacob's ears. Bright lights cast a pink glow through his eyelids. He tries to open them, finding he's unable to move any muscle or limb. Pressure is felt around his head, but no pain comes with it. Someone is speaking, but listening to their words is like trying to hear underwater. Jacob's body is being moved by something. Or someone. As he fights harder to open his eyes, everything goes dark and quiet again.

Louder, higher-pitched humming returns to his ears, this time with a stinging in his cheek and his head forcefully jerking to the side. Noel slaps his cheek again, speaking under his breath, "...can hear me, you need to wake up."

Jacob begins to regain feeling and weakly hisses as the burning in his cheek intensifies from Noel's repeated attempts to wake him.

"Dude. Dude. Okay. Stop." Jacob grunts, bringing a hand to his cheek. His throat is scratchy and he squints his eyes, moving his arm to shield them from the light. Forcing multiple blinks, he finally sees the room and Noel in focus. He's in a medical room lying on a tan bed. Given the fact that Noel stands beside the bed he's in, he must be inside Victor's facility. Noel stands, holding folded clothes under his arm, looking the most exhausted and worn that Jacob has seen him. The bags under his eyes are such a dark purple, they look nearly black. His hair looks thinner and lighter, and his skin is so thin that all his veins can be seen wherever his tattered and aged clothes don't cover.

"Sorry, I–" Noel presses his eyes closed and rubs his forehead as Jacob's thoughts fill his mind. Jacob has begun to panic as his hands vigorously rub his head. "Yeah, they, uh… They operated on your head."

Jacob hisses again as he touches a painful spot on the back of his head where he feels a small rectangular cut. "They took…" He hesitates.

"A brain sample, yes." Noel observes Jacob's buzzed-off hair. "You're probably only alive because of your healing abilities. Or luck." He pauses. "Or both."

"That's reassuring," Jacob mutters, sitting up, feeling a pain in his torso where he was stabbed as he turns to sit on the side of the bed. They stare at each other as Jacob contemplates asking Noel the question on his mind.

Sighing with disappointment, Noel says, "Yes. Victor is responsible for your dad's death."

Jacob lowers his head into his hands and sighs. The palms of his hands grow a tingling sensation.

"If your dad didn't cooperate with giving Victor your samples, he had Elliot prepared to…" Noel doesn't finish his sentence.

"Elliot killed my dad?"

Noel hums confirmation.

"Can he be any worse?" He says under his breath.

"Yes." Knowing it was rhetorical and not meant to be heard, Noel replies anyway.

Jacob moves his head from his hands, expressing determination in his face, and shifts himself off the table onto his feet. He looks at the clothes under Noel's arm and asks, "Are those mine?"

"Yes. Well, they're *for* you. They're David's. Yours were bloody and " Noel waits for Jacob's eye contact. They stare without speaking, allowing the hum of the lights to be the only sound in the room.

"Thank you."

Noel nods. He weakly raises his eyebrows to show he knows what Jacob wants to ask next and is waiting for him to speak.

"If I get the files from Victor's office, will it be enough to take him down?"

"My concern is whether you're prepared to do what it takes if it's not," Noel replies, handing him the clothes. As Jacob begins to put the jeans on under his medical robe, Noel continues, "Victor has what he needs from you now. The more time he has, the more it will work on him." Noel moves from side to side to keep eye contact with Jacob as he continues getting dressed. "Jacob. He's going to relentlessly test on more subjects until he gets the third strain to complete Vitality. Then, he intends to combine your sample with it and create subjects with all sorts of telepathic abilities who will be damn near immortal." He's leaning over to keep Jacob's attention while he ties his shoes. "He'll have an army of people who can do what Chloe does and hear thoughts like me. It'll be impossible to get to him. Are you listening to me?"

"Yes." Jacob stands. "That's why I'm going to stop him."

"You are the only one that can stop him." Noel's tone is serious.

"No pressure." Jacob pulls a hoodie over his head.

"No. Jacob. I mean you're the *only* one who can stop him. And Victor knows this." Waiting for Jacob to finish putting his arms through the hoodie and look at him, he pauses, then says, "If he was willing to kill your father, he'll be willing to…"

"I've put that together, Noel," Jacob replies, putting his hands in his hoodie pocket, finding his phone. He takes it out and shows it to Noel, saying, "They didn't confiscate this?"

"They *did*. But I know the code to his office and safe."

"Nice." Jacob chuckles lightly. "What happened to Elliot?"

"He's in another medical room receiving blood. He barely survived, even with the healing ability he got from you. All the blood loss from his eye."

Jacob scoffs. "And what about–"

Noel winces, hunching forward. He straightens his posture, scratches his arm and says, "I… I have to go. I can't be seen helping you." He runs out the door.

"…Theo…" Jacob finishes his question as he watches the door shut, then leans against the medical bed. He touches his fingertips together, placing his pointer fingers against his lips as he thinks. *The Wasteland.* He reaches into his hoodie pocket again, grabbing his phone, when the door to the room bursts open. Standing outside the doorway is Theo. He's wearing jeans and a long-sleeved shirt instead of his training gear, but still wears his back holster with his swords sheathed.

"Jacob, I–"

"Save it, Theo."

Motioning his arms at his sides, Theo says, "I didn't have a choice. I–"

"Didn't have a choice? I was *helping* you, Theo. I told you about the compound and you *choose* to bring Elliot there."

Theo's head drops.

"He killed their leader," Jacob speaks with a raised voice. "He could have killed how many innocent people there. *And* you helped him try to kill me. Just… Fucking leave, man."

"I know. I'm sorry. But want to help you, Jacob. I'm here now to help you." He's being genuine as he says, "Jade is waiting at a safe location we found on a hunt months ago. I told her I was going to get you and we'd get away from here together."

"No."

"We'll save your friends. We'll take whoever you wish and get away from here. From all of this."

"I'm not running away from this." Jacob stands from his lean. "But I agree, you and Jade should–" He stops when he sees a hand grip the hilt of one of Theo's swords. "Theo, behind–"

In a swift motion, the hand unsheathes the sword and swings it down, cutting through Theo's shoulder, through to the center of his torso. Theo's body spasms as his eyes widen in fear before losing all expression as he falls forward, slamming against the floor with the sword sticking out from his back. Standing behind him is Elliot.

He is smiling at Jacob. A bandage is wrapped around the top of his head, over his missing eye, and dark red blood stains where the hole is underneath. Trails of blood stream heavily down the left side of his face, down his neck to stain the top half of the medical gown he's wearing. On his left arm hangs a ripped-off IV line that is also dripping blood from inside his elbow.

Elliot chuckles silently, then gives a sarcastic frown with his lips as he says, "I should've…" He gestures a stabbing motion. "You know, like he did to you. Really missed the chance at a poetic moment there." He laughs and shrugs. "Oh, well. I can finally kill you now."

Elliot steps toward the door, stumbling from losing his balance.

"You killed my father," Jacob speaks. As his palms begin to tingle, he opens the fingers on this left hand at his side, feeling pressure in them as he thinks about bringing the sword sticking out of Theo to himself.

While swaying heavily, Elliot forces an arrogant smile and nods his head. His eyes turn to the sword as he sees it twitch in Theo's back. His head bobbles weakly as he forces a laugh and says, "You think you're fuckin'… You think that teleki–" he coughs as his knees give out beneath him. Barely catching his balance, he continues. "You think that mind shit makes you better than me?"

Jacob feels electricity through his wrist and forearms. "You're not looking so good, First Place. Even with you stealing my healing abilities," he says, taking two steps toward him.

"I'm fi–" His torso sways as he coughs, causing a gush of thick blood to burst from the bloody bandage, opening the clot and sending an aggressive flow of blood down his face and over his gown.

Jacob stays still, watching Elliot struggle to stand.

"I–" Another cough sends the blood rushing faster. He falls onto his knees, staring his eye at Jacob. "Help me, Jacob."

Jacob watches him losing blood. He thinks of everything this man has done to him and to others. Jacob scrunches his face and presses his eyes closed, clenching his fist as he angrily grunts, then rushes to Elliot.

Kneeling in front of him, Jacob rips off a portion of Elliot's gown that isn't covered in blood, folds it and presses it against the blood-spewing bandage. He grabs Elliot's left hand and presses it over the folded piece, saying, "Keep pressure on this." While holding Elliot's head and helping put pressure on the wound, Jacob looks frantically around them to find where Elliot's medical room is located.

Seeing a trail of blood drops, Jacob turns to Elliot to say, "We need to get you back to–" he stops when he sees Elliot reaching for the sword in Theo's back.

Jacob jumps to his feet. "Seriously?" He speaks loudly. Elliot's head slumps forward as the blood from his eye begins to flow again. His shoulders bounce as he releases a short chuckle.

Elliot's head bobs weakly as he lifts it to look at Jacob. His mouth opens to speak, then his eye rolls backward and he collapses forward, thudding onto the floor, landing with his head next to Theo's leg.

Jacob stands still, watching Elliot, waiting for him to move. His arms and legs twitch violently, smacking off the tile floor of the hallway, then his body goes still. A small puddle of blood begins to form under his face.

With his hands now gripping the phone in his hoodie pocket, Jacob sighs, stepping backward slowly from Elliot, keeping his focus on him, making sure he isn't moving or getting up. Once far enough away, he turns and sees the dorms up ahead. He walks past, making his way to the parking garage. All the lights in the facility are off except for a row of dim lights glowing down the hallway along the center of the ceiling. The training room looks eerie as he passes, like there's infinite darkness beyond the glass windows. The stillness and silence of the hallway feels like it carries whispers Jacob is unable to hear.

Notifications fill the screen of Jacob's phone, consisting of missed calls and texts from Chloe, Kyle, and Deante. He taps the most recent and calls Chloe.

A full ring doesn't sound before Chloe answers, yelling, "Jacob. Please tell me it's you."

"It's me." He hears her sigh in relief. The background behind her is full of yelling and commotion. The noise is high-pitched through the phone, causing him to pull away from his ear.

"Jacob, it's bad. They're–"

"Is that Jacob?" Deante is heard through the noise. "Let me… Put it on speaker."

The background noise blares louder. He pulls the phone further away and holds it near his chest. The sounds from his phone echo lightly through the hall.

"Dude, it's an absolute nightmare here." Deante sounds nervous.

"What's–"

"Trissa is on a rampage. She's been prepping the army all night and all day. They're gathering now to attack the city."

"Dammit," Jacob says to himself, away from the phone. "Put Trissa on the phone. I need to talk to her."

"O-Okay. I need to find her," Chloe says. Loud, indistinguishable voices yell through the phone as Jacob listens to Chloe trudge through a crowd of soldiers.

Trissa's voice cuts through the noise as she gets closer. Her voice is commanding. She's giving orders to someone. She stops and says, "What's this?"

"Hello?" Trissa speaks through the phone.

"Trissa. Please. You can't attack the city yet," Jacob speaks, panicked but assertive.

"No. That's not how this works, kid," she replies sternly.

"Please. You *can't* attack yet. I can still get to–"

"Do you know how many of my fucking people your city has killed? *Do you?*"

"Victor killed them, Trissa. *Not* the city. The people inside the walls are innocent."

"Isaac was innocent. Isaac was the one who convinced me to give you a chance. This discussion is over."

"Wait. Trissa. What about our deal? You said that we could bring our parents there to–"

A long pause lingers leaving Jacob to listen to the soldiers yelling and chanting.

"The deal stands, but I'm not waiting." Rustling distortion plays through the phone as Trissa pushes it away and gives it back to Chloe.

Jacob takes a large, sighing inhale, holding the phone against his chest.

"J-Jacob?" Chloe says nervously among the loud voices again.

"Chlo. Can you get back to Kyle and Deante?" He's pacing in the hallway, listening anxiously to the yelling and chanting through the phone.

"Yes, I'm heading there now." Chloe speaks breathlessly as she pushes back through the crowd of soldiers and jogs to their friends.

"Okay. We're all here," she says.

"We need to get our parents out of the city," Jacob speaks.

"What are you thinking, man?" Deante asks, still showing nerves in his voice.

"First, Kyle, while we're talking, get back onto my dad's laptop." Jacob begins. Kyle hums in agreement. "Log back into Volcan Enterprises under his name and find a way to open the main gates of the city."

"Can I do that remotely from the laptop?"

"Every time Garret drove me out of the city, I saw the guard's computer up. It looked like just a program that controlled the gates. Hopefully, you can find that and control it remotely."

"Got it," Kyle says.

"Okay." Jacob rubs his hair as he paces. "All of you will need to get to the wall as fast as possible. Kyle and Deante… Find a way to convince your parents to get in the car and drive to The Wasteland."

"Fuck. How are we going to do that?" Deante asks.

"I… I don't know, dude. Just give it your best pitch."

Deante mutters to himself.

"Chlo. Get back to the vehicle Garret gave us outside the walls. Drive to my house and bring my mom back with you. Please."

"Of course, Jacob," Chloe says compassionately.

"D… Get Renz's parents if you can."

"I will–"

"I found it," Kyle says. "There's an emergency override that will keep the gate open or closed when I activate it."

"Good. Do it," Jacob demands.

"It's going to draw attention. Who knows how long until someone else overrides the override."

"Once you activate it, move as quickly as possible. This is our only shot."

"You can count on us, bro," Deante says. "But… What about you? Where even are you?"

"I'm at the facility. I'm… I'm pretty far away." Jacob turns to the door to the garage and runs to it. "One of these other vehicles might have keys." He sees two vehicles parked inside the garage. Sprinting to the closest one, he opens the door and searches for keys inside. Chloe, Deante, and Kyle discuss their plans while Jacob searches. "Figures. Nothing," he mutters, slamming the door shut and running to the next vehicle. The driver's door is locked. The back door is locked. The trunk and the passenger side doors are locked. "Fuck!" Jacob's voice echoes through the large garage. "I have to make it on foot," he speaks into the phone.

"Oh. Cool. Nice. So, like, how long will that take?" Deante replies.

"It's going to be awhile. If I jog and run, maybe under two hours."

"*Two hours*?" all three of them yell simultaneously.

Jacob exits the garage and looks at the glowing, evening sky. Dark gray clouds sit in patches among the gradient of yellow and orange. He shuts his eyes, mentally preparing for his journey on foot. "Please, just focus on getting the parents out of the city before Trissa attacks. Don't worry about me. I'll get the files from Victor's office then come straight to The Wasteland."

"We got it, man."

"Be careful. And all of you text me and let me know you got them all back to The Wasteland."

"We will."

"I love all of you," Jacob says, then hangs up the phone and begins jogging.

CHAPTER 36

<u>TRISSA</u>

"**D**O YOU UNDERSTAND THE ORDERS?" Trissa leans over a large table with her hands on a map depicting the Conservation City of Pittsburgh and its immediate surroundings. She turns her head, meeting eyes with a roomful of soldiers in tan shirts and cargo pants. Some wear their bandanas over the lower half of their faces, ranging from forest green to dark brown in color. "I asked if you all understand the orders?"

"Yes, ma'am," synchronized voices respond with nods. Most of the room is standing at attention.

A nervous soldier speaks through his bandana, saying, "M-Ma'am… If we… If we just throw these grenades and Molotovs over the wall… We'll…" He drops his head and stops talking.

Trissa stands from her lean and pushes soldiers away from the table to get to the soldier that was speaking. "Remove your bandana," she commands the soldier looking at her boots. "Look at me and remove your bandana." Her voice is stern, but not loud. The soldier lowers their bandana and looks nervously at Trissa. "You're worried about innocent civilians, Marcus?"

He nods. "Y-Yes, ma'am," he speaks innocently. With shoulders the width of two people, a muscular stature, and standing nine inches taller than Trissa, he looks down at her upward gaze nervously.

In a quizzical tone, while pointing toward the door of the room, she asks, "Was Isaac innocent, Marcus?"

Marcus closes his eyes and sighs.

"We have two dozen sound bombs that we're throwing first around the walls. That was Isaac's idea. And that's their chance to figure a way out before the attack. If they don't, that's on them." She points at Marcus as she speaks. Turning back to the map, she raises her voice for the room to hear. "Alright. I want all of you to gather your weapons. Join your squads, and meet at–"

"Ma'am," Marcus walks to her, interrupting. He speaks with compassion, saying, "Replying to violence with violence fixes nothing. You lived in the old-world as did I. You know what it causes."

"I was barely a teenager back then and you're younger than me. Don't pretend you understood the political climate of the old-world. And if you did, you'd understand that comparing that world to ours now is laughable."

"We can't just kill innocent civilians. We should help them get to safety." Marcus speaks and watches her eyes squint, gazing into his soul. He wishes someone else in the room would back him up on this. After clearing his throat, he adds, "Ma'am."

Trissa inhales sharply. As she opens her mouth to reply, the radio on her shoulder hisses white noise, followed by a voice, saying, "Ma'am, those kids are here requesting we let them leave."

Rolling her eyes with frustration, she presses the button on her radio and says, "Let them go."

Another burst of white noise sounds, followed by, "Copy."

While holding eye contact with Marcus, Trissa yells loudly for the room to hear, "I am *not* ordering recreational murder of civilians, Marcus. I am merely telling you that after their warning, casualties are out of our control.

"We break through their walls, destroy their luxuries, and eliminate Victor Volcan. Understood?"

Marcus nods and mutters, "Yes, ma'am."

"Good." She speaks directly to Marcus. "Maybe you've forgotten how many of *our* innocent people have been abducted, murdered, used for experiments, and turned into Ghouls, so I'll forgive you for not appreciating the mercy they're getting with Isaac's plan."

Trissa turns once more to the room and yells, "Gather into your squads and meet me at the gates in half an hour." The soldiers grunt in acknowledgment.

CHLOE

"SIR, I… I don't know what happened, I–" Chloe watches the security guard at the gate of the city stammer and speak in circles to Garret in the passenger seat of the vehicle she's driving. "The gates opened, and then the computer froze up with 'overridden' flashing on the– Look, sir, you can see it right there on my screen." He leans to give Garret a view through the security window, showing his computer monitor flashing bold, red letters reading: OVERRIDE.

Chloe hides a smirk.

"It's okay, we're looking into it," Garret speaks strangely. His voice rises and shifts dramatically in pitch. "Be sure to keep a stern watch of the gate in the meantime." Garret sounds as though someone is moving a pitch lever back and forth as he speaks.

The guard lowers his eyebrows and says, "Of-Of course… Sir, are you okay?" He looks past Garret at Chloe.

Chloe shrugs and raises her eyebrows.

"I'm fine, just need to get to my office to get to the bottom of this security issue is all." Garret replies, most words carrying the higher shift in pitch. The guard continues to look confused while staring at Garret.

"We have to get to Volcan Enterprises," Chloe speaks hurriedly and drives into the city.

Stopped at a stop sign, she looks around for something familiar to guide her to Amber's house. On the empty passenger seat where Garret was sitting lay directions drawn by Deante. She grabs them, reads them over, then sets them back, resuming her drive to Jacob's home.

From a combination of nerves and the pressure of time, Chloe knocks on the front door of the Andersons' home rapidly.

Amber fiercely opens the door with her eyebrows lowered and lips snarled, ready to reprimand her son, when she sees Chloe standing alone on the porch. Her eyes look around for Jacob. When she confirms Chloe is alone, she asks, "Where is my son?"

"He's… He's okay," Chloe replies, waiting for Amber to make eye contact.

"That's Garret's vehicle. Where's Garret?"

Watching panic fill Amber's eyes, Chloe reactively says the words on her mind, speaking softly. "Amber, the city is in danger. Jacob is on his way to a safe compound outside of the city. We need to–"

"He's outside the walls?"

"Yes, but he's–"

Amber loudly sighs and covers her face with her hands and paces in the foyer. Chloe steps inside.

"Amber?" Chloe says in a calm voice. "Jacob asked me to come get you. He's meeting us at "

"I've been calling him. All day. He said he'd be home for dinner last night and just never showed." Amber's voice is shaking.

"I'm-I'm sorry, he–"

"Now you show up at my door without him, in Garret's vehicle, without Garret, telling me…"

Standing still and fidgeting her thumbs in her clasped hands by her waist, Chloe watches Amber steady her breathing while covering her eyes. She slides her hand down her face, looking at Chloe with a mixture of worry and anger. Her eyes are glossed over, waiting to drop a tear with her next blink.

"I…" Amber's voice stutters.

"Jacob is resilient. He's making his way to us," Chloe speaks.

"I know. It's just that… It's never been easy for me to not worry about him. Especially with all the ability stuff." Amber stops her pacing to wave her hand as she replies.

"I-I know why you worry so strongly."

Amber's head tilts. She holds a stare with Chloe.

Reaching in the back pocket of her faded jeans, Chloe hands Amber a creased picture. It's the picture Jacob found showing Ethan with a small child with pigtails.

"Where did you– How did you–" Amber's words are short and choppy.

"We found this… Well, Jacob found this in your old home outside the walls," she replies with soft words. "Is that Alice in the picture?"

Amber looks at Chloe with tears flowing past her freckled cheeks. Her lips are attempting to smile while trembling. She nods quickly at Chloe, then looks at the picture, focusing on young Alice and Ethan's smile. "He was at our old home?"

Chloe doesn't respond. She continues to watch Amber take in the photo.

Holding the picture in one hand and covering her mouth with the other, Amber closes her eyes, letting warm drops fall to her chin. She looks at Chloe as the corners of her mouth appear from behind her hand, revealing a smile. She speaks shakily, saying, "Yes… That's… Alice."

Chloe smiles, remaining quiet as she watches Amber gaze longer at the picture.

"We…" Amber sniffles. "During the outbreak, we… We lost her." Her shoulders tremble from quiet sobs. She looks at Chloe again, asking, "Does Jacob…" She's holding the picture up.

"No." Chloe shakes her head, then stops, saying, "Well… I think he put it together, but I don't know if he…" Stuttering, she says, "He hasn't brought it up again."

"We intended on telling Jacob. Ethan and I. But we finally healed from the grief. As much as we could. And Jacob was such a special… Happy boy. We…" Amber cries. Her glossy eyes look at Chloe with guilt as she says, "I never forgot about her."

Chloe rushes over to Amber and wraps her arms around her torso in a tight hug. "I know," she whispers as Amber rests her head on her shoulder.

"Thank you," Amber mutters then lifts her head. She touches Chloe's cheek and says, "She'd have been about your age."

With her eyes now filling with tears, Chloe smiles at Amber. Both of them look to the front door when a series of explosions bang outside.

"Amber, we have to–" Chloe begins to speak but stops when Amber's phone rings in the kitchen.

Rushing to answer, she holds the phone to her ear.

"Mom?" Jacob speaks. "Mom, are you there?"

"I'm here, sweetheart." Amber's voice is worried, but still saddened.

"Mom… Chloe is on her way to get you. There's a safe place outside the walls where–"

"She's here, Jacob."

"Oh… Okay. I promise I'll explain everything when I see you, just please hurry and get out of the city before it gets worse."

"You'll be there? At this… Place?"

"Y-Yeah, mom. I'm on my way there now."

Amber hangs up the phone. She looks at Chloe and says, "Let me just pack a few things." She walks up to her bedroom.

Chloe stands by the front door, watching the sky through the sidelight as flashes of orange and white flicker sporadically, followed by a delayed, faded crack or bang.

Soft thuds of Amber's footsteps come down the stairs as she walks toward Chloe. Opening the front door and stepping onto the porch, she waits for Amber. Just as she's stepping out the door, Amber freezes and says, "One more thing," then jogs back into the house.

Chloe steps onto the sidewalk and sees neighbors walking onto their front porches and peering out their front doors and windows. Faint yelling can be heard in moments of silence between bangs all around the wall.

"Okay," Amber says breathlessly as she hurries toward the SUV parked on the street.

Chloe drives slowly to avoid the people now running across the road and stopping to look for the source of explosions. The closer they get to the heart of the city, the more people are sprinting down sidewalks and crowding intersections, running and screaming with scared expressions. Amber mutters, "This is exactly like last time," as she leans over the dashboard, watching the panicked people gather as Chloe slowly drives through the crowd.

As they drive toward the open gate, Chloe pulls over and puts the vehicle in park and looks out the driver's window. Amber looks up through the windshield at Volcan Enterprises and asks, "Why are we stopped?"

Chloe looks at Amber with watery eyes and says, "I need you to do exactly as I say."

<u>DEANTE</u>

"DID YOU NOT hear me? I told you your son is infected. He needs you–"

"We heard you," Renz's mom speaks aggressively with his dad behind her. They're standing at the front door, and she's holding the edge, eager to close it on Deante. "This is the result of his own actions."

"His own act– *You're* the ones who chose not to give him the fucking vac–"

The door slams in Deante's face.

"Assholes." He kicks the door and walks to the street. He throws his hands in his hoodie pocket and drags the soles of his shoes across the pavement. "No wonder he never invited us to hang at his place."

He arrives home and bursts in the door. "What on Earth has you comin' in here making this kind of noise?" his mom yells as she enters the foyer.

"I..." He hasn't come up with a plan. Rubbing his head and humming, he stutters, saying, "I... Have a surprise for you."

"A surprise, huh?" She looks at him suspiciously.

"Uh... Yes." His eyes light up as an idea comes to him. Pointing at his mom, he says, "I'm taking you..." Singing to drag out the word while he finishes his plan in his head, he and his mom sway back and forth holding impatient eye contact. "We're meeting Jacob and Mrs. A at Pete's Grill." Deante snaps his finger and points at his mom.

She lowers her eyebrows and glares at him. After an awkward staring contest she finally smiles and says, "Okay. That sounds nice. Let me change my top and we can go."

"What?" Deante mutters then quickly says, "Yeah. Cool. Uh... I'll drive us."

She spins around and says, "Fine. But remember, you run another stop sign and I'll take away your permit myself. You hear me?"

"I hear you." Deante watches his mom go upstairs with widened eyes. He can't believe it worked. He exhales a large sigh of relief and waits by the front door.

KYLE

"YOU WERE OUTSIDE the walls *again*?" Kyle's mom stands next to her husband in the living room. Both have their hands on their hips, reprimanding Kyle with their eyes. "After you promised us you would stop with this rebellious act." She turns to her husband and speaks to him for Kyle to hear, saying, "It's those friends. I've known it all this time. We should've never un-grounded him so soon, this way he–"

"Mom!" Kyle yells, angrily. "This *cannot* be what you took away from everything I just told you."

His mom's eyes widen in shock and his dad gasps. They're not used to Kyle speaking out, let alone interrupting them. She attempts to respond, but stutters, muttering sounds instead of words.

"The city is about to be attacked." He puts strong emphasis on each word. "We need to leave and get to safety now."

Tisking, his mom says, "I really think you need another week in your room. Think about what you're saying and what influence these friends are having over you.

"And what kind of place is called… What did you say? *The Wasteland*?" She forces a sarcastic chuckle. "How would a place like that be safer than our city?"

"Whatever," Kyle huffs, throws his arms out and walks toward the steps.

Walking quickly to catch up to Kyle, his dad yells, "You apologize to your mother *right* now for that attitude, young m–"

Explosions roar outside. A cracking rings their ears as if a large firework exploded outside their window.

"Dennis, what was that?" Kyle's mom asks his dad in a panic.

They both look at Kyle, who stopped halfway up the stairs and watches them react from the railing. He's so angry with them, he's unfazed by the explosions.

Responding to their fearful expressions, he says, "We all just going to sit in our rooms and think about this, or…"

They burst past him on the steps and run into their bedroom. His mom is yelling instructions on what to pack to

Dennis. He pokes his head from the room and asks Kyle, "Do you know how to get there by vehicle?"

Kyle stares at him and shakes his head in disappointment.

Dennis stutters and says, "Y-You know, I… I only ask because… The… The wall you all…"

"Yes, I can get us there in the car, dad."

His dad shuffles back into the bedroom. Kyle stuffs his backpack with his hacking books, another laptop and tablet with The Wasteland's equipment, he figures he might as well see if he can hack into more of these devices while they're there.

He throws a spare hoodie into the backpack, tosses it over his shoulder, and waits by the garage for his parents. They show up, breathing heavily from their panicked packing. A deeper explosion roars from far away, followed by sirens screaming through the air.

"We need to go now," Kyle speaks demandingly to his parents, who are standing frozen by the door in the kitchen.

"L-Let's go," his mom says, nodding to Dennis. They run into the garage, leaving the door open for Kyle. He steps in and slowly closes the door while looking at the kitchen and adjoining living room, wondering if all of this will be here when they come back.

Will we come back? he thinks, taking one more look, then closes the door and gets in the car.

JACOB

"Y-YEAH MOM. I'm on my way there now," Jacob lies into his phone. The line goes quiet as he's standing at the top of the hill, looking down at plumes of gray smoke erupting from the city. He's going to Victor's office, but it's better she thinks he's going directly to The Wasteland. Flickers of orange light glow between buildings at the base of the streams of smoke. White flashes flicker over the edges of the wall near the towering Volcan Enterprises. Snapping sounds carry through the air in a delay following each flash of white.

Jacob continues to stand in place, watching new pillars of smoke appear after pulsing orange lights inside the walls surrounding the city. If he listens to the wind, he can hear diluted sounds of screaming and explosions traveling from the city to his ears.

Why couldn't you just let me help you? he thinks, envisioning an imaginary conversation with his dad.

He thinks about how serious and frequent his dad's lectures became regarding how important it was that his abilities remain a secret. They used to only occur on the quarterly blood draws until they became brought up on the rides to mixed martial arts training, and walks back from basketball, and even during dinner.

"You were afraid of him all this time," Jacob says aloud, watching the city's destruction unfold. With a large inhale, he closes his eyes, then exhales and looks beside him, vividly picturing his dad standing there, smiling at him.

Ethan smiles with comforting eyes. This is the dad Jacob remembers fondly.

Looking at his father, Jacob says, "I could've helped you. We could've stopped him together."

His dad gives an understanding smile and says, "I know, son."

Jacob hangs his head, then looks back at his dad.

Ethan says, "I'm sorry," then disappears.

As Jacob approaches the city's gate, he hears yelling, screaming, glass shattering, explosions, and gunfire all within the walls. A large group of soldiers from The Wasteland gather outside near the entrance, where one soldier is yelling orders and strategies.

"Make sure the buildings are clear, then destroy them. No homes are to be destroyed."

Jacob is walking between the huddle of soldiers and the wall when three soldiers run away from the huddle and bump into him. They don't acknowledge Jacob and continue running ahead into the city.

Large holes are blown open from the corners of buildings with fire raging inside, spewing dark-gray smoke. Bricks, pieces of furniture, and rubble are scattered across the sidewalks and streets. Jacob looks between buildings and sees soldiers throwing more explosives in the windows and holes already blown in the brick walls.

As Jacob jogs another block he watches soldiers demand a group of scared civilians across the street. While they're running through burning debris, a set of headlights quickly approaches them. Jacob opens his mouth to yell when the vehicle swerves to miss them, driving over the curb of the sidewalk and smashing into the wall of a small coffee shop.

Airbags deploy inside the vehicle as the glass of all the windows shatter. The car horn blares briefly, stopping when the driver's door opens and the man driving steps out holding his head with bloody hands. He looks up, revealing his bleeding nose, staring at the top half of the broken wall falling toward him.

Jacob stands across the intersection from him. He reaches his hand out toward the man, clutching his fingers. He feels resistance in his fingers as he thinks about grabbing the man's shoulder. Jacob pulls his arm toward himself, watching the man get pulled into the street as the slab of falling bricks crush against the sidewalk, barely missing him. A cloud of gray dust skims across the ground around the man as he looks and finds nobody next to him, shocked and confused as to how he got pulled away.

After seeing the man is okay, Jacob proceeds down the sidewalk toward Volcan Enterprises where he sees, up ahead, shards of glass covering the sidewalk from the large windows shattering in one of the many explosions. People in lab coats run from the building. Some are screaming; others are on their phones as they pass Jacob.

Inside, the large marble desk is split with a large crack running across the middle. Glass crunches under Jacob's feet as he steps through the large broken window. An employee pushes another employee in a wheelchair past Jacob while yelling at him, "You're going the wrong way, kid! You need to get out of here!" Jacob keeps his focus on the elevator at the back wall.

The button showing thirty-three seems unresponsive when pressed. Jacob taps his foot anxiously as he stares at the keypad next to the floor buttons. It can't be a lack of power because the doors opened to let him in. He thinks about the vision from Garret and the code he entered and types it into the keypad. Immediately, button thirty-three lights up and the floor below him vibrates. He watches the numbers change with each ding above the door. The doors open to the hallway he saw in those visions with an empty desk at the end.

As Jacob begins to walk past the dark office with his dad's name, an explosion sounds, rumbling the floor and flickering the lights. Small chimes ding as the fluorescent lights blink off then on.

He stands at the door to Victor's office. *Just get in, get the files, then get out,* he thinks to himself, stretching his neck and sighing.

Pushing the doors open, he sees the burning city through the large windows in the back of the office. The orange sun casts its light through the standing clouds of smoke into the room. Victor's desk sits in the middle. Sitting at the desk is Victor.

"You took longer to arrive than I anticipated."

CHAPTER 37

VICTOR EXITS THE ELEVATOR INTO the lobby. The receptionist says hello to him in her overly excited voice. He passes it off and turns to walk down the hall, toward the exit into the parking garage off the side of Volcan Enterprises. On his way, he sees Ethan coming out from one of the training rooms — as he hoped he would.

"Ethan." He stops him after he closes the door.

Hiding a sigh, Ethan replies, "Hey, Vic."

Victor looks around them to confirm nobody is nearby. "You should come with me."

"Where?"

"I want you to see what I've done with Vitality. I know it'll change your mind, Ethan. I have a subject who is showing–"

"Not today with this," Ethan interrupts and attempts to walk away, but is stopped by Victor pressing his hand against his chest.

"Do you no longer trust me, Ethan?" Victor asks sincerely.

"It's forgiving you that I'm struggling with more, Vic."

While slowly closing his eyes, Victor releases a long exhale through his nose. He drops his head then looks back at Ethan, speechless.

"*Why* would I support this?" Ethan speaks under his breath through his teeth. "You nearly made us extinct over your desperation for this fantasy of yours."

"This one… She's… She's projecting visions, Ethan."

"And where did you get this subject?" Ethan quizzes Victor. He knows the answer.

Victor's shoulders slouch in defeat.

"Yeah. Leave me out of it." Ethan walks away.

Yelling to stop him, Victor says, "It's Jacob's fifth birthday this weekend, right?"

Ethan stops walking but doesn't turn around.

"Are you and Amber doing anything for him? I got a little gift for him."

"If we do, one of us will let you know." Ethan still faces away from Victor. He hates that Amber is ignorant to all that Victor has done and is doing. He just hasn't had it in him to tell her and disappoint her.

Seconds of silence pass, then Victor asks, "Has he shown anything yet?"

Ethan's shoulders rise and lower with his breathing. He says a quick, "No. He's shown nothing," then walks to the elevator.

Victor enters the back seat of a black SUV in the parking garage. It begins to drive off as Garret speaks from the driver's seat. "You tried to invite Ethan, sir?" he asks, judging by Victor's silence and blank stares out the window.

"If you hadn't gotten to know me so well, so quickly, Garret, I'd assume you were watching me."

Garret delivers a soft chuckle. "He's missing out, sir," he says in an attempt to cheer him up.

"Who knows?" Victor scoffs. "Maybe I'm the fool. I thought things were going well with John Doe before that went south." He speaks under his breath.

Garret passes a glance in the rearview mirror. "This girl seems to be progressing well, sir. Hopefully she continues to defy the odds." His tone is positive.

"Yeah," Victor mutters.

"How is her mom progressing?"

"Our cancer treatment is preventative. Given after a diagnosis is too late and won't cure it. The chemotherapy is helping her, but we're only buying time."

"Does the girl understand?"

"She's seven, Garret. Probably not. And that's if the mother has explained anything to her."

Garret hums an acknowledgement.

Once they arrive at the facility, Victor walks through the hall past a large room that is under construction. It will become a large training room when it's complete. He knocks on a dorm room door, then enters a code on the pad next to it. A little girl with brown, braided hair and light blue graphic t-shirt comes running up to him with her arms held outward.

"Victor!" she exclaims.

He closes the door and kneels to meet her and wraps her in a hug. His eyes are closed, and his smile is genuine. "Hey, kiddo. How are you feeling today?"

"Good," she says, bouncing on the tips of her toes.

"No fuzziness or tingling in here?" he asks as he rubs the top of her head.

"Nope." She's smiling, holding back excitement. "You wanna see what I drew today?"

"Are you kidding me?" Victor speaks with a playful tone. "I *always* want to see your drawings."

"I know!" she says happily, scurrying past the small kitchenette to a bed littered with papers and colored pencils.

Victor walks over to the small couch on the wall opposite the bed. As he sits, she brings him a drawing of two stick figures with long hair. The smaller figure is purple with long brown hair scribbled over the head. The taller figure next to it is purple, too, but with a green dress colored over the stick body and curly yellow hair over the head. Little blades of grass are drawn haphazardly around their feet, and blue clouds are sketched in the sky.

"Tell me about this one," Victor asks. He smiles as she shuffles next to him, leaning on his shoulder as she points to the picture.

"That's me." She points to the smaller figure. "And that's mommy."

"I can see the resemblance," he says softly.

"Yeah," she says with excitement. "This is me and mommy after she's better and we're outside playing like she promised."

"Like she promised," Victor speaks softly under his breath, looking at the drawing. He jumps as her mother appears standing at the foot of the bed. She's in a hospital gown with an IV line running from her wrist to her shoulder.

She speaks to the little girl, saying, "Chloe. Victor here is going to give you a comfy room with movies and coloring paper and pencils, okay? You'll be safe there while mommy gets better in here." She coughs deeply. "Okay, sweetie?"

"Okay," Chloe answers her mom while scribbling on a piece of paper. Victor watches her act this out. This is verbatim, from days after they got to the facility.

"As soon as mommy's better, we'll have Victor show us to the nearest and safest park with a swing and playset. I promise."

"Okay, mommy."

"Do you know I love you, Chlo?"

"I love you, too, mommy."

Chloe's mom disappears.

"Amazing," Victor whispers. Speaking normally, he asks, "You still remember that like it just happened?"

"I remember everything since after I got here," Chloe answers confidently, still scribbling with a new color.

The serum gave her photographic memory, Victor thinks to himself.

Victor sees a copy of himself appear where Chloe's mom just stood. He's wearing a white lab coat and one of his many old polo shirts, saying to Chloe, "I'm going to do everything I can to help your mom get better."

"I know you are," Chloe answers him, she's leaning into her drawing, creating what looks like a swing set.

"How have you been feeling? Is your head fuzzy or burning?" Victor watches himself ask these questions he had already asked days ago. His jaw hangs open in awe.

"No, I feel good still."

"Good. We'll get you back to your room as soon as we're sure you are one hundred percent. Would you like me to bring you anything? Juice? A cookie?"

"A cookie!" Chloe bounces on her toes again. She looks at Victor in a lab coat as he disappears, then at the real Victor with a smile on her face.

He shakes off his shock and giggles, saying, "I… I'll bring you a cookie next time I come back, okay?"

"Okay!"

"Hey, Chloe." He slides off the couch and kneels next to her. "Can you show me again but in an outfit you haven't seen me in before?"

She shakes her head aggressively. "No. I can only show what I've seen. Otherwise, it looks all weird and stuff."

"Can you show me that anyway?"

Another copy of Victor appears. He's wearing jeans and a grey T-shirt with a distorted logo on the front. His face is normal, but his arms are different lengths, and his feet point to the sides.

Victor chuckles and says, "Okay, you can make him disappear."

She does.

"How about this. Can you make me appear but have him say something you haven't heard me say?"

She shakes her head again.

"No?" he asks.

She hums no, then says, "People sound funny if I haven't heard them say what they're saying."

"You've tried this already?"

"Yeah. All the time when I'm by myself. I still like to talk to them even though their voices are silly." She continues to hold the crayon with a fist and scribbles a blue sky.

Victor smiles politely at her.

"Wanna see that, too?" she asks with excitement.

"I sure do." He smiles.

An identical copy of Victor stands in the same spot as the others. He smiles at Chloe and speaks. His voice is spiking in pitch and tone, but the last word sounds like his normal voice, saying, "I'm always going to be here for you, kiddo."

He disappears.

Victor looks at Chloe, who has returned to drawing a swing set. He says, "Hey," and taps her shoulder.

She turns to him. She's smiling, but her eyes are glossy, holding a sadness behind them.

"I'm… I'm always going to be here for you, kiddo."

Chloe leaps into Victor's arms.

***   ***

VICTOR KNOCKS ON Chloe's door. He listens for movement inside but hears nothing.

"Chloe." He knocks again. "Please let me in. Even if you don't want to talk yet, I just want to see that you're okay."

Listening with his ear near the door, he hears shuffling. His shoulders slouch as he feels tension leave them when the steps continue to approach the door.

The door opens, and he sees Chloe with swollen bags under her eyes that are pink from crying. Her hair is disheveled and partly braided, with frays sticking out in all directions. She lets the door sit open and walks back to the bed she just exited and sits on the edge, returning her hands into the sleeves of her oversized hoodie.

Victor softly closes the door and walks to sit on the small couch, leaning over his knees.

"Chlo. I'm so sorry I couldn't do more help her," he speaks with empathy.

She hangs her head and sobs.

"I… I promise you, I tried everything."

"I know," she speaks, then sniffles, crossing her legs on the bed and pulling the corner of the messy comforter over one knee.

"Is there anything… Anything at all that I can do for you?"

Her head shakes as she looks down at her hands. Her thumbs rub in circles.

Victor gets up and walks over to her. He leans in to offer a hug when she stands from the bed and pushes him away.

"You're dying, too." Chloe says tearfully.

"I'm… I'm doing everything I can to stop that from happening, Chlo." Victor speaks softly.

"You said that about my mom."

Hanging his head with a sigh, he contemplates the best way to help her trust him. He says, "You've grown to understand how Vitality works now."

Chloe nods.

"You understand that when a serum perfectly alters a subject's DNA, we can use that DNA to make a perfect serum for that strain."

He's met with another confident nod. "That's how it can better humanity, right? It'll be safe to work on anyone?"

"Yes. And that's how I will be okay, Chlo."

"How?" Her eyebrows lower with frustration. "Who here has DNA that can help your heart?"

"It's not someone here. But there's a boy who has incredible abilities. One of them being a miraculous healing factor. I can use that to-"

"Where?" Chloe interrupts. "You said your facility outside of Columbus isn't functioning yet. Which means it's not someone from there. And I know everyone you have here. None of them have that ability." Stuttering her words, she says out loud, "I feel like you're lying to me."

"I am *not* lying to you. He's not from there, Chlo. Or here. He's in the city. In Pittsburgh."

"Why isn't he here already, then?"

"It's been complicated," he says, chuckling at her passionate frustration. He squeezes her upper arm and says, "I'm finally bringing him here soon. But I'm going to need your help with him when he gets here."

Her head jerks while holding her lowered eyebrows.

"He's not going to be open to giving samples. And I'm going to need *the* sample from him," he says while tapping a spot on the back of his head.

Chloe closes her eyes and softly winces.

"I know. I hated taking it from you, Chlo. I was extra careful to ensure I didn't lose you while taking it."

Pressing her eyes closed, a small tear falls down her cheek as she looks back at Victor and says, "How can I… What would I do to help?"

"He only trusted his dad with this stuff. His dad is gone. Which means he'll only listen to his mom now. Get close to him and build his trust. He'll eventually invite you to meet her. Then, you can get close to her, too."

"Okay," she says quietly. "But what if that doesn't work? What if he doesn't want to get to know me?"

Victor smiles as he wipes a drying tear from her freckled cheek. "I'm very confident he'll want to get to know you."

Tilting her head, she hopes he'll continue.

"The more trust you have from her, the more leverage we have at our disposal. This will work, I just need you to be prepared that we may need to become... Persuasive," he says delicately, watching her reaction.

Chloe gazes at him curiously, waiting again for him to elaborate.

"You would've done anything to save your mother, right?" Victor asks in a cautious tone.

She lowers her eyebrows and nods slowly.

"If all else fails, that may be what it takes to get him to agree to give the samples we may need from him." Victor pauses. Chloe's lowered eyebrows relax as she offers another gentle nod. "That's not asking too much of you?"

"I can't lose you, too," Chloe says.

Victor nods and smiles. He holds his arms out for a hug. She leans in and squeezes him. He feels her shake lightly and sob.

After the hug, he looks at her and says, "We'll do whatever it takes? Together?"

She nods and says, "Whatever it takes."

CHAPTER 38

A GRADIENT OF RED AND orange dimly stretches across the sky through the large windows. The floor shakes as an explosion flashes white light on the towers of smoke and dark clouds. Jacob stands inside the office doors, watching Victor sit casually in his desk chair. Victor wears a confident grimace but with his hair disheveled and scruffy beard unkept. His eyes are cold, staring back at Jacob with the dark veins protruding to his forehead and temples.

Putting his feet on the desk and leaning in his chair while interlocking his fingers behind his head, Victor says, "You weren't expecting me to be here, were you?" Jacob remains still, watching as Victor continues smirking while lounging in his desk chair. "I have to say, son, gathering Outsiders to destroy the city you live in, just to get to me, was *not* something I predicted you to be capable of."

"How could you do it?" Jacob squeezes his fingers into his fists.

"Risking innocent lives just to, what, capture me? Kill me?" The desk chair slams upright as Victor stands, clasping his hands behind his back. He walks toward the window, looking at Jacob. His suit jacket is thrown over the chair at his desk. His black button up shirt is tucked into his pants with the top two buttons unbuttoned. With a sarcastic expression, he adds, "Bold."

"You killed him!" Jacob screams, extending his arms at his sides.

"Grow up, son," Victor barks defensively. His eyebrows scrunch with frustration. "You're telling me you coordinated an attack on our city but came up here with a plan to bore me to death?"

Jacob's face twitches with anger. "I had nothing to do with the attack on the city. That's all your doing."

Victor scoffs and paces side to side.

"You've been testing on them. Killing them. Turning them into Shriekers." Jacob continues. "Taking them from their fami–"

"They're Wasted, for fuck's sake!" Victor screams. Saliva sprays from his lips. "You've seen for yourself the successes I've created. Don't pretend I haven't produced anything short of miracles. At the risk of what? Losing Wasted outside the walls that nobody would ever notice." Victor scoffs. "These infected and otherwise worthless humans were given a chance to better our species. I gave them that opportunity. *Me*." He pushes his finger into his chest.

"They're not Wasted. They're people. Just like us," Jacob speaks. His fists tighten as he yells, pointing at Victor, "People *you* infected."

Pressure fills Victor's chest as he hears Ethan's voice through Jacob's lips. His vision blurs as he envisions Ethan standing where Jacob stands. A tear falls from his eye as the dark veins visibly disappear. "This is my chance to fix my mistakes, Ethan," he says softly.

Jacob takes a half-step backward. He loosens his fists as Victor gazes through him in a trance. He watches Victor's eyes close, then open as the dark veins stem back to his temples from his eyes.

"Do you have any idea what it's like to have your best friend decide to let you die instead of helping you?" Victor speaks angrily.

Jacob stands defensively as Victor begins to pace in a circle around him. His palms tingle aggressively with static. Jacob speaks to Victor as he paces behind him, saying, "He wouldn't have let you die, Victor."

Another scoff leaves Victor's nostrils.

"He wouldn't. You were his best friend."

As he continues walking around Jacob, Victor says, "I often forget how spoiled your generation has become thanks to the safety of your world in the walls." Catching Jacob's scowl in the corner of his eye as he circles behind him, he continues. "The walls *I* gave to you. Your lives have become so sheltered you don't understand the reality of human relationships."

Jacob watches the faint reflection of himself and Victor in the window. Victor walks slowly behind him, looking at the back of Jacob's head. Turning his eyes to the right of the room, Jacob sees the vault behind the framed notebook paper is open and the stacks of folders he came to get sitting inside. Turning his eyes back to the reflection in the window, he says, "He would've helped you in better ways. He only wanted to stop Vitality after all the failures you've had from–"

Victor steps in front of Jacob, yelling, "Your father knew *damn* well that once a host's DNA successfully adapts to the new genetics, it allows us to reproduce that strain with one-hundred percent success rates. I told him when I had success, yet he still rolled his eyes at me." His eyes look coldly into Jacob's. "But even if he chose to not support Vitality and the successful subjects I created, he still knew that *you* had an extraordinary healing ability." He gently places his first two fingers under Jacob's chin and forces his head upward to hold eye contact. "All I needed was one sample from you. Not only did your father deny me your sample that could save my life, he lied and told me Better Human didn't work on you."

Jacob forcefully pushes Victor away from him. "A sample that could fucking *kill* me."

"You seem to have survived just fine." Victor laughs through his nose, pointing at Jacob's buzzed head.

Jacob thrusts his hand forward with his palm facing toward Victor. He feels pressure against his fingers and sees Victor's shirt ripple but he doesn't move.

"Cute," Victor rolls his shoulders. "I've got more than your healing ability in my DNA, kid. But I'm impressed you learned to control your abilities." He chuckles sarcastically as he pats the wrinkles from his shirt.

With lowered eyebrows, Jacob mutters, "What have you done to yourself?"

The veins leave Victor's eyes as he steps backward, holding his forehead. He hears Ethan's voice echo through his head, saying, "What have you done to yourself, Vic?"

Victor regains his composure quickly, inhales sharply through his nose, staring intensely back at Jacob while the veins remain gone from his eyes.

"What's happening to you?" Jacob asks with concern.

Ignoring his question and breathing heavily, Victor says, "I can fix my mistakes. Your DNA can better... Can save humanity. It can better the lives of–"

Bursting with frustration, Jacob screams, "The only thing threatening humanity is *you*, Victor."

An immense pressure fills Victor's chest and head as his heart beats heavily. His eyes blur as the dark veins leave his face. He hears Ethan's voice through Jacob again. Slightly hunching over and catching his breath, he looks ahead at the blurry room. He sees the outline of Ethan where Jacob is standing.

Seeing Victor bent and breathing heavily, Jacob takes the opportunity to rush to the vault and grab the folders. As he turns around, he sees Victor holding his hand out weakly. He speaks with compassion and the veins remain missing from around his eyes, saying, "Jacob. You need to stop them…" His head drops.

Looking at the folders, then back to Victor, Jacob begins to speak forcefully, saying, "I'm stopping *you*, Vic–".

The ding of the elevator chimes faintly through the walls. Jacob's head whips to the door, listening as several footsteps begin to approach. He hears Victor breathing steadily and turns his head to see Victor standing over him, the dark veins back around his eyes that are burning a gaze into his pupils.

"You had every chance to make this easy." Victor's tone is dark and evil. He grips his right hand over Jacob's face, squeezing each fingertip deep into his temples and cheeks as if trying to grab bone. Jacob groans with an exhale, dropping the folders to the floor, scattering the pages at their feet. He grips Victor's forearm and wrist with his hands, unable to budge his tightening grasp. He lets go and sends the hardest punch he can into Victor's ribs. Remaining unphased by the hit, Victor barks, "Instead, you chose to be stubborn like your father."

Victor thrusts his arm forward, pushing Jacob back, causing him to stumble and fall into the wall next to the doors. As he stands back up onto his feet, dragging his back against the wall and rubbing the pain from his face, the doors open.

Jacob's heart skips a beat as he watches Chloe and his mom walk into the office.

With an evil chuckle, Victor watches Chloe guide Amber across the room to him while he straightens his posture and fixes the sleeves of his shirt. He turns his attention to Jacob, who is watching in shock as Chloe holds her hand against his mom's upper back.

"What… What are you doing?" Jacob stutters.

Laughing with confidence, Victor says, "Son, I almost feel bad for–"

"Chloe," Jacob intentionally interrupts Victor. Chloe turns Amber to stand next to Victor, then she stands on the other side of him. She crosses her hands in front of her waist and drops her head. "Chloe!" Jacob screams. She looks at him with tears in her eyes. He says, with fear in his voice, "W-What is happening?"

Without replying, she looks back at the floor.

"Mom?" Jacob looks at Amber, hoping for a sign there's a plan they made and left him out of.

She gives him a worried smile and weakly says, "Jacob."

Jacob looks back at Chloe with concern and anger in his eyes. She hangs her head downward, looking back at him through strands of her hair.

"The ignorance of betrayal," Victor speaks in a playful tone. "This is what I mean when I say you're sheltered in my cities. 'How could sweet, polite, innocent Chloe do this to me? We were friends.'" He mocks Jacob's voice and rubs the back of Chloe's head, then points to himself saying, "Her loyalty lies with *me*, Jacob. *I* saved her. *I* gave her a meaningful life. *I* gave her amazing abilities."

Jacob glares at Victor, who stands between Chloe and his mom, staring coldly back at Jacob with the veins around his eyes now nearly black, stemming to his ears and hairline.

Jacob's stare becomes angrier the more Victor speaks. His palms are pulsing with electricity.

"I required a way to *convince* you to cooperate," Victor explains without being prompted. "After your father's evasiveness of the subject, I figured that even my elaboration of events wouldn't be enough to get you to buy-in and offer a sample. So, I needed a plan. And what better way than the smile of a pretty, freckle cheeked girl to get to the heart of an Anderson boy. Am I right, Amber?" Victor nudges her. Her eyes close as she's frightened by the unexpected push.

Jacob steps forward, clenching his fists, stopping immediately as Victor tuts and shakes his head. He reaches behind his back, pulling a silver pistol from his waistband, and holds it against Amber's head.

"Think hard about your next move, son."

"Victor, stop," Chloe whimpers, passing a quick look at Jacob.

"I told you to control your feelings, Chlo. You did your part. Let me take it from here."

Chloe lowers her head again. Jacob sees teardrops falling to the floor.

Victor chuckles before adding, "Son, you'll love this. That whole story about her mom needing your sample — that was *her* idea. Came up with it right on the spot, too. Her mom died weeks before you got here."

Jacob breaks his stare at Victor and turns his head to Chloe. He looks upon the top of her head, at the messy braid and strands of hair hanging over her lowered face. Small trembles of her head and shoulders show she is sobbing. With a sniffle she looks up, slowly, as if she's nervous to find Jacob will be looking at her. She scrunches her eyes in shame when she sees he's staring back at her. She speaks, weakly. "Please, Jacob. Give him a sample."

Looking back at Victor, Jacob demands, "Just take whatever samples you need. Let them go."

Laughing, Victor says, "Look at your head, son. I already got what I need from you." With an additional chuckle, he says, "And with Garret being my successful third Neuro Strain subject, Vitality is ready to be completed."

Jacob's mouth opens with shock. *He said Victor didn't know.*

Victor manages to show a more menacing smile as he says, "You believe everything anyone tells you, don't you, son?"

Chloe's head whips up, looking at Victor with angry eyes. She says with a shaky voice, "You… You told me we only would have to do this if he didn't give you the sample."

Without looking at Chloe, he keeps his eyes on Jacob, replying, "He still needs to learn there are consequences for his actions. That he can't just go and launch an attack on *my* city. Plan to steal my life's work and use it against me." He pushes the nose of his pistol into Amber's neck. She winces with fear. Jacob feels tingling through his forearms as he keeps himself still. Victor's darkened eyes look deep into Jacob's as he says, "I'm going to take everything from you. And then I'm going to kill you."

"Stop this!" Chloe pulls on Victor's arm but he doesn't budge or acknowledge her.

Jacob turns his focus to the gun. He can use his ability to pull it from Victor's grasp. Keeping his hand at his side, he tightens his fist, feeling pressure against his palm as if he has a grip on the slide.

Before he can pull it away, Victor's eyes turn angry as he yells, "What did I tell you about interfering? You think I don't feel what you're trying to do?" In a quick motion, he reaches his arm toward Jacob with his fingers stretched wide. When Victor closes his fingers into a fist, Jacob feels pressure squeeze his entire body.

A grunt leaves Jacob's lips and he scrunches his face in pain as the pressure grows tighter, pushing his arms into his sides and his legs together.

"This is but a fragment of the power you are capable of. But you're weak." Victor speaks through gritted teeth, twisting his fist and raising his arm slowly toward the ceiling.

Jacob begins to lift off the ground onto the tips of his feet.

"How naïve of you to think you learned control of your abilities. I've had your sample for merely hours and yet I'm stronger than you." He raises his arm higher causing the tips of Jacob's feet to lift inches off the ground.

"Victor, stop!" Chloe screams while punching Victor's arm.

Victor drops his hand to his side.

Coughing as he barely lands on his feet, Jacob hunches with his hands on his knees, relieved that the pressure overwhelming him is gone. *How did he do that?* He thinks as he remembers pulling Elliot and how much anger and strength it took just to do that.

Amber's back is arched forward as she whimpers. Victor wraps his arm around her, pulling her against the gun in his other hand.

"Mom. It's going to be okay," Jacob speaks after a short cough.

"Don't lie to your mother, son."

"Victor, don't do this. Nobody here needs to get hurt. You have everything you need," Chloe begs.

Speaking in a softer tone, Victor looks at Chloe, saying, "I wish it went differently, too, but Jacob is in our way now, Chlo. He wants to stop us. He is in our way. You can see he doesn't understand what we've accomplished."

Chloe nods with tears falling down her cheeks.

"We are going to save humanity. Whatever it takes. Right?"

Chloe closes her eyes, pushing out a stream of tears. She sniffles with a large inhale, opens her eyes, looks at Victor, and with a quivering lip, replies, "Whatever it takes."

With an arrogant smile, he says, "I admittedly had hope for you, son." Victor looks at Jacob. "Unfortunately, you're just like your father; unable to see the forest through the trees." He uses his thumb to pull back the hammer of the pistol.

Stepping forward and lowering his hands, Jacob says, "Let… Just let her go." He exhales, adding sincerely, "Please, Victor. She has nothing to do with any of this."

The room is silent as Victor stares at Jacob. Speaking softly, Amber says, "Victor… We've known each other forever."

Unfazed and keeping his eyes on Jacob, Victor replies to her, "We have, Amber. You can thank your husband and your son for how it all came to an end."

Jacob sees Victor's hand begin to squeeze the pistol. Desperate to buy time, he steps forward, yelling, "Wait. She knows nothing about what's going on. You have no risk if you let her go." His chest heaves quickly from his rapid breathing.

Victor stalls but doesn't reply.

Feeling tingling throughout his arms, Jacob watches Victor's movements intently. He glances at Chloe, who is now staring at him. Her eyes are red from crying. He looks back and stares, waiting for any sign of hope from her.

"You're hoping she's going to tell you that your mother here is a projection, aren't you?" Victor says playfully after seeing the fear in Jacob's eyes.

Waiting for a reaction, Jacob gets only a slight shake of her head. He turns to Victor who is holding his evil grimace with the veins around his eyes so dark his skin looks purple at his temples.

"Let's clear it up, shall we?" Victor shrugs, briefly removing the gun from Amber's neck. She sighs as her shoulders drop.

Jacob opens his tingling hand at his side, ready to pull the gun from Victor who quickly resumes aiming the gun at Amber. "Tell us something they wouldn't know, dear. Specifically, something Chloe wouldn't know." His voice is unpleasantly chipper.

"W-Wha… I don't understand." Amber stutters, tensing her shoulders again.

"Say something Chloe wouldn't know. If your voice breaks, we'll know you're a projection. If it doesn't, we can continue," he speaks while smiling at Jacob.

Jacob's heart pounds heavily in his chest. Chloe is looking at him with her lips twitching.

"Victor, please. Please just let them go." Chloe says weakly, turning to him.

"We're waiting, Amber," he says impatiently.

Amber drops her head and releases a long sigh.

"Alice," she speaks through short chokes.

The room falls silent, revealing the fighting that continues outside as explosions softly rumble and cracks of bullets sound through the glass. Jacob, Victor, and Chloe look at Amber, waiting for her to continue.

"Ethan and I had a daughter…"

"What?" Jacob mutters. Even though he found evidence of this in their old home, hearing it from his mom — hearing this secret his mom and dad kept from him out loud makes it real.

"She… She didn't survive the outbreak." Amber drops her head and softly cries.

Victor scoffs lightly and looks at Jacob. "Well. Well. I see that even *you* didn't know that, son." Without empathy, he holds his gaze with Jacob and asks Amber, "What happened?"

Sobbing, Amber hangs her head, staring at the floor. "She was at… My parents were babysitting when it all… We… When we rushed over to get them, they…" She gets choked up and sniffles. Victor keeps his emotionless, cold eyes on Jacob. Amber continues. "Their house was overrun with infected people."

Ignoring Amber starting to cry, Victor adds, "Tell them who rushed to pick you and Ethan up when the outbreak started. And who helped you try to save Alice."

"You did." Amber whimpers through her cries.

Jacob stares at his mom who has tears dripping onto the floor. Her voice didn't break. It's actually her. Chloe truly betrayed him. He whips his head to Chloe, gesturing his arm toward his mom, and says, "How could... Why would you do this?"

"I..." Chloe chokes from her trembling throat. "I'm sorry, Jacob."

"*Your* decisions are what led you here, son." Victor speaks over Chloe, touching the pistol to Amber's head. "*Your* decisions are why this is going to happen."

Victor nudges the pistol harder against her head, indenting her skin around the nose of the gun. Her eyes tighten, forming wrinkles at the corners of her eyes and temples. Jacob sees Victor's grip tighten on the handle. Tingling stretches from his fingertips to his shoulder like shards of glass flowing through his veins.

Chloe sees Jacob open his hand, fingers spread wide, beginning to step forward. "Jacob," she says, gaining seconds of his attention. She shakes her head, then rushes in front of Victor, standing between him and Amber. She pushes Amber toward Jacob.

Stumbling, Amber sprints the short distance to him, squeezing his right arm tightly and reaching across his torso, pulling his left hand over and gripping it tightly. Her squeeze is strong and forceful.

Jacob watches intently as Chloe wraps her hands around Victor's. The muscles in his face twitch as he is attempting to comprehend what she is doing. She caresses the back of his hand and slowly pushes her right hand underneath his, grabbing the top of the pistol.

Lips moving as if trying to mutter words, but making no sound, Victor's eyes sharpen and eyebrows lower. As she pushes her left hand inside his on the gun, joining her right hand, Chloe immediately begins pulling repeatedly to take it from Victor. She grunts with every attempt as her elbows snap back as if pulling on a short rope. Victor doesn't budge while Chloe uses all her strength to free the gun from his grasp, failing with every pull.

"Let… Go!" She yells through gritted teeth as her body heaves and whips without affecting Victor even slightly. "You have to… Stop, Victor…" Her braid bounces between shoulders, breaking strands of hair loose and fraying.

Losing patience, Victor tightens his grip around Chloe's hands and shakes downward, yelling, "Enough!"

Her whole body freezes. Her eyelids twitch. Color leaves her cheeks as she realizes she can't remove the gun from his grasp. She turns her head to Jacob as a tear falls over her freckled cheek.

Jacob tries to lunge forward as his mom tightens her hold on his right arm and left hand. She's squeezing as if she's trying to grab his bone. He jerks his shoulder to push forward, realizing she has him anchored to the ground with her strength. Angrily, he looks at her, speaking through gritted teeth. "Mom? How…"

She shakes her head at him, adding pressure to her hold.

His eyes bounce rapidly between hers. "No…" He mutters quietly, turning his head toward Chloe and attempting to rush over to her again, only to be jarred back from his mom's unrelenting hold. "Chloe. Stop." Choked words leave his lips.

"Forgive me, Jacob," he hears Chloe mutter and watches her force a slight smile at him.

Holding a stare with Jacob, more tears slowly leave her eyes. She turns her head back to Victor who is staring coldly as every ounce of emotion has left him. Her elbows jerk back as she pulls herself toward him, pinning their hands and the gun between their stomachs.

The dark veins around Victor's eyes are pulsing. His mouth is still open as if ready to speak, but he continues to say nothing.

Chloe's shoulders shift around as she removes her right hand from his and touches Victor's cheek. Raising onto the tips of her toes, she leans close to him and says, "Let this be the last time you hurt someone." She drops back onto her heels and brings her hand back inside his hands.

Victor's eyes slowly close. His torso twitches violently as a muffled, yet loud bang cracks through the room. A bright flash escapes through their fingers covering the gun, lighting up Chloe's t-shirt and Victor's button-up. Her body jerks, as both of their eyes open wide with shock. Weak breaths escape their lips.

Jacob's heart sinks as his breaths stutter watching them both stand frozen. He sees Victor's hands struggling to take control of the pistol lodged between them. Amber pulls down on him again as he tries to leap forward to stop what's happening. "Let me go! Stop this!" He screams as he jerks his arms and torso with all his strength, unable to break from Amber's grasp.

The veins around Victor's eyes vanish and tears reach over his eyelids as he mutters in a weak breath, "Chloe... Don't..."

Another loud muffled shot rings out, causing both Victor and Chloe to shudder. Jacob jumps at the sound. He's leaning and pushing forward, pulled back by his mom who is still gripping his arm and hand like a vice.

"Stop…" A breathy whisper leaves Victor's lips.

Victor's eyes release a stream of tears as Chloe's face softens and eyes weaken. The gun clangs onto the floor. Chloe's hands fall to her side and she drops to her knees revealing two wounds in the middle of her torso flowing blood. Her head weakly looks up and she falls backward.

The grip on Jacob's arm fades, causing him to stumble and break his focus on Chloe. He looks over where his mom was just standing to find her gone. He drops his head and closes his eyes, feeling pressure fill behind them.

"No," Victor mutters. "No. No, no." He drops next to her and presses his hands on her torso, desperately trying to stop the bleeding while Chloe is struggling to breathe. "Chloe, why?"

With weary eyes, struggling to speak, Chloe weakly raises her trembling arm, reaching for Victor's face. He leans in to let her touch his cheek. Short wheezes leave her lips.

Jacob watches the puddle of blood grow underneath Chloe. Before it touches the pistol, Jacob walks over and picks it up off the floor. He sees Victor push harder on Chloe's wound that continues to pulse more blood from under her t-shirt.

A rush of lightheadedness travels between Jacob's temples. The outside of his vision blurs to white, joined by a warm pressure behind his eyes. His heart palpitates when he looks at Victor trying to save Chloe. Sadness fills his chest while anger rushes through his veins. The grip he squeezes into the handle turns his knuckles white.

"I'll make this right. I'll help you. I'll–" Victor speaks between rapid breaths.

"I didn't want…," Chloe speaks in a breathy whisper. Her hand falls from his cheek.

"It's okay… It's–"

Chloe tries to push herself up with her elbows. She loses her balance and begins to cry, saying, "I didn't want to believe you were hurting people." Her body heaves as she coughs, and tears fall from her heavy eyes. "Promise me you'll stop."

"I promise. I will be better, Chlo. You'll see."

Chloe moves her eyes to look at Jacob. A warm tear traces the side of his face as he stands, gripping the pistol in his palm, looking into her dying eyes. She says, "Nobody else needs to die." She holds a stare with him, then turns her eyes back to Victor.

While looking at Victor, she struggles to bring her hand to touch his, still desperately holding pressure on her chest. Almost reaching his hand, her arm drops to the floor, and her head slumps to the side as her short breaths stop.

Victor hangs his head and hunches over her, sobbing quietly. He holds his breath as he hears grinding metal from the pistol arming. He looks up to see Jacob aiming the gun between his eyes. The veins are still gone, but his eyes are bloodshot from crying. They hold eye contact with each other for several seconds, then Victor lowers his head back down.

Jacob's lip trembles and his outstretched arm shakes. He feels his finger twitching on the trigger as he thinks about pulling it and stopping Victor permanently. His insides vibrate with emotion while his arm sways from the pistol's weight as he aims at the top of Victor's head. *Nobody else needs to die.* Chloe's last words echo through his mind.

He thinks about everything that led to this moment. Victor killing his father. Victor lying to get him to the facility. Victor manipulating him to get his samples. Victor sending Elliot to hunt him down. Victor planning to use his mother to blackmail him. All of this leading to Chloe dying.

Jacob looks behind him at the files scattered across the floor. The files his father needed to stop Victor once and for all. Proof of everything Victor has done. These files and the videos from his dad are everything he needs to put a stop to him. He looks back at Victor and listens to his short, crying breaths.

Nobody else needs to die. He looks at the files once more, then back at Victor mourning.

With each heartbeat, Jacob's pulse sounds like a bass drum slamming between his temples. A bead of sweat runs down his spine under his hoodie. His eyes fight to resist but turn to Chloe.

Her body is still. Her head turned away from Jacob with her messy braid lying against her shoulder. The tip of her hair being touched by the slowly growing pool of blood underneath her. Her arm lies at her side. The hand he held is resting in her blood.

The hand he'll never get to hold again.

Another wave of light-headedness washes over him as his heartbeat stutters.

"I'm sorry," he hears Victor mutter in a soft breath.

Blinding light flashes in front of Jacob as he squeezes his finger, erupting an ear-piercing bang. Red rain forms a temporary cloud then patters against the floor following the thud of Victor's body.

Jacob falls to his knees, dropping the pistol at his side.

An unknown amount of time passes as Jacob remains on his knees with his unblinking eyes staring at Chloe's body. His limp arms at his sides are the only things keeping him balanced and upright. The sun completely sets, leaving the room dim and dark except for a blinking lamplight on the desk and flickers from the fires still raging outside. The volume of yelling and explosions diminishes over time and travels farther away until it stops.

A muffled ding from the elevator meets his ears, then seconds later footsteps run rapidly down the hallway — neither fazing Jacob. He hears the doors burst open, followed by Trissa's voice, saying, "There he is."

A gasp is followed by his mom's voice muttering, "Oh no." Thier voices sound as if he's hearing them with his head underwater. "Jacob. Sweetheart," he hears her mutter, then feels her arms hug him from behind.

EPILOGUE

THREE DAYS LATER

THE SOUNDS OF THE WASTELAND jar Amber awake. "This place never sleeps," she mumbles to herself, staring at the arched ceiling of her small hut. Rays of sunlight shine through the tiny square window into the bedroom-sized space. She stretches, slides her legs off the bed and into her sandals, then turns her gaze to her small, wooden nightstand holding the photo album she grabbed before leaving with Chloe. Setting it on her lap, she opens to the first page and passes her eyes over pictures of a young Jacob playing in the yard, sitting on the couch while smiling in his dad's arms, and laughing on a swingset. She turns all the pages to the back, where she added the single photo of Ethan with a small child with pigtails. Amber smiles, feeling goosebumps under her skin. She sets the album back, stands, and walks outside.

Far off in the horizon are thinning towers of smoke reaching into the sky from the burning city. Villagers smile at Amber as they walk past. Knocking sounds from one hut over, where she sees Deante leaning his ear on the door of Jacob's hut, waiting for a response. He mutters something, but she can't make out what he said. With her hands in her robe pockets, she walks toward Deante.

Seeing her making her way toward him, he shrugs his arms with disappointment, saying, "He won't answer me."

"He will," Amber speaks with a smile to assure him.

"I didn't even see him yesterday," Deante replies in a defeated tone.

"I saw him in the afternoon. He was heading to Chloe's grave again." She rubs his shoulder to console him. "He'll come around, D, he just needs some time."

"I know. I just…" He looks at his feet.

"How is Renz doing, sweetheart?"

Looking at her with sadness, he says, "They're saying he's okay, or 'as expected,' but he's not himself at all. His eyes turned gold. He's strapped in a bed by his wrists and ankles and just jerks and hisses. They said it could be anywhere from a few weeks to two years until he becomes normal."

"I'm sorry, D." She rubs his shoulder harder.

Heavy boots hit against the ground approaching from behind. "Good morning, Amber." Trissa says happily.

"Good morning, Trissa," Amber replies with a smile.

"Is everything to your liking? Are you comfortable? Do you have all that you need? Food, water, clothes–"

"Everything has been excellent, thank you." Amber's eyes squint as she maintains her pleasant smile.

Trissa pauses as she looks at Jacob's hut. Meeting eyes again with Amber, she says, "Is he…"

"He will be okay."

"He saved us from a horror that could have gotten even worse," Trissa speaks confidently.

Deante speaks up, saying, "Last I saw him, he kept saying he doesn't deserve praise. He said Chloe does."

Trissa replies with a warm smile.

Amber says to Trissa, "I can't thank you enough for getting her body out of the city for Jacob. It really means–"

"It's the least we could do, Amber."

"Have you heard any updates from the other compounds? Has the news done their part?" Amber's voice is anxious.

"We got word that Johnstown's Conservation City has been broadcasting Ethan's video, along with photos of Victor's files and… And his body. Hopefully in another day's time we'll hear reports from our farther compounds."

Amber sighs in relief.

"There's still no word on how they'll govern the cities going forward. Only talks that it might change."

After a short pause, Amber asks, "And the rebuilding of our… Of Pittsburgh's Conservation City?"

Trissa sighs with remorse. "We have the survivors in safe areas that weren't damaged by the attack. We're diligently working to repair the damages and recover any casualties promptly."

"Have you found Garret?"

With a concerning smile and eyes, Trissa says, "None of the survivors or bodies we've found match the description you gave to us."

Disappointment fills Amber's eyes, but she shakes it off and says calmly, "Thank you. For everything."

"No. Thank *you*." Trissa smiles while looking at Jacob's hut again. The sounds of the compound shine through the pause in their conversation. Trissa sighs as her smile fades, then says,

"So, all that time, she was supposed to bring you to Victor as blackmail for Jacob, but she sent you to me instead."

Amber forces a tight smile and nods.

"Did she say what changed her mind?"

"We were in the vehicle when she gave me directions and told me to come here. She held her hand on the door and asked me about Alice," Amber's eyes become glossy. "Then she stared at Volcan Enterprises, eventually saying she had a bad feeling and needed to help Jacob."

They all turn and look at Jacob's hut.

"She said she always believed Victor loved her. Because he always told her he did." Amber looks away from Jacob's hut and back at Trissa. "She said Jacob was the first person who made her *feel* loved."

Trissa watches a tear slowly fall to Amber's cheek. "Your son has a big heart." She's given a smile from Amber. "If any of you need anything at all, please do not hesitate to ask." She nods to Deante and Amber, then walks to the main street.

Amber watches as villagers carry food, clothes, and supplies around the compound, smiling and helping each other. Children from the city are playing soccer with children from the compound. City residents and Wasteland residents laugh in conversation. Amber smiles, knowing how proud Ethan would be in this moment.

She looks at Jacob's hut, then at Deante, and says, "I'll go check in on him. Why don't you go wake up Kyle and get some breakfast with him?"

"Oh, he's awake. He barely sleeps anymore. He spends all his time digging through Victor's files and videos on the intranet, or whatever he calls it."

Chuckling, Amber says, "Well then, why don't you get breakfast and bring it to him?"

"You'll let me know that Jacob's okay?"

"Of course." She pulls him in for a hug, then watches him walk toward the cafeteria.

Amber steps onto the small porch of the hut and knocks lightly on Jacob's door.

"Jacob. Can I please talk to you?" she yells softly with her face close to the door. She tests the doorknob and finds it turns fully, opening the door.

"Jacob?" she says, cautiously peeking into the room.

An identical tiny window casts rays of sunlight into the same room setup as her hut and the others. She steps inside to see his bed is made. His wardrobe cabinet is open and empty. The nightstand next to his bed is cleared, except for a folded paper on top.

Amber sees the folded paper has 'Mom' written on it. She opens the note. It reads:

Mom,

I need to be sure that Vitality is stopped.

Tell Trissa not to send anyone to come find me. Tell Deante, Kyle and Renz I'll be back when it's all over.

I can't let her die for nothing.

I love you, Mom,

Your boy, flying to Mars

Amber inhales slowly and looks at the rays of the sun shining into the room. She closes her eyes, dropping tears onto the note, blurring the ink where they land.

She reads the note once more, folds it, and places it in her robe pocket, squeezing it tightly.

With a strong exhale, Amber walks out onto the small porch, takes one more long look at Jacob's empty hut, then closes the door.

ABOUT THE AUTHOR

J Donald grew up and resides outside Pittsburgh in Southwest Pennsylvania. With a love of dark, immersive stories, his passion has been to write a story of his own. That passion is delivered in his debut novel, A Better Human.

Outside of novels, he also enjoys writing music, deep conversations about the universe with the people he loves, discussing easter eggs in the MCU, and watching his son grow up and discover the world around him.

Follow and interact with J Donald across most social media: @jdonaldwrites. To join his mailing list or for media relations, contact: jdonaldwrites@gmail.com.

www.ingramcontent.com/pod-product-compliance
Lightning Source LLC
Chambersburg PA
CBHW070306310726
48976CB00005B/1599